F

LARGE PRINT

Central Support Unit
Catherine Street Dumfries DG1 1JB
tel: 01387 253820   fax: 01387 260294
e-mail: libs&i@dumgal.gov.uk

Dumfries and Galloway
L I B R A R I E S
Information and Archives

UK

CUSTOMER SERVICE EXCELLENCE

24 HOUR LOAN RENEWAL ON OUR WEBSITE - WWW.DUMGAL.GOV.UK/LIA

HOW TO BREAK YOUR OWN HEART

HOW TO BREAK YOUR OWN HEART

Maggie Alderson

WINDSOR
PARAGON

First published 2009
by Penguin
This Large Print edition published 2011
by AudioGO Ltd
by arrangement with
Penguin Books Ltd

Hardcover ISBN: 978 1 445 85563 9
Softcover   ISBN: 978 1 445 85564 6

British Library Cataloguing in Publication Data available

Printed and bound in Great Britain by
CPI Antony Rowe, Chippenham and Eastbourne

For Barbie Boxall

Acknowledgements

As well as my adored agents, Jonathan Lloyd and Fiona Inglis, and my wonderful publishers, Julie Gibbs and Mari Evans, I am greatly indebted to the following people: Bruce Palling for his oenophile expertise; Paul Levy and Charlie Mount for some specifics on champagne, and Richard Juhlin's book *4000 Champagnes*; Mark Connolly for taking me to L'Atelier Joël Robuchon; Jocelyn Hungerford, for rhymes and chimes; Stephanie Donaldson for her horticultural knowledge; Barry Goodman for the matches game and Val Garland for playing it so hilariously; Henri Krug for the lunch at Tetsuya's, where we drank Clos de Mesnil. And in fond memory of my late friend Alan Crompton-Batt, who introduced me to Krug twenty years ago.

1

'Do you always sleep in separate beds?'

Kiki's question took me so much by surprise that I'd answered her truthfully before I had time to think about it. I hadn't had any coffee yet, my brain wasn't in gear.

'Yes,' I said and turned the tap on to full blast to fill the kettle. I wanted to drown out any possible further discussion of the subject.

But Kiki hadn't finished.

'Do you think that's normal for a happy couple in their mid- to late-thirties?' she asked brightly, leaning round me over the sink, forcing me to look at her.

I switched the kettle on and deliberately moved away to bustle around with mugs and coffee pots. I really wasn't in the mood for an in-depth discussion of my marital relationship before 9 on a Sunday morning. And especially not after the amount of wine we had consumed at dinner the night before. My head was pounding.

I wasn't used to getting up so early at the weekend, but Kiki had woken me like a puppy, bouncing up and down on the end of my bed, insisting I go for a walk with her. Which was when she'd discovered that Ed and I slept in separate beds. In separate bedrooms.

I glanced out of the window. It was a perfect March morning, as she'd said. The sky was bright blue with little white clouds scurrying across it and the catkins on my neighbour's tree were dancing in the breeze. A walk through the fields and woods would probably clear my head, I thought, as long as the conversation didn't continue in the same vein.

But Kiki wasn't ready to let it go.

'Amelia,' she said, walking over to the dresser where I was pouring milk into a Cornishware jug. She put her hand up to my face and gently turned my chin so I had to look at her. 'Stop running away from me. This is serious. How long have you and Ed been sleeping separately?'

I sighed deeply and pushed her hand firmly away from my face. 'It's none of your bloody business where we sleep, Kiki,' I said, starting to feel really cross. 'I've had enough of this. You've woken me up at the crack of dawn on Sunday to go for a walk, and I'm happy to do that, but not if you are going to give me the third degree about my sleeping arrangements.'

'OK, OK,' said Kiki, raising her hands in surrender. 'I'll shut up now, but I am going to make you talk about it one day.'

'Sugar, dear?' I asked in a deliberately over-bright tone and with a fake smile, as I held a mug of coffee up in front of her, my little finger raised genteelly.

'Two, thank you, sweetie,' she said, returning my ironic grin and then sticking her tongue out. I stuck mine out back at her.

*   *   *

Kiki kept her promise and our walk passed very pleasantly, with conversation no more intrusive than a post mortem of the various hilarities of the night before and what we each had coming up

2

socially in the next week—always a rich vein of conversation with her. There were also frequent diversions as Kiki discovered yet another wonder of the English spring to squeal over.

'I love all the mud here,' she said, lifting up each of her brightly striped Paul Smith wellies in turn to admire the thick clods sticking to the soles. 'We don't get much mud in Australia, because it's so dry. I love this oozy mud. Listen to that—a proper squelch.'

I laughed. Kiki had lived in London on and off for years, with stints in New York and back in her native Melbourne, but she still took great delight in all the little details peculiar to England. It was just part of the insatiable enthusiasm for living which made her so popular.

With her background and money—she was from an Australian brand-name family—and not forgetting her exquisite gamine looks, she would never have been short of friends, but Kiki's appeal went way beyond the fiscal or the physical.

As my husband Ed said when we first met her at a dinner party a few months earlier, Kiki didn't just seize the day, she got it in a half nelson and squeezed it into submission. His other pronouncement on Kiki was that she didn't so much meet people as recruit them. We'd been enlisted immediately.

We had met her that night, she'd decided we were OK, according to some value system entirely of her own, and we'd seen her at least once a week ever since, whether we liked it or not—and I was a bit more enthusiastic than Ed. But while Kiki's bossiness could be overwhelming, I was glad she'd forced me to go for a walk that morning. The

3

woods were heavenly in the early spring sunshine, and we got back to the house an hour later with our heads clearer and our arms full of branches of pussy willow and catkins to take back up to London.

My neighbour was in her garden as we walked past, examining the green shoots that were appearing in her flowerbeds, so I stopped by her gate to say good morning.

We'd only had the cottage a few weeks and I hadn't had a chance to get to know her properly yet, but I was quite fascinated by Mrs Hart. She was very old—the man in the village shop had told me she was ninety-five—and seemed to live entirely independently.

She spent a lot of time in her garden and it was lovely, even in winter. There always seemed to be something flowering and I was hoping she might be able to give me some tips for my patch. I had big plans for it.

'Been for a walk, Amelia?' she said, smiling, when she made it over to the gate, taking her tiny little steps. 'I bet it was splendid in the woods this morning.'

'Yes,' I said. 'It was glorious down there.'

Kiki joined me by the gate and I introduced them. 'G'day, Mrs Hart,' said Kiki, waving cheerfully. Mrs Hart waved back.

'Hello, Kiki,' she said. 'Lovely to meet you. But you must all call me Hermione. Those are splendid catkins you have there, Amelia.'

She put out an ancient hand and gently touched them. 'Those are female hazel catkins. You can tell by the red flowers at the tips. They are much more spectacular than my birch ones.'

I was impressed by her knowledge, but as she spoke I was distracted by a small thatch of long white hairs on her chin. They were glinting in the sunshine and they really bothered me.

Mrs Hart—Hermione—had such a marvellous face, fine-boned, with very lively blue eyes, and the bristles were such a shame. She was always nicely dressed, but her bright coral lipstick was a bit skew-whif, so I could only presume that she couldn't see the bristles. She certainly wasn't gaga, so it had to be her eyesight. If I ever got to know her better, I thought, I would say something. It was what I would want someone to do for me.

'Anyway, I'll let you girls go,' she was saying. 'Have a lovely day and do call and see me next time you're here, Amelia.'

'I will,' I said. 'I definitely will.'

Ed still hadn't come down when we got in, but I could hear him moving around upstairs.

He appeared—dressed, shaved and immaculate, as he was every morning—just as I'd put a large pile of thick bacon sandwiches on the table. I got up and poured two strong cups of coffee, with just a splash of milk in each and put them down at the place where he always sat.

As he reached the table, Ed pulled me to him and kissed my cheek, then he nodded at Kiki and sat down, helping himself to the food but still not speaking.

'Morning, Edward!' said Kiki, in the tones of a bossy nurse to a groggy patient.

'Hurrmph,' said Ed, which was quite chatty for him in the morning.

Then he started glancing nervously round the room and I picked the *Sunday Telegraph* up off the

5

dresser and dropped it by his plate.

'Hanksh,' he said, or something similar, not looking up, his gaze fixed on the front page as he took hurried little sips of his first coffee. I put a hand on his shoulder and he reached up to squeeze it, not taking his eyes off the paper.

I was used to Ed's silent morning routine and it didn't bother me in the slightest, but Kiki clearly wasn't prepared to let it pass unremarked.

She put her bacon sarnie down and leaned back, studying him with her eyes narrowed and her head on one side. Then she looked over at me and raised her eyebrows questioningly.

'Ed doesn't really speak before noon,' I said, laughing. 'Do you, darling?'

I reached over and ruffled his hair and he smiled up at me blearily. He looked a bit like a three-toed sloth in the morning, I decided. A very elegant three-toed sloth with beautiful hair, wearing a hand-made shirt.

'And the two cups of coffee?' she said.

'Just his little routine,' I replied, smiling indulgently.

'Right,' said Kiki, nodding slowly. 'Just checking.'

The three of us were settled into eating breakfast and reading various bits of the papers when our other houseguest appeared suddenly at the bottom of the stairs, after practically falling down them. He looked terrible.

'Oh, look,' said Kiki. 'Early man.'

'Shuddup,' said Oliver, slumping down in a chair, his eyes half closed. He looked like a spoilt Caravaggio cherub, with black curls, heavy beard growth and the mascara he had been wearing the night before smudged beneath his eyes. He didn't sound very angelic though.

'I feel like total shit. Did you have to make me drink that much last night, Amelia? It was the fucking brandy that did it. Filthy piss. Why'd you open that shit, Ed? It's fucking horrible.'

Ed grunted. It sounded like 'armagnac', but it was hard to tell.

'Why did you drink it then?' I asked Oliver, handing him a mug of coffee. He was wearing my flowery silk kimono, which he must have found in the bathroom, and was having problems keeping it closed.

'I drank it because I'm a total drink slut, but all that wine turns your stomach to shit, and my breath smells like it as well. Why don't you have decent piss in this house, like vodka? Or tequila? Midori would be better than that cack.'

He slapped Ed on his upper arm with the back of his hand, provoking another grunt.

Rolling his eyes in response, Oliver took a deep drink from his mug and then stood up and ran to the sink, the kimono flapping open.

'Bleeeucccch!' he said, spitting it out. 'What did you give me coffee for, Amelia? I fucking hate coffee. Haven't you got any tea? How can you drink that shit? It's disgusting.'

'Oh, do your nightie up, Ollie,' I said. 'We don't want to see the entire sausage counter at breakfast. Sit down and I'll make you some tea.'

Meanwhile, Kiki had stood up and was sidling behind the table towards where Oliver was now sitting. As he gazed vacantly into space she suddenly thrust one of the bottles from the night before under his nose. There was still an inch of

7

red wine in the bottom, I noticed, and a few cigarette ends bobbing in it.

'You fucking bitch,' said Oliver, jumping up and wrestling the bottle away from her. 'You are such a cow. Go on, *you* smell it!' he said, pushing it towards her face.

Kiki shrieked, grabbed the sash from his kimono and pulled it off, dancing off into the sitting room twirling it behind her like an Olympic gymnast. Oliver followed, waving the bottle and shouting profanities at her.

I heard a crash as, I presumed, they tripped over the ottoman, followed by shrieks of laughter and foul insults from both sides. I wondered where the wine bottle had figured in the impact with regard to the white linen loose covers on my sofas, but carried on eating my bacon sandwich. I'd sort it out later.

Kiki and Oliver carried on with their mutual abuse, with thwacking sounds suggesting they were now hitting each other with copies of *Wine Spectator*, *Decanter*, *Cigar Aficionado*, and whatever other magazines were in there, until they clearly tired of it and the noise stopped. The next thing I heard was the TV coming on.

'Ooh, look,' said Oliver. 'It's *Hot Property*. I love this. And I think this bloke is quite a hot property himself, in a Topman-suit estate-agent kind of way. He can take down my particulars any time.'

They roared with laughter. Ed sighed deeply and stood up, gathering the business section of the paper and his second cup of coffee and then coming round to my side of the table. He put his free arm around my shoulders and kissed my neck.

'It's all a bit too hilarious for me at this time of

day, Melia, my darling,' he said, sleepily. 'I'm going to take this up to my study. Give me a call when they're going and I'll come and see them off. OK?'

I nodded and smiled up at him as he stroked my head with his hand, and then I was left sitting alone at the table. Which made it a normal morning, in one way.

*   *   *

Kiki and Oliver left on the train for London about an hour later. Oliver had to get back to town early because he was flying off to Brazil that evening to do the hair for the new advertising campaign for a major fashion label, which was what he did for a—very lucrative—living. Kiki I had gathered in our relatively short acquaintance, just couldn't stay still anywhere very long.

'Thanks so much,' she said, tossing the giant-sized Hermès Birkin bag which was her weekend tote out of the car boot and on to the pavement as if it were an old bin-liner. 'I rather love your country idyll, but I need a few lungfuls of carbon monoxide now to even things out. I'll call you when I've re-toxed. We'll go out this week. We'll do something fun.'

I clicked my heels and saluted. 'I look forward to getting my orders, Frau Commandant,' I said.

'She is a bossy cow, isn't she?' said Oliver, giving me a surprisingly warm hug and two bristly kisses. 'Thanks, babe. I've had a great time. Kiki told me you were a good woman and you are. I'm glad we've finally met. But that husband of yours seriously needs a kick up the arse. What a grumpy git he was this morning. So much for Mr Suave in

9

his Savile Row suit. Is he always like that?'

'Oh, don't take any notice,' I said. 'He's just hopeless in the morning. And you weren't exactly Sally Sunshine yourself first thing, I might remind you. Ed's like an old car, he needs a while to warm up. He gets better and better as the day goes on. You'll get used to him—and he is worth it, really he is.'

'Yeah, he was all right at dinner, I suppose. Quite funny for a posh twat.'

He grinned at me, winking one of his freshly kohled and mascaraed eyes before jumping on to the train and blowing me another kiss through the window.

I stood and watched as the train pulled out, pondering what Oliver had said about Ed being grumpy. It was a bit rich coming from him, I thought. He had quite the foulest mouth of anyone I had ever met, and it had taken me a while to get used to him when he and Kiki had arrived at the cottage the day before.

She'd been telling me ever since I met her how much I was going to love her 'gay husband', as she called him, but for the first hour or so, I'd found it hard to see what there was to like. He was so unbelievably rude. But as the day went on, I had gradually fallen under his spell. Oliver was funny, original and always said exactly what he thought. He didn't play games with you, and it was quite refreshing once you got used to it.

'Are you this frank with everyone?' I had asked him, when he'd told me that the all-white-and-beige interior I had so carefully chosen for the cottage was 'tediously fucking obvious Farrow & Boring . . .'

'No,' he'd said, his eyes mischievous behind their thick layer of make-up—which I'd also got used to surprisingly quickly. 'Only people I like.'

'Blimey,' I said. 'What do you say to the ones you don't like?'

He shrugged. 'I ignore them. Bunch of fuckers.' Remembering that, as I drove back to the cottage from the station, made me reflect how people were sometimes put off by Ed when they first met him. I should have been used to it, after fifteen years, but it still always surprised me.

I was so accustomed to Ed's funny little ways and I loved him so much despite them—or even because of them—that I had to remind myself how he might appear to someone who hadn't met him before: frankly, a little odd. And the same went for certain aspects of our relationship, I supposed. Like what Kiki had said about us sleeping in separate beds.

I was still quite cross with her about that. It had been such an intrusion on our privacy and it had stuck in my mind ever since she had brought it up, like an annoying little stone in my shoe, because I couldn't deny it. Ed and I didn't share a bed—or even a bedroom—any more. Not in the cottage and not in the London flat either. I couldn't remember when it had become a formal thing, but it had been quite a while.

It had started because he seemed to work later and later at night in his dark little study and to get up later and later too, whereas I liked to go to bed reasonably early so I could get up and have a run around the park in the morning before work.

Rather than him disturbing me at three or four in the morning, when he eventually went to bed, and then me waking him when I got up at seven for my run, he'd started sloping off to sleep in the spare room. And over time that became 'his' room and our bedroom became 'my' room.

It had all happened so gradually I hadn't really given it much concentrated thought—although, in my heart, I always knew it wasn't right for a couple our age. I had tried to talk to Ed about it when he'd climbed into bed with me one Sunday morning, with something other than sleep on his mind, but he had just made light of the whole thing, telling me jokingly it was the time-honoured 'aristocratic' way.

'Louis XVI and Marie Antoinette had separate bedrooms,' he'd said. 'So we're just living in our own little mini Versailles.'

'They also had about fifty people watching them get dressed each morning,' I reminded him.

He'd laughed and pulled me closer, nuzzling into my hair.

'Well, we won't go that far, but it does make sense for us both to get a proper night's sleep, doesn't it, Amelia? And it's not like we don't have regular sex, which is a lot more than poor old Louis and Marie Antoinette could say.'

Regular was the word for it. Ed had very clear ideas about when we should celebrate that part of our marriage, just as he did about everything else in our life together. And that particular conversation had ended right there, because Sunday morning was one of those times.

He was simply a man of habit, my husband, I told myself, as I carefully backed the Volvo estate into the narrow garage, but not in a boring way; in a quirky way. He was a true eccentric, as the

12

brilliant often are. And with this in mind, I found myself shaking with laughter when I walked into the kitchen.

Sitting on the table was a rather shabby grey velvet elephant. It was wearing my flowery kimono, and a pair of large dark glasses were balanced on its trunk. The *Sunday Times* 'Style' section was open in front of it, at the fashion pages; on one side was a bottle of brandy, and on the other, my tube of mascara.

I heard Ed's feet clattering down the wooden stairs as I leaned against the table laughing.

'Good heavens!' said Ed, as he appeared, now clearly fully awake. 'Look at Mr Bun. I think he's had a bit too much to drink. Whatever is he wearing?'

'Oh, you daft bugger,' I said, putting my arm around his waist and shaking my head.

'What?' said Ed, in the tones of offended innocence he always assumed when Mr Bun got up to his tricks. 'What a very silly elephant he is. I caught him earlier, trying to plug your hairdryer in.'

'What a very silly elephant *you* are,' I said, turning to look up at his dear face, my arms still around him.

He smiled down at me and then, coiling my long ponytail around his hand, he pulled me to him and kissed me tenderly.

2

We got back up to London later that afternoon, and I ran straight out to Selfridges food hall to pick up something for dinner. Having that temple of gastronomy just a ten-minute walk from our flat was one of the multifarious joys of living, as we did, on Mount Street, in the heart of Mayfair. About the same walk in the other direction would have taken me to Fortnum's.

I knew how lucky I was to live there, and hardly a day went by that I didn't send up a little prayer of thanks that the man I had fallen madly in love with, at the age of twenty-one, came from a family which owned such a residence. Especially one with four bedrooms.

As a result of this equivalent of winning the love lottery, W1 had been my postcode for my entire adult life. Had I been reliant on the pathetic salary I got from my job in a nearby art gallery, I would have still been living with my parents in Maidstone. No thanks.

When I got back with the provisions, Ed was already holed up in his study, as usual, reading proofs for his next client newsletter for Bradlow's Bottles, his bespoke wine business.

The 'journal', as he called it, was a quarterly account of his travels around France in a classic car, which he changed frequently to keep things interesting, visiting tiny independent vineyards, from where he bought the best vintages and sold them on to his customers over the following years, at a very healthy mark-up.

You had to be a 'member' to receive the journal, which was exquisitely printed on linen paper, and even to buy wine from Bradlow's Bottles, a detail that made a particular kind of competitive wealthy man desperate to join.

I never quite understood Ed's vetting procedure, but not everyone who applied was accepted and, as you couldn't get those particular vintages from anywhere else, serving wine with Ed's imprimatur on it—they arrived in lovely wooden crates, with a 'BB' sticker on each bottle— was the last word in insider chic among certain elite circles.

This exclusivity, combined with Ed's very amusing writing style, the eccentric nature of the people and places he encountered on his travels, the anorak-y details of the wine, the cellars, the food, the hotels and the cars, plus his genuine connoisseurship, had turned the journal into a cult male read.

He had been approached many times over the years by newspapers wanting him to turn the journal into a column, and by supermarkets wanting him to do upscale wine ranges for them, but he always said no.

Ed was adamant that the whole set-up should stay as it was—'capriciously exclusive' was his term—and it certainly seemed to work. What had started out as a hobby when he was still a student had grown into a very successful business. Ed was raking it in.

So, I reminded myself, as I often did, settling down to read on my own, after we'd finished dinner and he had returned to his study, I could hardly resent him spending so much time on the

15

thing which kept me in the manner to which I had become so luxuriously accustomed.

I'd certainly had plenty of time to get used to it. Bradlow's Bottles had been at the heart of our relationship since the day we met fifteen years before, in the south of France.

He'd been down there on one of his early wine-buying forays, when he was still just selling cut-price plonk to university pals as a way of subsidizing his own passion for the seriously good stuff. I was doing a year at the university in Montpellier, as part of my French degree.

I could still remember so clearly the first time I ever spoke to him. He had rung my lodgings and, by sheer fluke, that morning I was in and my cow of a landlady was out—which was very lucky, because there was no way Madame Marchand would have passed his message on to me. I'd already had several promising flirtations wrecked by her disinclination to tell me when a young man had telephoned, back in those days long before mobiles, texts and emails.

'Is this Amelia Herbert?' an unfamiliar male voice, with a very English accent, had asked when I answered the phone.

'Oui,' I said. 'I mean, yes . . . who's calling, please?'

'My name is Ed Bradlow—I'm at Magdalene with your brother, Dick, and he gave me your number when he heard I was coming down to Montpellier. I'm here to look at some wine and I wondered if you'd like to come out with me for a day?'

I was rather bewildered. What did he mean by 'look' at some wine? Go to an off-licence and look

16

at the labels?

It didn't appeal to me particularly, but something about Ed's voice was terribly likeable and made me realize how homesick I was for some British company. It was the first time in my life I hadn't been at home for Easter.

'What did you have in mind?' I replied, hoping it was vague enough not to reveal my ignorance.

'Well, today I'm going to see a vineyard about 60 Kilometres from here, up in the hills. I think it will be a lovely drive and it would be really nice to have someone to share it with. I've been travelling on my own already for a fortnight . . .'

'I'd love to come,' I said impulsively, although I had an essay deadline looming. That could wait, I decided. Ed appeared less than half an hour later in a red open-top Jaguar. I was deeply impressed—my brother and his other friends drove round in terrible old bangers—and Ed's broad smile and firm handshake put me immediately at my ease.

'What a beautiful car,' I said, sinking into the cream leather seat and running my hand over the highly polished walnut dashboard—and then holding tightly on to it as Ed took off at high acceleration. 'Is it an old one?'

He turned and smiled at me again. Although he wasn't film-star hunky handsome—in fact, he looked rather skinny under his striped shirt—there was something about Ed's face which was as instantly appealing as his voice had been on the telephone.

'1962,' he said, proudly. 'I'm glad you like her. I got her last month and thought I'd bring her down to France for a spin on this trip.'

17

'Do you come to France a lot then?' I asked.

'A couple of times a year—for the wine.'

'Oh,' I said, suddenly remembering something my brother had mentioned. 'Are you the one who buys wine direct from the growers and sells it on to them all at great prices? Dick told me about you. He brought some bottles of red home for us at Christmas, actually. It was very nice.'

I didn't go on to tell him that my father had liked it so much he'd drunk himself into a foaming rage, which had led to the upending of the Christmas pudding on to the dining-room floor. I pushed that unhappy memory down to fester with all the similar ones and smiled at Ed.

'That's me,' said Ed, turning his head to me and smiling back. 'And I hope we are going to find some rather marvellous wine to buy today. I've had a tip-off about this grower from someone whose opinion I seriously respect, and I'm rather excited about the Languedoc in general at the moment. Actually, I need to see exactly where we are going. There's a red notebook in the case on the back seat—could you get it for me?'

I turned round to see an old leather suitcase which seemed to be full of maps, folders and notebooks. I did a double take when I noticed there was also a stuffed toy back there, a grey velvet elephant wearing a knitted scarf, propped on the seat next to the case.

It was, of course, the creature I would later come to know so very well as Mr Bun, Ed's constant companion since he was sent to boarding school aged six. At first sighting, though, it seemed highly peculiar—or a little pretentious—for a dashing young man like Ed to have a cuddly toy in

18

his car, but I said nothing, just found the red notebook as instructed and pulled it out.

'That's the one,' he was saying. 'Now open it up at the page where the corner is turned down.'

I did as he asked, and found a page of notes in elegant loopy handwriting—fountain pen—with the name of the vineyard in neat capitals at the top.

'Those numbers and letters at the bottom of the page are the map reference,' said Ed, passing me a map and a compass from a pocket in his door. 'How's your navigation?'

'Well, I was a Girl Guide . . .' I said, feeling somewhat nervous, but wanting to please.

'Great stuff,' said Ed. 'I know the way as far as there'—he pointed to a dot on the map with a very long, multiply-hyphenated name—'but after that it's up to you.'

I did really well getting us up into the hilly country and I loved bowling along with the top down. It was a beautiful April day and the air smelled of wild thyme up there. Everything seemed perfect until I realized we were completely and utterly lost.

I kept quiet about the first few signposts which meant nothing and a couple of villages which bore no relation to anything I could see on the map, but secretly I was really starting to panic.

Playing for time, I just carried on randomly saying 'Left again' and 'Right, here', as though I knew what I was doing, for fear of how Ed might react. I'd had too many experiences of my father going nuts when my mother or brother messed up the map-reading to be casual about it with a total stranger.

After another couple of signposts that might as well have been in Swahili for all they meant to me, Ed started to laugh. It began as a chuckle and then became such a belly laugh he had to pull the car over. He turned to me, still grinning.

'We're completely arseholed, aren't we?' he said, looking sideways at me, his elbows on the steering wheel.

I nodded, still slightly terrified that the laughter could turn to shouting at any moment, but he just put his hand on my shoulder, threw his head back and roared. I started to laugh too.

'Oh, that's so funny,' he said, getting the words out with difficulty. 'I started to wonder about thirty minutes ago, but I didn't like to say anything because it seemed rather rude to question a Girl Guide's map-reading skills, but when I realized we had gone past the same signpost twice, I really started to wonder . . .'

He was now helpless with laughter, spluttering and gesturing at something with his left arm. Whatever he found so funny, he was laughing too hard to get the words out.

'What?' I asked him, as he carried on flailing his arm around like a madman.

I turned to look—he seemed to be pointing at a signpost.

'Same . . . one . . .' he got out between gasps. 'Th—th—third time . . .'

Then I lost it too. Partly out of relief at the way he had reacted. He really didn't mind. He really did think it was funny that I had got us so lost. I was amazed.

'Oh, that's hilarious,' said Ed, wiping tears of laughter from his eyes. 'Your brother is so hearty and I just assumed you'd be similar. Oh, that's so funny . . .'

'Ed,' I said shyly. 'I've got something to tell you.'

He looked at me with his head on one side and his eyebrows raised expectantly. His grey-green eyes were still bright with amusement. I looked into that fine-boned face and felt my stomach do a funny little backflip thing.

'I failed my map-reading badge . . .'

For a moment he just looked at me and then he started again—a completely uninhibited, shouting laugh—and so did I.

After that Ed took over the map-reading and declared that my new job was Music Monitor. I was very happy about that and had great fun going through his box of cassettes and putting on my favourites, with a lot of winding backwards and forwards to find particular tracks, most of which we sang along to together.

He had all the stuff you would have expected to find in someone's car in 1992—Elvis Costello, Talking Heads, the soundtrack from *Betty Blue*—but also some other things that were less obvious, but which I secretly adored. When I found Shirley Bassey's *Greatest Hits* and put on the theme tune from *Goldfinger* at extra volume, Ed turned to me and beamed.

My stomach did that thing again.

Eventually we found the vineyard, and the owner appeared, smiling, in the open doorway of the farmhouse when he heard the car turn into the yard. It was a wonderful old place with the main house on one side, flanked by rambling outbuildings made from the same weathered grey stone.

Monsieur Fabre didn't seem at all bothered that we had arrived three hours later than Ed's appointment and laughed almost as much as we had when we explained how lost we'd been.

He had greeted us in reasonably good English, but when I described our beleaguered journey in French, the tiniest lift of his bushy white left eyebrow indicated to me that he was suitably impressed with my command of his language, and not another word was exchanged in English. After six months living there I could read such tiny calibrations of the Gallic face.

Although his accent was terrible, Ed's French was pretty good—good enough to appreciate quite how fluently I spoke it. I could tell he was impressed and was secretly delighted, but once we got into the tasting, which took place in an old stone barn full of wooden barrels of wine, it was Ed's turn to shine.

Until that afternoon, I hadn't fully appreciated the sensuality of wine, but I could see the pleasure Ed got from exploring each one, assessing and comparing the appearance, the legs—which was something to do with how it stuck to the sides of the glass, as far as I could tell—the nose and, finally, the taste, and it was a joyous thing to see someone doing something he so clearly adored.

Mr Fabre was clearly as impressed with Ed as I was, and after a full tasting of the wines it was already early evening and he invited us to stay for dinner.

With lively conversation, delicious food and a lot more wine, dinner was a jolly affair. Then, as I helped clear the table, I heard Monsieur Fabre ask Ed if 'you and your charming young wife' would like to stay the night, as it was a long way back to Montpellier in the dark.

'Especially with Madame Bradlow's navigational skills . . .' he added, chuckling heartily.

So without feeling any explanations were necessary, we did. We stayed the night together in a beautifully simple French bedroom, in an old iron bed made up with starched linen sheets.

With what felt like buckets of wine inside me— and not at all used to drinking so much—I fell asleep the moment my head hit the pillow, so there was no question of any hanky-panky that first night. And there was no risk of it in the morning either, because when I woke up, Ed wasn't there.

After a moment of feeling slightly rejected, I decided it was a relief. I'd only known him a few hours and I wasn't even entirely sure what I thought about him. I definitely liked him, but I didn't quite know where to put him in my head yet. He wasn't like anyone else I knew.

I lay there for a while listening to the sounds of the French country morning and thinking about him, this virtual stranger I had just shared a bed with.

He was a very self-contained person, I decided. It didn't seem to bother him what anyone else might think of him, so when he did engage with you, it seemed particularly sincere and meaningful somehow. Most of the time he seemed to be somewhere else, then he'd smile suddenly, looking you right in the eye, and it felt like a blessing, like a baby's guileless grin.

And he did have rather a beautiful face, I decided. Not in a flashy, obvious way, but his were very refined features which grew on you. It was an

23

old-fashioned kind of face, with those high cheekbones that look almost bruised, a narrow nose and a sculpted mouth. His mother must be a real beauty, I thought.

I stretched sleepily and then jumped out of bed, throwing open the shutters on to the most beautiful view, the sun just starting to burn the mist off the vines.

As I stood at the open window, clutching a sheet around me, there was a knock on the door, then Ed came in carrying a large jug of steaming water. He put it on the floorboards in the corner of the room, next to a wrought-iron washstand, and fished a large bar of soap out of his pocket.

'Your bath, mademoiselle,' he said, smiling in that sweet way of his.

He was already dressed and shaved, his wavy brown hair neatly combed into its side parting.

'When you've finished, just chuck the water out of the window,' he said. 'Good for the grapes. I'll see you downstairs. I think we're going to have rather a marvellous breakfast.'

As it turned out, I didn't share Ed's appetite for boudin noir at that time of the morning, but I enjoyed watching him tuck into it as much as our hostess clearly did. I was already finding Ed's enthusiasm for food, wine, France and life in general very infectious.

As we drove away from the vineyard later, waving back at our new friends Monsieur and Madame Fabre, he looked over and smiled at me, his once-neat hair blowing all over his face. 'Come with me, Amelia,' he said, turning his head back to the road. 'I've got another two glorious weeks of this before I have to get back to Cambridge, and

I'd love you to share them with me. It's pretty good on my own, but it would be so much more fun with you.'

He paused and then glanced at me again. He looked quite serious. 'Anything would be more fun with you, actually,' he said, quietly.

I didn't have to think before I replied. This was what I had come to France to find. Adventure. Romance. Possibly even love. Possibly even sex. My essay would just have to wait.

'I'd love to,' I said, nodding enthusiastically.

Ed peeped his horn happily in response.

We stopped briefly in Montpellier so I could pick up some clothes and tell my horrid landlady not to worry about me. She sniffed dismissively and looked out of the window at Ed sitting in his red open-top car, sunglasses on, his elegant face turned up towards the sun.

'*Bonnes vacances*,' she said, with pungent irony.

I pulled a face at the door as I closed it behind me and ran back to the car.

3

From the moment we roared off from that dull little street, I was thrilled I had gone with Ed. It was early April, the countryside was springing into life and, driving out into the country, weaving north and east towards the Rhone, the landscape was glorious. I was even captivated by the flat plains with leafy vines stretching for miles.

'Look at that!' shouted Ed joyously, as we bowled through it. 'Gallons and gallons of wine, as far as the eye can see. So much wine, so little time . . .'

Although it seemed to me that we were doing our best. We were certainly getting through it at the many vineyards we stopped at and, while I was feeling a little dizzy with all the driving and tasting, Ed seemed completely clear-headed.

It did cross my mind as we sped off from yet another cellar that the combination of wine and a powerful car was not an ideal one, but Ed seemed to spit out most of the wine he tasted; something I hadn't quite got the hang of yet.

And that was just one of many ways he impressed me. He was amazingly organized, with bundles of annotated maps and guides bound up with elastic bands in that old suitcase on the back seat, along with the colour-coded notebooks and folders of press cuttings, and he always knew exactly where he wanted to go each day.

When we arrived at each new vineyard, we would sit in the car for a moment and take in the general scene. Ed would have his ongoing notebook in his lap and would scribble down first impressions in his flowing script—it was all part of remembering the wine, he explained to me, to put it in a context. Other times he would snap the book shut without writing a word and we'd drive off again.

'Wasn't feeling the love there,' he'd say, by way of explanation. 'Neither was Mr Bun.'

He turned round and looked at the grey velvet elephant, to whom I had now been formally introduced. 'No, he definitely didn't like it either. Let's try the next one.'

We spent the second night in a hotel in the main

square of a small town and, after dinner in the restaurant downstairs, we had once more fallen immediately asleep, road weary and wine sated. And the following morning, I'd woken up again in an empty bed. Well, empty except for the velvet elephant, who was propped against the footboard at the end of the bed looking at me.

'Bonjour, Monsieur Brioche,' I said. '*Ça va?*'

I felt too peaky to wonder what it meant that Ed wasn't there in its place and stumbled downstairs to find him immaculately turned out and eating yet more boudin noir for breakfast. I sipped a café crème and nibbled unenthusiastically on a croissant, marvelling at his constitution.

We didn't do so much tasting that third day— and I made sure I spat everything out, as Ed did— so by the evening I had recovered enough to look forward to dinner, and as we walked into the restaurant, I was distinctly aware that something was different between us, a shift had taken place.

Mind you, the venue was enough to put anyone in a romantic mood. The restaurant was in a lovely old mill set in beautiful gardens, with the mill stream running through them. Ed had a press cutting about it in one of his folders and I noticed it had two Michelin stars, which was probably why he'd booked the table before he left England.

The maitre d raised a discreet eyebrow when the two of us turned up.

'Ah, Monsieur Bradlow,' he'd said. 'I see you are now requiring a table for two. Let me quickly make arrangements.'

And so we had ended up in the most beautiful spot, next to a window looking out over the darkening garden. The dining room was fit only

27

with candles, and I sat there with a stupid grin on my face, as the sommelier quietly opened a bottle of Krug's Clos de Mesnil—no flashy pops in a place like this—Ed's favourite champagne.

He held the glass up to his nose, sniffing purposively. 'Such a surprising oriental spicy nose,' he said, a satisfied grin spreading across his face. I was still getting my head around his particular use of language in regard to wine, but I was eager to learn. I sniffed my glass too. 'Then toffee, honey, coffee, linden, cream, butterscotch, sun-ripened oranges . . . It's got everything.' He took a deep sip and held it in his mouth, swilling it around for a few seconds. I was glad he didn't make the sucking noises he made during tastings.

He swallowed then sighed deeply, his eyes closed. 'Such power and breadth and so silky in the mouth.'

I had to smile. I wasn't sure I could detect everything Ed was describing, but it certainly tasted delicious. 'Mmmm,' I said, slightly surprised, after I had swallowed my first mouthful. 'You can taste it for ages after you've gulped it down, and it sort of changes on your tongue . . .'

Ed beamed at me and reached across the table to squeeze my hand. 'You're a natural,' he said. 'We'll make a proper wine buff out of you before the end of this trip.'

I felt something akin to a small electric shock when he touched me. Although we had spent two nights in the same bed, it was the most intimate gesture he had yet made to me and, to cover my self-consciousness, I started talking again.

'How did you become such a connoisseur?' I asked.

28

A shadow crossed Ed's face. 'As a child, I spent every August in Provence with my parents. Not a million miles from here actually. There were vineyards all around the villa and I used to entertain myself by visiting them on my bicycle and pestering the men who made the wine. It amused them to have an eight-year-old boy who wanted to taste with them and, just by hanging around, I learned a great deal.'

'Didn't your parents mind you drinking alcohol when you were eight?' I asked, trying to hide how shocked I was.

Ed shrugged. 'They didn't know. They were so caught up in themselves and their social lives, they didn't even ask where I'd been all day.'

'Where did you live when you weren't in France?' I asked, eager to find out more about what had made Ed the singular person he was.

'Boarding school. My parents lived in Hong Kong—I was born there—but they sent me to school in England when I was six. I went back to Hong Kong for Christmas every year, they came over to London for the Season each summer and then we spent August down here in Provence. Now, what are we going to eat?'

He clearly wanted to move on from that subject, so I didn't push him. As the daughter of the deputy headmaster of a boys' boarding school, I had a good idea what that kind of education involved in emotional terms—not a lot—and although I was now fired with curiosity about his exotic-sounding family, I knew it wasn't the time to press him further.

The food and wine were amazing that night, but even Ed seemed to eat and drink a little less than usual, and as we walked back to the car along by the millrace, he put his arm around me for the first time. And then, just as we reached the old cast-iron gate that led out to the car park, he pulled me over into the darkness under a flowering chestnut tree and kissed me.

It was a beautiful kiss. Very tender and tasting deliciously of the exquisite things we had eaten and drunk together. That was what Ed smelled like, I thought, as I buried my head into his neck.

He never wore aftershave, because he said it interfered with wine-tasting, and he smelled instead like the distilled essence of fine wine and brandy, of duck *confit* and goose-liver pâté good bread, white peaches, raspberries still warm from the bush, Normandy butter and the best cheeses. I pressed my cheek against his, breathing in his delicious scent and feeling an intense sense of homecoming.

Back at the hotel everything continued in this new mood. Instead of the two of us falling into bed already unconscious, Ed undressed me as though he were unwrapping a box of exquisite chocolates, stopping to admire what he found at each layer and arranging my long hair so that it fell down over my naked body.

Then he made love to me very slowly, with what seemed like hours of kissing and stroking, until I felt I was going to die from wanting him. He paused to put on a condom—I was impressed with how responsible he was—and then he entered me quite suddenly, taking me almost by surprise.

Then it seemed as if, just as I was getting used to the delicious sensation, his back arched, he cried out, and I realized he had come. He kissed me tenderly on the lips and then fell immediately asleep beside me.

I lay there for a moment feeling a little stunned, it had all ended so suddenly. I squeezed my legs together a few times, trying to regain the sensation, but it was gone. I curled up against him and fell asleep too.

*   *   *

I woke in the morning to find Ed sitting on the bed, fully dressed, shaved and immaculate as usual, and smiling down at me. He lay by my side, took me in his arms and kissed me. There was a delicious smell in the room and I raised my head off the pillow to see a large tray on the end of the bed.

'Breakfast,' he said, standing up and taking his clothes off again.

He was about to get into the bed when he noticed the velvet elephant sitting at the end of it, looking back at us.

'Hmmmm,' said Ed, reaching down and moving it on to a chest of drawers, facing the wall. 'Not for elephantine eyes, I don't think, Mr Bun. And close those big ears, please.'

Then he climbed back into bed beside me, pulled up the tray and started to feed me pieces of croissant dipped in hot chocolate, until his fingers found their way into my mouth and then I was gently biting and sucking on them and we forgot about the breakfast.

This time his love-making was more urgent, and as he finally collapsed on top of me, kissing my neck as his body continued to shudder, I knew I

31

was a goner. I had fallen in love.

*   *   *

The rest of the trip continued in the same blissful way and, two weeks later, when I really did have to go back to Montpellier, we agreed that when I'd finished my last term there, he—and Mr Bun—would drive back down to get me. It already seemed only natural for us to be together. All three of us.

We spent that entire wonderful first summer winding our way slowly back up through France, stopping at what seemed like every vineyard on the way. And as we drove and laughed and ate and laughed and drank and laughed and made love and laughed, we got to know each other better every day, until I found it hard to remember what life had been like before I knew him.

And as Ed told me more about his life and family, I began to understand why he seemed so much more self-sufficient than most people our age. On top of being an only child, cast adrift from his mother—and, more crucially, his ayah—to go to prep school across the world at six, when he was twelve, his father had died suddenly.

His mother, Dervla, who was much younger than her late husband, had then moved to South Africa. From what Ed told me she sounded a bit of a handful, but coming as I did from a classic nuclear family—two parents, two children, one dog—who lived in a new-build executive home in Maidstone, Ed's background, while sad, seemed very glamorous to me and an essential part of the attraction of the man I had fallen in love with.

32

It also made me a bit nervous at the prospect of him meeting my parents, but the point came when I knew it would have to happen. They had been pretty unhappy about me not coming straight home when I'd finished at Montpellier in June—especially as I was going to be trailing around France for weeks with someone they had never met. So I had mollified them with the promise that I would bring him back to visit at the end of the trip, and I'd also asked my brother Dick to put in a good word for Ed, which had seemed to do the trick with my father in the short term. It was the kind of man-to-man talk he understood. But by the time we were on the cross-Channel ferry heading back to Dover and I knew it was only a matter of hours until we would all be under the same roof, I was starting to feel really jumpy.

I was a bit worried that Ed would think my family were terribly dull and suburban—he was so sophisticated compared to anyone else I knew—but my greatest concern was what state of mind my dad would be in.

My father could be charming and amusing company, but if he was having one of his black days and things weren't going exactly as he thought they should, the atmosphere could quickly turn very ugly in our house. It was the unpredictability of his moods that made it so stressful.

As we drove through Dover, I looked feverishly out of the car window for a phone box. I wanted to call my mum to see how things were before we arrived, so I could be prepared. I finally spotted one and asked Ed to pull over.

'Hi, Mum,' I said enthusiastically, very relieved she had answered and not Stormin' Norman, as my brother called our father, although his real name was Paul. 'Just to let you know we have landed on British soil and we should be with you in under an hour.'

'Oh, hello, Amelia love,' she said. 'It's good to know you're back safely. We're so looking forward to seeing you.'

I tried to read the signs in her voice, the messages hidden underneath the pleasant chitchat. I could tell by the bright tone she was using that my dad was within earshot. There was always a slight tension in her speech when he was around, but she didn't sound overly stressed. Hopefully, that meant he was calm.

'I'm bringing Ed with me, as we discussed,' I continued, fishing for more information. 'Is that still a good idea?'

'Yes, yes,' she said. 'Of course. We're really looking forward to meeting him. I've got the spare room all ready. Dick's here as well, so it will be quite a party.'

I could have danced with relief that Dick was going to be there. Things were always better at home when he was around.

'Great,' I said. 'Can't wait. See you soon.'

And I rang off smiling, happy with what passed for a deep and meaningful conversation between me and my mother. Although I loved her dearly, that was about as close as we ever got to being real about things with each other, because when you lived in a state of constant tension, as we all did around my father, the only way to cope with it was always to pretend everything was lovely. Reality was way too scary to deal with. When Mum and I got going, we made Pollyanna look like a

34

miserable old pessimist.

I tried to keep my head in that mode as we got closer to Maidstone, but despite my best efforts, I couldn't stop my thoughts galloping off, wondering if there was any way I could warn Ed about my father before we got there. I could feel my pulse starting to race from the tension of it, until I knew I had to say something.

'There's something I've got to tell you,' I blurted out, eventually.

Ed's head snapped round and he looked at me. 'Are you OK?' he asked, looking very concerned.

I had to get on with it. I took a deep breath. 'Yes, I'm fine, it's just . . . well, the thing is . . . it's my father.'

'Oh, that's a relief,' he said, glancing back at me, this time smiling sweetly.

'Whatever do you mean?' I asked him, puzzled.

'Well, go on and I'll see if I'm right.'

'It's just, well, my dad can be a little . . .'

'Difficult?' said Ed.

'Yes,' I said, looking at him in amazement.

'It's OK, Amelia,' he said, taking my hand and holding it on his left thigh while he drove. 'Your brother gave me a bit of a tip-off about that.'

I was astonished. 'Whatever did he say?'

'He just said that if I was planning on meeting your folks, I might want to pack a bulletproof vest because your old man has a hair trigger on his temper. Is that it?'

'Pretty much,' I said, intensely relieved that I didn't have to do any more explaining.

'I think I'll be able to deal with him,' said Ed, squeezing my hand and then letting go of it to change gear. 'I know all about deputy

35

headmasters. They're always the really crazy ones. They take their frustration at not being the top man out wherever they can and, in your dad's case, it seems to be at home.'

I looked at the side of his face in astonishment. He had the whole sick picture bang on. Without me needing to go into tiresome explanations of the thing that made me most uncomfortable in my life, he seemed to understand it completely. I felt a new rush of love for him.

I sat there for a while, humming with happiness that I had met such a wonderful man. Then I remembered his slightly odd initial overreaction to me saying I had something to tell him.

'Ed,' I said, tentatively. He turned and smiled at me. My stomach turned over, as it always did when he looked at me that way. That smile really was adorable. 'What on earth did you think I was going to tell you before? You looked terrified.'

'Oh,' he said, laughing sheepishly. 'You sounded so worried, I thought you might be about to tell me you were pregnant, or something like that. You know, every man's worst nightmare, getting the lovely young girlfriend knocked up . . .'

He smiled at me again, but not his normal radiant beam, it was more of a nervous rictus. I was really puzzled. 'Well, that's hardly likely, is it?' I said, as lightly as I could. 'I'm on the Pill and you always use a condom as well . . . You'd have to have supersonic sperm to get me pregnant through all that.'

'Well, you can't be too careful, can you?' said Ed, laughing and squeezing my leg.

I said nothing. I'd always thought an accidental pregnancy between two people who were very much in love was terribly romantic. Really, I couldn't think of a nicer way for a child to be conceived than through unbridled passion like that. Maybe that was just a girl thing, I told myself. Ed would probably want to plan his family with the same precision he brought to his wine-buying trips.

'Cor blimy,' he was saying, shifting around in his car seat. 'Can we stop talking about that subject? You're getting me all hot and bothered, and I imagine we will be very separately billeted at your parents' place tonight, so I won't be able to do anything about it. I don't imagine your father would tolerate any corridor creeping.'

'No,' I said, laughing too. 'He's probably installed a tripwire alarm system ready.'

And then we reached the turn-off for Maidstone, and I was so distracted giving Ed directions to my parents' cul de sac, hidden deep in a soulless labyrinth of new housing developments, that I forgot all about it.

4

The visit started well enough. Everyone was on their best behaviour—apart from the bloody dog, which tried to shag Ed's leg while we were having a slightly tortured time drinking tea in the sitting room from my mother's best china cups. I wished we'd just had mugs in the kitchen, like we normally did, but I knew she was only trying to make it super nice for my sake, so I did my best to look relaxed while feeling as tense as a spring.

Ed did a good job gently extracting Monty, a

particularly foul-smelling and charmless Westie, from his trouser leg, but then my father's beloved pet proceeded to put on another canine display, dragging its bottom backwards and forwards across the carpet with a unique humping motion, until Dick administered a light kick when neither of my parents was looking.

It was a risky move on Dick's part, because Monty was the object of my father's unconditional love in a way neither of his children had ever been. My mother was surprisingly soppy about the dog too—probably because it was the one member of the family who never triggered my dad's rage. And even I had to admit it was a very useful distraction mechanism. If things started to get unbearably fraught, you could divert attention to Monty, ascribing to him all manner of anthropomorphic thoughts and motivations.

'Oh look,' said Dick, after the kick had sent the poor creature whining to the closed door, which it was now viciously scratching. 'Monty thinks it's a waste to stay in on such a lovely afternoon. He thinks it's time for a walk with Dickie, don't you, Monty boy? Anyone else want to come?'

I leapt to my feet, thrilled to have been thrown a means of escape. Dick really was the business like that.

'I would love to come,' said my mum.

'Yes, me too,' said Ed. 'A walk would be lovely after all that driving.'

But my father had other plans for Ed. 'No, Edward,' he said, planting one of his hairy hands on Ed's slender shoulder, 'let them go. You stay here with me, so we can get to know each other. I'd like to hear what you have to say about New

World wines . . .'

My heart sank, for so many reasons. I would have dreaded the thought of Ed being left alone with my father in any circs, but with the subject for discussion now laid on the table, it was potentially catastrophic.

I already knew exactly what both of them felt about New World wines. My father was a big enthusiast for cheap plonk from the colonies, while Ed thought that no vintage produced outside France was worthy of discussion, let alone drinking. He was categorical about it.

Even with my very limited knowledge of wine, I thought Ed's position a little extreme, but that was how he felt—end of story. And I already knew that when Ed's mind was made up about something, there was no point in arguing with him. In that moment it occurred to me for the first time that he and my dad were almost a match when it came to obstinacy. Ed was just a lot more charming about it.

I thought quickly. 'Ed,' I said, brightly. 'Can you just help me get my bag out of the car? I need to change my shoes.'

He sprang up like a ninja and we were out of the room together before any objection could be made.

'OK,' I said, going into full crisis-management mode as we walked across the short gravel drive to the car. 'Dad thinks wine from Chile and South Africa and probably Chad is really, really super, OK? I know you hate it, but can you just pretend to go along with him? Please? He's even more stubborn than you are, so don't bother trying to argue. For my sake?'

Ed answered by pulling me towards him and kissing me passionately by the car, while I opened one eye to make sure my father wasn't watching out of the sitting-room window.

*   *   *

Dick's idea of a walk involved, as I had strongly suspected it would, not much more perambulation than it took to get from the car park to the door of one of his favourite country pubs.

Mum and I left him there and said we'd come back and find him after we'd had a proper stroll with Monty. We set off on one of our well-trodden family routes, down a path which ran along the edge of a beautiful meadow and into some woods. I breathed in the sweet late-summer English air and felt the tension of the day begin to subside.

'Ed seems very nice,' said my mum.

'Oh good,' I said. 'I'm so glad you like him. Of course, you haven't really had a chance to get to know him yet, but I'm pleased your first impressions are good.'

'He has lovely manners, and he's very nice-looking, I must say.'

We walked on for a bit without saying anything else, apart from the usual nonsensical asides to Monty that we ritually employed to fill up the space where a conversation might normally be.

'Oh, what a clever puppy!' exclaimed my mum when he caught a stick.

'Look, Monty!' I said in equally excited tones, as I threw the stick again.

'So how have you been since I last saw you?' I asked casually, and deliberately not specifying whether it was 'you' in the singular or the plural.

'Oh, we've been fine,' said my mum, her voice rising very slightly, so I knew things hadn't been fine. I had been worried about leaving her alone with my father for the entire summer holidays. Normally, I would have been at home for most of them, working in a kitchenware shop in the town and just being there for Mum the rest of the time.

'Has Dad been able to relax and enjoy the break, or has he been worrying about work?' I asked, lightly, which was as close as I was going to get to asking the real question, which I could never actually ask.

'He's been a bit anxious about things,' said my mum, looking down. 'Here, Monty, catch . . . Oh, what a clever boy you are!'

She glanced at me. 'I went to stay with Jill for a week, while you were away.'

I sighed. So it had been that bad. 'How is Jill?' I asked. She was my godmother, who lived in Devon, and she had long been my mother's survival line when things with Daddy dearest got just too ugly.

'She's very well,' said Mum, smiling in a way that seemed much more genuine than her normal social face. 'We had a lovely time just going for walks and cooking and reading. Just pootling quietly. It was glorious.'

I put my arm around my mother's shoulders and gave her a squeeze. It was the best I could do. There was so much to say, I couldn't even start. If we opened that floodgate, we would never be able to close it again. But in that moment a tiny hug was enough between us for me to tell her I loved her and knew what she went through with my shit of a father. We didn't have to put it into words. We knew.

She smiled at me softly again and I could see tears in her eyes, before she blinked them away and resumed her usual determinedly composed mantle.

'So,' she said. 'Do you think you are serious about Ed?'

'Gosh,' I replied, taken off guard. 'I'm not sure. Well, I think he is probably the most serious boyfriend I've ever had. He's . . . he's just so lovely. I feel so comfortable with him. He makes me laugh, he's very thoughtful and he rather spoils me. I do really like him.'

'I'm so pleased for you, Amelia. You are at the right age to feel like that about someone.' She paused and gave me a resigned look. 'Let's pray your father likes him as much as I do,' she said. 'I'm sure he's giving him the third degree right now. I hope it doesn't put Ed off.'

And then the conversation at any real level was over and it was back to telling Monty how terribly clever he was and look, how amazing, here was another lovely stick, until we went back to find Dick.

His eyes had a distinct glaze to them when we found him leaning on the pub bar. He was near the bottom of a pint of real ale of some kind, and I strongly suspected it wasn't the first.

'Hello, you two,' he said in his habitually jolly tones. 'Care for a heart-starter?'

Mum had a gin and tonic; I had a ginger beer—now I had been introduced to the delights of serious wine, I didn't fancy a glass of pub red—and we sat down at a table in the corner. Dick lit up another of the extra-strength cigarettes he almost chainsmoked.

'Better get a few more tabs in before we have to go back home,' he said conspiratorially. He didn't smoke in front of our father, who heartily disapproved of it. It was one of the many things in our family we all pretended didn't happen.

'So, tell me, Mum,' said Dick, blowing a long plume of smoke into the air. 'What do you think of Amelia's new bloke, then?'

'I was just telling her how nice he seems,' said Mum, smiling sweetly at us both.

'Yes, he's a good man, Bradders,' said Dick. 'Our Meals is a savvy girl. He's quite a catch, you know.'

'Really?' said Mum.

'Yes, half the girls at Cambridge have been chasing Bradlow and his bucks.' Dick looked at me and started laughing. 'Don't pretend you didn't know. . .'

'Well, he's clearly not short of a few bob, driving that car,' I said guardedly. 'And he has been very generous with the trip we've just been on, although of course it was all research for his business . . .'

'What do you mean, Dick?' asked my mum, cutting in.

'Bradlow's very nicely set up for a twenty-three-year-old. His dad died years ago and he got loads of cash, plus a huge flat bang in the middle of Mayfair, if you don't mind, and on top of that he's making stacks of money with all this wine he imports. Little sis here has really landed on her feet if she bags Bradlow.'

'Well, that's not why I like him,' I said, defensively. 'I'd Eke Ed just as much if he had no money . . .'

Dick put his hands on my shoulders and looked deep into my eyes with his own slightly addled ones. 'But a little lubrication to smooth your passage out of Maidstone wouldn't exactly hurt, would it?' he said.

I looked straight back at him without saying a word. Even through the haze of the drinks and the smokes, the rugby banter and the forced bonhomie, my hearty brother could be quite perceptive.

*   *   *

I drove us home. Mum and I had both insisted Dick wasn't up to it, so he sat in the back with the window open, smoking feverishly, while I made inane chat with Mum in the front, trying to ignore the butterflies that were beginning to swirl in my stomach.

I dreaded to think what might have gone on in our absence. I wouldn't have been surprised if we'd pulled up in front of the house to find Ed gone, just a cartoon plume of exhaust smoke left behind as he disappeared into the distance, but in fact I was very pleasantly surprised. We walked in to hear gales of manly laughter coming from the dining room. Dick and I exchanged a look of mutual wide-eyed wonder and went to investigate. Ed and Dad were sitting at the table with several bottles of wine and a row of glasses in front of them. My father was sitting in his carver chair, sniffing a glass of red wine, a tea towel tied round his eyes.

'Now that is definitely the Argentinian Merlot,'

44

Dad was saying. 'It's got that big hearty bouquet. I'd recognize it anywhere.'

'Are you sure?' said Ed, turning and smiling conspiratorially at us.

I was delighted to see them getting on so well but simultaneously beginning to worry what would happen if Dad was wrong about the wine he was holding. He'd never been a very good loser, and the family games of Monopoly and Scrabble had long been despatched to the attic by my mother. Even Cluedo was risky with him.

'OK, Paul,' said Ed. 'Have a look.'

Dad whipped the tea towel off his head and Ed presented the bottle—it was the Argentinian wine.

'There!' said Dad. 'I was right!' He beamed when he saw the three of us standing in the doorway. 'Ah! There you all are. We're having a very interesting tasting here. So far I've got—what is it, Edward?—five out of six right. It was just that French red which threw me off course. Told you they were tricky wines, those French ones, didn't I, Edward?'

Ed nodded. 'Very tricky, French wine,' he said. 'You never know what you're going to get . . .'

He caught my eye over Dad's head and winked at me. My stomach turned over with delight.

It was a miracle, but Dad's good mood continued right through dinner and even having quite a bit more of the various wines to drink didn't set him off. By the time he and Mum went up to bed, he was clapping Ed on the shoulders and telling him what a good chap he was.

I was almost in shock, I was so relieved, and Dick was equally impressed.

'Don't know how you did it, Bradlow,' he was

saying, as the three of us celebrated in the kitchen with a glass of the French wine.

'Aaaaah,' said Ed happily, as he savoured his first mouthful. 'Depth and complexity. Subtle richness. Quiet assertion. Such a relief after all those frightful tarry New World plonks. Give me Catherine Deneuve over Kylie Minogue any day.'

'So how did you do it?' said Dick, from his position by the open back door, out of which he was blowing his smoke.

Ed chuckled. 'Well, your sister here tipped me off about how your Dad feels about New World wine, so I just went with that. He'd also been talking about the car, so I let him drive it down to the off-licence for a test spin, and then I got one decent bottle of French, one Argentinian, one foul bottle of South African cack, one Aussie and one New Zealand, and we tasted them all, with me subtly rigging the results and swallowing as little of the New World cough mixture as I could get away with.'

'Nice work, Bradders,' said Dick, nodding in appreciation.

'Well, as I told your sister earlier, I've had plenty of experience with grumpy teachers and, like most of them, your dad is a pussycat as long as you play it all exactly by his rules—or at least if he thinks you are.'

I just gazed at him in silent awe. For the first time in my life I felt I had an ally in the battle of my family life who wasn't already a hopeless part of it.

So, a year later, when Ed asked me to marry him, producing a large diamond solitaire ring from his pocket, after we had spent an afternoon tasting champagne in the Krug cellars near Reims, I didn't hesitate to accept.

My parents were delighted when I rang to tell them. And after I hung up, I laughed at the horrified expression on Ed's face as I passed on my father's special engagement message to him: he was going to lay down a few cases of that Argentinian Merlot ready for his first grandson.

At the time, I had assumed it was the prospect of the cheap New World wine that had horrified Ed—it wasn't until years later that I realized it had been the grandson part of it too.

5

'I don't give a damn if you are going to send it round by tame ostrich. It is now 10.15 a.m. on Monday 12 March—one quarter of an hour after the agreed time and date—and as I have still not received your remuneration, I will be sending round the bailiffs to remove my painting forthwith . . .'

I tried in vain to block out the sound of my boss's voice. Christopher was one floor up from me, but his honking tones were so loud and offputting I had already messed up three of the envelopes I was addressing—and I knew that, if he found out, I'd be in for a similar roasting to whoever was on the end of the phone. I really couldn't be bothered.

I could just imagine it. 'Do you know how much each of those tissue-lined envelopes cost me, Amelia?'

47

'Tiss-yew,' he would say, hissing like a snake.

And I did know how much they cost actually, they were 40 pence each. I knew, because it was me who had to order them from Smythson and try, humiliatingly, to weasel a discount. I fished the spoiled envelopes out of the bin and put them in my handbag, to be on the safe side. It just wasn't worth the hassle.

So why did I work for such a monster and his equally repellent son, Leo? Because in my own way, I enjoyed it. After growing up with my father, I was used to dealing with difficult men—indeed, it was almost a game to me and more than worth it to spend my days surrounded by amazing works of art and the interesting people they attracted.

C. J. Mecklin and Son was one of the most well-known art galleries on Cork Street, and their list of artists was extremely impressive. If you weren't edgy enough to be with White Cube, you were with Mecklin's. Artists who showed there got rich. Just not quite as rich as Christopher James Mecklin, or 'CJ' as he styled himself.

I'd worked there for nearly five years, lured away from my previous position at a less prestigious Mayfair gallery after we'd met at a drinks party. He'd taken me for lunch at Le Caprice and done his full oily number, promising great things, telling me how my 'marvellous language skills' would be such an asset to the gallery, and implying I'd be practically running the place in no time.

In fact it had turned out to be little more than a souped-up receptionist's role and I had long ago realized that my association with Ed's business, with its super-rich clients and the potential for cut-price prestige wine for private views, was a large part of my appeal to Christopher. Yet somehow he managed to keep me believing that I was permanently on the brink of a thrilling promotion, so I stayed.

Really, he was such an operator—with me and everyone else—I couldn't help rather admiring him. Indeed, observing CJ, or Creeping Jesus, as Ed called him, on one of his deadly charm offensives with a potential customer was so impressive I sometimes wondered if that was what kept me working there. It was great sport.

And, really, I reflected, as I addressed another envelope, although it could be tedious, my job suited me for all kinds of reasons. Not least of which was I could walk there from home. That, combined with the status of the operation—which played well with Ed's snobby clients and made me sccm likc much more of a go-getter than I really was—made it a perfectly acceptable package for me.

I put down my fountain pen and massaged my right hand, which was starting to ache from the strain of writing addresses in my best calligraphy; Christopher thought printed labels were beyond the pale.

I stretched in my seat behind the reception desk and then got up to take a stroll around the room. We had a wonderful show on, one of my favourite Mecklin artists, a lovely old chap who specialized in almost abstract landscapes of the Cornish coast where he lived.

I was gazing at a tiny, jewel-like watercolour in the far corner of the room when I heard a commotion at the door and spun round. There'd been a ram raid on another gallery a few doors up the month before, and it had left us all a bit jumpy, but this seemed to be someone simultaneously pressing the security buzzer and banging on the window.

I walked over quickly to check them out through the plate-glass door and saw a familiar figure standing there. A neat head of shiny black hair and an enormous pair of white sunglasses above a vintage Chanel suit told me it was Kiki.

'Jeez, what's with all the security?' she was saying, as she pushed past me. 'You think anyone would want to steal these things? They're hideous.'

'Will you shut up?' I hissed at her. I could already hear heavy footfalls coming down the stairs and I knew CJ was on his way. I didn't need the aggro.

'Is everything all right down here, Amelia?' he said, in his most sinister smoothie tones, gliding across the parquet floor towards us. Sometimes I was convinced his Lobb brogues had wheels in them.

'Oh, yes,' I said. 'The, er, doorbell got stuck. I'll have someone come and look at it.'

'Hi,' said Kiki, brazenly looking him up and down. She'd never been to the gallery before, which had suited me fine, and so far I'd managed to dodge her requests to be put on the private-view invitation list.

'Hello,' said Christopher, icily. 'Can we help you?'

'Oh, I've just come to take Amelia out to lunch,' she said cheerily, linking her arm through mine, 'but I thought I'd check out the gallery first.'

He fixed me with a cold, enquiring stare.

'Um, Christopher, this is my very good friend Kiki *Wilmott*, from *Australia*,' I said, hoping he would catch my drift. A tiny flicker in his saurian eyes told me he did.

For someone who read—and re-read—the *Sunday Times* Rich List with the reverence most people reserved for a religious text, as he did, 'Wilmott' in an Australian context was a name which meant something. Something with a great many noughts on the end.

'Ah, Miss Wilmott, how lovely to see you. Let me show you the work . . . Now this is a very special piece . . .'

'Oh yeah, very nice,' said Kiki, in devastatingly dismissive tones. 'But you see, the thing is, Chris, I only buy Australian art.'

'Ah, yes, very wise to concentrate on one area,' he replied, not missing a beat. It was a bit like watching a Wimbledon final, they were both such masters of the social volley. 'So many collectors make the mistake of lessening the effect of very good individual pictures by buying too disparately,' CJ was droning on. 'I don't know if Amelia has told you, but as well as all our premier British names, we are also widely considered London's leading gallery for prestige contemporary Australian artists. Lesley Pinecliff, you may know . . .'

He was Australia's greatest living artist and of course Kiki knew him. She'd already told me she had a flat full of his paintings.

'Oh, yeah,' she was saying. 'Les is a great mate. Love Les. I'll have to get Amelia to bring you over to see my collection some time.'

'That would be delightful, and of course we

51

must put you on our private-view list . . .'

'Oh, I already have actually, Christopher,' I lied, to both of them.

'Right,' said Kiki, clearly fully over the chitchat. 'Nice to meet you, Chris. Can I take this girl off your hands now?'

'Of course,' he said, smiling broadly at her and bowing slightly. 'Do come in and see us again,' and then, turning to me, he added: 'Have a nice long lunch, Amelia dear.'

Which I knew translated as: Go out and whore yourself to get this rich Australian bitch to give us some money.

I smiled sweetly back, thinking: Dream on, fuckface.

*   *   *

'Christ, what a dickhead,' Kiki was saying, the door of the gallery barely closed behind us. 'He's so oily I thought I might slip in it. Why on earth do you work for him? It's not like you and Ed need the money.'

I hurried her down the street, hoping Christopher hadn't heard any of it and electing not to answer any of her questions.

'Right,' she said, stopping on the corner of Burlington Street. 'Cecconi's or the Wolseley?'

'The Wolseley,' I said firmly. I loved Cecconi's, and Ed and I often went there for dinner, but hideous Leo Mecklin had a regular table at lunchtime. It was so close to the gallery he didn't have to waddle his chubby legs very far to get there, and having him so near might put me off my lunch.

'If you think Christopher—or Chris, as you called him'—I laughed out loud at the memory— 'if you think he's bad, you should meet the son. Christopher is oily, but Leo is more like toxic lard. He's foul. Luckily, he's so lazy he hardly ever comes into the gallery.'

'The Wolseley it is then,' said Kiki, not bothering to ring ahead. When we got there she just strolled casually in, certain she'd be given a table, and we were—a great one too, in the inner ring, right opposite the front door.

'Thanks for a great weekend, Amelia,' she said, raising the glass of champagne which had been sent over to our table by Jeremy King, one of the owners. 'It was a riot. Your Ed is hilarious when he gets going. I loved that story about getting accidentally locked in a cellar where he had been taking a sneaky look, but what's with the silent-treatment morning thing?'

'Oh, Ed just isn't very communicative before midday,' I said, shrugging. 'I explained all that to Ollie already. He wasn't always like that—in fact, he used to be quite a morning bird—but now he stays up very late working most nights and when he gets up he just likes to be quiet until his brain gets into gear. There's always so much going on there, he needs to let it warm up slowly.'

'Yeah,' said Kiki, raising her glass and draining it. 'And the amount of grog he puts away, he must feel like shit too. Does he always drink that much?'

I laughed and shook my head simultaneously. 'You do like to cut to the chase, don't you, Kiki?' I said. 'No edging carefully around the subject for you.'

She just shrugged. 'I'm Australian—but he does

cane it, doesn't he? Be honest.'

'Ed is a wine broker, Kiki, a connoisseur, he has to drink for work—and you and Oliver weren't exactly restrained with the vino yourselves this weekend, and you don't even have an excuse. I thought Ollie was going to suggest a drinking game with Ed's St-Emilion at one point.'

'Yeah, isn't he great?' said Kiki, chuckling fondly.

'Yes, he's very funny,' I answered, choosing my words carefully, 'once you get used to him. I found his foul mouth rather offputting at first—not to mention the make-up—but he's actually really nice when you get beyond that.'

'He's incredibly clever too,' said Kiki, smiling like a proud aunt. 'It looks like he's going to be doing his own hair-care range without having to go through all the hassle of opening a salon. All the magazines are fighting over the exclusive and Selfridges want to launch it with five windows. It's going to be huge.'

We carried on in this vein for quite a while, with Kiki updating me on the latest developments in her social life—and a lot seemed to have happened since our last conversation on the subject just the day before.

But while it was all pleasantly distracting and I always found just being in the Wolseley a treat, I had the distinct feeling there was another agenda, which Kiki hadn't got round to yet. It wasn't like her to be circumspect, and I was seriously hoping it wasn't going to be my marital sleeping arrangements again.

That topic had been nagging away at me ever since she'd brought it up the morning before, and it made me very uneasy. I knew it wasn't right, but I just didn't want to examine the reasons for it too closely, or any of the other unwelcome associated thoughts they brought up.

With all that swilling around in my head I had pretty much tuned out of what Kiki was saying. I was feeling increasingly on edge, waiting for her to bring up the real subject she wanted to talk to me about and, in the end, I couldn't stand it any longer.

'Kiki,' I said, firmly, putting my hand on her arm. 'It's lovely having lunch with you and everything, especially on a gloomy Monday like this, but what do you really want to talk to me about? Go on, be a proper Aussie, spit it out.'

She looked at me for a moment and then her shoulders slumped inside her Chanel jacket. She suddenly looked about half her normal size, which was pretty small to begin with. It was quite alarming.

'Whatever's the matter?' I asked, sincerely concerned.

'Oh, Amelia,' she said, sighing deeply. 'It's just my place.'

'Your place in Holland Park?' I asked. I'd never been there, which was a bit odd now I thought about it, considering that we'd been friends for quite a few months.

'Not just in Holland Park,' she nodded, looking glummer with every moment, '*on* Holland Park . . .'

'You mean, the actual road Holland Park?' I said, impressed. It was one of the nicest streets in London; Ed had several clients who lived there. 'Wow. How fab. So what about it?'

'You've never been there, right?' she said.

I shook my head.

'Well, there's a reason for that. I don't invite anybody to my place. Not friends, not even lovers—especially not them.'

'Why ever not?' I asked.

She leaned across the table towards me. 'Because it's a total shithole,' she said, abruptly.

'But surely it's one of those gorgeous villas . . . ?' I continued, still not understanding why she was so upset.

'It is. I've got the whole ground floor. It's got three bedrooms, two reception rooms with twenty-foot ceilings, and a big garden too. The problem is *me*, Amelia. I live like a pig and I don't know what to do about it.'

I still didn't understand what she was getting at.

'Haven't you got a cleaner?' I asked tentatively. Somebody with her money would have been able to have a full staff, I thought. Ed and I had a very nice lady who came three times a week, plus the cleaner for the cottage, and we weren't nearly as grand as Kiki.

She laughed bitterly. 'They usually last about fifteen minutes,' she said. 'They turn up, realize how bad it is and bale out. I want a housekeeper, but the agency won't send any more people over. The last one came three months ago. It's serious, Amelia.'

I could see she had tears in her eyes. 'I think I've got rats,' she said.

'Rats?' I squealed.

'Well, either that, or it's a very small squatter,' she said, regaining her sense of humour. 'Who likes to shit on the kitchen floor. Anyway, I've been to your flat and your cottage, and you really seem to know how to live like a grown-up. Your places are clean and tidy and nice to be in. They smell lovely, and you have flowers and milk jugs and ironed tea towels—so I was wondering if you would consider coming over to my place and helping me get it into some kind of shape, so that I might be able to get someone to come and work for me . . .' Her eyes filled up again.

'It's either that, or I'm just going to leave it. Throw away the keys and never come back. I mean—how can I ever expect to find a proper boyfriend, let alone a husband, if I can't let them see where I live? And it can make you feel like some kind of hooker, if you only ever see men at their place or in hotel rooms . . .' One tear fell out of each eye and rolled down her cheeks.

I took her hand.

'Of course I'll help you,' I said. 'I'll come over after work today and have a look. Then we can decide how we'll get started.'

*　　　*　　　*

Nothing could have prepared me for the scene that awaited me when I got to Kiki's place that night. I had to squeeze round the front door just to get in because of all the, well, *crap* was the only name for it, in the hallway.

There was a snowdrift of post and junkmail behind the door, which was why she could hardly open it, then, once you were in, all you could see were cardboard boxes and piles of bulging black rubbish bags.

There was a fold-up bicycle—or part of one—

57

some kind of vacuum cleaner, which seemed to be in pieces, and piles and piles of old newspapers cascading out of the cardboard boxes. They didn't look as though they had ever been read.

The smell hit you the moment you got inside too, the stale stench of old newspaper, dirty laundry and rotting garbage. It was horrid. You really couldn't bring a potential boyfriend in there; she was right.

'Jesus, Kiki,' I said. It was no time to make polite conversation. 'I see what you mean. But don't worry, we can do something with this.' Maybe with the help of the SAS, I thought to myself.

As we walked further into the place—which underneath all the mess, I could see was gorgeous—it just got worse.

The drawing-room floor was littered with junk: scattered heaps of books, shoes, bits of discarded clothing, dirty plates, empty mugs and wine glasses, magazines, more newspapers.

Incongruous among the chaos were strangely neat piles of carefully hand-labelled videos. They were stacked up on every flat surface, including the armchairs and sofas, and there seemed to be some kind of filing system. One chair seemed to be for old movies, another for episodes of *Inspector Morse* and *Rebus* and a third one was devoted to *The Simpsons*.

It was bizarre in the extreme, but it didn't seem like the time to ask questions, so I just looked around and made mental notes.

She certainly hadn't been kidding about the art collection. Every room had paintings covering the walls—all of them crooked—and in the drawing

58

room alone there were several Lesley Pinecliffs, and loads of work by other major Australian artists which I recognized from the gallery. Creeping Jesus would be foaming at the mouth if he could see them, I thought.

The dining room was another war zone. The beautiful old French table was covered in heaps of what appeared to be bank statements and other financial papers, with a great many unopened envelopes among them, all mixed up.

The kitchen smelled terrible, and it didn't take long to work out that the fetid odour was emanating from the piles of ominously full black bin-liners propped around a large, overflowing pedal bin. It may have been my imagination, but I thought I saw something moving in one of the bags. I shuddered. There was no way I was touching those.

The bathroom was relatively civilized, I was relieved to find. The loo was clean, at least, and the towels looked fresh—in fact, they looked brand new; they still had Conran Shop tags hanging from them. The shower rail was bedecked with exquisite underwear, giving it a rather festive air.

The first bedroom we looked in was like a Tracey Emin installation, full of clothes dumped on the floor and the bed, as though the contents of twenty-five jumble sales—or designer sample sales—had been forklifted in through the window. But like an island in the chaos, there was a professional-looking ironing board set up and ready to use in the corner.

The beautiful black and white tweed Chanel suit Kiki had been wearing at lunch was lying in a heap

59

on the floor, where she had clearly just stepped out of it. I picked it up and put it on the bed.

Kiki's own bedroom was dominated by a very large—very unmade—bed, covered in more books, and the floor was strewn with treacherous sliding piles of magazines and catalogues, making it difficult to walk. Definitely not the place for gentlemen callers.

In the corner there was a lovely old-fashioned kidney-shaped dressing table with a floral chintz skirt and a matching stool, but the glass top was littered with make-up and cosmetics, all mixed up and lidless.

I pictured my own make-up drawer, everything filed in separate Perspex boxes according to use, caps all on. Maybe I could help Kiki, I thought.

'What do you reckon?' she asked, in a small voice. 'Is it worse than you thought?'

'Thinking is what I need to do,' I said. 'Can we sit in the garden?'

It was getting dark, but I knew if I didn't get outside soon I would run screaming from the premises as her prospective cleaners had done. My head was starting to feel itchy from the sheer scale of the chaos in there.

The garden was overgrown, but a haven compared to inside. I perched on a dirty white metal chair and took some deep breaths.

'Do you think we can clear it up?' said Kiki.

'Nothing is impossible,' I said, diplomatically, although I was actually starting to think that her idea of throwing away the keys wasn't such a bad one. 'But it's such a big job, we're going to need to take some radical measures. A superficial tidy-up is not going to sort this out.' Her eyes were filling with tears again. I took her hand. 'Don't panic, Kiki, we'll take it slowly, step by step, but I've got to ask you: how did it get like this?'

'I just can't get organized,' she said, sounding wretched. 'I've got some kind of block about it. We always had maids when I was growing up, and my dad's accountants did all the financial admin, and now I just don't know where to start, so I don't do anything. I'm not a naturally tidy person, so I didn't really notice at first, but over time it's just spiralled out of control and even I can see I can't go on like this.' She paused and took a few deep breaths, which seemed to pull her together a bit.

'The thing is, Amelia, I've never lived anywhere this long before. I've never stayed in any flat longer than eighteen months since I left home. My chaos is the reason I keep moving. I always use one of those unpacking services, which sort it all out for you, so it's fine for a while, then, when it gets too bad, I move again. But I love this flat and I love London and I've been here three years now and that's the result in there. Armageddon.'

I looked at her. It was really hard to take in, because Kiki was always beautifully dressed and perfectly groomed. That evening her short black hair was neatly pulled back with a narrow Alice band, and she was wearing a pea-green cashmere cardigan with a pair of dark denim jeans, a vintage silk scarf as a belt and zebra-print ballerinas on her dainty feet. Kiki always looked immaculate and she smelled lovely too, of tuberose.

I thought about that room full of tangled-up clothes and I just couldn't put it together.

'But what I don't understand is how you always look so chic, Kiki,' I said. 'How do you emerge

61

from all that cack looking like Holly Golightly's sexier little sister?'

She managed a smile. 'I always have my ironing board up,' she said. 'You can put anything on once it's had a press and a spritz of Fracas. That was one useful thing I did learn from my mum. And I always use shoe trees.'

We looked at each other and laughed until our stomachs hurt.

6

Ed was highly amused to hear about Kiki's domestic arrangements when I met him for dinner that night at Scott's, one of our regular spots, not far along Mount Street from our flat.

'So she's a fully paid-up filth packet, is she?' he said, chuckling, swilling the brandy in his glass, holding it up to admire the colour and then sticking his nose inside. 'That is surprising,' he continued, when he lifted his head again, a beam of satisfaction on his elegant face. 'She's always so chic, and I've never heard of an Australian filth packet before. I thought it was a uniquely British species, the well-bred slattern. That bizarre inverted snobbery about not appearing to care how you live, as though the dirtier you are the grander you must be. I've never understood it.'

'I don't think it's like that with Kiki,' I said, cutting a chocolate in half. 'I think the grooming uses up all her organizational energy and she's just chronically untidy and chaotic in every other regard. There's not a surface in the whole place that isn't covered in crap—it's hard even to find somewhere to put your feet down on the floor—so she can't even start to get sorted out, and it's just got worse and worse over time.'

'That is a shame,' he said. 'Poor Kiki. What a horrid pickle to get yourself into. I do feel sorry for her—but what has it got to do with you, exactly?'

'Well, she's asked me to help her sort it out, and I've said I would.'

He put his head on one side and studied my face. 'But why does she think you're qualified to sort out her mess?'

'Because she's been to the flat and the cottage and seen that we live like civilized adults,' I said, starting to feel a little defensive.

'That's true—we do, and I'm very grateful for it,' he smiled and raised his glass to me, before draining it. 'Because it is all thanks to you, my beautiful, capable Amelia. But I just wonder if sorting out someone else's chaos is really what you want to do with your spare time. I thought you wanted to spend all these spring weekends working on your garden down at the cottage.'

'I do—but I feel so sorry for Kiki, and it just comes naturally to me to be organized, it's no effort, so I feel I should help her. And I think it might be fun, Ed. . .'

He leaned across the table and took my hand. 'You're just too nice, Amelia,' he said, shaking his head and looking at me lovingly. 'Do it if you think it will be a hoot, but I just don't want you to be used by some spoilt little rich girl. Kiki is great fun, but I work with these people, remember. I know what they're like. They exist on a different plane from we normal folk and they get awfully used to other people doing their dirty work, you know.'

I nodded. 'Tell me about it,' I said. 'CJ wants me to ask you to get him some Krug for the next private view, with a "family" discount, that was how he put it.'

Ed laughed heartily and, catching the waiter's eye, he pointed at his brandy glass.

*   *   *

Whatever Ed's misgivings, I really enjoyed planning how I was going to sort Kiki's place out. I'd been thinking about it every morning as I jogged round the park—which was when I always had my best ideas—and had come up with what I thought was an excellent action strategy.

I arranged to meet Kiki early on Saturday morning at Julie's *Café* to go through it, without the chaos of her place to muddle our heads, and she was already waiting when I got there. That was a good start. Kiki was usually at least forty-five minutes late for everything.

'Oh, no,' she said, shaking her head, when I walked in. 'I don't know if I can do this.'

'What's up with you?' I asked. 'We haven't even started and you're already freaking out.'

'But look!' she said, gesturing at me.

'What?' I said, looking around me for the cause of her distress.

'That thing you're carrying—it's making me feel ill.'

'This?' I said, holding it up. 'It's only a clipboard, Kiki.'

She shuddered and backed away in her chair, making a crucifix shape with her fingers.

I sat down and waved it in her face.

'Now stop it,' I said. 'I could be digging manure into my garden in Winchelsea, but I've stayed in town just to help you, so you'd better start co-operating. I've brought this stupid clipboard for a very good reason—there's not a single flat surface in your place that we could write on. OK?'

Kiki nodded like a guilty child and took a sip of her cappuccino.

'Right,' I continued. 'Before we go over there I need to ask you some questions.'

'OK,' she said, in a tiny little voice.

'First of all—what are all those newspapers in your hall?'

She shrugged. 'They're just the daily papers and the Saturday papers and the, er, Sunday papers.'

'Right,' I said, nodding. 'Do you mean *all* the papers? As in the *Times*, the *Guardian*, the *Telegraph*, the *Independent* and the *Observer*?'

She nodded. 'And the *Mail* and the *News of the World*,' she added.

'OK,' I said, trying to keep my voice neutral. 'And do you actually read them?'

She shook her head, looking absolutely terrified. I tried not to look incredulous.

'So why on earth do you get them all?' I asked, tentatively.

'Because my father says you have to look at the papers every day, or you'll get left behind . . .'

'Hmm,' I said. 'And I imagine he has a very large desk and a very efficient secretary who lays them all out ready for him and clears them away again each night?'

I knew about that, because I had to do it every day for Creeping Jesus.

She nodded.

'OK,' I said firmly, but warmly—or at least that was the effect I was trying to achieve—we are going to go to your newsagent on the way to the flat and we are going to cancel them all. From now on you can buy one paper a day—one, OK?—but before you do that, you will put the old one into the paper recycling basket we are going to get you, whether you have read it or not. Unless you're planning on doing a lot of *papier mâché* no one needs a hall full of old newspaper. Got it?'

She nodded again. 'I think I need another coffee,' she said, in a pathetic little voice.

That was when it really sank in that clearing and organizing Kiki's flat was going to take a lot more than my clipboard, a couple of rolls of bin-bags and a man with a van out of the Yellow Pages. A degree in counselling would have been handy.

She was visibly empowered when I stopped and cancelled her newspapers on our way over to her flat, which was encouraging—although the newsagent didn't look so happy, I'd probably wrecked his early retirement plans—but when I started hauling the cardboard boxes containing all the old papers out of her hall and on to her front path, Kiki got quite panicky.

'Hang on,' she said, trying to snatch something out of the box I was heaving along. 'That's a *Telegraph* magazine. I must keep that.'

'No-you-mustn't,' I said, holding my hand up in front of her face in the sign language signal for 'no'.

'But . . .'

'There is a new one out today, Kiki. A lovely new *Telegraph* magazine. You can have that as a reward when we've done this. This is an old one.

It's over, yesterday's papers, let it go.'

She looked so distressed I thought she might have an anxiety attack, but I had to carry on.

'Right then,' I said, after we'd hauled all the boxes outside. 'Now the bin-bags. What is all this?'

Kiki looked nervous and said nothing, so I tipped one out on to the floor. I picked a few things up, and it quickly became clear they were clothes—serious designer clothes—tangled up like old rags, with some damp towels mixed in with them. There were eight bags, I counted.

I looked enquiringly at Kiki.

'They're, um, clothes, I don't, er, want any more,' she said, haltingly.

'OK, that's fine—so why are they still in the house?' 'In case I do want them?' she asked tentatively.

'This is really good stuff, Kiki,' I said, sifting through and finding a Malo cashmere sweater, a YSL top and two pairs of Chloé trousers. 'Wow. You could get serious money for these on eBay.'

She shook her head, looking anxious again. 'I don't want any money for them.'

'Well, a charity shop would love them then. Would you be happy for a charity to have them?' She nodded. 'OK, help me carry them to my car,' I said.

She got that distressed look on her face again.

'We have to get them out of the house now, Kiki,' I said. 'Or we never will.'

That left just the fold-up bike and the pieces of vacuum cleaner. 'Ever going to use that? Or get that mended?' She shook her head. 'OK, out they go,' I said.

I'd already arranged for a recycling service to

come later that afternoon, so I stacked them up against the wall next to the old newspapers and went back into the house—making Kiki wait outside.

I gathered up all the post that was behind the door and quickly sorted it into two carrier bags, one for real mail and one for junk. I nipped along the hall to put the proper letters on the dining table, then I went back outside, closing the door behind me, and chucked the bag of junkmail on top of the newspapers for recycling.

I saw a flash of anxiety cross Kiki's face as the bag flew past, but I distracted her by taking her hand and leading her over to the front door.

'OK,' I said. 'Go back in.'

The door swung open when she pushed it, like a front door should, and Kiki stepped inside. She gasped, then turned round and grabbed my hand.

'It's amazing,' she said. 'It's all gone!' She started jumping up and down with excitement. 'It's all gone! All the crap! I've got a hallway! Yippee!'

She skipped up and down it, flailing her arms with glee, and then hugged me. 'Oh, thank you, so much,' she said.

'It's only the hall, Kiki,' I said. 'But it has made a big difference, and that took us exactly seventeen minutes; I timed it. That's how easy it is, once you start. It's just the starting that's hard.'

She nodded enthusiastically. 'OK, what's next?'

'Your clothes,' I said firmly.

Her face fell. 'Oh, can't we leave them until later? Look at me—I can get dressed fine, the way things are. Let's do the kitchen instead, shall we?'

'No,' I said, firmly, still with no intention of touching those sinister rubbish bags. 'You do dress

68

beautifully, that's true, but I don't think you really want to have your lovely clothes lying around in heaps like that, do you? And you might not be late all the time if you could get dressed without having to iron everything first . . .'

She hung her head and sighed deeply, the energizing triumph of the transformed hall already evaporated.

I took her hand and made her come into the bedroom with me.

'OK,' I said, bending down and scooping up armfuls of clothes. 'First we are going to put them all on the bed. Actually, you can do that. I need to get some things from the car.'

I came back to find her posing in front of the mirror, holding various dresses up to herself, all the other clothes still on the floor.

'Kiki?' I said, irritated and remembering what Ed had said about spoilt rich girls. 'You've got to help me here. This is my weekend, remember? I'm not going to do it all for you, I'm just showing you how.'

'Sorry, miss,' she said, throwing them on the bed. 'What's that thing you're holding?'

'It's a temporary folding surface,' I said, in a deliberately officious voice, erecting the wallpaper table I had brought with me. 'You carry on putting things on the bed and I'll start folding. If you find anything too dirty, put it in this carrier bag and we'll drop it at your drycleaner's later. Where do you go?'

'I don't really have a drycleaner,' she said sheepishly.

I narrowed my eyes at her. 'Is that why those bags of clothes were out in the hall?' I asked.

'Were they just dirty?'

She nodded, looking very guilty. 'I've got a washing machine, but I don't really know how to use it. I wash all my undies by hand anyway, and I've never been very good at picking clothes up from drycleaner's . . .'

'Don't tell me that's why there were towels in there as well,' I said.

She made a guilty face.

I put my head in my hands and shook it. 'All right,' I said. 'Let's keep going. Once you've got it all on the bed, start sorting it into categories— trousers, skirts, dresses, jackets, tops, knits, etc. And I'll show you how to work the washing machine later.'

It took us over an hour, but finally we had all Kiki's clothes folded into neat piles and I produced the bag of assorted hangers I'd bought at John Lewis in my lunch hour the day before.

To make a point, I sat on the bed and made her hang it all up herself in the—mostly empty—built-in wardrobes, and then we filed all the T-shirts and knitwear on to specific shelves.

'Wow,' said Kiki, stepping back and admiring our work. 'I can't believe the difference. Thank you so much. I could never have done this on my own. It looks like a Prada boutique.'

I smiled to myself. Anyone else probably would have said it looked like a branch of Gap. Ed was right about her living on a different plane. Still, I was rather enjoying myself. I got some Post-It notes out of my handbag and marked each shelf with its contents.

'Those stickers are temporary,' I said. 'They're just to get you used to putting things back in an

70

ordered way, so you won't need to rake through all your clothes to find one cardigan. OK?'

She looked at me with a bemused expression on her face. 'Is this what your wardrobe is like?' she said.

'Yes,' I said, shrugging. 'But without the sticky labels—or the really beautiful clothes.'

'Who did it for you?'

'No one,' I laughed. 'I've always done it like this. It never occurred to me not to.' I consulted the masterlist on my clipboard. 'OK,' I said. 'That's the clothes done—where are your accessories?'

Looking sheepish, she led me through to the third bedroom, which I hadn't seen inside before. When she opened the door, it was like Selfridges handbag department, there were so many designer bags strewn across the bed.

I decided they could wait—at least she could see what she had—and she hadn't been kidding about the shoe trees either. There was a small conurbation of shoes on the floor of that room, every one with its shoe tree in and arranged in neat pairs. About 120 of them.

I was temporarily lost for words and just spread my hands in disbelief.

'So how come you can do it for the shoes, but not anything else?'

'I guess I just love my shoes,' said Kiki, sliding off her ballerinas and slipping into a pair of purple velvet pumps with dizzying heels. 'Aren't they gorgeous?'

'They sure are,' I said, wishing I had tiny feet like Kiki and a fraction of her shoe collection. 'But I don't think they should be on the floor like this.'

I made a note on my clipboard: I was going to

get someone to build her a whole wall of shelves specially for shoes and bags in the bedroom with the wardrobes, so that could be her dedicated dressing room and this could be a proper spare room.

By five thirty, when the man-with-a-van arrived to take away all the recyclable detritus—and I'd booked Rentokil to sort out the kitchen—we'd at least made a start on every room, except the dining room. I'd decided that the morass of financial admin could wait for another day, when we were both feeling stronger.

For the final assault of this session we moved back into the drawing room. We'd had a stand-off earlier in the day about getting rid of all the old magazines that were lying around in there, which I'd won after threatening to leave, but nothing prepared me for her emotional attachment to the home-recorded videos.

'Right,' I said, approaching the pile of *Morse* episodes holding a black bin-liner.

'What are you doing?' she said in a tone so sharp it brought me up.

'Well, you can't tell me you watch all these,' I said.

'I might,' she said, her voice still tight. 'And, anyway, they're all sorted already, we don't need to touch those.'

I dropped the bin-liner and sat down on the floor. There was no room on any of the chairs. They were all covered with more videos.

'All right, Kiki,' I said. 'Let's talk about this. What exactly are all these?'

'What do they look like?' she said. 'They're videos of TV shows and films that I really love, and I am not throwing them out, so forget it.'

I felt adrenaline flush through my system. I was so furious at her rudeness, I felt like telling her to get stuffed. I didn't very often let myself get angry—I'd spent too much time dodging my dad's temper tirades to have any desire to indulge in my own—but her tone and attitude really pissed me off.

I had spent my entire Saturday sorting out her crap when I could have been in my lovely garden in the Sussex countryside in the spring sunshine, and she was treating me like some kind of serf. I should have listened to Ed. I was about to get up and stomp out when something stopped me.

Although it had meant sacrificing my weekend, I'd found sorting out Kiki's chaos strangely rewarding. On top of that, I just never liked leaving anything unfinished. It went against my nature.

That was probably why our flat and the cottage were so nice to be in, I reflected. Whether it was unpacking the shopping, clearing up after a dinner party or sorting Ed's receipts, I always carried on until the job was done. He had always said he thought it was one of my special qualities. So, however rude she was being, I wasn't going to leave this job half done. It just wasn't my style.

So I took a few deep breaths and looked steadily at Kiki. I decided to let her break the silence, and she did—she burst into tears. I was so amazed, my anger left me as quickly as it had come. She was clearly in serious distress. I went over and put my arm around her.

'It's OK, Kiki,' I said. 'Just let it out, whatever it is. Let it go.'

She carried on crying for quite a while, before she started to speak. I groped in my bag for some tissues and gave them to her.

'I know it's stupid,' she said, between sniffs. 'But I have to have these videos. It's just I'm so scared of being on my own and, whenever I am, I put on one of these and I feel OK.'

'Do they remind you of someone?' I said gently. There had to be more to this than just watching old TV shows and, sure enough, that question provoked another attack of wailing. Bull's-eye, I thought.

'My dad,' she said. 'He loves TV. It's his great relaxation and, when I was a kid, I used to be allowed to watch with him in his den. It was the only time I ever had on my own with him. So when I'm alone and sad, I feel like he's with me.'

'Does he like *The Simpsons*?' I asked, noticing a stack of them next to the sofa. By reputation, Gary Wilmott was something of a business tyrant. It was hard to imagine him watching a cartoon.

'He loves them,' she sniffled. 'He always says Lisa is me—small, smart and bossy.' She managed a smile.

'Well, you don't have to throw your videos away, Kiki,' I said, thinking perhaps I had been a bit hasty about it. 'But maybe we could just come up with a better way of storing them, so they don't fill up the whole room?' She nodded. 'Maybe you could just get the entire *Simpsons* and *Morse* collections and everything else you love on DVD, and that would take up a lot less room, wouldn't it? Better quality too.'

She looked at me as though I had just invented penicillin.

'That's such a great idea,' she said. 'A lot of these tapes hardly work any more, I've watched them so many times.'

'Well, then,' I said. 'Let's make a list, right now—on my dreaded clipboard—and we can order all of them from Amazon tonight and you'll have them on Monday. Then you can store them in those nice cupboards on either side of the fireplace there—and you'll have your drawing room back.'

'I can have a drinks party,' said Kiki, her face brightening.

'You sure can,' I said.

There was nothing like the prospect of a party to energize Kiki, and she immediately grabbed my clipboard and starting scribbling a guestlist, which seemed to have reached 150 names in a matter of moments.

'Hang on a minute,' I told her, grabbing the clipboard back. 'Not so fast.'

I unclipped the sheet of names and handed it back to her. 'Put that on your fridge, as your motivation—and when this place is completely finished, then you can start inviting people.'

Then I went to the kitchen and opened the bottle of champagne I had pinched that morning from Ed's home supply.

7

Ed and I arrived early on the night of Kiki's party four weeks later, so I could show him around before the hordes descended. I'd brought him over for a look right after my first clear-out, so he could see it in a relative 'before' stage, the greater to appreciate the full transformation, and it was clear he did.

'Amazing work, Agent Amelia,' he said, as I showed him the home office I'd created in the large hall at the back of the flat. My fiendish plan was that by having all her admin out in the hallway, rather than in a room she could close the door on, she couldn't just forget about it.

'I'd ask you to create a home office for me like this, you clever girl,' he said, kissing my forehead, 'but you already have.'

Then I took him to see the makeover I was most proud of the bedroom with the wardrobes, which was now a proper boudoir dressing room. We'd got rid of the bed, replacing it with a lovely old chaise longue, hung a huge gilt-framed mirror on the wall opposite and moved the dressing table in there from her bedroom. Kiki loved it. She called it 'Planet Kiki'. And, as a concession for good behaviour, I'd let her keep her beloved ironing board up.

'Look, Ed,' she was saying, prancing up and down by the wall of specially built shelves, which was quite an achievement in the heels she was wearing. 'Look at my darling shoe children, they each have their own little house on Planet Kiki. Isn't it great?'

She took down a pair of vertiginous gold sandals and, after regarding them with satisfaction, she changed into them, putting the shoes she had been wearing before back in their place. I smiled to myself. She was a quick learner.

Then she pulled down a grey shoebox from a

top shelf and turned to me.

'These are for you, Amelia,' she said, handing me the box. It had 'Christian Louboutin' written on it.

I opened it to find a glorious pair of peep-toe high heels in black satin, with the delicious red soles I had so often admired on Kiki's feet. I checked the side of the box and was amazed to see they actually were my freakishly large size. I didn't know serious designers even made shoes that big. I was thrilled.

Kiki was grinning at me.

'Go on,' she said, nodding and smiling encouragingly. 'Put them on.'

I kicked off my flats and climbed into them, holding on to Ed's shoulder for support, then I took a few tentative steps. I never wore heels and felt like a baby giraffe.

Kiki was clapping with delight. 'They look great on you,' she said, grabbing my hand and leading me over to the mirror to admire my new look. 'Look at yourself, you glorious Amazon. I was sick of seeing you in flat shoes, girlfriend. Get out and strut your stuff, Amelia. You're gorgeous and you don't make enough of it.'

I looked at myself. Even though I was wearing the muted green Jigsaw dress and beaded cardigan that was my staple cocktail-party outfit, I could see that the shoes had given me a whole new look—and I liked it.

As I was admiring myself, I caught sight of Ed's face behind me, and he didn't look so thrilled. I wondered for a moment whether I should take the shoes off, but after glancing back at myself in the mirror I decided to keep them on. I liked the way they looked—but I really loved the way they made me feel.

It was only when I went to give Ed a kiss on the cheek, to snap him out of his grumpy disapproval, that I realized my new shoes made me inches taller than him.

He kissed me back. 'Don't worry, Melia,' he said, his face softening again. 'I just won't stand next to you tonight.'

*   *   *

Maybe it was the shoes, maybe it was all the champagne—Veuve Clicquot, supplied by Ed, of course—but I had a wonderful time at that party.

I knew quite a lot of Kiki's friends already, because so many of them were Ed's clients, or the kind of people who hung out with Ed's clients, that is, various combinations of witty, smart, famous, grand, beautiful, ambitious, well-connected or just plain opportunistic. And most of them were good value at a party.

The freeloading opportunists, in particular—Ed called them 'the courtiers'—made careers out of being good company, and I was having a very funny time hopping from group to group and catching up on all the latest gossip and chat. It was a great night, and I was particularly delighted—and somewhat amazed—when my brother Dick appeared.

'Dickie,' I said, trying to run over to him through the braying throng in the drawing room and nearly breaking my neck in my new shoes. 'How lovely to see you. I didn't know you knew Kiki.'

'I don't,' said Dick. 'Well, I didn't until three minutes ago, but now she seems to be my new best friend.'

I laughed. Dick had clearly been recruited. 'But how come you're here?' I asked, reaching up to kiss his cheek.

Even now I was in my heels, he was taller than me, one of very few men in the room who was. Dick was a very big man in every way—not fat, just big. He had an enormous head, and his hands were to scale, about the same size as the rugby balls he was so adept at catching and holding on to. His glass of champagne looked like a toy in his massive paw.

'I'm here because Ed called me,' he said, draining the glass in one mouthful and stopping a passing waiter for a refill. 'Told me how many crates of pop he was supplying for this do, so I reckoned I'd be nuts to miss it.'

'Ed rang you?' I said, mystified.

'Yes, I was a bit surprised too, but you know me, never one to miss a booze-up. Apparently, Kiki had rung Ed and asked him to invite some friends of yours as a surprise, so he called me. Secret Squirrel.'

'Aha,' I said, as it all became clear. Kiki's social engineering was a complex matter; it was probably part of her permanently ongoing plan to expand her circle of friends.

Sometimes I thought she wouldn't rest until she had met every single person who lived in London, had lunch with them and added their names and numbers to her BlackBerry and her Rolodex, and their birth dates to her birthday book. It was the one area in her life—apart from her shoes—that she was organized about. Mainly because every new friend was a possible conduit to more new friends.

I really didn't know how she managed to keep so many pals going at once, especially the way she seemed to make all of us feel like we were each her very best and dearest one. I had never been able to do that. Ed and I were very social—it was an integral part of his business, and of the gallery—so I knew a lot of people, but they weren't really friends.

I still kept in touch with some of the girls I'd been at school and university with, but they were all so tied up with young children these days I hardly saw them any more. My closest pal, Louise, had moved from Fulham to Cornwall a couple of years before with her growing family, including my special goddaughter Posy, and since then I had pretty much existed in a private universe with Ed. I think he actually preferred it that way, having me to himself, but one of the things I liked about Kiki was the feeling that she was becoming the proper girlfriend I so needed.

'Seems a great girl, Kiki,' said Dick, taking in the room. 'And clearly very popular. By the way, she says you "did" this flat for her. What does that mean?'

'Oh,' I shrugged. 'I just helped her sort it out. She's a little chaotic.'

Dick laughed fondly and put his arm around me. 'Still little Mrs Tittlemouse, eh? Still playing house with your toy dustpan and brush?'

'Yes, thanks, brother dearest,' I said sarcastically. 'And are you still living in grotesque bachelor squalor?'

'Yes, thanks, Amelia Jane,' he replied, using the full name I hated. 'Do you think there might be any suitable wives for me at this event?'

I glanced around the room. It was full of beautiful women of all types and ages.

'Positively brimming with them,' I said. 'Perhaps you could go and talk to some of them . . .'

Dick pulled a face. 'They all look too scary,' he said. 'Richard Paul Herbert,' I said, shaking my head, 'I'll never understand how you can launch yourself headfirst into a roiling mass of human muscle, sweat, bums and teeth on the rugby field and be too shy to chat up a perfectly nice woman at a civilized party.'

'But rugby is fun,' said Dick. 'Girls are much scarier.'

I sighed and shook my head at him.

'Spoken to Mum recently?' I asked, deliberately changing the subject. Dick's ongoing single status was one of the many areas in my family where you had to tread carefully. A little teasing was OK, but then it was time to move on quickly before anyone actually felt something.

'Hmmmm,' mumbled Dick. 'Last week, I think. You?'

'Oh, I speak to her every couple of days,' I said. 'She seems OK. Stormin' Norman has been behaving himself, because the school got a glowing report from the inspectors. I'm going to have lunch with her next week.'

'That's nice. Give her my love. I know I should go down and see them, but I'm still getting over Christmas.'

I rolled my eyes at the memory. Christmas in the Herbert household was always particularly fraught. If we made it through to Boxing Day without anything being thrown, it was a really good year. The last one had not been good.

'Don't worry, Dick,' I said. 'It will soon be his birthday . . .'

Dick crossed his eyes and pulled a face like Munch's scream, one of our large repertoire of private jokes at our father's expense. Making light of it had always been our defence against his volatile personality, and I was laughing so much as Dick clawed the air and pretended to gasp for breath I hardly noticed that someone had joined us, until Oliver's unmistakable tones reached me.

'Hello, you old tart. That is the ugliest fucking dress I've ever seen, but I like your shoes,' he was saying, thrusting his stubbly chin into my face to kiss me. 'You actually look quite sexy in those.'

He pulled away, and linking his arm cosily through mine—Oliver was always touching you, which I found endearing, and Ed loathed—he looked Dick up and down like a farmer appraising a prize bull, which is what he rather resembled.

'So, who's man mountain then?' he said, narrowing his heavily kohled eyes. 'He doesn't look like one of Kiki's usual pretentious friends.'

'Oh, hi Ollie,' I said. 'Actually, this is my brother, Dick Herbert—although most people call him Sherbet.'

'Is that right?' replied Oliver. 'Pleased to meet you, Sherbie—and who are you?'

In one move Oliver had unlinked my arm and turned his eyes to someone who was standing slightly behind Dick. He stepped forward and I nearly choked on the large mouthful of Veuve Clicquot I had just swallowed. It was Joseph. Or

Joseph James Renwick, to give him his full name, which was etched on my memory, just as it had been in my teenage diaries, along with a lot of embarrassing variations on Amelia Jane Renwick and Mrs Joseph Renwick. He was my brother's best friend from school and the first boy I had ever kissed.

I hadn't seen him for years and was so surprised I felt a blush rising up my neck. He'd lived in America for ages—Washington, I remembered—and I'd hardly thought about him since he moved there, but seeing him again so suddenly had spun me right out. He had been a spectacularly nice kisser.

'Amelia,' he was saying enthusiastically, and he sidestepped Oliver to come over to me. As he put his hands on my upper arms and gave me warm smackers on both cheeks, I felt the blush rise from my neck up to my cheeks. Actually, I think it may have gone down as well.

'Well, I'd hate to interrupt . . .' said Oliver pointedly, and I felt him brush past me as he went off in search of fresh quarry to insult and flirt with.

'Joseph!' I managed to splutter out. 'Gosh, how lovely to see you. It's been so long. Don't you live in Washington now?'

He smiled broadly at me, his dark-blue eyes crinkling behind his glasses. He still wore the same kind as when I had last seen him, small, round wire frames. John Lennon glasses, we'd called them when we were teenagers, and they suited him now just as they had then. I was glad he hadn't changed them for something more angular and modern. It would have spoiled the memory of the night I had kissed him behind the rugby club at Dick's eighteenth birthday party. It was still surprisingly vivid, I realized.

'I did live there,' he was saying. 'But I'm back in London now. I'm a professor at LSE, international law.'

'Bloody hell, that makes me feel old,' said Dick. 'My best friend is a professor. Aren't professors meant to be ancient?'

'We are ancient,' said Joseph. 'Well, you are, Sherbet. I'm a child prodigy and so is Amelia, of course. What are you up to these days? You're looking lovely, as always. Sherbet tells me you don't have any kids yet, that's probably why. Are you planning to?'

'Maybe,' I said bluntly. I hated that question. I found it incredibly rude and intrusive and it made me a lot less thrilled to see Joseph than I had been, although I couldn't help thinking he was just as gorgeous as ever to look at. 'Have you got kids?' I asked, to return the insult.

'Yes,' he said. 'Two. Well, maybe, two, or three.'

'That's lovely,' I said, thinking it was a pretty strange answer, but I didn't pursue it, in case there was some kind of tragedy involved. Whatever he meant, it didn't seem like light cocktail-party chitchat material.

'So, if I remember correctly, you married Sherbet's friend from that unfortunate university in the Wash,' Joseph was saying.

My heart sank a little more. I had forgotten all that tiresome Oxford-Cambridge bollocks. Dick's crowd had loved all that. I'd preferred the anonymity of my London university, where you didn't feel defined by where you happened to be taking your degree.

84

'Yes, I married Ed Bradlow. He's here somewhere, and I'm sure he'll be delighted to tell you the results of the last ten Varsity matches.'

'Yeah, and we beat you car-builders soundly in the last Boat Race,' said Dick, warming to a favourite theme.

'Oh, did you cheat, then?' said Joseph.

I took it as my chance to scarper. I was relishing the sophistication of Kiki's world and realized that I didn't want to be reminded of my gauche teenage years, when an invitation to watch the Boat Race or some ghastly game of rugby with Dick and his friends was the height of my social ambitions. In fact, now I was over the initial thrill, seeing Joseph again was way too big a reminder of my Maidstone maidenhood for my liking.

So as they carried on trading friendly insults, I allowed myself to be sucked into the fast-flowing tide of the party. But as I moved away something made me turn back for another look at Joseph. I did it without thinking and jumped with surprise when I realized he was also looking back at me. I froze as our eyes locked.

It can only have been a fleeting moment, but it felt like an age as we gazed at each other. Nothing was said, there wasn't even a shift of expression on his face, but as I whipped my head away again it felt like we'd had an entire conversation at some kind of cellular level. And not the kind of conversation a happily married woman should be having with another man.

I felt so flustered I pushed my way out of the room and locked myself in the loo in the hall to recover. I took some deep breaths to steady myself and looked at my reflection in the mirror with the

85

intensity brought on by drinking several glasses of champagne in quick succession.

I examined my face, trying to see it as Joseph just had. Did I look very different from the girl he had kissed all those years before? More wrinkled around the eyes, I supposed, but not radically different.

I still had exactly the same hair, very long, very blonde, straight and parted in the middle. I probably looked pretty much the same, and now it seemed he still had the same visceral effect on me too. I had written him off years ago as an embarrassing teenage crush, resulting mainly from proximity, yet here I was, a thirty-six-year-old married woman, flustered like a schoolgirl by one penetrating glance.

My eyes closed, and for a moment I lost myself in the memory of that melting kiss twenty years before. Then they snapped open again as I remembered what it had led to. Joseph's girlfriend's best friend had come round the corner and caught us at it, then all hell had broken loose.

The repercussions of that one stolen snog had gone on for months, as the girlfriend and her posse bullied me at school, spreading vile rumours and not letting up even after Joseph had left for Oxford without a backwards glance.

It had been so foully unjust that all the blame for that kiss was taken out on me when he was the one being unfaithful to his girlfriend. It had been the unhappiest time of my life, and I hadn't recovered from it until I left school and started a new life at university myself. Not until I'd met Ed, really.

Joseph Renwick had been nothing but trouble

for me when I was a teenager, I told myself, and I wasn't going to allow his disruptive energy into my life again.

I drank handfuls of water from the cold tap, smoothed down my hair and sprayed myself with a bottle of Jo Malone eau de cologne Kiki had put in there for her guests. Taking a few more deep breaths, I squared my shoulders and finally felt ready to go back out into the party, where I intended to give Joseph a very wide berth.

My first instinct was to look for Ed, and my heart surged with affection when I found him in the dining room, sitting at the table with an ageing rock star, a hedge-fund billionaire, the deputy editor of a Sunday newspaper and the younger son of a supermarket dynasty.

They were all Bradlow's boys and they were sitting rapt as Ed told them a story of how he had uncovered a stash of incredibly rare old armagnac in the cellar of an obscure château on his last trip to France.

It was all true—I knew because I'd been with him at the time. I wondered if he had told them the bit about me distracting the sleazy old retainer upstairs, at great risk to my girlish honour, while he had a good snoop around in the cellar before the *marquis* came in from shooting.

It was classic Bradlow's stuff. The journal was very male interest in its content and appeal and, although I had often been his accomplice in this way over the years, I only ever made cameo appearances when it added to the story.

Not that I went with him much any more. I'd long come to the conclusion that one decaying French château was pretty much like another, and

I was less fascinated by alcoholic wine-growers than Ed seemed to be. But I still appeared occasionally in the journal in my Bond Girl role—'Heady Bouquet' was my name.

It was a bit patronizing, but I didn't let it bother me. Ed was very impressed by Ian Fleming, and it seemed to resonate equally deeply with most of his clients. And, as I always reminded myself, I had been living very nicely off Ed's business for fifteen years, so I was hardly in a position to complain.

None of them had noticed 'leggy blonde beauty, Heady Bouquet', as Ed always described me in the journal, standing by the double doors, but I could see the competitive glint in their eyes as he told them that the story of the armagnac would be the main feature in the next journal when it was sent out in a couple of months' time.

Hearing about something before everyone else was major currency in their particular elite, and they were all leaning in towards him so far they were practically sitting on his knee.

Ed was as much a player as Creeping Jesus in his way, I thought. I knew what would happen next. One of them would say he would buy the whole lot outright, then the others would try and top him—with the deputy editor desperately trying to memorize the details for the paper's diarist.

Ed would refuse, saying he had to offer the armagnac fairly to all his members, but gradually he would allow them to 'persuade' him to put aside a few bottles each—for a premium—which would be delivered several weeks before the journal went out. He was masterful, my husband. And, as a result, we were probably several thousand pounds richer than we had been half an hour before. Or

Ed was, anyway.

I melted away before any of them saw me. I didn't want to ruin Ed's pitch, especially as I knew he enjoyed that fly-fishing part of his business, as he called it, almost as much as he enjoyed buying the wine.

After that I strolled around the flat a bit, admiring my handiwork and looking for someone new to talk to who wasn't Joseph Renwick. Heading back down the hall I was surprised to see an all-too-familiar squat figure pushing through the crowd.

It was Leo Mecklin, my boss's indolent son and the supposed 'deputy gallery director', although the only thing I had ever seen him direct were waiters to bring him more food and drink.

'Hello, Leo,' I said, in tones which did nothing to conceal my undelighted surprise at seeing him there.

'Oh, hello, Amelia,' he replied with an equal lack of enthusiasm. 'Yes, that's right—Christopher said you knew Kiki.'

I shuddered inwardly. I hated the way he called his own father Christopher; it was so wrong.

'I didn't know *you* did,' I said, with barely disguised hostility. I had long since stopped trying to get on with Leo. There was no point.

'You might be surprised who I know, Amelia,' said Leo and practically pushed past me into the drawing room.

What a monumental tosser, I thought, and was glad to hear Kiki's laugh shrieking out of the dressing room. I turned carefully on my towering heels and went in there to see what the joke was.

'Oh, here she is!' she cried, when she saw me in

the doorway. 'Come here, darling, I want you to meet everybody.'

She gripped me tightly round the waist—she could barely reach any higher—and addressed the small crowd in the room.

'Now everybody, this is my marvellous friend Amelia Bradlow. You all know clever Ed Bradlow with the wine, don't you? Well, she's married to him, which is great, but what I want to tell you is that it was Amelia who created Planet Kiki for me. She did this whole flat. So if any of you need your places sorting out, Amelia is the only person to do it. She's a clutter-clearing genius.'

The assembled crowd—and there were quite a few of them standing around and draped over the chaise longue—made suitably enthusiastic noises. I was so surprised I couldn't think of anything to say in response. I had only organized Amelia's place as a favour, and I wasn't planning on doing the same for a bunch of total strangers. I stood there grinning like a self-conscious goon while she introduced me to all of them, and it was mostly a blur, although I did recognize a few names.

There was the former wife of an infamous junkie aristocrat; the current wife of the rock star Ed was talking to; an actress who had been in an early film with Hugh Grant; and an antiques dealer who made the social pages even more often than his wealthy customers.

They all seemed delighted to meet me and I smiled back at them, dazedly. Then, not releasing her python grip, Kiki steered me out of the dressing room, announcing that she was going to introduce me to 'everyone' else.

I managed to stop her—after several equally

gushing meets and greets in the hall—just as we were about to go through the drawing-room door.

'Kiki!' I said. 'Hang on a minute—what are you doing?'

'I want everyone to know how clever you are,' she said. 'It's about time you got some credit for what you do, Amelia, and as neither your employer nor your husband seems to give you any, I'm going to.'

'Well, that's lovely,' I said, deciding to ignore the wider implications of what she had just said; it was a classic Kiki shock statement, and this was not the time or the place to argue it out. 'But please will you stop telling everyone I'm going to do their places for them? I only did this for you because you're my friend and I care about you. I'm not going to do it for anyone else.'

Kiki put her glossy head on one side and raised a sculpted eyebrow. 'Well, maybe you should,' she said.

I finally escaped from Kiki's grasp when she ran into her Melbourne pal, Jan Delmo, and let go of me to throw her arms around her. I fled back to the dining room to find Ed.

He was still there, as I knew he would be: that was his party style. After an initial bit of milling around to check out the scene, he'd find a commanding spot and stay there for the rest of the evening, letting people come to him. They always did. But on this occasion I was delighted to see he was on his own, with just a glass and a bottle of champagne for company. I smiled when I saw it was vintage Krug. He would have put half a case of that in with the rest of the less rarefied delivery, for his own consumption, and for any clients who

91

showed up. Ed left nothing to chance and, still, after so many years, there was something I found enormously reassuring about that. I sank down into the chair next to him and put my head on his familiar shoulder. He put his arm around me and kissed me on the forehead.

'How are you, Heady Bouquet? Having a good time?'

'Lovely,' I said. 'But my feet are killing me.'

Ed chuckled. 'That'll teach you to wear stupid shoes. I like you in your elegant flats. You don't need to trick yourself out like a tart. Leave that to Kiki.'

'Oh, don't be so horrible, Ed,' I said. 'She's just a naturally girly girl, and high heels are all part of it.'

'And she needs the height . . .' he added, stroking the length of my thigh. I pinched him on his flabby middle bit and made him jump. He pretended to pull my hair and then coiled it round and round his hand, as he liked to do.

After that we sat in companionable silence for a while, enjoying a little oasis of calm in the shriek and hum of the party. Nestling into his neck I breathed in that familiar smell which I still loved as much as I had the first time he'd kissed me all those years before.

In the same instant the memory of the other kiss which had been on my mind earlier in the evening came rushing back into my head. I batted it away like an irritating fly, then I kicked off the shoes and wiggled my toes, suddenly feeling exhausted.

'You never told me Dick was coming,' I said eventually. 'You sneaky old thing. Did you see him?'

'That was Kiki's idea. She thought it would be a

nice surprise. She's very sweet like that, and she clearly adores you, even if I don't like her shoes | . . .' I pinched him again and he laughed. 'And yes, I had a long chat with Sherbet and that weaselly friend of his, Joseph Renwick. I didn't invite him, by the way—your brother brought him along.'

'Do you really think he's weaselly?' I said, trying to remember if Ed knew about my unfortunate romantic history with him. I was fairly sure he didn't.

I tried to put it out of my mind as I sat there with my beloved husband, but it kept sneaking back in. It made me feel guilty and uncomfortable, as though I were being mentally unfaithful to Ed just by remembering it. Because the truth of it was that I still couldn't think about that twenty-year-old kiss without a serious frisson.

'I don't like the cut of his gib,' Ed was saying. 'I never have.'

'So you wouldn't have him as a Bradlow's member, then?' I said, teasingly and to keep things light.

'Definitely not,' he said.

I was surprised he felt so strongly but decided not to pursue it any further. I really wasn't that interested in Joseph Renwick.

8

I'd been at work for precisely half an hour the next morning and I'd already had two phonecalls that had put me into a total spin. And my head was on the fragile side anyway, after all the champagne.

The first one had come in on the main gallery number at 10.03 a.m. It was as though someone had been waiting for us to open.

'Is that Amelia?' said a woman's voice I didn't recognize. She sounded quite young, and not like the kind of person who usually rang CJ Mecklin & Son.

Their voices divided pretty evenly between old-school RP, Mockney, elocution lesson, posh Aussie and Russian. This was more of an unreconstructed estuarine accent. What Creeping Jesus would charmingly call 'common'. And Ed, for that matter.

'Yes,' I said, tentatively.

'This is Janelle—I met you last night at Kiki's party?'

Janelle? Janelle? I racked my brain. I had no idea.

'She said you do clutter-clearing,' continued Janelle, whoever she was. 'Anyway, I love what you've done with her place and I want you to come and do mine.'

I was so surprised I didn't say anything. Janelle did.

'She told me you charge £500 a day—is that right?'

I think I squeaked. Kiki had been telling people I charged money for clutter-clearing? I didn't know whether to laugh or cry. The cheek of that woman was unbelievable. On the other hand, a different part of my brain was reminding me, I didn't make much more than that in a week at the gallery—and that was before tax.

'Hello?' said Janelle, starting to sound a lot less self-assured. 'Are you still there? I mean, I can pay

94

more . . .'

'No, er, gosh, but . . .'

'I know, I know, Kiki told me you are incredibly busy, but I'm desperate, so if I say £600 a day—cash—could I jump your queue?'

She really did sound desperate, and I didn't know how I was going to tell her that Kiki was actually bonkers and I wasn't really a professional 'clutter- clearer' at all, because I was starting to feel sorry for this Janelle person. Plus, the money was making my head spin.

'Er, where do you live?' I asked her, playing for time.

'Hampstead,' she said.

I took a couple of breaths before I said anything else, trying to process the situation but having difficulties. 'I am very busy,' I said to Janelle, slowly, trying to work out what I was going to say as I went along. 'But perhaps I could do something at the weekend. Would that be possible for you?'

'Can't you come any sooner?' said Janelle, now sounding quite pathetic. I had a strong suspicion I was going to need to have some tissues at the ready if I did meet up with her. The image of Kiki weeping over her *Simpsons* videos came into my head.

'Well, I could come and do an assessment this evening, if you like,' I suggested, amazed at how together I sounded.

And as I put the phone down, her address and phone numbers recorded in my diary, I realized that perhaps now I really was a professional clutter-clearer. How the hell did that happen? Oh, yes—Kiki. My meddlesome little friend. I'd have to sort her out quickly before she pulled any more of these stunts.

I reached for my mobile—I had learned the hard way not to make personal calls on the gallery phone—but before I could even look for her name it rang. It was Oliver, another big surprise, as I didn't even know he had my number. I only ever saw him with Kiki.

'Morning, bitch,' he said, with his usual charm. 'It's Ol. Got your diary handy?'

'Yes,' I said, tentatively.

'All right, which of these can you do at 8 p.m. at Kiki's place?'

He reeled off some dates.

'I can do most of them,' I said cautiously. 'But for what?'

'I'm going to cut your tragic hair off,' he said.

I was so surprised I couldn't think of anything to say.

'Hell-oo-oo . . .' said Oliver. 'Anybody there?'

'I'm still here,' I said, spluttering a bit. 'But I'm in shock. What do you mean, cut my hair off? And what do you mean, tragic? How bloody rude! I like my hair, thank you very much . . . and so does Ed.'

'I'm sure he does, I've heard about men like that . . .' he laughed. 'It is lovely hair, darling—for a twelve-year-old. But you, Amelia, are a beautiful, grown-up woman and you need a grown-up haircut. I'm sick of seeing you with it tied up in a pathetic ponytail, or hanging down like Joni fucking Mitchell's on a bad-hair day.'

I went quiet again, trying to take it in. I couldn't, so working according to the theory that if you can't say something nice, say nothing, I continued with the silent treatment. He broke first.

'I'm not going to labour this point, Amelia,' he

said, in a softer voice which he didn't use very often. 'But a lot of women would cut off a leg to have me cut off their hair, and I'm doing this because I like you and I want you to look as gorgeous as I know you can. I can't bear to see potential wasted. Trust Ollie, OK?'

'OK,' I said, but not because I had any intention of actually letting him cut off my hair. I'd decided it was easier to appear to go along with him for the time being and then I could just keep cancelling arrangements until he and Kiki got bored and forgot about this latest crazy plan—because I had no doubt that she was involved in it as well.

Between this and telling everyone at the party I was a 'clutter-clearer', Madame Kiki really was getting seriously out of order, I realized, but I'd think about that later. Right now Oliver was talking again, in his more usual hectoring tones, so I tuned back in.

'And Kiki's taking you clothes shopping to say thank you for doing her place, so you're a lucky bitch and you don't want that shit hair to ruin it, do you? Good party, wasn't it? I didn't get home till five this morning . . .'

And after a short recap of exactly what he had got up to between leaving Kiki's party and eventually going home—which was a lot more information than I really needed—we agreed on a date to meet at Kiki's place and he rang off.

I sat back in my chair, my head reeling. I really did hope they would forget about my hair, as I was absolutely certain I didn't want it cut off. I thought my hair—naturally straight and naturally blondish, properly blonde with help from my friends at the John Frieda salon, round the corner from the flat—was my best feature. So I wore it long because I was proud of it, but also because Ed really loved it.

I didn't think he was some kind of weird, long-hair pervert, as Ollie had implied, but it was true that he did have a bit of a 'thing' about my hair; he had since we had first got together. He was always playing with it, winding it round his hand and then letting it fall down again, and he always liked me to wear it loose when we went out together, to show it off. And when we were in bed, for that matter.

But when I was left to my own devices, it did end up tied back in a ponytail most days, quite often with a red rubber band dropped by a postman which I had picked up off the pavement. Sometimes I just had to get it out of my face that minute.

I went into the loo at the back of the gallery and had a look in the mirror. Maybe a ponytail wasn't the most sophisticated style for a woman my age, I thought. I took the band out and let my hair fall around my shoulders and down my back. It was exactly the same as it had been since I was a teenager, if not younger. I'd never really had any other style.

That was what my hair had been like when the sixteen-year-old me had kissed Joseph Renwick, I remembered with a slightly nauseous pang. That had been so weird, seeing him like that last night. Quite disturbing. I consciously put it out of my head and went back to looking at myself.

It had looked like this when I'd met Ed and that's how I'd worn it for our wedding too—I certainly didn't have one of those awful bridal updos. That was my hair and I really couldn't imagine it any other way.

I knew it still attracted men's glances as I walked down the street, but perhaps, I suddenly thought, I was in danger of turning into one of those tragic women who look like hot stuff from the back and then turn round to be a scary old disappointment.

I shuddered slightly and tried to catch myself out in the mirror, peeping over my shoulder through the open door of the loo to try and get the back view and then turning around properly. I was so engrossed, it took me a moment to realize Leo was watching me.

'What *are* you doing?' he said, in his most snide voice. 'Auditioning for a hairspray advert? Or just admiring your crowning glory? Lovely Amelia Bradlow and her famous long blonde hair . . .'

He came up beside me and tapped me on the top of the head with his rolled-up newspaper, which I could see was the *Daily Sport*. Typical.

'Well, you may think you look like Anna Kournikova,' he said, so close to my ear I could feel his hot wet breath on it, 'but just remember Donatella Versace for the front view, OK? Now can you get out of there? I need to drop my load.'

'*Charmant!*' I said, smiling brightly as I stepped aside to let him past. '*Bien merder . . .*'

'And fuck you too,' I distinctly heard him say, after he slammed the door in my face.

I stuck my middle finger up at it, slapping my bicep with the other hand. Not very ladylike, but a satisfying nicety I had picked up from my brother.

*   *   *

99

It was still only 10.45 but, after all that had happened, I decided I needed a breather. I was feeling increasingly jaded from the night before and I really didn't want to be in the gallery when Leo opened that lavatory door again in about twenty minutes' time.

I knew exactly what he'd do. He would go back upstairs, leaving it deliberately ajar, so I would have to go over to close it. He was so disgusting. I'd probably have to clean up in there with the lavatory brush too. I shuddered.

I grabbed my coat and bag and buzzed up to Christopher on the intercom. 'I'm popping out to collect some envelopes from Smythson,' I said, when he answered. 'Leo is looking after the gallery.' And I was out of the door in moments, before he could even reply.

I strolled idly down Bond Street, trying to see how my hair looked at a casual glance in the shop windows. I thought it looked rather good, swishing from side to side as I walked. Then, without really thinking where I was going, I crossed Piccadilly, walked along past the Ritz and then turned left into Green Park.

The moment I was inside those railings, I slowed down and breathed more deeply. I loved that park and felt a sense of ownership of it because I lived so near and ran round it so often. Hyde Park was actually closer to the flat, if you took the subway under Park Lane, but there was something about the quiet, contained space of Green Park which I particularly loved.

It was really starting to feel like spring now, and the trees were finally coming back to life. I wondered how my garden was doing down in

Winchelsea. I hadn't been there for a couple of weeks, so it was probably completely different from the last time I'd seen it. Mrs Hart's garden—or Hermione, as I was learning to call her—next door definitely would be.

If I took on this clutter-clearing job from Janelle, whoever she was, I thought as I walked, we might not get down there that weekend either, and Ed would definitely not be happy. As he kept saying, what was the point of buying a cottage in the country if we didn't bloody go to it?

And it had been me who'd wanted it so badly. I loved our flat in Mount Street, but it didn't have a garden—not even a balcony—and I had been desperate for one. The park was lovely, but it wasn't the same as having your own outdoor space.

I just wanted somewhere I could go outside with my coffee in the morning, I had told Ed repeatedly, until eventually he had caved in. I'd driven him mad over it, really.

We'd had to go the second-house route because there was no question of selling Mount Street and moving to somewhere in London that had a garden. Apart from the fact that Ed was very attached to the Mayfair flat as the only place that gave him an ongoing sense of home, we couldn't sell it because it was bound up in some kind of family trust. They couldn't chuck us out, he assured me, but it wasn't legally 'ours'.

Everything to do with Ed's family and their money was tied up tightly with red legal ribbon as far as I could tell. Ed had told me years ago this was because his mother was a terrible spendthrift and, being much older, his father had wanted to protect her—and Ed—from destitution, in the event of his death.

As it turned out, he needn't have worried about Ed, who was as brilliant with money as his father had been, but over the years I had come to see his point about Dervla. I'd had plenty of opportunity to watch her in action, as she still came over every summer for the Season, and stayed with us in what she very much still considered to be 'her' flat.

In all honesty, those annual visits were another reason I'd wanted the cottage so badly. I needed somewhere to escape to which I could really call my own. A lot of the furniture in the flat dated back to when Dervla had last decorated it in the seventies and I wasn't allowed to change it. In that way and so many others, she was quite demanding.

At seventyish—not that she would ever reveal her age—Dervla was still beautiful, in a fabulous-bone-structure way, and expected everyone to swoon at her feet and do everything for her. A lot of them did, which just encouraged her. She was also still intending to bag herself another trophy husband, and her endless pursuit of wizened old men she was convinced were loaded was absolutely exhausting to be around—especially as so many of them seemed to be under the impression that she was a wealthy widow who could bankroll *them*.

We still had a couple of months before she descended upon us that year and, now I was out in the fresh air and thinking straight again, I was cursing myself for agreeing to go and see Janelle that night. It had been one thing doing it for Kiki, but I didn't want to get involved in the mess and filth of a total stranger and end up frittering away those precious pre-Dervla weekends on this ridiculous clutter-clearing nonsense.

But she had sounded so desperate, poor thing, I told myself, it would have been cruel to say no—although, if I were really honest, the prospect of earning—00 a day for something I found so easy was also pretty hard to resist.

It wasn't like I went without—Ed paid all the bills and I had my own copies of his credit cards to use for everything else—but my salary from Mecklin's was a joke, and it was exciting to have the prospect of some decent money that was really my own.

So, I reflected, sitting down on a bench and tilting my head back to enjoy the spring sunshine, perhaps it was worth missing a few weekends in Winchelsea for that.

Thinking about Janelle reminded me of the only possible explanation of how she had come to ring me—Kiki must have been handing out my work number with the bloody canapés the night before. Damn cheek!

It was odd she'd given them the gallery number, though. And what had Oliver said? Something about her taking me shopping? There was way too much Kiki puppeteering going on. I got my phone out.

'Hi, Kiki,' I said.

'Hello, darling,' she replied, her voice several tones lower than usual. 'Wasn't it a great party?' She lowered her voice even more. 'I'm still in bed.'

I had the clear impression she wasn't alone there.

'Oh, well, I won't keep you then,' I said. 'It's just someone called Janelle rang me today and I wondered how she got my number . . . Hmmm, Kiki?'

But before she could reply, I heard some kind of giggly scuffle going on, and then my phone went dead. I rang back on her home number and then again on the mobile but they both went straight to voicemail, so I left a message asking her to ring me and walked back to the gallery.

Creeping Jesus was standing behind my desk when I got back, with a face like a pickled walnut.

'There you are!' he practically shouted, before returning to his more usual, deadly measured tones. 'I don't employ you so I can stand behind this desk and answer the telephone, you know, Amelia.' He stood and looked at me for a moment, his eyes narrowing to slits. 'So where are the envelopes then?' he said finally.

I was so surprised by his reaction—I'd only been out for half an hour or so—that I completely forgot my story about going to Smythson and just looked back at him blankly.

'Aha,' he said, nodding his head. 'A little amnesia, I see. So where exactly have you been, Amelia, while I acted as your social secretary?'

'But Leo was down here,' I said, stupidly. It had seemed funny at the time, going out while Leo was in the loo.

'Leo was in the lavatory, as you well knew, and then he had to go out to a legitimate appointment. I'm still wondering where you've been.'

'The envelopes weren't ready,' I mumbled, suddenly remembering my cover story.

'No, they weren't,' said Christopher. 'Because we didn't have any ordered. I've just rung Smythson to check. So where were you really, Amelia? Coffee? A little shopping?'

I looked at him and wondered what it took to

make someone so pathetic that they went to the trouble of checking up on some stupid little excuse, when they were always telling you how busy and important they were.

'I went out to get some fresh air, Christopher,' I said. 'I've got a headache. I just needed to go outside.'

'Well, I don't pay you to go out for walks,' he said, 'so I will dock an hour from your wages this week. I don't like liars, Amelia. Next time you have a headache on my time—take an aspirin.'

And with that, he turned and stomped back up the narrow wooden stairs to his office.

I went and sat down in my chair, feeling an initial numbness quickly begin to melt into absolute fury. On top of all the little indignities and bad temper I had suffered from Christopher over the years, not to mention the total absence of the promised promotions, this latest verbal assault seemed completely unacceptable.

I took a few deep breaths to try and recover myself, so I could think straight, then I happened to glance down at the desk and saw that a whole page of the telephone logbook was covered in Christopher's spiky scrawl.

There were various names and numbers with my own name next to all of them, in larger and larger writing, down the page, as he had clearly become increasingly furious about taking messages for me.

As I stared, it gradually became apparent to me that while I'd been out—maybe it had been nearer an hour, I now realized—at least six people had phoned for me on the gallery number and, while I didn't know any of them myself, I recognized all their names as friends of Kiki's.

One of them was Rosalyn, the actress I'd met in Planet Kiki when she'd been telling everyone how they should hire me as a 'clutter-clearer'. There was only one way Rosalyn could have got my number—and only one reason why she would be calling me.

As I was sitting there, simultaneously understanding that this list of personal calls was what had made Christopher so furious—and that they were probably all clutter-clearing enquiries—the phone rang again. I grabbed it, sure he would try and get to it first. I heard him pick up just after me and I knew he was listening in.

'Oh, hi,' said a male voice, with the kind of Chelsea accent which usually rang the gallery. 'Is that Amelia? This is Charles Dowdent. We met at Kiki's party last night . . .'

It was the antiques dealer guy.

'Oh, hi, Charles,' I said brightly and quickly, all too aware of old Flapping Ears upstairs and not wanting Charles to say anything that would reveal why he was calling. 'Lovely to hear from you,' I continued. 'I think I know what it's about, but I can't really speak right now. So why don't you give me your number and I will ring you back tonight?'

He gave me the details and rang off. I waited until I heard the click as CJ put the phone down upstairs, and that was it. My former fury had subsided into an icy clear-headedness about the way both he—and Leo—had spoken to me that morning and so many other mornings. I knew exactly what I had to do.

I tore the page with all the names and numbers out of the phone log and put it in my handbag.

106

Then I put my coat back on and walked out of the gallery.

With no intention of ever going back.

9

Fifteen minutes later I was happy to be sitting in a rattling Northern Line tube carriage on the way up to Janelle's flat, knowing that my mobile wouldn't work down there. I needed a little while to sit with my thoughts.

CJ had already called me twice before I had even made it from the gallery to Piccadilly Circus underground station, which was less than five minutes' walk, so he clearly knew I'd gone.

I hadn't answered, of course, although I knew I would have to return his calls pretty soon, or he would ring Ed to report me missing and, for various reasons, I didn't want to tell Ed what I'd done yet. In fact, I needed to get it absolutely clear in my own head before I discussed it with anyone else.

As the tube train rumbled along and I pondered the morning's events, it quickly became apparent to me that it was the prospect of being paid for clutter-clearing that had finally given me the guts to walk out of the gallery.

Christopher—and Leo—had been treating me like shit for years and, locked in some kind of cosy inertia, I'd let them, but now I had the prospect of doing something for myself, I'd finally had the courage to stand up to them. It was really exciting—and absolutely terrifying. Then, working on my father's tightly held principle that you should always do first the thing you want to do least, I forced myself to make the call to Christopher the minute I came up at Hampstead. So I felt pleasantly rewarded for my diligence when I got the answer machine.

I left a succinct message saying that for personal reasons I was resigning from my post and would not be returning to the gallery. Then I heard myself thanking him for employing me and hoping that the business would continue to prosper.

It was out of my mouth before I could stop it. I certainly hadn't planned on doing anything so gracious. Kiki would have told him to get fucked, I thought—in fact, she probably would have sprayed it on the windows—but there I was thanking him for the 'opportunity to work at such a prestigious gallery. . .'

I plodded down Hampstead High Street, fuming at myself for being such a wimp, but when you have grown up being told that everyone is judging your father's professional abilities by your behaviour—with the implication that the entire family's livelihood depends on it—you do become something of a world-class goody-goody.

But it was done, I'd said it, so I tried to put it out of my mind and to concentrate instead on my new challenge. Who was this Janelle? And what on earth was I going to find at her flat that was making her so desperate?

I stopped at a mini-mart on the way to buy some of the tools of what appeared to be my new trade: a roll of bin-liners and a box of tissues. She'd already burst into tears of gratitude when I'd rung her after leaving the gallery, to see if it was OK for me to come over right away, and I had a feeling there was going to be a lot more of the same to come when I got in there. I was a bit nervous about it because it was one thing dealing with that kind of emotional outburst from a friend—even one as normally ebullient as Kiki—quite another doing it with a stranger.

I needn't have worried. It was obvious from the moment I walked through her front door—or, rather, squeezed through; it was no easier getting in there than it had been at Kiki's place—that Janelle's problem was not so much disorganization as full-blown shopping addiction.

The things blocking her hallway were carrier bags of every imaginable colour and provenance. I took in Harvey Nichols, Topshop, Burberry, Louis Vuitton, Prada and Jimmy Choo in one glance. And it was clear that none of them had been opened since she had brought them into the flat.

The other thing that made total sense from the moment I walked in was where all the money for this shopping—and to pay me £600 a day cash—came from. There were framed gold and platinum discs right along the walls.

And when I saw her, a tiny peroxide blonde with high cheekbones, beautiful full lips, almond eyes and the gorgeous dark-golden skin of mixed race—or a very good spray tan—I realized immediately she was one of the Honeypots, a girl band who'd had about seven number-ones before splitting up in volcanic style.

Not being aged nine myself, the mother of pre-teen daughters, or even a fan of weekly magazines, I just hadn't immediately recognized her famous name.

109

'So how long have you had a shopping addiction?' I asked her, settling into one of the three sofas crammed into her sitting room.

It still had the price tag on the arm and the cushions were still in plastic wrapping, which was lucky, as the rest of the room was pretty filthy. The carpet looked as though it had never been vacuumed.

'I'm not no addict,' protested Janelle, clearly offended. 'I've never been in rehab. Two of the other girls in the band have been, but not me. I think you've got me mixed up with Shanelle, or Lorelle.'

'Well, how long have you been shopping like this?' I tried again, gesturing at the spanking-new stuff all around us. The side table next to me had no fewer than four table lamps on it, all still wrapped in the plastic they had come in, like a mini Christo installation.

There were numerous mirrors and pictures propped against the walls, many of them also in their original packaging, and all the flat surfaces were crammed with porcelain figurines, silver photograph frames and other overpriced knick-knacks.

She just gazed at me blankly.

'There's nothing wrong with your flat, Janelle,' I said. 'You're not disorganized, as such, it's just too full. You can't tidy up because there's nowhere to put all this stuff you've bought and you can't clean because you can't get round it.'

She continued to look at me brightly with her surprisingly green eyes. Contact lenses, I realized. And no sign of a light on behind them.

'The sofas,' I said gently. 'Do you really need

three? And four table lamps for one table? And all those mirrors?'

She looked around the room and I could see it still wasn't registering with her. It was as though she were blind to it all.

'Come on,' I said, standing up. I took her hand and led her back into the hall. 'These carrier bags, Janelle,' I said. 'What's in them?'

'Just clothes,' she said, her voice getting a little higher. 'Some shoes and bags . . .'

'Have you ever taken any of them out of the carrier bags?' I asked.

She shook her head, and a frown started to form between her perfectly arched eyebrows—well as much of a frown as the Botox would allow.

'That's not normal, Janelle,' I said firmly. 'When most women buy something new, especially from shops like these, they can't wait to get it home and try it on. So all this makes me think it's the shopping itself that gives you a buzz, rather than the clothes as such—or the lamps, or the sofas, or the knick-knacks . . .'

Finally, I could see she got it. The tears started to flow silently down her cheeks, and I already knew from my very short career as a clutter-clearer that they signalled a breakthrough.

As I had done with Kiki, I said nothing, just tried to look sympathetic and let her get it all out, as she spluttered her story between gulping sobs— how she still couldn't get over having so much money after a difficult childhood with her single mum and how she just kept spending to prove she really had it.

And maybe because, deep down, she didn't really think she deserved it, I thought to myself, so

111

she was subconsciously trying to get rid of it all. Ed had a name for clients like that: he called them 'HBB-LSE'—High Bank Balance Low Self-Esteem—and, according to him, their confusion about self-worth meant you were doing them a service by taking their money from them.

'The thing is, Amelia,' she was saying, still sniffing and dabbing her exquisite surgically adjusted nose with one of my tissues, 'what I can never tell anyone is that I'm so flipping lonely. Everyone thinks I'm a pop star and I've got it all and I have got the money and the gold discs, and I know I'm not ugly and I'm proper A List and all that, but even if I ever met a nice bloke, how could I bring him back here?'

I was beginning to understand that there was more to this clutter-clearing malarkey than just tidying up a bit, but for the time being I wanted to stick to what I knew—which was how to make a chaotic home liveable again. So I took her back into the sitting room to discuss some practical steps we could take.

The first task would be taking any unworn stuff back to the shops where she'd bought it. Then we would have to do a thorough inventory of the rest of the flat to establish what she really loved and really needed—and then I'd put the excess on eBay for her. Or she could have a celebrity charity auction, I suggested. Then we could have the place professionally cleaned.

The other news I was going to break to her at a later point was that I was going to find her a proper shrink to sort out the more deep-seated emotional stuff. She clearly needed it. But in the meantime, to help her feel we were making progress, I made her put all the carrier bags from the hall into five bin-liners, which we hid behind one of the sofas. Then I made her wait outside the front door while I vacuumed the filthy carpet that was revealed underneath.

Janelle couldn't stop smiling when I let her back in and she stood in the cleared space by the front door. She kept opening and closing it just for the hell of it, grinning at me.

'It already feels so different,' she was saying, as I told her we'd done enough for the first session and got my diary out to make our next appointment.

'Here, let me pay you,' she said, and I watched her brown fingers with their ridiculously long French-manicured nails take a wad of new £20 notes from an oversized white Chanel handbag.

I didn't want to count it in front of her, but I could see it was a lot.

'That's £600 for today,' she said, looking nervous. 'Is that OK, or do you need a deposit for the rest? I'm just so grateful you could see me at such short notice . . .'

I felt distinctly uncomfortable. I'd only been there about three hours—it wasn't even a full day. I was about to argue that I couldn't possibly take that much money for so little work when I remembered one of Ed's cardinal rules of business: the more you charge, the more they will respect and value you.

He also believed it made clients more likely to recommend you to their cashed-up pals, because massive prices gave you a high 'BQ', or Bragging Quotient.

This approach certainly worked for him and, now I thought about it, Christopher Mecklin seemed to operate on similar principles. It must be standard practice in that kind of luxury market, I decided. So I smiled at Janelle, told her not to worry about a deposit and zipped her money into my handbag.

I went straight from Hampstead to Fenwicks, where I bought myself a new outfit—a lovely floaty skirt and a top embroidered with sequins, much more expensive than the kind of things I normally bought—paying with Janelle's money.

As I handed over the crisp notes, I felt a flush of the excitement which I realized must have been part of Janelle's addiction. Unlike her, though, I went straight home and changed into my new things.

*　　　*　　　*

Ed was out somewhere when I got back and not answering his mobile, so I didn't have a chance to tell him about leaving my job before we met for dinner with one of his favourite clients at St Alban. It was a very jolly night and definitely not the right occasion to bring up the big change I had made so impulsively in my life.

I just smiled and played my part as the real-life Heady Bouquet, looking interested while they talked obsessively about wine, cigars, restaurants and cars. By the end of it I could have gone on Mastermind with the Bentley Continental GT as my special subject, but that male-interest stuff didn't phase me. Growing up in the all-male context of the school my father worked at, I'd been immersed in it since childhood.

He and my brother were very much boy-men—

rugby, cricket, Formula One, classic cars, boats, trains, aeroplanes, snooker, even hideous boxing, were the dominant themes in our household. My mum and I had our shared interests too—mainly baking, needlepoint and watching bonnet dramas on the telly—but it was the manly pursuits which dominated.

The whole family would decamp to watch Dick and the rest of the school rugby team on freezing Saturday mornings and, if the Monte Carlo Grand Prix clashed with a Dickens adaptation on TV, the cars always won out. It's just the way it was in my family, so normal to me, and Ed's Boy's Own dinner conversation slotted right into the same mould.

By the time we got home that night, I was just too full and snoozy to launch the job-leaving conversation, so after giving Ed a quick hug and kiss, I was relieved to fall into my bed while he shuffled off to do yet more tinkering in his study.

10

I woke up at my usual time the next morning and was about to jump out of bed when I suddenly realized I didn't have to. It was quite a shock, and I flopped back down again, staring up at the ceiling as a wave of anxiety passed over me.

Walking out of Mecklin's had seemed the only possible thing to do at the time, especially with the golden carrot of Janelle's cash waiting for me up in Hampstead, but now I wondered if I hadn't been a little hasty.

My so-called clutter-clearing had worked for Kiki, I could see exactly what I needed to do for Janelle, and all those other people who had called me would no doubt be similar, but that didn't mean it was definitely going to burgeon into a proper career. I should have done a feasibility study and a business plan first—whatever they were.

Because, if it didn't work out, I might end up just kicking around the flat getting in Ed's way— then I'd be completely financially dependent on him, and that really scared me. I didn't want to turn into his mother. Or mine. Because, while my wages from the gallery had never been much more than play money, it had at least given me a sense of independence.

On top of all that, I just wasn't looking forward to telling Ed what I'd done. Not because I thought he really cared whether I worked at Mecklin's or not—he loathed CJ even more than I did—but because I knew how much he disliked sudden change.

I'd figured out quite early in our relationship that Ed was someone who liked to have things planned, and I understood why—a lonely little boy alone in a foreign country, dumped in the unloving arms of an English prep school, Ed had developed routine as his coping mechanism. To feel secure, he absolutely needed to know where he was in life, and it didn't seem particularly weird to me. My father was a man of routine to a much more extreme degree. But unlike dull old Daddy dearest, Ed wasn't remotely boring.

Bowling along French country roads with him in one of his open-top cars, music playing, wind in your hair, alcohol in your bloodstream, you felt wild and free, but Ed always knew exactly where he was having dinner that night.

He did in London too. We only went to certain restaurants—all within walking distance of our flat—and if he had his way, we would have gone to the same one on the same night each week. I wasn't prepared to go that far, but I didn't object to the limited choice of venues. The ones we did go to were so lovely, and there was actually something terribly nice about being really known in them, as we were.

Ed only had to sit down in Scott's and a waiter would bring him a vodka martini, shaken not stirred. Ian Fleming had also been a regular there in his day and the connection thrilled Ed. We ate there at least twice a week, every week.

Such a proscribed life might sound tedious, but I could see that having this structure in place allowed his brilliant, original mind to run free. Either that, or he really did have borderline Asperger's Syndrome, as Kiki had once laughingly suggested.

But while I understood it, I did rather wish it didn't have to extend to our sex life as well. I knew it was good going that a couple who had been together for fifteen years still had regular scx—but I just would have preferred it not to be quite so regular. The marital act of love always took place on Sunday mornings and every other day on trips to France. I wondered sometimes if he scheduled it into his itineraries when he was planning them.

Thursday, Medoc
AM: Lafite, Pichon-Lalande, Pontet-Canet.
Picnic lunch.

PM: Margaux, Palmer and RauZan-Ségla.
Dinner: Le Chapon Fin.
After dinner: intercourse, missionary position,
  condom.

Always with the bloody condom. How I had come to hate those nasty rubber things. I was on the Pill when I first got together with Ed, but he still always insisted on using them. I'd gone along with it at first, but once we were married I'd suggested it might be nice to have bareback sex occasionally.

'Pregnancy is a woman's responsibility—contraception is a man's,' he'd said when I'd pressed him on the subject.

I'd been rather impressed with his responsible attitude at the time, until I'd realized that it was because he wanted absolutely no risk of me ever getting pregnant accidentally—or, 'accidentally'.

I had understood it when we were first married, but I always assumed that once we were a little older and his business was really established, children would be the inevitable next stage. I raised the subject whenever it seemed appropriate—usually when yet another set of friends had their first baby—but he remained intransigent. I had reached the point where I could hardly bear to think about it. What if he never changed his mind?

Lying in bed that first morning after leaving the gallery, with that great unthinkable floating around in my mind, combined with my increasing anxiety about what I was going to do with the rest of my life—and how I was going to tell Ed about it—I was starting to feel as if my head was going to

118

pop. Finally, I threw off the covers and headed out to the park for a run.

It was heavenly out there. The spring air smelled sweet, and the sun was warm on my arms, burning through the morning chill. I could see it was going to be a lovely day, and my anxiety lessened with every step I ran.

I was hoping Ed would be up when I got back to the flat, so I could get the big announcement over, but when I peeked into his room at five to nine he was still fast asleep. I looked at his dear face, so peaceful on the pillow, and felt a pang of sadness that I no longer woke up looking at it every morning. I sighed and remembered yet again what Kiki had said about that.

She was right: we were way too young to be sleeping in separate bedrooms, and then that just reminded me all over again about the other unresolved question—the real elephant in the bedroom. Not the grey velvet one, but the baby issue. I would have to bring it up with him again, I thought, some time soon, but not today. First I had to get through telling him the news about quitting my job.

I kissed his cheek then, closing his bedroom door carefully, started to get on with my day. By ten, when I was showered and dressed and starting to feel twitchy again, I reckoned it was late enough to start phoning people.

My first call was to Kiki.

'Darling!' she cried. 'I hear you've left that stupid gallery at last—that's fantastic news. And Janelle is thrilled with you. I think you're going to get a lot more work out of her too, all those music-business bunnies are total basket cases . . .'

119

I was practically speechless. 'How on earth do you know I've left the gallery?' I asked when I'd recovered.

'Charlie Dowdent just called me,' she said, carelessly. 'You didn't ring him back last night, so he tried you at the gallery again this morning and that hideous Chris gave him very short shrift apparently, so I gave Charlie your mobile numero. I expect he'll ring soon. He's very keen to talk business with you . . .'

'Why did you give everybody the gallery number in the first place?' I asked, wanting to get one thing straight among the many questions roiling around in my head.

'Did I?' she replied, in a voice of such faux innocence, it had clearly had exactly the intended result. 'So,' she continued, before I could pursue it. 'How is London's hottest celebrity clutter-clearer today?'

Thoughts whirled around in my head. I could have been furious with Kiki: she had manipulated the whole situation for reasons I couldn't entirely understand, although I guessed it was partly just for the sport of it and perhaps because she really couldn't bear to see CJ exploiting me the way he did.

There was no doubt she had been unbelievably Machiavellian, but now I'd got over my early morning panic, I was really excited again about the idea of launching my new career. Thanks to Kiki, I had £600—well, £320 after my shopping spree—in crisp notes in my handbag, and the prospect of more to come. And never again would I have to address three hundred envelopes by hand, or clear up after Leo Mecklin's visits to the loo.

'Actually, Kiki,' I said, 'I'm great, thank you, really great—and all thanks to you. So thank you very much, and I'm just about to ring all my other potential clients, so I'd better get off the phone.'

'That's fantastic,' said Kiki. 'You are very welcome—but before you go, sweetheart, Ol rang you, didn't he? He's going to do your hair, and I'm taking you shopping—did he mention that? For one of the more attractive women I know, you really are the worst dressed and, while it was fine for that hideous art gallery and Ed obviously doesn't give a toss, it won't work for your new career. So Kiki is going to give you a new look as a thank-you for everything you've done for me.'

'That's very kind of you,' I said, not sure how to react to such a grossly backhanded compliment. 'I had no idea I was the worst-dressed woman in London, so thanks, that's lovely, but a shopping trip won't be necessary. I bought some new things yesterday, with the money I got from Janelle. It was great fun.'

'Oh God . . .' Kiki groaned, 'I hope they aren't too *floaty* . . .'

They were, of course. I couldn't see what her problem was. I loved wearing floaty skirts, they made me feel more feminine and less—what had Kiki called me?—less Amazonian. I decided I had to give her a serve of her own bluntness back.

'So, Kiki,' I said in a mock-innocent voice, 'enough about me. Let's talk about you. Who exactly was in bed with you when we last spoke? Hmmmm?'

But I was no match for her. She answered with nothing more than a filthy giggle and then, refusing to take no for an answer, she forced me to arrange a day to go shopping for what she called my new 'work wardrobe'.

After we rang off, I sat for a moment, working up the courage to make my first call to one of my potential new 'clients'—a word I was still getting used to with regard to myself—but before I could make the first call, my mobile rang. I was rather relieved to find it was Dick—someone reassuringly familiar in my strange new life.

'Morning, little sis,' he said, with his usual cheer. 'Where the hell are you? I just rang the gallery and, when I asked for you, the bloke who answered said, "No one of that name works here." Pompous arse. What's going on?'

I couldn't help laughing. 'I've left,' I said. 'Those two creeps were rude to me one time too often.'

Dick chuckled. 'Good going, sis, you gave them the finger. Bloody brilliant. Wish I could do that with my job half the time, but never mind, I'm always grateful they don't give me the sack. Anyway, I'm just ringing to say thanks for a top party the other night. I would have rung you yesterday, but I felt too ill.'

'Oh dear, was it like that? Did you kick on somewhere with Joseph?'

'Yes, but no. I ended up joining some friends for dinner, but not with JR, I lost him somewhere along the way—but he's the reason I called actually.'

'JR?' I said, confused, before remembering it was Dick's nickname for Joseph, dating back to the mid-1980s. Dallas-era.

'Yes, he wants us all to get together,' Dick was saying. 'You know he's just moved back here from the US and everything, and he's pretty lonely, I think, and he rang last night to say he'd really love us all to have dinner to catch up on old times and all that. So when are you two free?'

For a moment I was thrown. I loved my brother and I could see he was trying to do the best for his pal, but how could I tell him how little I—let alone Ed—wanted to see his dear friend? As far as I was concerned, Joseph Renwick was someone slightly embarrassing from a previous life and I had no intention of making him part of my current incarnation.

And, as well as that, I had too much going on with leaving the gallery and starting my own business, and I just couldn't face explaining it all to Dick. So I was weak and cowardly and made vague excuses about the next couple of weeks being a very busy time for us and promising that I would get back to him about it. Which I had absolutely no intention of doing.

It wasn't how I would normally behave, but I didn't feel too guilty, because I knew Dick would forget all about it in a couple of days anyway and, at that moment, I had more important things on my mind—like the rest of my working life. So I fortified myself with a strong cup of coffee, took a deep breath and made my first client calls.

The first conversation was similar to Janelle's initial approach. It was with Rosalyn, the actress, and she turned out to be another successful single woman living alone in a flat she couldn't let anyone see. I made a mental note to pack tissues for that appointment.

The next was more interesting: this one was the wife of a banker who couldn't cope with the mess

123

he made in their Notting Hill house. She wanted me to come and clutter-clear him by stealth. That sounded like an interesting challenge.

I had two call-waiting bleeps while I was speaking to her and then the moment I hung up, it rang again. It was Charles Dowdent. He really did want to talk to me, I thought.

'I'm so sorry I didn't call you back last night,' I started to say, but he hardly let me get a word in.

'I want to have lunch with you,' he said, bluntly. 'You and I can do business and I want to get on with it. How about today?'

I was a bit taken aback. I was used to the social niceties in a commercial context with Ed, who did his biggest deals over dinner, and even at the ghastly gallery we had gone through the motions. I couldn't imagine what was making Charles Dowdent so keen but, starting out as I was, I knew that I needed to follow every lead that came my way.

'That would be lovely,' I said, and we arranged to meet that lunchtime at the Bamford café in Sloane Square.

When I put the phone down my head was spinning. I hadn't even been in my new career for twenty-four hours, and already I had three confirmed clients at £500 a day—I'd decided the £600 Janelle had paid me was a one-off, I hadn't entirely abandoned my conscience—with the prospect of 'doing business', whatever that meant, with another.

After that, I couldn't wait another moment, I had to tell Ed what was going on. Plus, I didn't want to give him a heart attack when he finally emerged from the bedroom in his bleary morning state and found me still at home.

I made two macchiatos with the elaborate kit we had in the kitchen—Ed said it was the Bentley Continental of coffee machines—and took them through to the bedroom. Moving Mr Bun, so I could put them on the bedside table, I bent down and kissed Ed tenderly on the mouth.

'Wake up, sleepyhead,' I said, stroking his hair, as he blinked slowly back to consciousness.

'Melia?' he said, smiling at me sweetly. He took hold of my hand and kissed it, and I felt a surge of love for him.

Ed could be detached to an extreme but when he did engage with you, I couldn't imagine anyone being more affectionate.

'I brought you some coffee,' I said. 'I know you normally like to be up and dressed before you have it, but this morning you're having it in bed.'

'Am I ill?' he asked, still smiling sleepily. 'Am I in the San?'

'No,' I laughed. 'But I think I am.'

He sat up and rubbed his head. I handed him his first coffee, and he sipped it gingerly, blinking at me and the room in general. I had no idea how late he had worked after we came in from dinner, and I knew I had to give him time to come to.

Eventually I could see his eyes were starting to focus. He shifted over, patting the bed next to him, and I sat down on it.

'Why are you at home, Melia?' he asked, turning to look at me. 'It's Thursday, isn't it?'

'Yes, it's Thursday, and I'm not at work because I have left Mecklin's. I couldn't stand it any more and, yesterday, I'm afraid I just walked out, Ed.'

I took the empty coffee cup out of his hands and

125

passed him the second one. He sipped a few times before he said anything. I held my breath.

'Good,' he said, eventually. I was so surprised I just gaped at him. 'I've been wondering how to tell you I thought you ought to leave that place,' he continued. 'I don't know why on earth you stayed there so long. Creeping Jesus has really pissed me off, the way he treated you, not to mention trying to scam discount wine all the time, he's such a cheapskate—and when I saw that hideous Leo Mecklin at Kiki's party, I thought, my beautiful wife is just too good for these people. I'm delighted you've left.'

I was so relieved I threw my arms around him and buried my face in his neck. Then something else really amazing happened. Ed made love to me. I felt a flash of irritation as proceedings were interrupted, as they always were, to put the bloody condom on, but then I just surrendered to the comfort of my husband's familiar body.

After that, I found it quite hard to stop giggling. It was all so extraordinary—I was at home on a Thursday morning, Ed was wandering around the flat in his pyjamas and we'd had sex, on a weekday, in England. We were both on a bit of a high. Ed brought Mr Bun into the drawing room to join us, always a sign he was in a playful mood.

'What shall we play, Bun, my good friend?' he was saying to the toy, as he flicked through our CD collection. He pulled one out and showed it to him. 'How about this? You agree? I'm so glad.'

The strains of 'Diamonds Are Forever' launched out of the speakers at high volume, and Ed took me in his arms and waltzed me around the room, throwing in a few dramatic lunges as the music dictated. He was a surprisingly good dancer.

'I still can't believe it, Ed,' I said to him as he tangoed me up and down the room. 'I was terrified to tell you what I'd done. I thought you'd be upset that I'd been so impulsive.'

'Why? It was totally the right thing to do. I know I can be a bit fussy, but I'm not always a complete stick-in-the-mud, you know, Melia. Who was the man who broke into that cellar in Alsace? Me. Who pretended to be a buyer for Waitrose to get into that closed tasting in St Emilion? Me. Who endured the advances of a mad old count to get into his family cellars in Montélimar? Me. Oh yes, inside this staid wine-broker's body beats the heart of a slightly less handsome and a lot less fit James Bond.'

I giggled. I loved Ed when he was silly.

'I've had an idea,' he said, coming to an abrupt stop and looking at his watch—a vintage Rolex (watches were another obsession). 'Let's go to Paris to celebrate. Now. We're too late to get there for lunch, but if we go in the next couple of hours we'll be there in time for dinner. I'll ring L'Ambroisie, I'm sure they'll fit us in. We can stay at the Crillon.'

He was beaming at the prospect. My face must have fallen visibly.

'What?' he said, looking puzzled.

'Can we go tomorrow?' I asked.

'But we're celebrating today,' he said, looking surprised. 'It's not the same if we don't go now, this minute. What's the problem?'

'I've got a lunch date,' I said, feeling pathetic.

'Well, cancel it,' said Ed.

I sighed. I could cancel Charles Dowdent, I

127

thought, but I didn't want to. He was so superkeen to see me, and I didn't want to put him off while my business—if that's what it was—was still in its infancy.

'Who's your lunch with?' he asked.

'Charles Dowdent,' I said, wishing I hadn't as the name came out of my mouth.

'What? That hideous social-climbing knocker boy who shags rich divorcees and lonely widows so he can sell them overpriced French furniture? He tried to crack on to my mother once before he found out she has limited funds. What on earth are you having lunch with him for?'

'He wants to work with me,' I said, cautiously.

'You are joking, aren't you?' said Ed, still smiling, but not quite so brightly. 'You've just got away from two of the most unpleasant reptiles in Cork Street—why ever would you even countenance going to work for the Pimlico version of the same species? Actually, he's even worse than they are. At least they sell good paintings. And he dyes his hair.'

'I wouldn't be working *for* him, but he seems to think I might be able to work *with* him . . .' I said slowly.

'Whatever do you mean, Amelia?' he said, in a bewildered voice. 'I really don't understand.'

I wished I'd never mentioned stupid Charles Dowdent, or working with anyone. I should have just shut up and cancelled him while Ed was getting dressed and gone off to Paris for a lovely jolly. But it was too late now: I'd said it, and I was going to have to tell Ed what I was planning to do sooner or later, so I plunged in.

'I'm going to do clutter-clearing,' I said,

'professionally. People were so impressed by what I'd done at Kiki's place they want me to work for them. I've already got three clients, and Charles Dowdent seems to think we can work together in some way. So I'm having lunch with him to find out what he's got in mind.'

Ed's face fell as I spoke, all the good humour draining from it. 'I don't know what to say,' he said, shrugging. 'You're telling me you are going to demean yourself cleaning up the mess made by spoilt brats who don't know how to live like civilized people? Are you going to polish their shoes? Bring their ironing home?'

He shook his head, and something about the expression on his face—a trace of snobby contemptuousness, behind the genuine disappointment—triggered the same feeling in me that had made me walk out of Mecklin's the day before. I spoke before he could.

'I'm getting £500 a day for it, Ed. It's a fantastic opportunity. I'm not giving it up.'

'Well, you might want to think a little further about that,' said Ed, 'because it's not what I ever envisioned a wife of mine doing. And I don't think a glorified cleaner is quite the image I want her to project to my clients either. So you go and have your lunch with ghastly Charles Dowdent—who, incidentally, I turned down when he applied to join Bradlow's—and I will go to Paris for dinner anyway. On my own.'

And with that, he stalked out of the room, slamming the door behind him. I heard another slam as he went into his bedroom, and decided to leave him to it. He'd never spoken to me like that before, or slammed a door, not once in fifteen

129

years of marriage, and I was so stunned I didn't know if I was more angry, hurt or surprised by his reaction.

I smiled bitterly as I remembered how stupidly nervous I had been about telling him I'd left my job. That had turned out to be no problem, and it had never occurred to me that my new-found profession would be. I had naively thought Ed would be delighted for me to have discovered my vocation at last.

Focusing on how much I enjoyed doing it, how lucrative it might be—and the not insignificant fact that it seemed to help people feel much better about themselves—the délassé implications of clutter-clearing had never crossed my mind. Sometimes, I thought, Ed's eccentricity verged on the irrational.

For a moment I considered going to try and talk it through with him, but then something hardened deep inside me. He could sit and stew with his stupid snobby hang-ups, I decided.

I glanced at the clock on the mantelpiece and saw it was already 12.10, so I grabbed my bag and headed for Sloane Square.

11

My lunch was a disaster. It was clear from the moment I sat down that Charles—I could never call him Charlie—Dowdent saw me entirely as an opportunity for him to make money. It was pretty insulting, but at least I was spared from him flirting with me, which really would have been unbearable.

I could see, though, that even with his tinted hair and overtanned, over-Botoxed skin, he would have appeal for certain women of a certain age. He did have the remnants of a good face and the dyed hair was quite luxuriant.

Plus, he had the Chelsea Eurotrash look that those women loved down to an art form. He was Mr Sardinia from the slightly curling toes of his Tods loafers, through his ironed jeans, navy blazer and white shirt—open at least two buttons too low—to the sunglasses on the top of his head. I wouldn't have been remotely surprised if he'd produced a man bag.

Fortunately for me, he knew I was not only married, but married to someone potentially useful, and it was quickly apparent that Ed was an appealing part of the package Charles thought I could deliver to him.

'When Kiki told me what you were doing, I immediately saw how we could work together,' he said, picking bits of salad off his plate with hairy fingers and stuffing them into his mouth. 'Your clients and mine are the same people, Amelia,' he was saying, as he chewed. Not attractive. 'You sort their places out—they need new furniture, you call me in. Simple. I'll cut you 10 per cent of any sales I make and you can do the same for me, if I pass any clients your way. Sweet, yah?'

He sucked his middle finger in a way I was sure he had developed as a flirtation technique, but which had subsequently become a habit. I hoped he wasn't going to shake hands with me at the end of the lunch.

'Then there are all your husband's customers, of

course,' he said, looking beadily at the Gruyère soufflé which had just been put down in front of me. 'They're a perfect fit for both of us, as well. Between us, it's a dream three-way.' He paused with his fork in mid-air. 'Can I try that?' he said and, before I could even answer, he had plunged his fork into the unbroken top of my soufflé and scooped a large forkful out of the centre. 'Mmmm, that's good . . .' he said and when I saw the fork was about to return for another visit, I lost all my appetite.

I pushed the soufflé towards him and gathered up my bag.

'Actually, Charles,' I said. 'You have it, I'm not very hungry today. And as for your proposal, I think I am still too much at the early stages of building up my client list to start sharing them with other people. So thank you so much for thinking of me, but I'll just carry on solo for the time being.' I looked at my watch. 'And I'm afraid I have a dentist's appointment I forgot about when we made this date, so I'll have to dash.'

Then I got up and walked out. I had for a millisecond thought about handing him a tenner towards my half of the bill—which is what the deputy headmaster's daughter normally would have done, fair play and all that—but I decided against it. He'd invited me for lunch, he was eating it, he could pay for it.

I glanced back just as I was about to walk out of the café door and he was bent over the soufflé stuffing it in.

I powerwalked towards home, furious with myself for being so keen to kickstart my new career that I'd jumped at his presumptive demand

132

that I meet up with him immediately. Not to mention having my first ever proper, big, door-slamming row with my husband over it. But I was still very cross with Ed as well.

He had been right about Charles Dowdent being dreadful, and I should have cancelled the stupid lunch, but I still thought he had been really unfair and rude about my new career. I knew it might have been different if I had explained it all to him a little more tactfully, perhaps in one of his favourite restaurants, over something complicated involving foie gras and a glass of Château d'Yquem, but sometimes I just wanted to get on with things.

I felt I spent rather a lot of my life tiptoeing around Ed's sensitivities and, this time, just for once, I felt it was about me, not him. I wanted things on my terms for a change, and the result had been slammed doors as if he were a spoilt teenager. Not right, not fair.

I stomped along Sloane Street and Cadogan Place feeling seriously grumpy, but after I turned into Pont Street, my attention was distracted by the gorgeous bags in Anya Hindmarch's boutique. As I gazed through the window at them I remembered what Kiki had said about my wardrobe. I adjusted my focus so I was looking at my own reflection. Did I really look that bad?

I was wearing my favourite old jeans. I'd had them a few years and I had no idea what label they were, but jeans were still the thing to wear, weren't they? Kiki often wore them. Hers mostly had straight legs, but surely it didn't matter if mine were bootleg, did it?

I looked down at them, and then noticed I was

wearing loafers on my feet. I hated having anything in common with Charles Dowdent, so maybe I did need some new shoes, as well.

But my top was lovely. It was my new one. Sort of Indian-y and sparkly. It was a bit 'floaty', as Kiki had said, so I had one of my little cardies from Jigsaw over it and then just a normal navy jacket. But that was a bit like Charles Dowdent's too, now I thought about it. Maybe Kiki was right. Maybe I did need a wardrobe overhaul.

My eyes shifted back to the bags. They were absolutely glorious, and I could see they were a lot more fun than the one I was carrying. It was a simple black shoulder thing by Ferragamo that Ed had bought for me in Duty Free one time. I'd had it for ages, and it worked perfectly well for everyday, but now I looked at it again I had to admit it wasn't very exciting, certainly not compared to the kind of bags Kiki carried.

On a sudden impulse, I pushed open the door of the shop and went in. I came out again ten minutes later carrying a brand-new handbag. In leopard-print ponyskin.

I had tried to buy another plain black bag, as I thought it would go with more things, but the very glamorous young woman who served me convinced me to get something more fun. A 'statement', she'd said, and as I swung along the road with it, I was delighted I'd listened to her. Buying it had used up the rest of my Janelle money and then some, but I didn't care; it had really cheered me up. I was just walking under the Wellington Arch, wondering whether to go straight home or detour into Green Park to try and clear my head, when my phone rang. It was Ed.

134

'Melia?' he said, in a very small voice.

'Hello, Ed,' I said, coldly. I wasn't quite ready to forgive him yet. That door-slamming really had been a step too far.

'Don't be cross, Melia,' he said. 'I'm sorry. Really, really sorry. I was horrible to you. I was wrong. Please forgive me.'

'Oh, OK,' I said, still irritated, but starting to soften as I heard the sincere regret in his voice. 'You were horrible and unkind to me—and I think door-slamming is pathetic—but I will give you another chance, if you promise never to slam doors again.'

'I promise,' said Ed. 'Scout's honour.'

'You weren't in the Scouts!'

'I'll join . . .'

I had to laugh.

'All right,' I said. 'You are forgiven, and I have to admit you were absolutely right about Charles Dowdent. He is completely hideous. He was so awful, I didn't even stay to finish my food.'

Ed chuckled. 'I told you he was a creep,' he said. 'And I do really promise I won't slam any more doors. It was pathetic. I was jealous, OK? But listen—I'd better be quick, I'm just about to go under the Channel. I'm not even in France yet, but I'm already miserable without you. Will you come and join me, Melia? There's a ticket for the 16.45 waiting for you at St Pancras. I've got a table at L'Ambroisie. Please come. We'll always have Paris . . .'

It was one of our little repertoire of tension breakers. How could I resist him?

*   *   *

135

I was delighted I'd gone to Paris, from the moment I arrived at the glorious Crillon—and we even had sex again, right after I got there. I didn't know when we had last had sex twice on the same day, and I liked it. A lot. There was another condom involved, of course, but at that point I wasn't complaining.

On top of that, I got my chance to talk to Ed about my career plans in the setting of one of his favourite restaurants, after all—his very favourite, in fact. But while he clearly was making a big effort to be nice about it, I could see he still wasn't entirely thrilled by the prospect of me being a professional clutter-clearer.

I tried to explain that it was more of an executive role and that I wouldn't actually be doing any cleaning or any of the grubby stuff, but I was making it up as I went along—I really didn't have any properly formed plan and, as I talked, I realized I needed one. If I could get him on side, that was something Ed could really help me with.

'It's more like interior decorating,' I said, in a moment of inspiration. That was a profession his mother had once dabbled in—or at least she had persuaded Ed to pay for her to go on a very expensive residential course about it in Florence—so I thought it might be more acceptable. It seemed to work.

'Oh,' said Ed, relaxing back in his chair and practically purring with pleasure as he looked around the candle-lit dining room. 'Well, put like that, maybe it's not such a bad idea, and I have to agree the money is astonishingly good.'

He had the warmth back in his eyes as he

136

looked at me, over his glass of La Mission Haut-Brion '75.

'I just don't ever want to see you leaving the flat with any rubber gloves in your tarty handbag.'

My new bag was the only cause of slight tension on that trip. He hadn't said anything until we were about to leave for the restaurant, clearly keen to make amends for the earlier unpleasantness, although I'd clocked the way he looked at it when I'd first arrived.

'You look absolutely beautiful,' he'd said, when I emerged from the bathroom. 'I've always loved you in a little black dress—it sets off your hair so wonderfully—but are you really going to take that awful bag?'

'Why not?' I asked, picking it up and checking out my reflection in the full-length mirror, and deliberately ignoring the word 'awful'. I thought it went perfectly. I had my Louboutin shoes on too and felt, for once, like *une vraie Parisienne.*

'Well, it looks like something Diana Dors might have carried, and with those shoes as well, don't you think it's all a bit much?' He frowned a little. 'Did Kiki give you the bag too?'

'No, she did not!' I said, a little louder than necessary, but just managing to hold back from sounding fully cross; I wasn't ready for another row. 'I bought it myself with the money from my first client and I love it. I think it's really fun, and it's the only bag I have with me, so you're stuck with it, but I'll change my shoes, if it's going to spoil your entire night.'

Considering I was still hoping to get him onside about my new career at that point, I thought it was worth the compromise and judging by the way things had gone at dinner, I was right. By the time we were on our way back to the hotel, snuggled up together in the back of a taxi, he was being quite funny about it, asking me if the bag needed a bowl of milk, how often it would need worming and things like that. By the time we pulled up in front of the Crillon, he had named it Pussy Galore.

*   *   *

On the way home the next day, half-dozing on Eurostar, as it rattled through the bleak flat fields of northern France, I was wondering what to do about Kiki's proposed shopping trip and wardrobe makeover, which was in my diary for the following week.

In the light of Ed's reaction to one new handbag—and his earlier one to the shoes Kiki had given me—a radical new look really didn't seem such a good idea just then. Not because I was prepared to have my entire life dictated by his little quirks and prejudices, but in these crucial early stages I desperately wanted Ed's active support for my new work venture. I wanted the benefit of all his years of business experience to help me build mine up, so there was no point getting him offside now over irrelevant issues—especially as it seemed to be getting off to a most brilliant start. Even while we were on the train my phone kept ringing with people wanting to book consultations with me, which all helped to impress Ed that it was a serious proposition.

'What a lot of untidy people there must be in London,' he said, smiling fondly at me. 'With lots of lovely spare money.' He looked thoughtful for a moment. 'You're going to need a bigger diary for all those appointments,' he said. 'Or actually, maybe you should go space age with it, have it all on your Batphone. I tell you what, when we get back I'm going to go out and get us each one of those iPhone thingies. It's about time I got into the twenty-first century. I'm so out of date I'm practically using a quill and a tom tom. I've been meaning to do it for ages, so let's get digital together, shall we?'

Half standing up, I leaned across the table, put my hands around his cheeks and gave him a big snog, right there on Eurostar.

'I say, Heady Bouquet,' he said, as I pulled away, his cheeks adorably pink. 'I am most awfully glad you left your job.'

12

The days after we got back from Paris, as I darted around London visiting all my new clients, were like a crash course in the many and various kinds of chaos people manage to mire themselves in.

My first appointment was with the wife of the untidy banker, who I had met at Kiki's party. That was a bit tricky, as I didn't really feel I could start going through someone's private possessions without their permission. So I suggested we got the rest of the house into a state of exquisite perfection, in an attempt to inspire him to want to be tidy himself—and kept it that way with the help of a daily housekeeper, which she could easily afford and which I also reckoned she really needed.

I'd sussed out early on in that appointment that she was actually very disorganized herself—and not a little lazy—and was using her husband's mess as an excuse to hire me. I went along with her. As long as we got results, it didn't matter how we did it.

The next day I encountered my second shopping addict, although in this case her purchases were not bags and shoes but works of art, which she was unbelievably precious about. Monica—another pal of Kiki's—lived in a one-bedroom flat in Regent's Park, but the limited space clearly didn't stop her seeing herself as a female Charles Saatchi.

There were paintings hanging floor to ceiling in every room, loads more propped against the walls, with sculpture and more conceptual pieces on every other surface. You could hardly walk about for mini-installations by artists I had never heard of, although she talked about them with great reverence, and I was terrified to put my mug down in case what appeared to be a coaster was actually the work of some rising art-world star.

I suggested we should hire a qualified curator to do a complete inventory and, during that process, she could choose the ones she wanted to live with for the next six months and all the others would be put in a secure art-storage unit. Then she could change the display twice a year and open the flat as a by-appointment museum, I suggested, which went down very well—as I had known it would.

I hadn't been a professional clutter-clearer for much over a week yet, but I had already figured out that sizing up your clients and understanding exactly what would appeal to their particular variety of vulnerable self-esteem was a large part of being successful at it.

And after so many years of manoeuvring around the Zeppelin-sized egos in my own personal and professional lives, this way of working came very easily to me. I was pandering entirely to my clients' weaknesses and vanities, but I was also helping them, which made me feel good—and being paid for it. Double kerching! As Ed liked to say.

After that appointment I headed over to Bayswater to see Rosalyn, the actress. It was a lovely, spacious flat and, as she showed me round, I got more and more puzzled. It didn't seem cluttered at all. A bit untidy in places but nothing out of the ordinary, and I couldn't really understand why she had called me—until I asked her to show me the one room we hadn't been into.

Her stricken face said it all.

'The study?' she said, sounding as if I had brought up an unmentionable taboo, and then out it all came.

Her problem was focused entirely on financial admin—and it was all crammed into that one room. So crammed in, the only way I could get the door open was to hold a mirror through the gap and use a broom to shift the piles of paper that were jamming it shut.

'OK,' I said, surveying the devastation within. 'Let's go back to the sitting room and have a chat.'

She admitted her study was like that because for months she had just been opening the door and throwing in anything that looked like a bill, a bank statement or a letter from the Inland Revenue. The tears finally flowed as she confessed she hadn't done a tax return for five years. She didn't even have an accountant and couldn't sleep at night for worrying what was going to happen when the taxman eventually caught up with her.

I had to bite my lip not to smile when she sobbed, 'And I haven't got a TV licence either . . .'

This had all blown up in her mind to the point where she saw her whole flat as some kind of catastrophe when, really, the rest of it was fine. Sometimes, she said, the whole thing weighed on her so badly she checked into a hotel for a night to get away from it.

It was time for action, but once we went back into the study and I took in the great piles of mixed-up papers and unopened envelopes that had drifted like sand dunes against the walls and furniture, I could understand why she had been having trouble sleeping. For a moment I felt a little daunted, and I was not at all afraid of a little financial admin.

I did all of ours—not Ed's business stuff; he had a professional bookkeeper for that—but all the household finances, council tax, insurance, the car, that kind of thing. My mother had shown me how to balance a cheque book and keep things filed when I was fourteen, and it had been second nature to me ever since. I did it once a month and even enjoyed it in a Uriah Heep kind of way.

Rosalyn's study was overwhelming simply because of the sheer volume of it, and it was hard to see where to start, but I didn't want to leave until I had given her some sense of hope that I would be able to sort it out for her. So I used what I was beginning to think of as my bin-liner trick. I got out my trusty roll and we stuffed every single bit of paper in that room into bags.

Then I sent Rosalyn out to wait while I piled them up in one corner behind the door so that when I brought her back in—*et voil*—she had a room again, with a desk and bookshelves, even a floor. Like Kiki and Janelle, she was amazed by the difference.

And just putting the stuff into the bin-liners, we had come across several cheques she had never banked—the total would more than pay my fees, I was pleased to note—plus she had found a lone shoe she'd been searching everywhere for, which had been buried under the heaps of paper.

Once again, that first small change worked wonders and, while I knew we would still have to sort through all that paperwork, which was not a very appealing prospect, I was confident that Rosalyn's life was already starting to change for the better.

And so, I realized, as I left with a cheque for £500 in my wallet, was mine.

*   *   *

My final appointment on Wednesday afternoon was the follow-up with Janelle and I was amazed by what I found at her flat when I got there.

'Amelia!' she said, giving me a huge hug at the door. 'Come in, come in, I've got so much to tell you. You are such a genius. Look at this.'

She took my hand and led me through to the sitting room, where I saw that the pile of bin-liners, containing her unopened designer carrier bags that we had stuffed behind one of her sofas, was now three times as high as it had been when I had left the week before.

'Wow,' I said. 'You have been busy.'

'Yeah,' she said, her alarmingly green eyes dancing with excitement. 'And there's loads more to come.'

'You don't have to get rid of everything you own, Janelle,' I said, a bit alarmed at what I might have started. 'There is a happy medium.'

'It's not all mine,' she said, jumping on to the sofa—quite an achievement in jeans as tight as the ones she was wearing—and grabbing one of the bags. She opened it and pulled out a pair of bright-pink sequinned hot pants. 'These are Lorelle's, and this bag'—she produced some egg-yolk-yellow moon boots—'is Shanelle's stuff.'

I was bewildered, although I did recognize the names as those of her former girl-band colleagues.

'What have you got all their stuff here for?' I asked.

'The charity auction,' she said, looking at me as though I should know all about it. 'It was such a brilliant idea, Amelia, and it's going to be so amazing. Look, it's in the papers today.'

She handed me a copy of the *Sun* and there it was.

A TASTE OF MONEY!
Honeypots reunite for charity audion, rumours of tour!

'Good going, Janelle,' I said. 'You got right on to that.'

I didn't want to tell her I had completely forgotten ever suggesting she could have a charity auction of her unwanted stuff.

'Well,' she said, 'I felt so much better just

144

getting all that crap out of the hall, I had this big surge of energy, and the brilliant thing was, it gave me the excuse I needed to call Lorelle. We've been friends since we were five years old and I hadn't spoken to her since the band broke up. So I rang her and suggested we did a charity auction of our clothes, like you said, for our old school where we met, and it's just gone on from there. Turns out we were all really sad and missing each other and now—don't tell anyone, we haven't released it officially—we are reforming and we are going to do a new album and a tour. And it's all thanks to you.'

I was about to open my mouth to say I couldn't possibly take any credit for any of it, but Janelle had started talking again.

'Who's your agent?' she said.

'My agent?' I replied, bewildered all over again.

'It's just that the magazines are fighting over the exclusive about how the auction came out of your clutter-clearing my place, and my agent wants to speak to yours to discuss who we should place it with.'

'Magazines?' I said, dumbly.

'Yeah, I'd like to do it with *Grazia*, because they've got more class than *Heat* and I've done *Hello!* so many times, but I'm just gonna tell her, take the one who offers the most, because I'm going to give it all to the school fund anyway. So, who shall I tell her to call?'

'Give her my number,' I said, my head whirling.

After all that excitement, I insisted we get started clearing the rest of the place and, within a couple of hours, we had arranged for one sofa to go back to Heal's and filled several boxes with

145

knick-knacks ready to be flogged on eBay, all money raised to go to Janelle's old school.

She helped me down to the car with them and, as we said goodbye, she handed me a wedge of crisp banknotes. I looked at it for a moment and then pressed them back into her hand.

'Put it towards the school fund,' I said. 'That's my donation.'

She gave me another big hug and said she'd 'see me at the photo shoot'. I didn't even ask her which photo shoot, I decided just to let it all unfold, like some crazy flume ride—and it did.

I hadn't got far down Haverstock Hill when my phone rang. It was Janelle's agent, calling to discuss which magazine we should place the story in, but it soon became clear that wasn't the only reason she'd called me.

By the time we rang off, we'd agreed a date for me to go and sort out her office, which she said was such a 'cesspit' she had to have all her meetings in café, which was a huge waste of time— plus, she'd put on half a stone drinking endless lattes she didn't really want. Then, she reeled off a list of names of clients who she said would also be contacting me.

Kiki had been right—London badly needed its clutter clearing.

13

The next day was supposed to be our big shopping expedition, and I met Kiki in the café on the ground floor of Liberty's as we had planned, because I thought it would be easier—and kinder—to explain face to face that I wasn't ready for the wardrobe makeover yet.

'Oh boy, have we got work to do,' she said, shaking her head, when I walked in. 'We'd better not dawdle too long over this coffee.'

'What are you talking about?' I said, sitting down.

'Well, it's all a bit random, Amelia, isn't it?'

'What is?'

'You—your outfit. You've got Sloane Ranger shoes, yummy-mummy jeans, a top that looks like it's on holiday in Goa and a jacket that should never have left Cheltenham. Nice bag, though— when did you score that?'

She reached over and grabbed Pussy Galore, nuzzling it against her face and purring.

'Last week,' I said proudly. 'It is gorgeous, isn't it? I got it from Anya Hindmarch. And this top's new as well. It's by Antik Batik. I think it's lovely, and it's got a matching skirt . . .'

'It is lovely, Amelia,' said Kiki, in surprisingly gentle tones, and putting her hand on mine. 'But it just doesn't work with the rest of your outfit. Like I said before, you need to look more pulled together if you want to be taken seriously professionally. Mind you, I'm hearing great things about you on that front. Monica says her flat is going to be a museum, Janelle says you have reunited the Honeypots, and Rosalyn said you found cheques for—,000 while you were tidying up her place. Is that all true?'

I nodded. Kiki high-fived me across the table.

'Way to go, baby girl,' she said, grinning broadly. 'I knew you'd be a star.'

'Well, thanks to you,' I said. 'It's still early days,

147

but I am loving it and you've reminded me—I'm going to check out the stationery department here to see if they have any nice filing boxes for Rosalyn's place to help keep her motivated once we've sorted her out.'

'You can do that another day,' said Kiki, in her bossiest voice. 'We haven't got time now. I thought we'd start here to get a feel for what suits you, then we might head over to Dover Street Market to pick up some statement pieces. Then on to Selfridges for jeans, shoes and basics.'

'Actually, Kiki,' I said, taking a breath and determined to be firm with her, 'it's incredibly nice of you to do this for me, especially after what you've already done setting me up in business, but I think I need to take it slowly on this wardrobe-makeover lark. I'm not really ready for a whole new look in one go.'

'Why ever not?'

I wasn't going to tell her the real reason was Ed—and anyway, it wasn't just about him. 'Well, it's just too much change for me all at once,' I told her. 'It's quite scary working for myself for the first time and if I suddenly get all new clothes as well, I don't think I'll know who I am any more.'

Kiki looked at me steadily. She was wearing the heavy-rimmed 1950s-style glasses she appeared in sometimes. I strongly suspected they were just for effect, and they were certainly having one on me. She was reminding me uncomfortably of my father in telling-off mode. He looked at you over his glasses like that. Joseph Renwick used to do a very funny impersonation of him doing it, I remembered, and his face flashed into my head suddenly, looking back at me at Kiki's party. I felt

148

myself blush at the memory. It was all too much; I was squirming in my seat.

'It's Ed, isn't it?' said Kiki quietly, her gaze not breaking mine. 'He didn't like it when I bought you those shoes, and you're worried he'll freak out if you come home looking like a twenty-first-century woman, rather than the mid-twentieth-century version he seems to prefer. Hmmmm? Am I right?'

I had to hand it to Kiki. She was as tactful as a nightclub bouncer, but she was spot on once again. Ed's feminine ideal was pretty much Miss Moneypenny. He'd bought me several cashmere twinsets over the years, and I had a drawer full of Hermès scarves.

'No,' I said, hoping it sounded more convincing to her than it did to me. 'I just want to take my new life one step at a time. OK?'

She leaned across the table towards me. 'Look, Amelia,' she said. 'You did something amazing for me with my flat. I really feel my life has changed since you sorted it out. I used to live with a slight feeling of panic permanently in my chest, and that has gone—completely gone. You did that for me, so now will you let me do something for you? I think you need this as much as I needed to be told to get rid of those stupid videos . . .'

She was looking at me so kindly and intently over those silly glasses, and while it made me feel quite uncomfortable, I could see she was completely sincere. Then, as I looked back at her, wondering what to say, something strange happened. My eyes filled with tears, and when I opened my mouth to answer her, I realized my throat was all achey and closed.

149

She squeezed my hand. 'It's OK, Amelia,' she said. 'Just this once, let me look after you. OK?'

I was so horrified that I might be about to burst into tears in public, I just nodded.

*   *   *

In the end we had a really great day. Although I was still adamant I didn't want her to buy me anything, I did agree to try things on and found it was a lot of fun. She took me over to Dover Street Market—by a route which took us perilously close to C. J. Mecklin & Son—where she put me in all kinds of peculiar garments by Comme des Garçons, Balenciaga and Boudicca.

And while I had no intention of ever wearing clothes like that, I could see that they looked rather good on me, in a weird kind of way. Being tall, I realized, meant you could get away with quite extreme styles.

'See,' said Kiki, when I came out in an almost backless black satin dress by Lanvin which had looked like a sack on the hanger. 'You look amazing in that. It's sickening actually. I'd love to be as tall as you. And why don't you wear more black? It looks great on you. Put these shoes on.'

They were a ridiculously high pair of silver platforms that I wouldn't have been seen dead in—they looked like something from *Dr Who*—but I was happy to go along with her for the lark.

I put them on, looked in the mirror, and it was suddenly quite strange. I felt like I was looking at someone else, someone rather amazingly glamorous. It was exciting, but also slightly terrifying. I didn't feel up to being the woman I was looking at in the mirror. She was me, but I wasn't her.

'Unbelievable,' said Kiki, looking at my reflection. 'I think I hate you.'

Then she came behind me and lifted up my hair so it hung like a bob just above my shoulders. It made my face look quite different, more bony and sculpted. More grown up.

'That's the next thing,' she said.

After that, I felt so unsettled I hurried to get back into my own things again. When I was dressed I stopped and looked at myself in the mirror inside the changing room, and for the first time I really understood what Kiki meant about my clothes.

Compared to the glamazon I had momentarily been transformed into, I could see I was pretty frumpy—and the only difference between me and that other woman I had glimpsed in the mirror was the clothes.

'All right, Kiki,' I said, when I came out. 'You're right. I do need to change my look. I get it now, and I do want new clothes. Today.' She grinned at me, and I realized she must be feeling the way I did when I had just cleared someone's hallway. 'But I don't feel ready for silver platform shoes and backless dresses,' I added. 'Can you help me look less frumpy without looking freaky?'

She took me off to Selfridges, where we commandeered a changing room and several assistants to bring us things from all over the store. Sending them off on quests like a little potentate in red high heels, Kiki was in her element.

'OK,' she said, coming back to the changing room carrying armfuls of clothes. 'I know you love

151

jeans and a tailored jacket, so let's stay in your comfort zone, but with these jeans and this tailored jacket.'

She picked out two garments from her pile and I obediently put them on. The jeans were in the very dark denim colour she always wore, quite high on the waist and very narrow right down to the ankle, and while they were different to what I was used to, I could see right away that they really showed off my long legs.

The jacket—black, just to the top of my hip and with wide, oddly short sleeves—was more challenging, but after Kiki had me try it on over a stripy T-shirt, with the jeans, I totally got it, and after that I was open to anything she suggested.

After an hour or so we had narrowed it down to the dark jeans, a wide-legged white pair, a pile of assorted long-sleeved T-shirts, the black jacket and a double-breasted bright red one like a reefer jacket. There were also a couple of floral-print silk dresses which she was trying to persuade me could be worn over jeans or on their own, belted or loose.

'But how come these don't count as floaty?' I asked her.

'Trust Auntie Kiki!' she said happily. 'The fabrics are modern. OK, next stop, shoes. Some very frivolous flat sandals and perhaps some red ballerinas—they'd be gorgeous with your new handbag.'

In the end, after protesting that it was too much, I let her buy me the jeans, the jackets, the T-shirts and the dresses as her thank-you for doing her place, but I insisted on paying for the shoes myself.

I got three pairs, all variations on the basic ballerina style, in wonderfully fanciful colours. I'd hardly had a pair of shoes that weren't black, brown or navy since I was a child, I realized, apart from trainers, and flip-flops for holidays, and it felt really reckless.

Finally, the crazy spree over, we stopped on Oxford Street to say goodbye and I gave Kiki a huge hug before she got into her taxi.

'Thank you so much,' I said. 'I love my new clothes. I really didn't know how much I needed to do that. Thank you for being so bossy.'

'You are so welcome, Amelia,' she said, smiling up at me. 'But I still don't think you realize quite how much you have done for me. So I'm going to force you to let me be as helpful to you as you are to me. Just trust Auntie Kiki, OK?'

I kissed her again and headed home down Duke Street, happily swinging my bright yellow Selfridges bags.

I felt a little like Janelle when I dropped them all on my bed, but unlike her I immediately opened them and tried everything on again. Ed was going to be out late that night doing a cellar inventory for one of his best clients, so I had great fun putting on different combinations of my new things and parading around the flat striking poses.

And as I looked at myself in the big mirror in Ed's bedroom, wearing the narrow-leg dark denim jeans, a tight and shiny dark blue T-shirt and the Christian Louboutin heels Kiki had given me at her party, I was relieved he wasn't in.

If these new clothes made me look as different as they made me feel, the effect would be striking—and while he was being great about my new business, I was fairly sure he wasn't ready for the wardrobe makeover as well. I'd have to

153

introduce it slowly, piece by piece.

I was so caught up in trying on different looks I hadn't noticed how late it was until my mobile rang. Reaching for the handset, which was lying on the bed, my eyes fell on my alarm clock and I saw it was nearly midnight.

It must be Ed, I thought, ringing to say he'd decided to stay the night at the client's house in Richmond, but when I picked the phone up the display said 'Dick'.

'Dickie bird,' I said, surprised and immediately a little concerned at how late he was ringing me. We had a strict not-after-9-p.m. rule in our family. 'Is everything OK?'

'It's not Dick, actually,' said a deep voice. It was familiar, but I couldn't quite place it.

'Oh?' I said, now feeling quite worried. 'Well, you're ringing on Dick's phone—so who is it?'

'It's Joseph Renwick,' said the voice. I sank down on to the bed, in something like shock. It was a combination of instant deep anxiety about Dick and that irritating effect Joseph Renwick seemed to have on me.

'Is Dick all right?' I asked.

'Yes and no,' said Joseph.

My heart was pounding. Now I knew something bad had happened.

'He's been in a fight,' said Joseph, his voice heavy with concern.

'A fight?' I said stupidly. 'Is he hurt?'

'Not as much as the other bloke . . .'

'Oh God, what happened? Where is he?'

'He's in A&E at Saint Mary's. I'm with him, but so are the police.'

'Oh God,' I said again, starting to feel quite

154

nauseous.

'Do you think you could come?' said Joseph, gently.

'Oh, of course,' I said, flustered. 'I'm sorry, I'm just so shocked, I can't think straight. I'll come immediately.'

I grabbed my bag and literally ran out of the flat and raced down the stairs, which seemed quicker than the lift. It wasn't until I had jumped into a taxi, which had been coming along the street from Berkeley Square, that I realized I was still wearing the Louboutin heels.

*   *   *

A kind nurse directed me to the side room where Dick was, but when I got there Joseph was sitting on a chair outside the closed door.

'Amelia,' he said, his face lighting up when he saw me. He jumped to his feet. 'It's so great you're here.'

'What's going on? How is he?' I asked, hardly noticing that Joseph had put his arms round me and was giving me a tight hug.

'He's all right,' said Joseph, letting go of me again. 'He's not going to look pretty for a while, but he hasn't lost any limbs.'

'Can I see him?' I asked.

Joseph shook his head.

'The cops are in there at the moment, taking a statement. They made me wait out here. . .'

'Oh sod that,' I said. 'He's my brother.'

And I pushed open the door and marched in. Two very surprised policemen looked up at me. I ignored them.

'Dickie,' I said, running to the bed on my perilous shoes, shocked at the state of him. His face was like a big red hamburger with slitty eyes. 'Whatever's happened to you?'

'Hello, Meals . . .' he groaned. 'Had a bit of a disagreement. South African bloke. Bigger than me . . .'

'Oh Dick,' I said, wanting to kiss him but not able to see any bit that didn't look too painful to touch. 'You are such an idiot.'

I squeezed one of his feet through the hospital blanket.

'Er, excuse me, young lady,' said one of the policemen, 'but we are conducting an interview here . . .'

'Oh, I'm so sorry,' I said, looking at the two of them properly for the first time. And as I did, I realized they were already looking at me, and in a very particular way.

Then I remembered what I was wearing. I had been in such a hurry to get there I hadn't even stopped to put a jacket on, so I was basically wearing skintight clothes from the clinging T-shirt down to my very high-heeled feet. And it was clear they appreciated the effect.

Maybe it was the shoes, maybe it was the adrenaline, but the next thing I knew, I was looking at that policeman from under my eyelashes and pouting shamelessly.

I stepped forward towards him with my hand—and my chest—out. 'I'm Amelia Bradlow, Dick's sister,' I said. 'I'm so sorry to interrupt, but I was just so worried about him. I had to see him. Do you think you will be very long? Should I go away?'

I did everything but lick my lips at him, then I

turned my gaze on the other one, who was shifting uncomfortably in his seat. They looked at each other and then back at me.

'Well, I think we've pretty much finished actually,' said the first one, clearly the senior officer. 'We can leave it for now. We've got Mr Herbert's details, and we can always find him if the other party wants to press charges.'

'Oh,' I said, in my newly acquired Marilyn Monroe whisper 'you'd better have my number as well . . .' And I took his notebook and wrote it down, with a bit more simpering. That time I actually did lick my lips. He went quite pink. It was hilarious.

'We'll leave it there for now, Mr Herbert,' said the policeman to Dick, in a much brisker voice. 'But do try not to get into any more pub brawls. We won't be so lenient next time. You're on notice.'

'Right you are,' croaked Dick, wincing as he moved his painfully swollen lips.

It wasn't until I turned to wave a coquettish goodbye to my new policemen pals that I realized that Joseph was standing in the doorway watching, a look of barely contained amusement on his face.

We left it a few moments after they'd gone then he came into the room, closed the door, and we all cracked up—even Dick.

'Oh bloody hell, don't make me laugh—bloody painful—but really, sis, that was quite something.'

'Way to go, Amelia,' said Joseph, holding up his palm. I gave him a high five. 'You played those two like a couple of trout.'

I giggled. 'I don't know what came over me,' I said. 'I just couldn't resist it.'

157

'I know what came over PC Plod,' said Dick, speaking much more clearly all of a sudden. He must have been laying on the pitiful croaking for our friends from the Met, I realized. 'Raw lust. I don't know what you're wearing, but you look like Olivia Newton-John at the end of *Grease.*'

'Oh, I think she looks a lot better than that,' said Joseph quietly.

My head snapped round to find he was looking at me with that steady gaze of his, the same way he had looked at me at the party. I swallowed awkwardly and my mouth felt dry. I licked my lips again, but out of nerves this time, not flirtation. Something about that look was so grossly inappropriate—but why couldn't I just ignore it?

I was greatly relieved when a nurse bustled into the room, followed by a doctor, who put some X-rays up on a lightbox by the wall.

'You've been very lucky, Mr Herbert,' he said. 'Judging by the size of the bump, that bottle clearly came down very hard on your head, but it hasn't fractured your skull. You've got six fractured ribs, though, which won't be much fun, but the rest is just severe bruising and a few cuts. You'll survive—painfully, but you'll live.'

'Just an average game of rugby for you then, Sherbet,' said Joseph.

The doctor turned to look at us for the first time, and he did a classic cartoon double-take. At me.

'Hello,' he said, some kind of primitive light flaring in his eyes, 'are you Mr Herbert's wife?'

I shook my head. 'Just his sister,' I said. 'There isn't a wife yet.'

'Well, he's going to need a bit of looking after in

the next week. Reckon you can do the ministering-angel bit?'

I nodded.

The doctor turned to Joseph. 'Don't suppose you'd like to hit me over the head with a bottle, would you?'

They laughed heartily together while I stood there feeling slightly like a piece of meat or a blow-up doll and marvelling at the power of tight clothing over apparently intelligent men. It was extraordinary. Kiki really knew what she was doing when it came to the male of the species, I thought, and not for the first time.

The doctor said he was going to keep Dick in overnight so that he could have some morphine to alleviate the worst of the pain, and I promised to come and take him home the next day. We left him waving at us with one arm, as the nurse was putting a needle into the other one.

As Joseph and I rode down in the lift, I suddenly felt exhausted. Now the adrenaline had worn off, my feet were killing me, and I was starting to feel quite uncomfortable about what had happened up there.

I'd never knowingly used my sexuality to manipulate men like that, and I wasn't sure if I felt empowered or cheapened by it. But once I'd started, it had seemed almost obscenely easy, and pointless to stop. I knew there were women who did that stuff all the time, but I never had. It didn't quite seem like fair play to me.

On top of all that (not to mention what had happened to poor old Dick) there had been the disconcerting look I had exchanged with Joseph—again. It was all a bit too much to take in at getting on for two in the morning, and my head was starting to throb.

I blinked and rubbed my temples with my fingers, and as the lift came to a stop and we stepped out into the hospital lobby, I felt Joseph's hand resting lightly on my shoulder. I turned to look at him.

'Tired?' he said, softly. I nodded. 'Me too,' he said, smiling gently.

Now he was looking at me normally, I felt relaxed with him again. He was just silly old Joseph Renwick, I told myself. As familiar as someone's old pet you've known for years. I didn't know why I had ever allowed myself to get so mixed up about seeing him again. All that snogging nonsense was in the past. He was just hopeless Dick's slightly more together friend.

We agreed to speak in the morning to work out a roster to look after Dick, and then he walked me out of the hospital on to Praed Street and hailed a taxi. I pecked him lightly on the cheek and climbed in.

Then, as the taxi took off towards Mayfair, something made me look back, and I saw Joseph still standing on the pavement where I had left him, his hands deep in his jeans pockets, gazing after it.

14

Looking after Dick—I did a morning visit each day and Joseph went round after work—kept me up in London that weekend, but by the following Friday he was much better and we finally got down to Winchelsea again, just Ed and me.

The closer we got to Rye on the train, the more excited I felt at the prospect of properly getting to grips with my new garden. Having a garden to nurture—particularly a vegetable patch—was one of the reasons I had badgered Ed so relentlessly about getting a country cottage. I had fantasies about growing all our food for the weekends, gathering it in trugs and entering my giant onions in the village show. Not that I knew anything about growing vegetables.

My parents certainly weren't great gardeners. Keeping the garden fearsomely neat with lots of mowing, strimming and trimming was about the extent of it for them, and my father was like Genghis Khan when he got hold of a pair of pruning shears.

My mum would ask him to 'shape' a tree or shrub, and he'd go at it wildly until everything in the garden looked like a stunted lollipop. Then he'd stalk around it like an avenging conqueror admiring his handiwork. Thought you'd grow, did you? Ha!

Dick and I used to laugh about what would happen if he ever got his hands on a chainsaw. I think he would have quite enjoyed napalming the entire garden actually, and I had often reflected that he might have been happier with a career in the army, where constantly barking commands would be seen as normal rather than 'eccentric'— to put it politely.

I knew the boys at the school used to call him the Führer, and I remembered seeing some of Dick's friends goosestepping around with their

161

arms in Nazi salutes, fingers across their top lips, doing impressions of Dad's shouty voice.

Somehow Dick was able to take all that in good spirit—or at least he was good at putting on a show. All part of his hearty rugby persona, I suppose. I found it a bit hurtful, but it just went with the territory when your father was a deputy headmaster, and we had to deal with it.

It was worse for Dick, though, because he actually went to the school where Dad worked, and one of the things I had always liked about Joseph Renwick was that he had never done any of that kind of stuff; he'd poke gentle fun at Dad, but nothing nasty—and I knew the rest of the boys had given Dick a really hard time.

As a result, over the years I think he'd grown a hide thicker than a rhino's. Mind you, this was a great advantage in his eventual career, working for a major tobacco company. He really didn't care what anyone thought of him which, with that job, was pretty essential.

So there was no ringing Mum and Dad for horticultural advice to get my garden going. I was relying on *Gardeners' World* and a gorgeous pile of lavishly illustrated books Ed had bought me for Christmas from the list I had left at Hatchards, as was our annual custom.

I was staking out the back lawn with string on Saturday morning—as advised by *Country Living*, my other gardening oracle—to mark out where I thought the vegetable patch should go, when Hermione called over the hedge to me.

I'd gone round with a box of chocolates from Charbonnel & Walker when we'd arrived the evening before, as a gesture, and I could tell she

162

had really appreciated it. The people we had bought the house from had lived there all the time, and I could understand that a woman of her age, living alone, would prefer to have neighbours who were in residence more often than the odd weekend.

'Amelia, dear,' she said, when I went over to her. 'I can see you are a keen gardener. Would you like to come and have tea with me and see around mine?'

I practically vaulted over the hedge I was so excited. I'd only seen what I could scope from my bedroom window and the small area at the front that you could see from the road. I was gagging to see the rest, and it was no disappointment when I got in there.

The space seemed to unfold like a series of rooms, each with a different character and atmosphere, and while it was only just May something seemed to be blooming in all of them.

I also loved the fact that, although it had clearly been meticulously planned, Hermione's garden looked as though it could have grown that way on its own. It wasn't all manicured and uptight like my parents' painfully tidy plot. Plants tumbled over each other in a riot of colours, the lawn had camomile and wild flowers mixed in with the grass, and the paths were as much vegetation as paving stones.

An image of my father stalking his garden like a Cyberman, with a tank of deadly weedkiller on his back, spraying anything that dared to grow outside its allotted zone, came into my mind.

I loved it all, but most fascinating for me was Hermione's vegetable patch. It was in the far back left corner, so two sides of it were enclosed by her lovely old flint garden walls, with fruit trees espaliered—a term I had picked up from one of my glossy gardening books—up them.

The rest was neatly contained within picket fencing, and it was made up of a patchwork of small raised beds with wide walkways between them, which she explained to me was a method called 'square-foot gardening'.

'I don't need much of anything,' she said. 'But I want a long season of different things to pick, so I just plant a little of each—some courgettes, artichokes, lots of different salads and leaves, runner beans, potatoes, broad beans, fennel. Some of the salads just keep on going—they are called "cut and come again"—which is marvellous, and for the things which fruit once then finish, I plant a second crop, or something else altogether. I can eat from my *potager* most of the year.'

'Perhaps I should do that in my garden,' I said, feeling really inspired. The fences round her vegetable garden were painted a gorgeous muted grey-green, and it all looked so beautiful, with little wigwams of bean canes set up for the new growing season and her lovely old galvanized watering cans dotted around. Even her fork and trowel, stuck into the earth in one patch, looked as though they had come from the pages of a lifestyle magazine.

'I was just measuring out for my own vegetable patch when you called over to me, actually,' I said, in the confident tones of one seasoned greenfinger to another.

'Yes, I thought perhaps you were. Would you like some advice about it from an old codger, or would that be annoying?'

'Oh, no,' I said, enthusiastically. 'I would love your advice. I've been working up the courage to ask you.'

'Well, come inside and have some tea and we can talk about it.'

Hermione's house was as gorgeous as her garden, with the same feeling that it had become like that organically over time. There was nothing contrived-looking about it, just an apparently random collection of lovely old furniture and rugs, loads of books, and a wonderful mix of quirky paintings, photographic prints and other artefacts, including quite a few impressive animal horns, mounted on the walls. There were big vases of blossom and decorative leaves everywhere, clearly all cut from the garden—something else I keenly aspired to do.

I followed her out to the kitchen while she made the tea and then carried the tray back into the 'drawing room', as she called it, like Ed. My parents called it the sitting room and I knew it was a key semantic difference. I varied between the two. Ed had once told me that if I had ever called it the 'lounge', he couldn't have married me, which I had always found hilarious. I knew he was joking, but there was a little grain of truth in there.

Hermione held the teapot high as she poured the tea into my cup through a silver strainer and then passed me the milk jug—another class indicator Ed would approve of. It always drove him bonkers that my mother put the milk in first. I honestly didn't care. I preferred coffee anyway.

'So,' she said, passing me a slice of date and walnut loaf, which she said she had made that

165

morning. 'What are you intending to grow in your garden?'

I told her that in the first year I was going to concentrate on the vegetable patch and that I was hoping to produce enough salad and vegetables—all organic, of course—to feed us all weekend, with some to take back to London. I was also going to create a separate area devoted entirely to herbs, in the manner of the Chelsea Physic Garden. The following year, I announced, I would tackle the rest of the garden. I was very keen to grow a lot of dahlias, I told her, in a cutting garden.

Her eyes sparkled with merriment as I spoke and I realized how pretentious I sounded.

'Have you ever grown vegetables before, Amelia?' she asked me, gently.

I giggled a bit. 'I grew some mustard and cress on a flannel once . . .'

We caught each other's eye and both burst out laughing. Once I started, I couldn't stop. Because I didn't know her very well and it was the first time I had ever been in her house, I felt a bit hysterical, like you do when you get the giggles in class at school. But I couldn't help it. I was throwing myself around in her armchair like a lunatic and had tears of mirth coursing down my cheeks. Luckily, Hermione was laughing too, hooting like a little white-haired owl.

'Oh, I'm so sorry,' I said, wiping my face on the sleeve of my T-shirt, as I tried to recover. 'I'm such an idiot. I'm carrying on like I'm Sarah Raven and really I haven't got the slightest clue what I'm doing out there.'

'Well, there is quite a bit to it, Amelia dear,' she said, dabbing her own eyes with a lace-edged hanky she had taken from her sleeve. 'But I have an idea that might help, shall I tell you?'

I nodded enthusiastically.

'The thing about growing vegetables is that they need quite a lot of attention, especially in the peak growing season, so it would be very difficult for you to keep it all going just over the odd weekend.'

I think I must have looked crestfallen.

'But don't be cast down,' she continued. 'Because I have a very nice young man who helps me with the heavy work in my garden, but I don't let him have much of a go at the interesting bits like sowing seeds and planting out, and he is so keen it's a shame really. So perhaps you could hire him to help set your garden up and then look after it for you during the week, and I could show both of you what to do along the way. I would enjoy that very much and I think he would too—and you would have your vegetable garden and enough to eat all summer. What do you think?'

'I think that would be wonderful,' I said.

*   *   *

That evening, I was happily making dinner, listening to Radio 4, while Ed was holed up in his room working with the curtains closed, as usual. One of the many things I loved about the cottage was the chance to do some cooking, rather than eating out every single night, as we did in London, and I was making Jamie Oliver's roast chicken with fresh herbs, inspired by a big bunch of thyme, bay and rosemary picked for me earlier by Hermione.

I was just pushing the herbs and butter under the skin when there was a knock on the back door.

167

I opened it to find a young Greek god on the doorstep.

He was backlit by the setting sun, and his scruffy blond hair was like an illuminated halo around his head, his shoulders broad and square against the foamy pink of Hermione's cherry tree, which was blossoming behind him. I was lost for words.

'Hello,' he said, smiling shyly. 'Are you Mrs Bradlow?'

I nodded dumbly, wiping my greasy fingers on my apron and suddenly not really sure of anything as I squinted at the unlikely vision in denim before me.

'I'm Sonny. Mrs Hart said you might be needing a gardener.'

'Oh,' I said, my brain kicking in again. 'Yes, yes, come in.'

He stepped over the threshold, bowing his head to get under the low beam, and as I closed the door behind him, I saw that he looked even better without his Hollywood lighting.

He had a light growth of blond stubble on his chin, his cheeks were quite pink—partly from embarrassment, I thought, but also simple rude health and that thing called youth—and although he was wearing a loose plaid shirt over a T-shirt, I could see he had a powerful physique.

I asked him to sit down and sneaked a pervy look at his rear end, as he turned to pull out the chair. Glorious.

'Would you like some tea?' I said, my voice sounding false and weird to my own ears. I felt as I used to when Dick brought Joseph and the rest of the rugby team home for tea. All hot and useless and liable to knock things over.

He smiled shyly at me again, showing a row of white teeth, with just a little chip off one of the front ones, an imperfection that just made the total package more delicious. I had butterflies in my stomach just looking at him.

'That would be very nice—' he was saying, but I had already started speaking again.

'Or perhaps you'd rather have a beer,' I was stuttering. 'The sun is over the yard arm . . .'

Jesus, I thought, I sounded like my father. 'It *is* Saturday night, time to chill out . . .' I added, trying to make up for it, to sound young and cool. That was worse. What was happening? One minute I was happily cooking a wittily seasonal dinner for my beloved husband, the next I had been rendered a gibbering teenager by the arrival of a stranger at least ten years younger than me. Probably more.

'A beer would be great, thank you,' said Sonny, and I was glad of the distraction of getting it out of the fridge and finding the opener, while simultaneously being shamefully pleased that I was wearing my new tight jeans when I dropped it on the floor and had to bend down to pick it up again.

I grabbed the Campari and soda I had been drinking when he knocked on the door and sat down opposite him.

'Cheers,' he said, raising the beer bottle to me.

'Cheers,' I said, clinking my glass against it, in bold contravention of Ed's no-clinking rule. Ed thought clinking glasses was the absolute end— and not just because his were all Riedel crystal and cost at least £15 each.

Then I just sat there looking at him. I honestly didn't know what to say.

'So,' he said. 'About the garden . . .'

'Oh, yes,' I said, my mouth kicking in, double time. 'That would be really great because, you see, we live in London during the week and we don't even get down here every weekend, which is really annoying, and I would really love to grow some veggies—organic, of course—and I haven't actually got the first clue how to do it and Hermione—Mrs Hart—suggested that you might be able to help and she said that she could show you what to do and me as well, when I'm down here, which might be more often now because I've left my job . . .'

I was babbling like a madwoman, and there was a little smile at the corners of his mouth that I couldn't take my eyes off.

'That sounds great,' he said, putting me out of my misery. 'I work at Great Dixter two days a week, then on Thursdays I come to Mrs Hart. So I could come here on Fridays, if you like. Or on Saturdays. Whatever suits you.' I nodded frantically. 'Mrs Hart pays me £8 an hour, is that OK?' I nodded again. 'So, when do you want me to start?'

'Next Friday?' I said, finally gathering my wits. 'I'll come down early so we can all do it together. Would you like to see the plot I have in mind?'

We walked outside and I showed him round the garden. He made enthusiastic noises about my plans and then we walked up to the gate together.

'Well, it was great meeting you, Mrs Bradlow,' he said, putting out his hand to shake mine.

'Oh, please, call me Amelia,' I said, as I placed my hand in his, where it disappeared into a warm, dry, slightly rough cavern. I got butterflies again. This was very terrible. 'Hang on a minute, Sonny,'

170

I said quickly. 'I'd like you to meet my husband before you go.'

I went back across the lawn towards the house and called up to the open window of Ed's room. His head popped out.

'Do you want me, honeybun?' he said, blinking in the evening sunlight. He reminded me of Mole from *Wind in the Willows*.

'Yes. I want you to meet Sonny,' I said, gesturing towards him. 'He's going to be our gardener.'

'Hello, Sonny,' said Ed, waving. 'I'm Ed Bradlow. That's great news. Amelia has grand aspirations for us to be self-sufficient down here, so I look forward to eating it all. Yum yum. See you later.'

He disappeared back inside and I walked Sonny back over to the gate. He smiled at me again. I'd thought introducing Ed into the picture would calm me down, but it hadn't. Sonny's shy, gentle smile on top of his brute of a body just about did me in. And while I felt guilty for thinking it, I wished Ed hadn't said 'yum yum' to him.

'Well, thanks for the beer, er, Amelia,' he said. 'I'll see you on Friday. Is 10 a.m. OK?'

'That will be great, Sonny,' I said, in tones that sounded far more casual than I felt. 'See you then.'

When Ed came down for dinner an hour or so later, I still felt horribly guilty about my reaction to Sonny, as though I had been deliberately disloyal to him in some way, but I really hadn't felt as if it were in my control.

It had been a purely visceral reaction, which I had never experienced before, clearly entirely hormonally driven and nothing to do with my rational mind or how much I loved my husband. It

171

was as though several millennia of civilization and proper behaviour had been swept away with one sniff of young male pheromone.

This must be how dirty old men feel, I thought, when they see a young woman walking along in a short skirt—the same uncontrollable instinct that makes male dogs run miles to find the bitch emitting the delicious scent of fertility. Maybe it was being in the country in spring with all the animals and birds frisking around and plants springing out of the fecund ground. Nature in the raw was quite terrifyingly sexy, I realized, and it was certainly having a terrifying effect on me.

To make things even worse, Ed was incredibly sweet and loving over dinner too, so appreciative of the effort I had made with the food and excited about the wine we were drinking with it, a lovely Chambertin from a tiny vineyard Ed had recently discovered in Burgundy, which was perfect with the chicken.

He also asked me lots of interested questions about the garden and was fascinated to hear about my visit to Hermione's place and how I had found Sonny, all of which just made me feel worse. My heart hadn't betrayed him, but my body most certainly had.

Dinner over, Ed disappeared upstairs to work as usual, and after I had cleared up, I kicked around the house, not knowing what to do with myself. I turned the telly on but, typically, there was nothing to watch on a Saturday night, the one time any civilized person was likely to be in.

And that was how I found myself gazing out of the sitting-room window at where the vegetable patch was going to be and picturing Sonny there.

Possibly taking his shirt off in the sun. Wiping his arm across his forehead. Standing with one hand on a spade, the other behind his head, the muscles popping on his biceps, a line of dark-blond hair running down his stomach. Me taking out a long, cool drink for him, wearing a very skimpy summer dress . . . I could see it all as clearly as if I were watching a corny pop video.

I even went into the kitchen and took down his card, which I had tucked into the noticeboard next to the fridge, and punched the number into my new iPhone—Ed had kept his promise about that—kidding myself it was what a super-organized professional clutter-clearer would do.

I looked through some of my new gardening books, but that just kept Sonny at the front of my mind. Eventually, I went to bed and tried to read myself to sleep, but that was hopeless too. I was halfway through a novel and just a few pages on from where I picked it up was a seriously steamy sex scene. As I read, I felt myself get immediately aroused. I put my hand between my legs and found I was slick and wet. Desire pulsed in me in a way I had never experienced before, so strong it was like a presence in the room. There was no escaping it: I wanted sex and I wanted it now.

I got up to find Ed. He was fast asleep, an empty brandy glass on the bedside table next to Mr Bun.

I slipped in beside him and rubbed my breasts against his back, lifting my nightie and his pyjama jacket so my nipples grazed his skin, getting harder with every teasing stroke. I pressed myself against him lower down, hooking my leg over his hip, then I put my hand down to find his cock. It was completely soft.

I played with it gently, continuing to rub my nipples against him, which was making me mad with lust, then I started kissing his ear and cheek. He half woke up and turned his head towards me. He kissed me on the cheek, then brought up his arm and patted me on the shoulder. Three pats, like you would give an old dog. After that he turned away and gently pushed my leg off. He couldn't have made it plainer he wanted me to go away and leave him alone if he'd told me to piss off.

I jumped out of the bed feeling furious. Weren't men supposed to be the ones who wanted sex all the time? Yet here I was, still relatively young, not bad looking, or so I'd been told, with extremely erect nipples and as slick and wet as an oyster below, and he wasn't in the slightest bit interested. He'd rather sleep with his god-damned cuddly toy than make love to me.

I stomped back to my own bed and lay there for a moment, fuming. A vision of the woman I had seen in the mirror when I was wearing the Lanvin dress and the silver shoes flashed into my mind. What would she have done, I wondered? It was hard to imagine any man pushing her away.

I looked down at my nipples, still standing so perkily to attention, and pulled the thin lawn of my nightgown tight over them, so they were straining against it. I put my hand between my legs and explored, rubbing my finger over the bump of my clitoris. It was as hard as a pearl, but I could feel the desire ebbing away.

Then, finally feeling too rejected to be sexy, I rolled over and went to sleep. But my body wasn't prepared to leave it there—or my subconscious, or whatever it was—either way, something made me have an absolutely filthy dream. About Sonny.

We were having wild, abandoned sex in the garden, not on the lawn but down in the bare earth. We were rolling around in it like animals, grunting and growling and covered in mud, but when he came he threw his head back, and suddenly it wasn't Sonny any more. It was Joseph.

The dream was so intense I woke up with my heart pounding, a steady throbbing between my legs. It had seemed so real it took me a moment to be sure it had definitely been a dream, but once I was certain I closed my eyes and forced myself to go straight back to sleep.

Some things are too weird and confusing to dwell on and I was a grand master at not thinking about them.

15

The next morning it was clear that Ed had no recollection of what had happened between us the night before, and I certainly wasn't about to remind him. That way, the mortification could be mine alone.

But it did make me a little uneasy when he got into bed with me, according to his Sunday-morning routine, putting his wretched bloody condom down on the bedside table. Just a few hours before, I had been desperate for sex in a way I had never experienced before, but now it was being presented to me so plainly, I didn't feel so keen.

I was still a bit confused about that disturbing

175

dream—and the contrast between that wild rogering and the Sunday-morning routine that was now unfolding with Ed was stark. He'd taken off his pyjamas and was now removing my nightgown, prior to playing with my hair and arranging it the way he liked it down my body. Then he'd play with my breasts a bit and off we would go. It was practically choreographed.

But, as his hand slipped between my legs, a flicker of the lust from the night before returned, and I reminded myself that even this predictable married sex was better than no sex.

*   *   *

After our regular conjugal rites, we got up, I walked to the village shop for the papers, and we read them as we ate our bacon sandwiches, as was also our Sunday morning habit. Then Ed took the rest of them up to his study, while I hopped into the old Volvo estate we kept down there as a suitable country vehicle and took myself off to a car-boot fair just along the road towards Rye.

I loved boot fairs and was thrilled to find a beaten-up old watering can, nearly as quaint as Hermione's, for the princely sum of £1, plus a couple of old galvanized tubs that I thought would look lovely with plants in them. I stopped at a nursery on the way back and bought some bright-pink geraniums, a trowel, some fertilizer and a big bag of potting compost. I was capable of doing that much gardening on my own, I reckoned.

Of course, watering cans and garden centres did have the effect of bringing Sonny firmly back to the front of my mind, but I was relieved to find that the thought of him didn't seem to send me into quite such an uncontrollable erotic spin any more.

It had all been some kind of spring madness, I decided, as I drove home with the windows down, breathing in the sweet country air. Or maybe the first drink of the evening had kicked in just when he knocked on the door and I hadn't been thinking straight.

He was a very attractive young specimen, there was no doubt about that, and the horny-handed man-of-the-soil thing did have its own unique appeal, but I felt sure I was over my micro-infatuation. That was a relief.

Joseph Renwick's appearance in that bizarre dream was harder to explain, but must have been some kind of random throwback to my earliest sexual experiences, I decided, combined with seeing him in such weird circumstances around Dick's hospital bed the night I had discovered how to get my way through calculated cockteasing. It was all way too Freudian for me.

*   *   *

Ed was upstairs when I got back, still glued to his laptop, so I spent a very happy afternoon making mud pies with my potting compost, sploshing water into the tub of earth, mixing it all up with a bit of powdered blood and bone and then patting it down again around the plants. I felt like I was tucking the geraniums up in bed, like the children I didn't have.

'Night night,' I said to them.

'That looks lovely,' Hermione called over the

177

hedge to me, when I was standing back to admire my handiwork.

I went over to her.

'I got the tubs at the boot fair,' I said. 'Do you like them?'

'Oh, yes. They look very rustic. You might want to look out for another one to grow your mint in. Otherwise it will take over your whole herb garden—very invasive stuff. Did you speak to Sonny last night?'

'Yes,' I said, slightly too quickly. Damn. 'He popped round.'

'He's a charming young fellow, isn't he?' she said.

My head snapped round, too fast again, as I looked to see if there was any mischief in her eyes. Maybe a little; I wasn't sure. It could have just been her usual warmth.

'Yes, he seemed lovely,' I said. 'He's going to start on my garden this Friday—if that suits you. He's coming at ten.'

'Marvellous. I'll make a banana cake, that's his favourite.'

I looked at her again. It wasn't mischief in her eyes at all, I realized, it was twinkle. She found Sonny just as attractive as I did.

*   *   *

It wasn't until Ed and I were on the train going back to town on Monday morning that I realized there might be a problem with starting the garden that coming Friday. I might have to put Sonny off a week if I didn't get it sorted out right away.

The snag was that the coming weekend was my

father's birthday—which meant it was also Ed's birthday. They were born within two days of each other—10 May and 12 May—Taurus, both of them, and just as stubborn and intractable as people born under that star sign are reputed to be. And both with very fixed ideas about how their birthdays should be celebrated.

My father expected—or should I say, demanded?—that his entire family be in residence for the weekend nearest his 'special day', as he actually called it, a tradition that had been problematic for me over the years, as Ed felt equally strongly that I should spend the weekend nearest his birthday alone with him, preferably somewhere in France.

Most years I got round it in cahoots with my mum. She'd convince Dad that the weekend before their birthdays was 'his' weekend, while I'd convince Ed the one after was 'his'. Normally, it worked pretty well, but it was going to be impossible to pull off this year, when Dad's birthday fell on the Friday and Ed's on the Sunday. There was only one weekend to go round.

I was quite surprised Ed hadn't already mentioned it and knew I had better get in quick, before he sprang it on me that he had booked us in for three nights at the Colombe d'Or, because I had already committed us to going to my parents' place. I couldn't let my mother down, and I was hoping he would understand that.

'Ed,' I said, reaching across the train table and pulling down the edge of the *Daily Telegraph*, so I could see his face. 'You do know it's my dad's birthday on Friday, don't you?'

'Yes,' he said brightly. 'And it's mine on Sunday.

I was wondering when you were going to bring it up. What shall we do? What lovely treat are you going to lay on for me?'

I looked at him entreatingly, mentally begging him to throw me a lifeline, although, while my dad was just pathetic, I could understand why birthdays were a bit of a thing for Ed. He didn't remember ever seeing his parents on his birthday as a child. It had always fallen in the middle of the school term, and the best he could expect was a card with a Hong Kong stamp and a generous cheque in it. If he was lucky, a kind housemaster would organize a cake, but I suspected he'd cried himself to sleep clutching Mr Bun under the covers on many a birthday night at prep school.

Knowing this, I always made a big effort to spoil him, but I still really wished he didn't have to turn it into a tug-of-love with my father every year, even if he did it half-jokingly.

He had put his paper down on the table between us and was looking at me with an eyebrow raised and a cheeky look in his eye. He clearly thought it was hilarious. I didn't.

'Right,' I said, in the most resolved tones I could muster, 'we are going to my parents' house this Friday for Dad's birthday dinner. Full stop, no argument. We have to, and I've promised my mother already, so that's the end of it. You know I only do this for her anyway, because she's the one who'll cop it if I'm not there, so please try and be nice about it.'

I paused to collect my thoughts.

'OK,' I continued, hoping it was a good sign that Ed hadn't reacted, apart from sticking his tongue out and pulling a goofy face. I swatted his head with the paper and he shielded himself in mock fear. 'Ed!' I said. 'Will you take this seriously? You know what my dad's like about his stupid birthday. He's even worse than you.'

He pulled more faces. I threw the paper at him. 'Do you want everyone on this train to think you are a nutter? OK, we will need to arrive in good time for dinner on Friday, so I'll drive over from the cottage in the afternoon, and you can go down from London by train. We will leave early on Sunday morning and then we can do whatever you would like for your birthday. OK?'

Ed now had his lip curled in an exaggerated sneer, like Elvis Presley in a Savile Row suit.

'What does that face mean?' I said.

'It means,' he said, leaning towards me, 'that I am happy to pander to your sociopathic father— and to help out your lovely, put-upon mother—for one night each year, but I really don't want to wake up on my own birthday between polycotton sheets in a room with roller blinds. Nor do I want instant coffee for my birthday breakfast, and I particularly don't want to listen to your father shouting at your mother for more toast and telling me I really ought to shop at Lidl and take up golf. I love you enough to put up with it any other weekend, but not on my birthday.'

'Oh, Ed,' I said, starting to feel really cross. I was well aware of all the petty little things Ed found untenable about my parent's living arrangements and mostly it washed over me. But this was too much. He was semi-joking—but only semi—and they were still my parents, however suburban they were in his eyes.

'Sorry, I forgot it was your sixth birthday,' I

hissed at him. 'I wouldn't care if I woke up in an igloo on my birthday. In fact, I wouldn't care if no one remembered my birthday for the rest of my life. But you're going to be thirty-nine next Sunday, Edward Bradlow, so maybe you should grow up.'

I glared at him, and he glared back, crossing his eyes simultaneously, the corners of his mouth twitching. He clearly *was* half joking but at the same time I knew there was no point arguing with him about it. The more I argued, the more deeply he would entrench himself in his position.

'All right,' I said, sighing deeply at the thought of relaying changed plans to my mother, who already had her work cut out making sure my father was happy with every detail of his birthday arrangements. 'Is this acceptable? We'll get there early on Friday evening, as planned, but we'll leave on Saturday afternoon—not even twenty-four hours later. Then you can wake up on your birthday between your own starched linen sheets.'

I felt like adding 'alone, the way you like it', but it wasn't worth it.

'OK,' he said, smiling happily. 'That's perfectly acceptable, thank you. Perhaps we could go straight from your parents' place to St Pancras, hop on to my favourite little train, and then I could wake up on my actual birthday in the Crillon. Very nice sheets there. Then Sunday lunch somewhere lovely for my treat and home. . .'

'Consider it booked, you heinous old Taurus,' I said. 'But I might make you drink Blue Nun as a punishment.'

'That's all right,' he said. 'Your father will probably serve it at dinner anyway.'

He chuckled happily and went back to his paper.

It hadn't been the greatest start to my week, but the minute I turned my phone on things got so frantic I didn't give it another thought. By midday on Monday I had first appointments booked in with three new clients, as well as follow-up visits to all the people I had seen the week before.

It was after I had spent an entire afternoon and late into the evening posting Janelle's ghastly ornaments on eBay and the best part of another day sorting Rosalyn's financial paperwork into separate piles and then filing it all in order that I realized it might be time to start delegating.

With my fee of £500 for a first 'consultation'— on Ed's advice, that was how I structured it now, so I didn't feel I was overcharging for a 'day' that only actually lasted three hours—with a flat fee then negotiated for the rest of the job, depending on what was involved, I could afford it. I could hire a freelance bookkeeper to do all the financial filing, and use one of those eBay agencies for selling stuff. Even after paying them I'd still be ahead, and I could be getting started with the next client, which was the really lucrative bit—and there was already a waiting list.

Even more excitingly, Janelle's agent had somehow wangled it so that both *Grazia* and *Hello!* were doing 'exclusive' stories about how my clutter-clearing had led directly to the reunion of the Honeypots. I made a note to get Kiki's advice about what to wear for the photo shoots.

On top of all that, I now had to book Ed's birthday trip to Paris as well, and I actually found it quite hard to get excited about yet another ride on Eurostar and yet another night at the Crillon. It was a gorgeous hotel, but we always stayed there, and usually in the same room. It was lovely to be greeted as old friends by the concierge, the barman and even the chambermaid, but I couldn't help thinking it would be so much more fun to try somewhere else for a change.

The groovy Hotel Costes would have been fabulous, I thought. Kiki had stayed there on a recent dirty weekend and it sounded fabulous. Or perhaps a night in Oscar Wilde's old room at L'Hôtel, daringly over on the Left Bank. But I knew there was no point in trying anywhere new. Ed would have been bitterly disappointed and it really wasn't worth it. Not on his 'special day'.

Oh well, I thought, as I arrived back at Bond Street tube on Thursday afternoon after a second visit to the banker's wife in Notting Hill—at least I might get lucky at the Crillon. That was one of Ed's routines I *did* appreciate.

But when I got home and picked up the phone to book the restaurant for his birthday lunch, I rebelled. I had been about to call L'Ambroisie, because I knew that was where Ed expected to go, although Arpège or Le Grand Vefour might have been options, but I was heartily sick of all those restaurants. I'd been to them countless times and I wanted a change.

While I put up with the limited restaurant roster at home, in Paris—gorgeous, exciting, sexy Paris— I wanted some adventure. So I called Kiki to get the number for L'Atelier Joë Robuchon. She and Oliver had both raved about the London branch— sadly, outside Ed's geographically acceptable restaurant zone—and I wanted to try it myself in

184

the original Paris venue. And, anyway, it did have a Michelin star. Surely Ed couldn't object?

'Great idea,' she said, when I told her my plan. 'You'll love it—but you've got no chance for Sunday lunch at this short notice, so let me ring them. I'll get you a spot. They'll do it for me.'

With all that to organize and being so busy with work, I hadn't given the garden—or Sonny—a thought all week. It wasn't until I started packing for the weekend, ready for my early start down to Winchelsea on Friday, that I realized that, as well as something nice for my father's birthday and something chic for Paris, I would also need some gardening clothes.

That put me in a quandary. I knew in my heart that if the gardener had been more of an Eddy Grundy than a Calvin KIein model, I would have been packing some foul old pair of track pants without a second thought, but I couldn't help myself. I wanted to look good for Sonny.

Surely that was a natural way for any woman to feel, I told myself. It wasn't as if I was going to try and get off with him, but I knew I wouldn't be able to concentrate on the garden if I felt I looked middle-aged and frumpy with him around.

That meant I really wanted to wear my favourite new skinny jeans for gardening—but I wanted them for Paris too. I tried on my tired old bootlegs and realized I could never wear them again: they were only fit for a clothing bin. There was only one thing for it. I was going to have to hit Oxford Street.

It was Thursday late-night shopping, so I had plenty of time, which was a good thing, because now I had my head around having a new look for myself and some proper money of my own to spend there was so much great stuff I wanted to try on. I found some perfect skinny jeans in Zara—a fraction of the price of the ones Kiki had bought me in Selfridges—and once I'd started shopping, I went a bit nuts.

They had some great little summer jackets in there as well, so I bought two of those and then, starting to feel more confident, I tried on some dresses. I was amazed to find one that looked remarkably like the backless black satin Lanvin number I had tried on in Dover Street Market and, in an impetuous moment, I bought that too.

*   *   *

The next morning, Sonny knocked on the door about five minutes after I had arrived down at the cottage, and I was greatly relieved to find that I didn't turn instantly into a crazed nymphomaniac at the sight of him. He'd shaved, and maybe that was the difference, because it made him look even younger—about twenty-two, I would have guessed.

'Morning, Mrs Brad . . . er, Amelia,' he said. 'Mrs Hart was wondering whether you had any tools, or whether you would like to borrow hers until you get kitted out?'

I hadn't thought about tools. Well, not the sort he meant.

'Oh, gosh,' I said. 'That would be great.'

'OK. I'll go back round to her place and I can pass them over the hedge to you.'

As he set off back up the path to the garden gate, Hermione's head appeared on her side of the thick holly hedge that divided our gardens.

'Morning, Amelia,' she said, looking very perky, her coral lipstick clearly freshly applied. 'There's no point in you spending a lot of money on tools at this stage. While Sonny's doing both gardens, you might as well use mine.'

'Thanks so much,' I said, and then Sonny appeared at her side holding a large spade over his head. I took it from him and put it down on my lawn, and we carried on until there was also a fork, a rake and a strange object I thought might have been a mattock. It looked like something out of *Chancer.*

'Right,' said Sonny. 'Now for the humans.'

They both disappeared, and I wasn't sure what was going on until I heard the latch open on our garden gate. I looked up the path and saw Sonny walking towards me—carrying Hermione.

'Right you are,' he was saying. 'Nearly there . . .'

She was smiling radiantly and gave me a little wave with her walking stick as they progressed towards me. I waved back and then dashed to the garden shed to get her a chair. The best thing I could find was an old flowery sun-lounger that had been there when we bought the house, so I put it on the back lawn next to where the vegetable patch was going to be and Sonny settled her into it.

The rest of the morning was a blur, we worked so hard. From her vantage point on the sun-lounger, with an umbrella shading her from the surprisingly strong sun—Sonny's idea—Hermione ordered us about with great charm.

First we staked out the plot with bamboo canes and string. Then we divided it up into where the separate beds would go and started to take off the top layer of grass. That was hard labour, but

187

nothing compared to our next task, which was to bring over from her house wheelbarrows of old bricks that she was donating to my project. They were left over from when she'd had her greenhouse built twenty years before and she'd kept them 'just in case'.

It was quite tricky manoeuvring the loaded wheelbarrows all the way through her garden, up the side of her house, out of the gate, along the pavement, through our gate and then all the way down to the back of our house, and after we'd done it twice each, Sonny stopped, wiped his forehead on the back of his arm—just as I'd pictured him doing but, fortunately for my equilibrium, with a shirt on—and looked thoughtful.

I went inside to get us some cold drinks and when I came out with the tray, he was sitting on the grass next to Hermione and they were both grinning up at me conspiratorially.

'Sonny's had a marvellous idea,' said Hermione, patting him on the shoulder. 'Go on, tell her.'

'Well,' he said, squinting up at me in a way that gave me an inappropriate little flutter. 'As I'm going to be working in both your gardens and we are going to share the tools, I just wondered whether we should put a gap in the hedge here. It would save us loads of walking.'

'What do you think?' said Hermione, who clearly loved the idea.

'I think it's brilliant,' I said. 'As long as you're sure you don't mind losing part of the hedge, Hermione?'

'Pfff,' she said, flicking her hands in the air. 'Hedge smedge. We can always grow it again.

That's the joy of plants, they are so forgiving.'

So Sonny got to work with the pruning shears, and in no time there was a wheelbarrow-sized gap in the hedge between the two gardens, between Hermione's potting shed and where my vegetable patch was going to be. Once it was finished, we agreed that she should officially open it, so she tottered gingerly through the gap while we clapped and cheered, and then announced she was going inside to make us all some sandwiches.

'I'll ring my little gong when they're done,' she said. 'And you can come through Checkpoint Charlie and get them.'

Half an hour later we were sitting on the table outside her French windows eating our lunch, and it was all very pleasant. Hermione kept offering Sonny more food, and he never refused. It was a joy to watch him eat with such relish, hoovering up at least five ham sandwiches, several cheese ones, an apple and three pieces of her amazing banana cake.

I could see the delight in Hermione's eyes as she watched him, but she hardly ate a thing, just nibbled on some ham and drank a cup of weak China tea with no milk. Sonny emptied several large glasses of lemon barley water and I found it hard not to stare at his Adam's apple bouncing in his strong neck as he gulped them down.

When we'd finished, Hermione said she was going upstairs to rest, and Sonny and I went back through Checkpoint Charlie to the devastation of my back garden. I hadn't noticed how much damage we were doing while we were hacking away at it, but seeing it after a break, the torn-up lawn covered in piles of old bricks, it looked like a disaster area. I hung my head and sighed loudly when I saw it, feeling a bit overwhelmed.

'Don't worry,' said Sonny. 'It looks terrible now, but in a couple of weeks, you'll have a beautiful vegetable garden. I promise.'

He was smiling at me in that sweet shy way of his, and I knew he meant it. While I had mostly got over my embarrassing initial lust attack for him, the more time I spent with Sonny, the nicer I thought he was.

16

If I hadn't had such a lovely time in the garden with Sonny and Hermione, I don't know whether I would have survived the visit to my parents.

I got there at four so I would be able to help my mother with the final dinner preparations before Stormin' Norman got home. Everything would have to be perfect from the moment he walked in through the door just after 6 p.m., or we would all pay for it.

Mum was in the kitchen putting the finishing touches to his birthday cake when I arrived and was clearly delighted to see me.

'How has it been so far?' I asked her, as I sat and polished the glasses while she concentrated on icing 'Happy Birthday Paul' on top of a cake in the shape of a Formula One car, presumably a Ferrari, as it was covered in garish bright-red icing.

That was one of the 'surprises' he expected every year—a novelty cake. It was lucky Mum was such a handy sort of a person by nature. She could knit and sew and crochet and all that, so she had simply added cake decorating to her set of craft skills.

'It's been all right,' she said. 'He's in a pretty good mood at the moment, because the school has come out higher in the academic league tables in the year when he was acting head for three months—so do remember to congratulate him. And it looks like a record number of boys are getting into Oxbridge this year too, so he's pretty happy.'

That was a relief. I could remember once visiting my parents when the school had dropped in the league tables. A weekend in Gaza would have been more relaxing.

After that we spent a very pleasant hour, just Mum and me, setting the table, putting the 'Happy Birthday Dad' banners up in the hall and the dining room and arranging his presents in a display on the sideboard in the dining room, all according to unbreakable tradition.

Just before five, Dick arrived, having taken the afternoon off work specially. I was pleased to see that, after a couple of weeks, his face was almost back to normal and he was able to pass off his still-swollen black eyes to my mother as injuries sustained during a 'charity rugby match' which had got a bit out of hand. He'd pre-briefed me on the story.

It was all very jolly, but then the first problem arose. My mobile rang and it was Ed, saying that he was running late and wouldn't be at Maidstone until nearly seven.

I could have killed him—and told him curtly that he would have to take a taxi from the station

191

to my parents' house. I couldn't leave in the middle of Dad's celebrations to pick him up at the station, it wasn't possible. Ed wasn't happy about that and snapped at me. Lovely.

Hoping to avert more tension later, I found the mixed case of wine he had sent down as Dad's birthday present and opened two of Ed's favourite reds so they would be at the perfect drinking point when he arrived. I could pretend I'd done it specially for Dad, and everyone would be happy, I thought.

Then I took two bottles of champagne from the box and put them in the fridge to chill. Mum saw me and a funny look came over her face.

'I'm not sure I'd do that,' she said.

'But Ed's bought it specially for Dad's birthday. I thought we could have it for pre-dinner drinks. It's Krug . . .'

She looked pained and my heart sank. 'Your father has discovered Prosecco,' she said.

'Lidl?' I asked, tentatively. She nodded. 'Oh God,' I said. We didn't need to say any more. We had a shorthand where things like this were concerned and I understood immediately. When Dad 'discovered' something, everybody else had to love it too.

The thought of Ed being given a glass of budget supermarket Prosecco was so awful I almost started laughing, but I knew it wouldn't be funny when it happened. I took the champagne out of the fridge and put it back in the box with the rest of the wine.

'And I'd hide those other bottles you've opened too,' said Mum, bustling past with the centrepiece, a horrendous creation of red gerberas and white carnations. 'He's joined a wine club.'

I sank down on the nearest seat and put my head in my hands.

Dick came in, took one look at me and absorbed the whole situation in an instant.

'Incoming?' he said.

'Wine club,' I replied.

'G and T?' he said, holding his first finger and thumb wide apart, to signify how strong it might be.

I nodded my head vigorously.

Dick's kamikaze cocktail certainly took the edge off it all, and by the time Stormin' Norman arrived home, I'd stopped caring that Ed seemed to have turned his phone off. I'd have to try and warn him about the wine situation when he arrived. Perhaps by using Morse code.

'Isn't this lovely?' Dad was saying, as we stood in the hall after greeting him at the door with the enthusiasm he expected.

He had one arm around my shoulder, the other around Dick's, which wasn't easy for him, as we were both taller than him. We got our height from Mum's side of the family. He was a shortarse.

'Oh, and look at that lovely happy-birthday banner,' he was saying, as though he had never seen it before. 'Aren't you all sweet to me?'

As though we would dare not to be, I thought, but I kept smiling. As long as he stayed happy, we would all have a nice time, and Dad in a good mood really was great company, so it was worth it. Actually, it was worth it just to avoid him in a bad mood, but anyway.

'Now, what we all need is a drink,' he was saying. 'Joan, you bring the glasses, and I'll go and get a few bottles of something.'

He stalked off towards the utility room, which I'd discovered he'd commandeered as his new cellar, rubbing his hands, and Mum came through with a tray of champagne glasses—the saucer kind, which Ed said should only be used for Babycham, and even that was too good for them.

Dick and I stood in the sitting room mainlining dry-roasted peanuts and pulling faces at each other to our great mutual amusement, until Stormin' Norman appeared with two bottles of Prosecco.

'Have you ever had this before?' he was saying. 'It's terrific stuff. You'll never guess where I got it. There, try that.'

He handed me a glass and I raised it to him. 'Happy birthday, Dad,' I said.

'Oh, don't make a fuss,' he said, beaming with delight that everything was just as it should be— i.e. just as he liked it.

The Prosecco was OK actually. It wasn't sweet, just a bit thin and soapy. I thought it was fine, but I knew Ed would rather set fire to himself than drink it.

'What do you think?' Dad was asking, his slightly bulging eyes staring at me keenly. 'I bet your oenophile husband has never had this before. It's not French, you see, and I know what a snob he is about French wine.'

'I think it's very nice,' I said quickly. 'Delicious. What do you think, Dick?'

'I think I'd like a bigger glass,' he said, and everybody laughed. Dick always knew how to keep things light.

One thing I did notice about the Prosecco was

that, even in the stupid paddling-pool glasses, it was very easy to drink a lot of it, and by the time Ed arrived we were all half-cut—which was probably why I failed to get out into the hall before Dad, so I didn't have a chance to warn Ed what we were drinking.

'Ah, Edward,' I could hear Dad saying, as I realized my gaffe. 'Come in and have a drink—I know how fond you are of a glass.'

I jumped up as they came into the room, hoping to be able to race over and hiss, 'It's Prosecco . . .' in his ear under the cover of a welcome kiss, but it was too late. Dad was already proffering him one of the terrible glasses—I think they'd had them as a wedding present in 1965—and Ed was looking at it as though it were an alien artefact.

'Isn't it lovely, Ed,' I said loudly. 'Dad's bought a whole case of Prosecco.'

Dad turned on me, a deep frown beetling his brow. 'Oh Amelia,' he said furiously. 'You've *ruined* it. I wanted to see if Ed knew what it was, and you've *completely* ruined it. You really can be so stupid.'

I caught Mum's eye as I slumped back down on to the sofa—or couch, as my parents called it—another thing that made Ed twitch. She gave me a tight little smile and I nodded back at her. I wouldn't let her down.

'So, what do you think, then?' Dad said, smiling again as he locked Ed in his bug-eyed stare. He was standing so close to him, Ed was practically backed up against the bare brick fireplace.

Ed took a sip and I held my breath.

'Oh, that's very nice, Paul,' he said, smacking his lips and holding the glass up to admire the

195

colour—a sort of pale urine. 'Very refreshing. Cheers. Happy birthday.'

He looked over at me as Dad clinked his glass loudly and winked.

In that moment, I forgave Ed every single bit of his earlier birthday childishness, and he continued to behave perfectly throughout dinner. Under cover of taking his bag up to our room before we sat down at the table, I had been able to warn him about the wine club. He took it very well, and I flung myself into his arms.

'Thank you for being so lovely,' I said.

'That's all right, Melia,' he said. 'I've been a bit of an arse about this weekend and I'm sorry about that. I know you only do it for your mum, and I love her too, so I'll stick it out for both of you. As for your a-hole of a father, I really don't know how someone so utterly dreadful produced such a beautiful daughter, but I promise I will play along with him and his gruesome Romanian wine, or whatever it is, OK? For you and Joan and dear old Dick. Plus, I've got Paris to look forward to.'

'We'll always have Paris . . .' I said, and he laughed.

Then I took him over to my suitcase and showed him where I'd hidden two empty bottles of his wine—now decanted into the bottles that had previously held Dad's wine-club red, until I had poured it down the drain outside the kitchen door.

'Ah, Moneypenny,' said Ed, taking me in his arms and kissing me quite passionately.

*   *   *

So Ed behaved immaculately at dinner. But Dad

196

didn't. He was a little bit annoyed I'd opened the wine before he came home, until I convinced him I'd done it so it could breathe and would all be perfectly *à point* for dinner and to 'show' Ed. I knew I was being disloyal to my wonderful husband by saying that, but I just wanted the evening to go smoothly, for everybody's sake.

Ed played along brilliantly about the wine. Professing thrilled astonishment that a non-vintage South African Pinotage could be so 'opulent and perfumed'—to use his description—even though we both knew it was actually a Cos d'Estournel '90.

I didn't dare let Mum and Dick in on the secret, because I was already terrified I might burst into hysterical giggles at any point, as Dad got more and more puffed up about his bloody wine club. When he eventually proudly told Ed that the wine in question had cost him £3.99 a bottle, I had to leave the table in a hurry.

'That's marvellous,' Ed was saying, with ambassadorial diplomacy as I sped out of the room. 'It really is amazing the quality you can get these days. This tastes like a wine I would sell for nearer £150.

So it was all going swimmingly. Mum's food was delicious, as always, greatly enhanced by the wonderful wine, and Dad loved his presents, which he opened after the novelty cake had been produced, 'Happy Birthday' sung and the candles blown out, with him beaming like it was all a big *This is Your Life* surprise. Even though it was exactly the same every bloody year.

Then, when we were all having a glass of indifferent cognac—Dad's present to himself—Ed congratulated him on the school's results. I'd told

197

him about them when we were upstairs, keen to foster good relations between the two of them, and Ed had risen to the occasion.

'Ah, yes,' said Dad smugly, leaning back in his chair, a heavy mahogany carver—reproduction, of course. 'Yes, we're very pleased with the school. It's performing extremely well, and we have a very high level of parental satisfaction as well as our success in the league tables. But what I want to know is, when are you and Amelia going to produce a grandson I can educate there?'

'Oh, Paul,' said Mum in an indulgent tone, clearly hoping to move the subject on. She knew how sensitive I was about it.

' "Oh, Paul" what?' said my father, his thick black eyebrows forking down dangerously.

Mum said nothing. It was already too late.

'Well,' roared my father, his face now getting red, which was a very bad sign. ' "Oh, Paul" what? What's wrong with a man asking his son-in-law when he might be expected to produce a grandchild? It's hardly unusual, is it? What is unusual is for a healthy young couple to be married for—what is it, Amelia, fifteen years?—and not have bloody children. It's not like you can't afford it, is it?'

I just sat completely still, looking studiedly down at my plate, praying for it to stop. I looked up under my eyelashes and saw that Dick and Mum were doing the same. It was what we did when Dad went off on one at the dinner table, which had happened with great frequency in my childhood. Like every Sunday lunch.

I looked covertly to my left and saw Ed was still looking straight at my father in astonished

198

amazement. He'd never seen him quite this bad before.

'So, go on then, Edward,' bellowed Dad. 'What have you got to say for yourself? Is there a problem we should know about?'

'Now come on, Paul,' said Ed, in what I thought was an incredibly reasonable voice in the circumstances. 'That's a bit unfair. . .'

'DON'T "PAUL" ME!' shouted my father. 'You can call me Paul when you're a father—when you're a man, not some pansy wine-swilling snob.'

I'm ashamed to say I continued to sit there in silence. What can you say when your father behaves like that to your husband? There's nothing *to* say—except perhaps, Fuck off and die you hideous old psycho I'm never speaking to you again. But you can't do that, when your lovely mum is sitting there close to tears and you know she would be left with the old bastard and his fury.

So I just sat there mutely and so did everyone else, praying he would calm down. Very carefully, I reached under the tablecloth and found Ed's hand to squeeze. He squeezed it back.

Then, as usual, Dick saved our lives. We all had our roles in the catastrophe of our family and that was Dick's.

'Hey, Dad,' he said, like nothing unusual had just happened. 'I nearly forgot—I've got you another present. It's that Michael Schumacher Formula One computer game I was telling you about. Shall we go in your study and have a look at it?'

I think the three of us breathed out simultaneously when they left the room. I felt like bursting into tears, but I wouldn't let myself for my

199

mum's sake. She was so brave about Dad's temper.

'I'm so sorry, Edward,' she said, putting her hand on his arm. 'Paul has never been good after too much to drink, but he won't listen, he insists he can handle it. I'm so sorry about what he said.'

'You don't need to be sorry,' said Ed, taking her hand and kissing it.

I got up and started clearing the table. That was my way of dealing with it. Keep busy. Bail out. There was too much to say about what had happened even to start. My father's outburst was monstrous, but the subject he had brought up was even harder for me to deal with. What was really doing me in was that, while his approach was completely unacceptable, he did have a point.

My mother had asked me several times over the years in her own gentle way if Ed and I were planning to have a family, or if there was anything I wanted to tell her—were we having problems? But I was always evasive. I just found it too painful to talk about.

Of course I wanted children was the answer, but I didn't even know if I was fertile or not because, with his belt and braces approach to contraception, Ed had never given me the chance to find out.

I had considered secretly coming off the Pill and putting pinholes in all his bloody condoms, but it didn't seem right to conceive a child by stealth. And besides, eagerly anticipating the conception was meant to be something couples joyfully did together. Ha bloody ha.

Taking out my frustration rinsing the dirty plates, as my mum liked, under a steaming Niagara of hot water, I wondered yet again how I could have been so offhand about such a fundamental issue at the start of our marriage.

I remembered mentioning it to him quite casually early on—'when we have kids . . .' or something like that—and being surprised to find he was quite so set against it. But at twenty-five I hadn't freaked out, because there was plenty of time for all that and at that stage I was still so impressed with my new life with him, the flat in Mayfair, the eating out and all, I had other things to think about. Plus, I had been so convinced he'd come to his senses about it eventually, there really had seemed no point in fretting unnecessarily.

But, by the time I hit my early thirties, things began to feel a bit more pressing. Most of my girlfriends from school and uni days were having babies by then, and as each one became a mother, a kind of curtain was drawn between us.

My best friend, Louise, in particular, had made a big effort to keep me included and involved, and as a result I had a special relationship with her daughter, Posy, but in some ways that made it worse. Opening an envelope to find one of her gorgeous drawings just reminded me of what I was missing.

I was so wrapped up in these thoughts as I rinsed and stacked that I didn't notice Ed had come into the kitchen until he wrapped his arms around me from behind and nuzzled into my neck.

'Are you all right, my most precious Heady?' he asked.

I nodded. 'You can always rely on darling Daddy to make a party go with a swing,' I said bitterly. 'I'm sorry he was so appallingly rude to you.'

'As I told your mother, please don't apologize to

me. I can take it. You know how I am about teachers—water, duck's back, etc., etc. I just don't want you to be upset by the old tyrant.'

I sighed deeply and blinked hard, patting his hands, which were clasped around my waist, but staying resolutely facing towards the kitchen wall. I didn't want him to see how close to tears I actually was. Tears of frustration that he couldn't understand that what might be upsetting me was not my father's bad behaviour—although that was bad enough—but Ed's own attitude to the children issue.

I would have to bring it up with him again soon, I told myself, but once again this was not the time or the place. I just wanted to get through the hours until we could leave there and I could feel like an adult again.

'I'll be fine, Ed,' I said, when I trusted my voice not to quiver. 'We'll talk about this another time. Is Mum OK?'

'Yes,' he said. 'She was coming out here to see if you were all right, but then she stopped and asked if I wanted to talk to you first. She's so thoughtful like that. I really don't know how she stands living with him, so I'm going to go and make light and entertaining conversation with her—is that good?'

'That's very good,' I said, turning round to kiss him on the cheek.

He left and I leaned against the sink and let my head drop down. I suddenly felt exhausted. Surely, I told myself again, it was only a matter of time before Ed realized what we were missing out on as a couple or saw how unhappy it was making me?

But my father's outburst had reminded me, all too painfully, that perhaps nothing would ever change Ed's mind. After all, lovely though he could be, he was the most stubborn man I had ever met—apart from my dad.

So, drying my hands, smoothing down my hair and putting on a smear of the lipstick my mum kept in the cutlery drawer, in case of unexpected visitors, I readied myself to go back and join her and Ed in the sitting room.

For the time being I would deal with it in the best way I knew, resorting to my family default setting—which was not to think about it. Because what was there to think? If he didn't change his mind pretty soon, the only way I would ever be able to have children would be to leave Ed and find somebody else to have them with. And how could I possibly do that?

17

The next day didn't start out much better for poor Ed. As a big treat for my mum, who cooked seven breakfasts, two lunches and six dinners a week—my father had a takeaway curry every Thursday night—we were going out for lunch on Saturday. To a pub.

For Ed, it was the only thing worse than eating at my parents' house.

'If you can find me a pub where they have Château Lafite on tap, then I might like them,' he'd once told me, with heavy emphasis on the 'might'.

But I still had a fingering affection for a good old English pub. When I was young I had been thrilled to go to the various real-ale venues enthusiastically frequented by Dick and his friends, to binge-drink Archers and lemonade or whatever sickly concoction the girls were into that week, and I still loved the atmosphere of the old pubs in the countryside around Maidstone.

Driving out to one of our favourites, the Bell, in a small village about ten miles south, brought back just such happy memories, and I gazed out of Dick's car window at the countryside, which was springing magnificently into leaf in the May sunshine, remembering many previous excursions there as a child, teenager and student.

Adding to the sense of jollity was Dad's absence. He'd had to go into school that morning for some kind of sporting fixture so it was just the four of us, which was a great relief all round. Especially to him, I imagined.

I had long ago worked out that Dad experienced deep shame after an outburst like the one the night before, which had the unfortunate effect of making him even more bad-tempered the next day. He usually found a way to make himself scarce on those occasions, I'd noticed, and that morning I was particularly glad of it.

I felt as though every brand-new beech leaf, hawthorn blossom and bluebell we passed down the narrow lanes on the way to the pub had turned out just to say hello to me, and I was feeling almost overwhelmingly nostalgic by the time we got there. So really I shouldn't have been surprised to find Joseph Renwick waiting at the bar when we walked in.

Mum was delighted. She'd always adored Joseph, so I was relieved that her excitement at seeing him gave me the space I needed to compose myself. I was still confused about those intense looks that had passed between us at Kiki's party and in the hospital—and that freaky dream I'd had the previous weekend added greatly to my disomfort at seeing him again.

So I was happy to lose myself in the mêlée of excited hugs, back-slapping and hand-pumping that was going on—Ed doing his best to look enthusiastic—as it became apparent it was no coincidence that Joseph was there. He was down in Kent for the weekend to see his parents and was having lunch with us by prior arrangement with Dick. I wondered absently which of them had suggested it.

'So how were the birthday celebrations?' asked Joseph, as we sat down at a table in the garden—a bench table, Ed's idea of the third ring of hell in dining terms. 'Any major nuclear explosions?' continued Joseph, a knowing glint in his eyes.

With extensive experience of my father as his deputy headmaster, his history teacher and his best friend's dad, Joseph knew exactly what Stormin' Norman was like and had always managed to be real about it in a humorous way.

'Just a minor earthquake,' said Dick, slipping seamlessly into family damage-limitation mode. I felt Ed tense next to me, clearly anxious that the details of last night's outburst might be discussed again—and in front of somebody he disliked. So I quickly jumped in and told the story of what I had done with the wine.

As it was still news to Mum and Dick, it went down very well, and the whole table was soon shouting with laughter. Most importantly, I felt Ed

205

relax. Dick thought it was the best thing ever. The combination of alcoholic drink and outwitting Dad delighted him so very much.

'Oh, my darling sister,' he said, putting his arm around me and giving me a quite painful squeeze. 'You are such an excellent girl. Even to my ignorant palate, I thought that wine was pretty decent for a wine club. I was thinking of joining. That is hilarious.'

Looking across the table, I saw Joseph was also grinning at me. The sunlight was shining on to the lenses of his glasses, obscuring his eyes, but when he moved his head I clearly saw an expression in them I remembered from twenty years before. And from Kiki's party. And from the hospital. Affection, admiration and unabashed sexual attraction.

I looked quickly away. On top of everything else that had happened that weekend I really couldn't take on the confusing feelings that Joseph still seemed to inspire in me.

*　　　*　　　*

I felt almost as relieved as Ed clearly did to get on to Eurostar late that afternoon. He was smiling like a happy Buddha from the moment we cleared security at St Pancras. He loved that train as though the whole thing had been laid on specially for him, and his delight continued to grow as we arrived at the Crillon and were shown to our usual room.

'Ah, Heady Bouquet,' he said, pulling me into his arms as the porter closed the door behind him. 'This is more like it. Do you know, I don't think I want to wait much longer to be reminded how nice the sheets are here. I think we should go to bed right now.'

He undressed me slowly, approaching sex, like everything else, in his connoisseur's manner, and by the time I was naked under the covers, his careful attentions to almost every part of my body had worked me up into a fairly dizzy state.

But as he reached for the condom he had placed ready on the bedside table with his usual forward planning, I felt desire leave me in an instant. I could hardly remember what it was like to have sex without one of those hideous raincoats. I wanted to feel skin on skin—everywhere.

'Do you have to use one of those?' I said to him, as he started to roll it on.

He stopped and looked at me, puzzled. 'What?'

'Do we have to use a condom, Ed? It would be so nice to make love without one now and again. It's not like we're strangers having safe sex. I'd just like to remember what it feels like. A pre-birthday treat?'

He slumped back on to the bed. 'Well, it would hardly be a birthday treat if you got pregnant, would it?'

'It would for me,' I said, starting to feel really irritated, the suppressed emotions from the night at my parents' house suddenly welling up.

'Oh, Amelia,' said Ed, his voice getting tenser. 'You know how I feel about that subject. I've already had it this weekend from your father, and I really don't need it from you as well. You know my point of view. End of discussion.'

He sighed and threw the condom on to the floor. 'Well, I don't need that now, thanks,

207

Amelia.'

He got out of bed and started to get dressed. I watched him, speechless.

'I don't know where you have booked for dinner tonight,' he said, as he zipped up his flies, 'but it's already quite late. I'll be in the bar when you're ready.'

I lay there for a second, in some kind of shock, as a wave of anger rolled up inside me like nothing I had ever experienced before. It flashed through my mind in that moment that this must be what my father felt like just before he went off on one.

'Is that it?' I hissed at Ed. Then my voice got louder. I was shouting. 'Is that all you have to say on the subject? Your hard-on has gone down so subject closed? Well, maybe I've got a lot more to say on the subject of contraception and pregnancy—have you ever thought of that?'

I actually saw the colour drain from Ed's face with shock. I was pretty shaken myself. I had never shouted at him before—in fact, I wasn't sure I had ever shouted at anyone.

'I'm not going to discuss anything with you while you are yelling like a fishwife,' he said, his voice quiet but a little wobbly.

'Well, isn't that convenient?' I said, still raging in mad-Dad mode. 'You can only discuss the most important thing in our marriage when it suits *you* and if the appropriate conventions are observed. Well, life's not like that, Edward Bradlow!'

'Mine is,' he said, very quietly. 'And if you would like to have dinner with me—and perhaps discuss this in a more civilized manner—I will be downstairs.'

I threw a pillow at the closing door and then just

208

stayed there, kneeling naked on the bed, panting like a dog. I feared my eyes were bugging out, just like my dad's did.

I could feel the intense anger ebbing away, almost as quickly as it had come, but my heart was pounding, and I felt quite sick and shaky from the adrenaline rush it had triggered. No wonder my father was such a freak if he felt like this all the time, I thought. It was most unpleasant.

I took a few deep breaths and wondered what to do. Ed had generously—ha!—said we could discuss the subject further over dinner. Unbelievable! Perhaps he'd like to table an agenda, I thought, put it to the committee.

But I'd had enough of all that. For once in my life I needed to talk about this thing that mattered so much to me in a real and meaningful way, and I wasn't going to do it in hushed tones over a tiny portion of duck breast, with painful waiters hovering around.

I picked up the phone, dialled the number for the bar and asked the barman if he could kindly tell Mr Bradlow that his wife wasn't feeling well enough to join him for dinner and he should make his own arrangements.

The thing was, I'd been so busy before we left, I'd actually completely forgotten to book anywhere for dinner that night. It was a shocking oversight, and in normal circs I would have felt terrible about it, but now it seemed like some kind of perfectly set up revenge. He'd never get into any of the places he deemed 'acceptable' on a Saturday without a reservation. I hoped he'd end up at McDonald's. It would serve him right for being so selfish.

When I hung up, I still felt a bit wobbly and decided to have a bath to calm myself. As I stepped out of the bed my foot touched something cold and slimy on the carpet it was the bloody condom. Horrid, smelly, rubbery thing. Yuk. I wrapped it in a tissue and threw it in the bin, although part of me wanted to drape it over Ed's pillow.

I ran the bath, grabbed the miniature of Scotch from the mini bar, poured it over ice—sacrilege in Ed's opinion—slid into the deliciously deep, scented water and considered my situation.

In every regard apart from this increasingly pressing baby issue, I still really loved my husband. I respected him, I admired him and I relished his company. He made me laugh. He spoiled me. He was very good to my mother and mostly thoughtful and generous to me. I enjoyed the things we did together and the glamorous experiences we had through his business. I still fancied him too, when I got the chance, even despite the bloody condoms.

But his implacable attitude to my increasingly desperate desire to have a child just didn't seem fair. What had he said again? 'End of discussion . . .'

Why? Why was his opinion the final one?

And, I thought, topping up the hot water, if I was honest with myself, I was also beginning to resent sleeping alone in a separate bedroom, and the amount of time generally I spent on my own while he was holed up in his dark study with the door closed or gallivanting around France buying wine.

If we had a baby, I thought, at least I'd have someone to talk to.

I sighed deeply, feeling I'd reached a dead end in my thoughts, and after a few minutes just staring into space, I got out of the bath. Then, as an act of pure rebellion, I ordered room service, a style of eating Ed considered on a par with cannibalism.

I rather enjoyed my dinner. I sat up in bed and had a hamburger, with French fries and lots of ketchup, giving him a mental finger as I ate them. I watched a couple of rubbish films on cable and then, noticing it was past midnight, vaguely wondered where Ed had found to have a dinner that was worth fingering that long over on his tod. After that I read for a little while and then fell asleep.

*   *   *

I woke at 4 a.m. desperate for water—my mouth tasted horrible from the raw onion that had been on the burger—and it wasn't until I completely came to that I realized I was still alone in bed. Ed hadn't come back.

It was so strange I immediately rang his mobile, but it was turned off and that was pretty much the end of sleep for that night. Ed never stayed out late like this, it just wasn't his thing.

I did know people whose husbands went on cocaine-fuelled benders ending up in lap-dancing parlours at seven in the morning, but that wasn't Ed's style. He stayed up very late in his study at home, but never out. And he never took drugs. He said wine, armagnac, coffee, animal fats, work and being with me provided all the thrills he needed.

I kept trying his mobile, and when there was still no reply at 5 a.m. I really started to get worried.

Perhaps he'd been mugged while he was walking the streets of Paris looking for somewhere to eat. Or maybe he'd been knocked over crossing the road and looking the wrong way after drinking too much. I wondered if I should ring the concierge desk and ask them to start calling the hospitals for me.

I must have fallen asleep at some point, though, because I was woken by the sound of a key in the door. I sat up feeling really disorientated to see Ed walking in looking perfectly fine. I felt a surge of relief he was OK, followed by anger about what he'd put me through.

'Ed!' I cried out. 'Where the hell have you been?'

'I've been asleep,' he said, coldly.

'Where?'

'In another room,' he said.

'Another room here?' I asked, really confused.

'Yes,' he said. 'I felt I needed a little time to myself after what happened last night—and the night before, for that matter—so I managed to get another room here. I see you enjoyed room service.'

He pushed my tray out of the door with his foot and closed it.

'Where did you have dinner?' I asked, stupidly. It seemed the only thing to say.

'L'Arpège,' said Ed.

And then we caught each other's eye and we both started laughing. It suddenly seemed so funny, but really it was just a blessed release of tension.

'Well, at least you had a good dinner,' I said, meekly. He sat on the bed and took my hand. 'I would have enjoyed it much more if you had been with me.'

'I'm sorry, Ed,' I said. 'I'm sorry I blew up like that. It's just I really don't think you understand how serious I am about that subject.'

'It's OK,' said Ed, sitting on the bed and taking my hand in his. He sighed and stroked the side of my face with his other hand. The warmth was back in his eyes. 'You are right. I was dismissive about it last night, but I don't think you understand how serious I am about it either.'

We just looked at each other. Deadlock. What was I going to do, start shouting at him again? What would that achieve?

'Never mind for now, my darling,' he was saying. 'We will talk about it properly, but can we leave it for the time being? We've had a crap couple of days, but we're in our favourite city and there's a bright blue sky out there—so let's try and make today better, shall we?'

I nodded.

'Happy birthday, Ed,' I said in a very small voice. 'We'll always have Paris . . .'

*　　　*　　　*

After that disastrous start we had a great morning. He loved his present—a first-edition hardback of *Dr No*—and we had a glorious time drinking hot chocolate in Angelina's, where we always had breakfast in Paris, then strolling through the Tuileries and sitting in the sunshine watching the Parisian world go by.

Everything was great until we went back to the hotel to change for lunch. When we were in the lift on the way back down again Ed asked where we were going. I said it was a surprise.

He was clearly immediately put off by that idea, and I realized in that moment what a mistake it was. While I adored surprises, a lot of Ed's pleasure in the things he enjoyed came from anticipating the things he arranged so far in advance.

So I told him where we were going, hoping he could look forward to it for the half an hour or so until we got there, but that didn't help either. He looked completely bewildered.

'But I thought we'd be going to L'Ambroisie,' he said, frowning like a confused child. 'You know that's my favourite.'

'I thought it would be fun to try somewhere new . . .' I said tentatively.

How wrong I was. It was a disaster from the moment we arrived and were seated at what resembled a very chic sushi bar, with chefs preparing food in front of us.

'Is this a teriyaki restaurant?' said Ed, looking appalled. 'Are they going to start throwing knives in the air?'

He didn't look much happier when he was given a menu. I thought it all looked wonderful, but Ed hated 'fusion' food of any kind, and there were a lot of udon noodles and shiitake mushrooms mixed in with the *foie gras* and the truffles. He snorted when he saw the word 'coriander' in the description of one dish.

'Now there is an ingredient which has no place on a menu in Paris,' he said. 'What absolute nonsense to think an entirely alien flavour from another continent will meld perfectly with

214

indigenous ingredients. Ridiculous.'

It was a longstanding gripe of his, and I held back from offering my usual argument about black pepper being an alien ingredient. Not to mention the heinous bright-yellow curry powder so beloved of French chefs.

He also loathed having to give his food order directly to the *commis* chef at the bar in front of us and the wine order to the sommelier behind his shoulder. In the end he asked to see the maître d'.

'Do you think,' he said in his terrible French accent, stubbornly unimproved, in that English way, despite all the time he spent over there, 'it would be at all possible for us to have a table rather than sit at this bar? It's just I am dreadfully old-fashioned and I really like to sit and look across at my beautiful wife.'

I cringed with embarrassment. He wasn't rude, but why couldn't he just relax and enjoy having a new restaurant experience? But then I could also see that, much as I loved it, this sleek restaurant, with its Christian Liagre interior and post-modern menu, was totally outside his comfort zone. I had been an idiot to bring him here.

'I am so sorry, sir,' said the maître d'. 'But we do not have tables at this restaurant. Only the bar and the stools. I thought Madame Wilmott would have explained that to you when she made this reservation . . .'

'Sorry?' said Ed, lapsing into English, then back into French. 'Who made the reservation?'

'Madame Wilmott, of course. She is a good friend of Monsieur Robuchon . . .'

'Thank you,' said Ed, nodding and assuming a social smile. 'I quite understand. Thank you so

215

much.'

He turned back to me with steely eyes. 'Kiki chose my birthday restaurant?' he asked.

'No,' I said. 'I chose it, because I thought you would be interested to try one of the most highly regarded new restaurants in Paris. We were very lucky because Kiki was able to use her influence to get us in at short notice. I think it's wonderful.'

'Well, some of the food is very nicely made,' conceded Ed, spooning up some iridescent broth with a Japanese-style spoon, 'when it's not ruined with coriander and bloody lemon grass, and it is a damn fine wine list, but I just don't like sitting on these crippling bar stools and eating out of a bowl like a baby. I mean, when your country has the finest dining on earth, why would you mess with the formula?'

I took a deep breath and remained silent while thinking: 'Because sometimes change can make things more interesting . . .'

There was no point in saying it. As far as Ed was concerned there was a right way to do everything—from pouring wine, to making coffee, to making love to your wife. A right way that was the only way, and change simply meant spoiling it. Change was bad and that was it.

What had he said the day before about having children? 'End of discussion.'

I was just starting to hope quite keenly that his ridiculous intransigence wasn't going to lead to the end of us.

18

Kiki couldn't wait to hear how Ed had liked his birthday lunch when I saw her the following week. I'd gone over to her place after seeing a new client nearby and we were sitting having coffee in her kitchen—now always immaculate, thanks to her housekeeper.

'I thought it was wonderful,' I said, trying to dodge the question. 'I loved the interior and Ed thought the wine list was excellent. He had the most amazing *foie gras* in a kind of Japanese broth, it was extraordinary.'

'Mmmm . . . yum, I love that dish,' said Kiki. 'Did he like my card too?'

'Oh yes,' I said, thinking quickly. 'He asked me to thank you. He thought it was very amusing.'

Actually, Ed had opened Kiki's birthday card when we had got back from Paris on Sunday night and had thrown it immediately into the bin.

'Why are you doing that?' I had asked him, bewildered. 'Don't you think it was sweet of her to remember your birthday?'

'It's a technique,' said Ed, 'the birthday book. Everyone gets a birthday card and thinks how thoughtful Kiki is. No, thank you. I don't do friendship by numbers.'

I really didn't understand why Ed was getting so antagonistic towards Kiki. She brought nothing but joy to my life. I always had a great time with her— and I had her to thank for my fabulous new wardrobe and my ever burgeoning new business, which was still growing at a prodigious rate.

I had the bookkeeper and the eBay people set up now, and with Ed's sage advice, I had also decided to hire someone to be a basic physical clutter-clearer for me. The idea was that once I had done the initial visit and worked out the action plan, they would go in to do the drudge work, leaving me free to get on with more lucrative first consultations. Then I would go back at the end and see to the glamorous finishing touches.

'It's the simple economic principle of the division of labour,' Ed had told me, working out on the back of an envelope how much I could afford to pay someone. 'I don't grow or bottle the wine I sell; my expertise is knowing which wines people will want to buy. Yours is having the vision to see the best way to clear someone's chaos quickly— not actually doing it yourself.'

I knew he was right, and one of the reasons I'd gone to see Kiki that morning was for help with recruitment. I thought there must be somebody suitable among her ever-expanding group of acquaintances.

It was just the kind of networking challenge she loved, and she sprang up from the table to get what she called her 'mothership' address archive— as opposed to the little black book she carried in her handbag and the new numbers that went into her BlackBerry.

'I can't believe you actually still use that,' I said, when she carried the old Rolodex into the kitchen. 'It looks like something from a Humphrey Bogart film. Have you ever thought of going digital with your contacts?'

I held up my iPhone, which was fast becoming like an extra limb for me.

'Are you normal?' she asked me. 'It would take me a year to type all this into a computer, and only I could ever understand my cross-indexing system, so no one could do it for me.'

'I was only asking,' I said, putting my gadget away.

'Now,' she said, flipping through the index cards, her fingers flying like a concert violinist, 'what you need is someone a bit short of the old cashola, who looks OK, is practical and capable, but isn't smart enough to try and steal your ideas and contacts and set up in competition. Let me see . . .'

'Mmmm,' she said, coming to a stop and writing a name down on a piece of paper. 'This one's possible, an out-of-work dancer, but I think we can do better. Not sure how practical she is. Hmmm, don't think you want an underemployed freelance journalist—too nosy. Aha! This is perfect. Fiona Rembury—a very bored housewife. She doesn't really need the money, just something to do. Bit of a chalet girl, very capable, and very nice. You'll like her.'

She scribbled a name and number on to a piece of paper and pushed it across the table to me, but I didn't look at it. I was staring at a card on the Rolodex which I had caught sight of as she flipped it over. I held it up with my finger and turned my head sideways to read it. I hadn't been imagining it. Joseph Renwick.

'You've got Joseph's number in there,' I said, surprised.

'Oh, yes,' giggled Kiki. 'That delicious friend of your brother's. So nice of Dick to bring him to the party. Brainy and cute, just the way I like them.'

219

'You do know he's married, don't you, Kiki?' I said prissily. 'With children.'

'Yes, but they're all still in Washington DC and he's based back over here. Doesn't that tell you something? From what he's told me, that marriage is well past its sell-by date.'

'Have you seen him then?' I asked, astonished.

'Yes,' said Kiki, completely casually. 'We've had drinks a few times. He's very good company. Didn't you see him at the weekend? He said you had lunch or something.'

'We did,' I said, feeling vaguely disorientated. 'He was down seeing his parents as well, and he and Dick arranged it.'

I felt strangely unsettled. It just seemed so odd to have someone significant from my teenage years suddenly intimately involved with my adult life in this way.

'He said your father was dreadful to Ed while you were down there,' said Kiki, in her usual relaxed tones.

Now I really was amazed. But while it felt like an outrageous invasion of my privacy, there was a small part of me that was quite glad finally to be able to talk about it. But then I wondered how Joseph knew it was Ed my father had attacked. We hadn't told him that—Dick had just joked about a 'minor earthquake', nothing more specific.

'What exactly did Joseph tell you?' I asked her.

'He said he could tell by the state you and your mum were in at the lunch that your father had misbehaved. He said you looked "crumpled" and he knew from years of being friends with Dick and being at school under your dad what that meant. So he asked Dick about it later and got the whole story.'

'Gosh,' I said, still feeling simultaneously violated and strangely excited by what Kiki was saying. 'He really did tell you the whole story. You and Joseph must be pretty chummy.'

She shrugged. 'We get on really well, I like him enormously, but I think he wanted to talk about it because he was quite upset on your behalf. He said your dad is a classic shortarse mini-dictator and he has always been foul to you and your mother. Is that true, Amelia?'

I felt tears pricking my eyes and just nodded. If I wasn't careful I'd have to get my clutter-clearing tissues out. 'Yes,' I said. 'But it was Ed who copped it on Friday. It was pretty dreadful.'

'What did he attack him about?' said Kiki, taking my hand across the table. 'Joseph didn't tell me that.'

I felt a bit shaky. This was all stuff I thought I didn't want to discuss with anybody, but now the subject was out I felt oddly compelled to talk about it. I took a deep breath, the kind I encouraged my clients to take when we were close to discovering why their clutter had accumulated.

'He asked him why we don't have any children,' I said, brushing a treacherous tear from the corner of my eye.

'And why haven't you?' Kiki asked me, very gently. 'I've often wondered myself . . .'

And then the tears came. I sobbed and sobbed so much I couldn't even find my bloody tissues and Kiki brought the kitchen roll over. She sat down next to me and put her arm around my shoulder.

'Let it out, Amelia,' she said. 'Tell me. I'm not being nosy, it will make you feel better to talk about it.'

So I told her the whole story. How I hadn't understood when we got married quite how dead against having children Ed was and how I had always thought he would eventually see sense, but now I was feeling increasingly desperate that maybe he wouldn't.

Kiki put her arms around me and I sobbed on to her shoulder.

'Do you think Ed's position is reasonable?' she asked, when I finally recovered a little.

'Well, I can understand it, in a way,' I said, wiping my nose and sniffing. 'He had such a loveless childhood himself, and his only other close-up experience of family life has been with my parents, and that would be enough to put anyone off. But it's such a ridiculously black and white situation. I want them; he doesn't. There's no right or wrong, we just have different opinions—and needs—on the subject.'

'And you are simply going to give up and let him have his way?'

'What choice do I have? Our marriage is so great in every other way. It's just this one thing.'

She didn't say anything for a moment, just sat there with her arm around me, then she suddenly sat up.

'Look,' she said. 'I want to show you something. It's not pretty, but I think you need to see it.'

She picked up her pencil and a sheet of paper and drew a line which started out horizontally, then went gently upwards.

'OK,' she said. 'This is the graph of female fertility. That point there at the top is age twenty-three.'

She wrote '23' and then continued the fine again, now sloping gently downwards. Then she stopped again.

'This is thirty-seven,' she said, and then drew the line on in a downward angle that was almost vertical. She stopped drawing again and looked at me. 'How old are you, Amelia?'

'Thirty-six and three-quarters,' I whispered, looking at her graph in horror and then back up at Kiki. 'Is that really what happens?'

She nodded. 'It's not a gentle decline, like we all think. A friend of mine who is a gynaecologist drew this graph for me years ago and told me to tell all my friends. Female fertility goes into freefall at thirty-seven, and by the time you hit forty, it's a black ski run.'

'But what about Madonna?' I asked.

Kiki laughed bitterly. 'There are always statistical oddities,' she said. 'You might be lucky, like her, or you might be average, which is more likely. And that wasn't a first baby, either.'

For a moment I was too stunned to speak. It was even worse than I thought. I picked up the little diagram and just stared at it.

'How did I get to the age of thirty-six without knowing this?' I said, eventually.

Kiki shrugged. 'You'd be amazed how many women don't understand how brutally quickly fertility declines,' she said. 'We all spend so much time concentrating on *contra*ception most of us don't know the first thing about *con*ception. Remember all those articles in *Cosmo* about avoiding pregnancy? I reckon I could have done a Ph.D. on contraception by the time I was seventeen.'

'I didn't read those magazines when I was a teenager,' I said. 'My father doesn't approve of them.'

Kiki rolled her eyes. 'Oh, Amelia,' she said, smiling indulgently at me. 'What time machine did you just pop out of?'

It was my turn to shrug. 'I dunno. But if you ever met my father—which I sincerely hope you won't—you'd understand.' I looked down at the fertility graph again. I still couldn't quite believe it. 'What about you, Kiki?' I said. The great unmentionable subject was out in the open, so I thought I might as well go with it. 'You're a bit older than me, aren't you?'

Kiki laughed. 'Oh, I'm ancient, darls—forty-one—but none of this bothers me, because I'm not going to have children. Not my thing. So that's one little worry I don't have. It would be nice to have a boyfriend, possibly a husband, but a family of my own? No thanks.'

Before I could ask her anything else, she had turned her attention back to her Rolodex. 'Ooh,' she said. 'Here is another possibility for your helper. A very nice actor, never in work, very neat. I'll write his number down too and I'll just have a look to see if there is anyone else who might be good . . .'

The serious discussion was very clearly over, which was a relief. I couldn't take anything else in. But when Kiki was absorbed writing the numbers down for me, I folded up the fertility graph and put it in my handbag.

*　　　　*　　　　*

I left her place feeling really stunned. I needed some time to process what she'd told me, and I didn't want to do it with Ed around. I was frightened that in my shock I would blurt it all out and we'd just have another big row when what we needed was a calm and reasonable conversation about it. So I rang him and told him I was going down to Winchelsea that afternoon, to be ready for Sonny, who was coming the next morning.

'That's all right, my darling Melia,' said Ed, in his most affectionate tones, making me feel like an absolute heel for what I'd just been discussing with Kiki. 'Go and get stuck into that garden—but you do remember I can't come down this weekend, don't you?'

I had forgotten, actually—it was despatch time for the quarterly delivery of Ed's wine, and he always had to spend those weekends out at his warehouse in Acton supervising it. Immaculate service was all part of the Bradlow's brand image, and Ed delivered quite a bit of the wine himself in his current car, a lovely old Bristol.

There had been a time when I'd done the deliveries with him, but the thrill of visiting ageing rock stars in their gracious Surrey homes and property developers in Bishop's Avenue had long since palled, and these days I left Ed to it.

*   *   *

I was amazed when I got down to the cottage later that afternoon and saw how much Sonny had already done in the garden. At Hermione's suggestion he had worked right through the previous weekend, and the first three vegetable

225

beds were already built, with the fourth well along. It was really starting to look like a kitchen garden. I was so excited, I ran next door to see Hermione. She was sitting in a chair next to one of her own raised beds, a trowel in her hand, wearing a magnificent pair of gardening gloves, like chintz gauntlets which went right up to her elbows.

'Hello, Amelia dear,' she said. 'Are you pleased with your *potager*?'

'Oh, it's wonderful,' I said. 'I can't believe how quickly he's done it.'

'He's a real worker, that boy. That's what I so admire about him.'

'Yes, you're quite right,' I said, thinking he had other outstanding attributes to admire and well she knew it. 'Thank you so much for sharing him with me. You look like you're hard at work yourself. What are you doing here?'

'I'm planting out my courgettes,' she said, pointing to a perky row of little plants at her side. 'I plant the seeds in these coir pots and leave them to come up in the greenhouse where it's nice and warm. Then, when they're ready, I can pop them straight into the bed here, still in the coir, without having to mess them around too much. They're a great invention, cut the work of propagation by two-thirds. I've already let the worms work all the compost through the soil over the winter, so just a bit of the seaweed extract, some water, and off we go.'

I wasn't exactly sure what she was talking about, but I was sure I would get the hang of it eventually.

'You make it look so easy,' I said. 'And I have a feeling it isn't.'

'If you think of your plants as pets, you'll be

226

fine, Amelia. They need food, water, care and somewhere comfortable to sit. They need to be kept sheltered and not be interfered with too much while they are growing. That's it. Oh, and you can't leave them alone too long, as I told you before.'

'When will I be able to start planting things, do you think?'

'As soon as Sonny finishes building the fourth bed, you can put the earth in, and that's it, you'll be ready to go. If you order the earth today, you'll have it tomorrow. I'll do some planting plans for you tonight, and we can look at them in the morning.'

I was so happy and excited I kissed her on the cheek, and she smiled sweetly at me and patted my hand.

*   *   *

Sonny arrived promptly at ten the next day and got straight on with his bricklaying. I went out to say hi and to thank him for what he'd done already. Then, after spending a few minutes trying not to stare at his biceps working through his tight T-shirt as he picked up each brick, I went next door to see Hermione's plans for my garden.

'Now, I've put some treviso in here,' she was saying, pointing with a coral-painted fingernail at the sketch she had done. 'That grows very well, and it's terribly good in a salad, nice and bitter. Apart from herbs and lettuces, you're too late to plant seeds for a lot of this now, so I will give you the seedlings, I've got so many in the greenhouse. Next year we can do the planting together from scratch and I can show you all that.'

After lunch on her terrace—sausage sandwiches made by me and consumed with great gusto by Sonny—Hermione went up for her afternoon nap and I went back into my garden to see what I could do to help.

Sonny pointed to the back left corner of Hermione's drawing, where it said 'summer fruits' in her lovely cursive writing. 'See that space there?' he said. 'Next to Checkpoint Charlie . . .' He stopped and looked up at me. 'Why does she call it that? Who is he?'

I looked at him blankly for a moment, not understanding. 'It wasn't a person,' I said slowly, as I realized what was going on. 'It was a famous security checkpoint on the Berlin Wall, the only place you could go through from West Germany to East Germany . . .'

He still looked baffled. 'The Berlin Wall?' he said. 'Is that like the Great Wall of China?'

I did a mental calculation. When did the Berlin Wall come down? 1989? If Sonny was twenty-two, as I reckoned, he would have been four at the time. He really hadn't heard of Checkpoint Charlie. Bloody Nora.

'After the war,' I said, 'the Second World War'— I hoped he knew what that was—'the Allies divided Berlin in two. One half was aligned with what we think of as Germany—capitalist—the rest was in what they called East Germany, and it was communist. You weren't allowed to go from one to the other without all kinds of special documents. There were armed guards, razor wire and searchlights. It was terrible, and some families were split on either side. People got shot trying to get over it.'

Sonny was nodding. I had no idea if he had understood anything I said, but he seemed satisfied with my explanation.

He went back to the drawing and explained that, according to Hermione's plan, I would have raspberry canes and gooseberry bushes planted next to the hedge there, to get the best of the sunshine in that corner.

'You could start breaking up the earth now, ready to put them in,' he suggested, so I did.

It was quite backbreaking work, but as I concentrated on using the mattock—Sonny had shown me how to lift it up behind my head and then bring it down hard, in a display I had found something of a festival of erotica—my brain disengaged in a most pleasant way.

My whole world came down to my arms and the mattock and the ground beneath my feet, and once I got into a rhythm with the lifting and the crashing down and the heaving up, it was almost like a meditation.

Ever since I'd seen Kiki the day before, I had been obsessing on the awfulness of the weekend with my father and then with Ed in Paris, and the issues it raised—plus what she had told me about the imminent black-ski-run state of my fertility. It had all been swirling around in my head like some kind of poisonous soup, so it was a blessed relief not to think about anything for a while. I was all thinked out.

That evening, I was so exhausted I had a hot bath and crawled into bed at nine o'clock. I fell immediately into a dreamless sleep and didn't stir until I heard my mobile ringing the next morning. I stumbled out of bed to find it, realizing as I picked it out from my handbag on the floor that the muscles in my shoulders and arms were screaming. I felt like I'd been stretched on a rack. 'Aaaaagh,' I said into the phone. 'Hello?'

'Oooh, that sounded very primal, what's going on there?' said familiar tones. It was Kiki.

'Oh, hi Kiki,' I said, climbing painfully back into bed. 'Ow, aaaagh.'

'Whatever's the matter with you?' she asked.

'I was working in my garden yesterday and I really overdid it. Ouch. Oooh . . .'

'Are you and Ed down in Winchelsea then?' she asked.

I explained he was in London doing deliveries.

'Oh, you must be lonely down there on your own then, you poor girl,' said Kiki. 'Would you like some visitors?'

'How many visitors?'

'Oh, me and perhaps Ol?'

'That would be great,' I said. 'But bring some old clothes so you can help me in the garden. You'll enjoy it—both of you—trust me on that.'

I rang off, chuckling to myself, because I was planning a little stunt. I'd asked Sonny to work on Saturday and Sunday too, to get things finished, and I knew watching Kiki's and Oliver's reactions to him would be great sport.

Little did I know that Kiki had her own mind game planned for me that weekend. When they turned up just after lunch there were three people in the car. Kiki, Oliver—and Joseph Renwick.

I was practically speechless when I realized who it was, but greeted him as though it was the most normal thing in the world to have the first boy I had ever kissed show up unannounced for a jolly

230

weekend in my marital home. Actually, I felt severely conflicted about it.

I was very happy with Joseph staying neatly where he belonged—in my adolescent past. Every time I saw him, I couldn't help remembering what it was like to kiss him, and it was all too confusing. And it seemed especially inappropriate with Ed not around.

Kiki's eyes were twinkling so hard it was almost painful to look at her, but I managed to corner her in the pantry while the boys were unloading the car. I shut the door.

'You might have warned me!' I hissed at her.

'I thought you'd like a surprise—an old friend to see you.'

'He's my brother's friend,' I protested, 'not mine, but anyway, just tell me quickly, what are the sleeping arrangements? There are only three proper bedrooms here, remember—Ed's room is also his study, so I can't put anyone in there and I don't really want to sleep in it myself.'

'I could share with you,' she said. 'And the boys can have a room each. Or one of them can sleep on the sofa. It's up to you.'

I nodded. At least I had established that Kiki and Joseph weren't an item. That cleared up one thing, but I had another question. 'Why exactly have you brought Joseph down here, Kiki?' I asked her. She didn't know about my romantic history with him, so I couldn't see what her game plan was, but I knew she always had one.

'I like him,' she said, apparently ingenuously. 'He's good fun. And you know he's pretty lonely in London, Amelia. He's been away for a long time and I think he's really missing his kids. I thought it

231

would cheer him up.'

I decided to accept what she said at face value. Just another bit of Kiki's well-meaning social engineering, this time for Joseph's benefit.

I made some tea and then took them out to see the garden. Well, I took Kiki and Joseph—Oliver said he wasn't the slightest bit interested in some tragic old mud patch and that he was going to go upstairs for a nap. I wasn't about to tell him what he was missing out on.

'So this is going to be my vegetable garden,' I said proudly to the others when we got outside. 'And that bed over there by the hedge is going to be my summer fruits—raspberries and gooseberries. I dug that myself yesterday, that's why I can hardly move this morning.'

'Did you do the bricklaying?' asked Joseph, examining it. 'It's beautiful work.'

'No, I have a gardener who's done all that for me. He's just popped out to get something, he'll be back soon.'

'Why have you got a large hole in your hedge, Amelia?' asked Kiki. 'I'm sure that wasn't there before.'

'That's Checkpoint Charlie,' I said, enjoying the bemused looks on their faces. 'We put it there so my lovely neighbour Hermione and I can share the gardener and her tools, and visit each other without having to walk miles around to the front gates.'

'Is she the old duck we met the last time I was down?' said Kiki.

'Yes,' I said. 'But she's no duck. She's as smart as a whip. We'll go round and see her later, you'll love her. Oh, look, here comes Sonny now.'

He couldn't have made a better entrance if it had been directed by Sofia Coppola. The sun was behind him, just as it had been the first time I saw him, and he was carrying a bag of cement on one shoulder, which made the muscles on his arms and chest pop out.

Kiki whimpered. It's the only word for it. A sort of squeak and a moan combined.

'Holy shit, Amelia, where did you find him?' she whispered to me.

I chuckled. 'He's Hermione's toyboy. Hi, Sonny,' I called. 'Come and meet my friends, they're going to help us.'

'Too flipping right we are,' said Kiki. 'I've just remembered how much I love gardening.'

19

The rest of that afternoon was like Carry On Gardening. Kiki had taken one look at Sonny and run inside to change into her gardening gear, which turned out to be a pair of jeans cut off into very short shorts—which I later realized she had done there and then with my kitchen scissors—and a singlet, worn in the Charlie Dimmock style, perky nipples ahoy.

She wiggled, simpered and bent over at every possible opportunity, announcing that she was Sonny's personal assistant and had to stay at his side at all times so she could learn from him. He was very patient with her and just got on quietly with his work.

Joseph was clearly off on some kind of macho

fest of his own, lifting piles of bricks with one hand and taking his shirt off, quite unnecessarily, after just a few minutes. He did have a surprisingly good bod for his age, I couldn't help noticing.

An image of the eighteen-year-old Joseph, hot and sweaty in his school rowing strip on a summer afternoon, flashed across my mind. I pushed it away, only to have it replaced by the memory of how his stomach had felt when I'd put my hand up his shirt that fateful night we'd kissed all those years before. It had been as hard as cobblestones.

It looked as though it probably still felt that way, but now it had a line of hair down it that I really thought I'd better not look at. It was all too weird and wrong.

Kiki nudged me and jerked her head at him, waggling her eyebrows up and down suggestively. I threw a gardening glove at her and shook my head disapprovingly. But then we were both distracted by Sonny.

'Would you mind if I took my shirt off, Amelia?' he asked me.

'Of course not,' I squeaked, determined not to catch Kiki's eye.

'Oh great, it's just that Mrs Hart doesn't like it, so I always keep it on over there, but I wouldn't mind working on my tan.'

He smiled in that guileless way of his and started to pull his T-shirt over his head. Kiki stood upright for what seemed like the first time all afternoon, and the two of us blatantly stopped and watched him. I glanced over at Joseph and he was looking too.

It was a very tight T-shirt and Sonny seemed to get it stuck on his head, so for a few golden moments we had a ringside view of the best torso I had ever laid eyes on.

His chest was clearly defined into two mounds which were so curved they almost had a cleavage, and his stomach went down into his low-slung jeans like a kind of suit-of-armour plate of hard muscles. It was extraordinary. Not one of those awful Ninja-turtle stomachs you see on artificially pumped-up gym bodies but a naturally fit young male physique, hanging off the finest pair of shoulders you could ever hope to see.

And that was the moment Oliver looked out of the bedroom window into the garden. He'd missed out on the whole thing up till then, sleeping off his hangover upstairs, but we knew he was awake when we heard his unmistakable tones through the bedroom window.

'Jesus Christ, look at the tits on that,' he clearly exclaimed.

We all looked up at the window, and then I saw Sonny's head, now having emerged from the T-shirt, swing over to me and then to Kiki, to see who the voice had been talking about. I was secretly thrilled he had looked at me first.

'I think he was talking about you, Sonny,' said Joseph, who'd clearly clocked the whole thing.

'Me?' said Sonny, but before we could say any more, Oliver had arrived in the garden, panting for breath. He must have run down the stairs.

'Who the fuck are you?' he said to Sonny, standing right in front of him, his hands on his hips, his unshaven cheeks quite flushed.

'Oh, hi, Ollie,' I said. 'You've woken up, have you? This is my friend Sonny, he helps me with the garden. Sonny, this is Oliver. He's a hairdresser.'

235

'Hi, Oliver,' said Sonny, putting out his hand after wiping it first on the seat of his jeans. Lucky hand, I thought.

Oliver had a look on his face I'd never seen before. He looked transported.

'You are the most beautiful man I have ever laid eyes on,' he said. Then he took the large hand with dirt under all the nails that was being offered to him, raised it to his lips and gently kissed it. 'And I'm going to spend the rest of the day gazing at you.'

I looked anxiously at Sonny. I knew that Oliver could reduce quite sophisticated people to spluttering heaps with his outrageous frankness, and I didn't want Sonny to be too embarrassed. He might resign. But he just laughed.

'Be my guest,' he said, shrugging his perfect shoulders. 'And when you get bored of that, you can help with the work.'

I was expecting Ollie to start carrying on like Kiki had, removing most of his clothes, making crass innuendoes, constantly bending over, etc., but he didn't. He went very quiet. He sat on the wall of one of the finished beds, smoking a cigarette and following Sonny's every move.

After about ten minutes of that, Sonny stopped what he was doing and went over to him.

'Come on, lazybones,' he said. 'I want to get this garden ready for planting tomorrow morning and you can help. I'm going to start shovelling the earth into the beds now—there are two spades, so you can do it with me. And pick that cigarette end up.'

I watched in amazement as Oliver did what he was told. Then he spent the rest of the afternoon pitching dirt into my vegetable beds and chatting quietly to Sonny. Kiki and I kept looking at each other and opening our mouths in pantomime astonishment. Oliver was usually only quiet when he was asleep or sulking.

With the five of us working flat out, by just past six all four beds were full of earth.

'Let's call it a day, everyone,' I said, as we applauded Sonny shovelling the last spade of earth into the final raised bed. 'You have all done fantastic work, and I think we've earned ourselves a drink. I'm going to get Hermione, so would you chaps mind putting your shirts back on? And Kiki, could you go and get the drinks started? There's some cassis on the dresser, so we can have kir royale.'

When I came back through Checkpoint Charlie with Hermione, I saw that Sonny had got the sun lounger out of the shed ready for her, and he literally tipped Oliver out of it so she could sit down. Oliver just lay laughing on the lawn where he'd been dumped. I still couldn't believe the change in him.

I went inside to help Kiki with the drinks, and he followed me in.

'Amelia,' he said, in a stage whisper, 'can Sonny stay for dinner?'

'Do you really think he'd want to?' I replied.

I assumed that a twenty-two-year-old would have more interesting plans for a Saturday night than hanging out with a load of middle-aged people.

Oliver looked shifty. 'Well, he's already said yes . . .'

I pretended to clip him round the ear. 'You are

so naughty, but of course he can stay. I love Sonny.'

'So do I,' said Oliver and ran back out to the garden.

Kiki and I just looked at each other and laughed.

'Have you ever seen him like this before?' I asked her.

She shook her head. 'It's unbelievable,' she said. 'I've seen him in lust countless times—almost on a daily basis, actually—and he's as predatory as a great white shark, as you know, regardless of the sexual orientation or relationship status of his prey, but this mild-mannered, love-struck loon is a whole new look. I'm practically speechless.'

When we got outside with the tray, Hermione was sitting with the three men at her feet, looking completely at ease. I'd just poured champagne for everyone and was about to make a toast to the new vegetable garden when the phone rang. I ran inside to answer it and was a bit thrown to hear Ed's voice.

'Hello, my lovely darling,' he said. 'I just thought I'd ring and make sure you aren't too lonely down there.'

I felt quite guilty. I hadn't thought about him all day, we were having so much fun.

'Well, that's really sweet of you, Ed,' I said. 'But I'm fine actually. Sonny is here doing the garden, and Kiki and Ollie have come down too, to help, so I'm not lonely at all.'

Because I felt uncomfortable about it, I didn't tell him Joseph was there, too, and then, as I hadn't said it straight away when I mentioned the others, I just couldn't find a way to slip it in casually. I was fairly sure Ed wouldn't like him being there, and I hung up feeling very uneasy about my lie of omission.

I stood by the phone for a moment wondering whether to do what my father would do in such a situation, which would be to ring him back immediately and tell him the whole truth, right down to the fact that I had felt uncomfortable about it, but then I heard raucous laughter coming from the garden and ran back out so I wouldn't miss the joke.

*   *   *

We had a great night. I kept the food really simple, defrosting a big tub of Bolognese sauce I had in the freezer to make two lasagnes—I reckoned Sonny would need one for himself. Everybody helped, and he turned out to be as handy in the kitchen as he was in the garden. He even made the béchamel sauce for me, with Oliver stuck to his side at every stage.

'You've got to take the roux off the heat when you start to put the milk in,' I heard Sonny telling him. 'Otherwise it will go all lumpy.'

'What?' said Oliver. 'Like your stomach?' and he grabbed Sonny playfully around the middle, tickling him, as you would a toddler. Sonny just laughed and pushed Oliver away with a deft bump of his hips.

Kiki and I swapped another of our pantomime looks. She gestured with her eyes towards the staircase, and we told the boys we were going upstairs to change. We got into my bedroom, closed the door and fell on the bed shrieking.

'Oh my GOD,' said Kiki. 'I think that boy's gay.'

'I can't believe it,' I said. 'I've been lusting after him like a tragic old Mrs Robinson, and it turns out he's a flaming woofter all the time.'

I put my head on to my pillow and screamed while I drummed my feet on the bed. We laughed until we had tears running down our cheeks.

'How could I have missed it?' said Kiki. 'I'm the biggest fag hag of all time and he totally flew in under my gaydar. It never occurred to me— although, with him having that body, I should have known better. I am so embarrassed. I have never made a play for a gay man in my life before. Aaaaaaaggggggh!' It was her turn to scream into the pillow.

'But Sonny's such a sweetie, I really don't think he would mind,' I said. 'I'm not even sure if he'd notice. I mean, we don't know he's gay, he's just lovely to everyone. He treats Hermione like a queen . . .'

We looked at each other and then whooped with laughter again.

'Oh God,' I said, trying to get my breath back. 'Of course he does. Sweet gay men like him love old ladies. That's probably why he's so nice to me.'

We laughed some more and then there was a gentle knock at the door.

'Come in!' I said, and we sat up straight on the bed, like naughty schoolgirls. It was Joseph.

'Can I join you?' he said. 'I just went down to the kitchen and felt like I was ready to be planted in your new gooseberry patch . . .'

Kiki's hands flew up to her mouth. 'Are they kissing?' she asked.

'Not quite,' said Joseph. 'But it's all mighty cosy

down there.'

That set us off again. Joseph sat down in the armchair and regarded us with the affectionate bemusement of a man confronted with a pair of hopelessly giggling girlies. He shook his head indulgently.

'Sorry, Joseph,' I said, a little uncomfortable at having him in my bedroom but determined to get over it. 'I know we're behaving like thirteen-year-olds, but we had no idea Sonny was gay. We're in shock.'

'I was making a big play for him,' said Kiki, her eyes wide with horror.

'I did notice,' said Joseph.

'Oh shit,' she said. 'And I've just realized I wrecked my favourite pair of jeans for him, dammit. What a waste. Oh well, I'll just have to go to Glastonbury so I can get some more wear out of them.'

The rest of the evening continued in a similar vein, with me, Kiki and Joseph exchanging looks and nudges, as Oliver mooned shamelessly after Sonny and he appeared to play along.

But by the end of dinner there was no sport left in it, because the two of them were clearly holding hands under the table. I wondered momentarily what to do now about sleeping arrangements but decided just to let things pan out.

Now that it seemed Sonny and Oliver were officially an item, the rest of us got over our rather childish hysteria and the conversation became more normal. We were chatting about films we'd seen recently, with Oliver chipping in with bits of thrilling celebrity gossip he'd gleaned on recent shoots with the stars.

241

'What kind of a hairdresser are you?' Sonny asked him, looking puzzled.

Kiki replied for Oliver. 'He's one of the top three session stylists in the world,' she said, proudly.

'But what does that mean?' said Sonny.

'Well, I do a lot of hair for fashion shoots and advertising,' said Oliver, actually sounding quite modest, for once. 'But I also do personal cutting and styling for quite a few big celebs.'

'He did Madonna's new do,' said Kiki, ever the agent for her friends.

'Wow,' said Sonny. 'That's amazing. I love that haircut.'

Kiki and I swapped glances again. He definitely was gay.

'That reminds me,' said Oliver, turning to look at me intently. 'Talking of beautiful ageing blondes—I was going to cut your hair, Amelia, wasn't I?'

I said nothing. I had been massively relieved when that all seemed to have been forgotten. He'd cancelled the date we'd made after Kiki's party and, as nothing more had been said about it, I was happily hoping it had gone away.

'Oh, yes,' said Kiki, enthusiastically. 'I'd forgotten about that. You've got your new clothes, Amelia, and you're looking great, but your hair is still totally daggy.'

'I think Amelia's got beautiful hair,' said Joseph, which just made things worse.

I was seriously beginning to wish the attention would shift away from me.

'She has,' said Oliver. 'But she's got too much of it.' He put his head on one side, and as he narrowed his kohl-rimmed eyes, I could tell he was

242

seeing me as a head, not a person.

'Look at this,' said Kiki and, jumping up from her chair, she came behind me and lifted my hair until it was hanging just above my shoulders, as she had that day in Dover Street Market.

'Wow,' said Sonny, repeating what I was beginning to realize was his favourite word. 'That looks amazing.'

Joseph nodded. 'I see what you mean now,' he said, sounding surprised. 'I never would have imagined it, but somehow it shows your face off better, Amelia. Maybe you should have it cut.'

I gave him a dirty look—traitor.

'Got any scissors?' said Oliver, standing up and opening the dresser drawers. He pulled out my chunky kitchen shears and held them up. 'Anything a bit smaller than this?'

'I've got some nail scissors in my bag,' said Kiki.

'Hmmm,' said Ollie. 'Well, they might do, but they could be a bit small, and these are too big, but I might be able to do it if I use both . . .'

Then, horrified that they were going to go ahead with the game shears whether I liked it or not, I weakened and confessed there were some hairdressing scissors in the bathroom. Ed used them to keep his sideburns immaculate.

Kiki volunteered to get them—rightly guessing that I wouldn't—and Oliver disappeared upstairs with her, saying he needed to get his comb, and Sonny went out to the loo.

I looked over at Joseph, hoping he might be an ally, after all.

'Do you really think I should do this?' I asked him, feeling almost sick with trepidation.

He stood up and put out a hand to me. 'Come

243

over here,' he said.

Feeling very self-conscious, I joined him in front of the large round mirror on the wall opposite the back door. Standing behind me, he lifted my hair up as Kiki had done.

'See?' he said, looking intently over my shoulder at me. I was supposed to be looking at my hair, but I couldn't tear my eyes away from his gaze. Then he dropped my hair down again so it fell over my shoulders and on to my breasts.

'Pretty girl,' he said. Then he picked my hair up again. 'Beautiful woman.'

I looked at my reflection and then at his face in the mirror right behind me. I swallowed awkwardly as I felt his breath on my neck and realized that my nipples had gone hard where his hands had brushed them as he lifted up my hair.

I could feel them tingling and I could see them in the mirror, clearly standing to attention through my white top. What a horrendous giveaway. Just as I realized, I caught his eye in the mirror again, and he was looking at me in the same way he had at Kiki's party and at the hospital. I felt a blush sweep down my neck and quickly turned and sat down again at the table, folding my arms.

I was so confused and horrified by what had just happened with Joseph I hardly noticed that the others had come back, or that Kiki had put a towel around my shoulders. Then Sonny lifted the chair, with me in it, so I was sitting in the middle of the floor, and I went into some kind of terrified trance, like a rabbit caught in headlights.

Oliver sprayed my head with a plant mister and he was gently combing my hair when I suddenly heard a loud *snip*. I looked down and saw a piece of hair about two feet long on the kitchen floor. As I looked down, it was joined by several more.

That snapped me back to consciousness. My hand flew up to my head and I found that my hair now stopped not far below my jaw.

'Too late now,' said Kiki, smiling brightly, 'so relax. You've got one of the best hairdressers in the world working on your head. It's going to be fabulous.'

'Can I have a mirror?' I asked pathetically.

'No,' said Oliver. 'I never let my clients have mirrors.'

It seemed to go on for ages. First there was a lot of regular, measured snipping, then he seemed to go wild, stabbing madly at my hair with the scissors and cutting into it in what seemed like a random manner. It reminded me of my father doing the pruning.

'Careful, Ollie!' I said. 'You'll have my eye out doing that.'

Kiki laughed. 'Don't worry,' she said. 'It's just what he does. If you ever read a fashion magazine, you'd know he's famous for it. He goes into another zone. But he won't hurt you and it will look perfect.'

Finally, Oliver stopped cutting and ruffled my hair with his hands. Then I felt him draw a parting down one side and make a couple of adjustments with his comb.

'Finished,' he said, 'Sonny, can you get that mirror down off the wall for her?'

He brought it over to me, and I closed my eyes, too scared to look. Eventually, I opened one eye and squinted at myself. Then the other. I gasped. I looked amazing.

245

'Omigod!' I said.

My hair seemed to have dried as he was cutting it, and it was hanging in a perfect bob, to just below my ears. I turned my head and saw how it was gently sculpted into the back of my neck, but in a natural-looking way not like a 1960s space-age hairdo.

I didn't quite recognize the person in the mirror yet—she had a much longer neck than me, fuller lips and much better cheekbones—but I could see that the haircut really suited her.

'Wow,' I said after a while. 'Wow, wow, wow. It looks amazing, Ollie. Now I see why you're such a big deal. Thank you so much.'

I jumped up and hugged him. Then I did various twirls and poses while they all clapped and cheered.

I had a new look and I loved it.

*   *   *

I got a heck of a surprise when I woke up the next morning, my sleep disturbed by rain hammering on to the roof. I'd actually forgotten I'd had three-quarters of my hair chopped off until I stumbled into the bathroom, and I nearly fell over when I caught sight of my reflection in the mirror over the sink.

Of course, after a night pressed against a pillow and a fair bit of thrashing around as Kiki and I had fought over the duvet, it didn't look as sleek as when Oliver had finished with it. In fact, parts of it were practically standing on end. I wasn't at all sure I liked what I saw. I looked plucked.

Then, entirely on automatic pilot, I picked up a hair elastic to tie it back while I cleaned my teeth.

But there wasn't enough length to tie back any more. The surprise made me stop and look at myself again, properly.

I smoothed the rogue strands down and then pulled a comb through the rest of it. To my amazement, it bounced back perfectly into the bob shape. I looked at myself from each side and then grabbed a hand mirror to check out the back. I still loved it—but I was already worrying what Ed would say.

I tried to put it out of my mind and busied myself in the kitchen making mountains of bacon sandwiches in anticipation of Sonny's usual appetite, but Oliver came down alone, not even particularly hung over—for him.

Kiki, Joseph and I exchanged looks.

'Where's Sonny?' I said in the end. 'Isn't he coming down for breakfast?'

'Sonny went home last night,' said Oliver, a serene expression on his stubbly face.

We made no effort to hide our amazement.

'But you two were practically getting it on at the table . . .' protested Kiki.

'We were holding hands,' said Oliver primly like some kind of superannuated convent girl. 'We had one kiss on the doorstep and then he left.'

He paused and took in the look on our faces.

'What?' he said crossly, and sounding more like himself. 'Just because you lot are a bunch of fucking whores—well, maybe not Amelia, she's probably frigid—you all expected me to shag him on our first date? Well, some things are worth waiting for, you know. You should try it some time, Kiki.'

This time she actually was speechless.

247

20

By the time I got back to the flat on Sunday afternoon, I was getting so nervous about Ed's reaction to the haircut, I really didn't know what to do with myself. Although it was pouring with rain, I was beginning to wish I had stayed on in Winchelsea—possibly until my hair grew back.

I called him to let him know I was home, and he was in a great mood, which gave me some hope. The deliveries had gone exceptionally smoothly, and he'd been very warmly received everywhere he'd taken the wine personally.

He'd ended up staying the night with one client—the hedge-fund guy he'd been talking to at Kiki's party, who lived in a beautiful Georgian house down in Richmond Park—after an informal tasting of the wine had turned into a full-on binge.

Not that Ed or his clients would ever have called it that. They were 'connoisseurs'. If they drank the best part of a half-case of wine between two of them, it was fully to compare and contrast the finer points of the vintage, not to get very expensively shitfaced.

But I was glad he'd had a good time, because it made me feel less guilty about my own gallivanting, particularly that embarrassing moment with Joseph Renwick.

It was the champagne, I told myself. There's nothing like alcohol—particularly bubbly—for stirring up odd feelings, and if he had been a little inappropriate with me, he was probably just desperate for a bit of female physical contact now he was suddenly single again.

My own reaction was harder to excuse, but I tried to put it out of my mind, telling myself it was probably some kind of sexual frustration left over from the disastrous episode in Paris and then being around Sonny's pheromones.

By the afternoon, the combination of guilt over that and worry about Ed's likely reaction to the haircut was making me so jittery I was just wandering around the flat picking things up and putting them down again. I would have gone out for a run, always my best therapy, but it was still pouring with rain.

In the end I found comfort in sorting out my business receipts. Thanks to years of being around Ed, I had known from the start to keep them for everything that related to getting my clutter-clearing job done: phone bills, taxis, Oyster card, stationery, stamps, bin bags, tissues . . .

So far though, I hadn't been much better about it than one of my clients, just stuffing them into a carrier bag in my bedroom, and I needed to get them ready for my first visit to my new accountant, which was scheduled for the following week.

Once I'd done that, an activity I knew most people loathed but which I found strangely calming, I set about creating a proper home office for myself in the corner of my bedroom. I'd always kept all my bank statements filed with Ed's stuff in his study, but now I was going to need to keep my business stuff separate from his, so I dragged a table in from the spare room and put my new phone, my old address book, my pencil pot, a lamp and my trusty clipboard on it. It was a start.

Then I made a list of files and folders and other

things I would need to buy, to keep it as organized as I was supposed to make my clients. I'd already collected my business cards and letterhead from Mount Street Printers & Stationers, just along the road—Smythson had too many bad associations with my old job—and I was finally starting to feel like a proper businesswoman.

'As easy as ABCC . . .' it said on one side of the cards, the initials standing for 'Amelia Bradlow Clutter-Clearing'.

That had been Ed's idea, I remembered, turning one of the sunflower-yellow cards over and over in my fingers, as I sat at my new desk. Ed had come up with the name one night when we were having a 'business-strategy brain-storming think-tank' dinner, at his suggestion. It had been incredibly helpful. But thinking about Ed reminded me of my hair all over again.

For about the hundredth time that afternoon I went and looked in the mirror and wondered, with a slightly sick feeling in my stomach, what he would say about it. But as it turned out, the next person to see my hair wasn't him. It was his mother.

She arrived at the flat around nine that night, not long after Ed had rung to say he was going out for dinner with a client and that I shouldn't wait up for him. He hadn't said anything about Dervla coming and the first I knew was when I heard a long press on the buzzer.

'Hello, Amelia,' said an all too familiar voice, colonial RP on top of childhood elocution lessons. I always thought she sounded like someone from a particularly arch Radio Four play. 'It's Dervla. Can you run down with the money for this taxi, please?'

250

I was so surprised I just said yes, and grabbed my bag. It was lucky I hadn't just picked up a couple of £20 notes, because it turned out she'd got into the taxi at Bristol airport.

The fare was nearly £300 and the driver would only take cash, so I had to run to a cashpoint to get it, while Lady Bradlow—oh, how she loved that title, which I always longed to remind her was the result of a knighthood, nothing glamorously inherited—swanned inside.

'Oh, good heavens, whatever have you done to your lovely hair?' I heard her exclaiming as I headed down the street.

When I finally made it up to the flat again—quite a while later, because when I got back to the building I found she'd left all her luggage down in the hall, so I'd had to load it into the lift and then heft it in through the front door—she was happily ensconced on the sofa, shoes kicked off, telly on, a glass of single malt by her side, cigarette in her hand.

'Hello, Amelia dear,' she said, offering her pampered cheek for a kiss, while simultaneously blowing out a cloud of noxious smoke. She smoked menthols, which made it even worse. 'Whatever does Ed think of your hair? He's always adored those long blonde locks of yours. I can't imagine he's very keen on this boyish style.'

I decided to ignore it.

'So, Dervla,' I said, pouring myself a drink to match hers—I needed one after this shock, 'this is a surprise. Were we expecting you today?'

'Well, I do normally come in mid-June, as you know,' she said, 'but this lovely man invited me to Positano, and it seemed crazy to go back to South

251

Africa from there when I could get one of these marvellous new cheap fares straight here from Italy. Do you know, it was only £39?'

I just smiled politely. There was no point telling her it had cost more like £339 once you factored in the taxi fare I'd paid. This was classic Dervla financial logic.

'Amazing,' I said tightly. 'But Ed didn't mention you were coming tonight. I'm sure he'd have been here to greet you if he'd known . . .'

'Oh, I can't remember if I told him or not, but this is such fun, because I'll be able to go to Chelsea this year—you know how I normally miss it. Have you got tickets for tomorrow? I'm so looking forward to it.'

She meant the flower show, of course, and Monday was the super-exclusive Queen's private view which meant invites were as scarce as Willy Wonka's golden tickets.

Not surprisingly, we didn't have any of those, but we did have tickets for the slightly less glamorous but still very nice Tuesday, as the guests of one of Ed's clients, whose merchant bank was a sponsor of the gardens. I was so furious at her assumption that she was entitled to one of them I just got up and walked out of the room, taking deep breaths as I went.

God, she made me mad. She hadn't been with us for fifteen minutes and already she was in full free-loader mode. I didn't trust myself to stay civil, and as Dervla never listened to what anyone else said anyway, it didn't seem worth wasting my breath to explain, or complain—and anyway, I had to make up the bed in her room. Maybe I should just put on a maid's apron, I thought.

252

I was just getting some towels out of the airing cupboard for her when she appeared at my side. She took them from me without even saying thank you, just one of her gracious-to-the-little-people Raine Spencer smiles.

'Now, I'm just going to have a shower and then I thought we might have a spot of dinner?' she was saying. 'Where shall we go? I hear Scott's is fun . . .'

'I'm going to bed, Dervla,' I said unsmilingly, knowing full well she meant I was supposed to take her out to dinner. 'It's nearly ten o'clock, and I have to work early tomorrow and I really don't like eating this late. There's cheese and pâté in the fridge and plenty of fruit and crackers. Just help yourself. I'll see you in the morning.'

She looked at me with an expression I knew all too well. It was the kind of moue that you might see on a spoilt three-year-old who has just been told they can't have a second ice cream. At seventy-four—I'd looked at her passport while I was bringing the bags up—Dervla had never grown out of it.

*   *   *

Ed came to find me when I was having my shower the next morning, which meant he was up unusually early for him.

'Amelia?' he was calling. 'Have you really had all your hair cut off? Or has my mother finally lost it?'

I turned the water off and opened the cubicle door. I still had my shower cap on and was happy to put off the dreaded moment a little longer.

'Did you know she was coming last night?' I

asked him, as a diversion.

'No,' he said, shaking his head. 'Hadn't a clue. She sprang it on us with her usual lack of consideration. She rang me about ten last night to say she was here and wanted to have dinner with me, so she came and joined us for pudding at Harry's Bar. That's when she told me you'd had all your hair cut off. Is it really true?'

I must have looked guilty, because he reached over and grabbed the shower cap off my head. The look on his face said it all. He was horrified.

He just stood there staring at me with what looked horribly like tears forming in his eyes. Feeling as naked as it was possible to feel, I started to shiver in his gaze and reached out to get a towel.

'What *have* you done?' he said eventually.

He didn't look angry. He looked bewildered. Bewildered and hurt, which was much worse.

'Your beautiful, beautiful hair. You know I've always adored it, and now you look so . . . so ordinary.'

Ouch.

'I just wanted a change . . .' I said.

Suddenly, Ed threw my shower cap down on to the floor and kicked it at the wall. I flinched. It was very out of character for him—and reminded me all too vividly of my father's behaviour.

'What is it with you and change these days, Amelia?' he said, throwing his arms up in the air. 'Why do you suddenly want to change everything? You quit your job, you take me to a ghastly sushi bar for my birthday, you're wearing weird clothes and hooker shoes, you've got that hideous handbag, and now you've just cut off your wonderful hair on a whim without even

254

mentioning it to me first. Don't you care what I think?'

I took a wobbly breath and said nothing. I could feel my heart beating double time in my chest.

'Well?' he continued, his voice getting tighter. 'Do my wishes and needs count for nothing in this relationship?'

I couldn't believe my ears. As far as I could tell, just about everything in our lives was determined by his wishes and needs, his wish to eat out every night in the same bloody restaurants, his need to lock himself away in his study working the rest of the time, his need to have separate bedrooms. Even in the area that meant most to me in our relationship—having children—only his wishes seemed to count. And I couldn't even decide how I wore my own hair!

I was feeling very upset now, my emotions were churning me up, but it wasn't the anger I had felt in Paris. It was something more like fear—fear that if I said the wrong thing at this moment it could never be put right between us again.

I wanted to shout at him, like I had that time, to tell him he was a selfish bastard, as spoilt in his own way as his horrendous mother, and I was sick of running my life according to his ludicrous rules, but I just couldn't. It was like one of those dreams when you can't scream. My vocal cords felt frozen.

'Oh well,' he said, seeming to calm down a little. 'You've done it, so I suppose I'll just have to live with it until it grows back, but what I don't understand is—how on earth did you get it cut down in Winchelsea? Did the gardener do it with his pruning shears?'

He'd completely forgotten that Kiki and Oliver

255

had been down there with me, I realized. I felt a small pang of guilt, remembering how I hadn't told him Joseph was there as well, but if this was how little notice he took of what went on in my life, I thought, I wasn't going to worry about that small detail any more.

Plus, I was so outraged at his assumption that I would just grow my hair back because he said I should that I really didn't feel like tiptoeing around his feelings too much.

'Oliver cut it,' I said bluntly.

I could see the coldness settling in his eyes as he took it in.

'Kiki,' he said, nodding his head very slowly. 'It was Kiki again. Well, I'll tell you something, Amelia. I don't like the influence that woman has on you, so I think you had better decide which you want—to be friends with her or married to me.'

With that, he stormed out and I heard his study door slam. He'd promised he'd never slam a door again. That didn't last long. Sighing deeply, I turned to the mirror and wiped the steam off it with the edge of my towel. I swung my head a few times and watched my hair fall perfectly into place again. I still loved it.

Fuck him, I thought, as I looked at the sophisticated woman in the mirror. Fuck him and his door-slamming and his juvenile Bond girl fantasies. I wasn't a girl any more. What was it Joseph had said? 'Pretty girl. Beautiful woman.' That's who I wanted to be.

Feeling a little shaky, I pulled on my bathrobe and went to make myself a restorative cup of coffee, only to find Dervla already in the kitchen, tucking into my fat-free organic yogurt while

256

smoking a cigarette. She stubbed it out in the nearly empty tub.

'I take it Ed didn't like your hair, then,' she said brightly. 'Well, I did warn you. Men don't like big changes in their women, and they certainly don't like short hair. It makes them think of lesbians.'

It took all my considerable self-control not to tell her to sod off. Instead, I just made my coffee without saying a word and took it back to my bedroom. It was possibly the first time I had been glad I had a room of my own in that flat.

As I got dressed, I still felt shaken by Ed's reaction, which had been much worse than I had ever expected, but as I looked at myself in the mirror, wearing my new wide-leg white jeans and one of the stripy T-shirt tops, my hair a chic little cap on the top, I felt the upset harden into a kind of resolve: it was my hair, I loved it and I didn't care what he thought.

*   *   *

Fortunately, after that less than lovely Monday morning, I had a very busy week and resolved to throw myself into work as the perfect distraction from Dervla—and Ed.

I'd taken on Kiki's friend Fiona to be my assistant clutter-clearer and I was taking her to her first appointment with me that afternoon, which felt like quite a big deal. Then I had what was starting to feel like my usual roster of new clients to see and, later in the week, the first meeting with my very own accountant.

He'd sent me an email with a list of things I needed to take with me, which included bank statements, previous tax returns, investments, pension schemes and the like, which I needed to sort out ready.

So on the Tuesday afternoon, when Ed and Dervla were out enjoying the Chelsea Flower Show—something I had been really looking forward to myself, but it was worth giving the hideous cow my ticket, just to have some peace—I knew I could spend some undisturbed time in Ed's study finding what I needed.

I hadn't been in there for a while and was quite shocked to see the mess it was in. For years I had sorted it out for him once a month, filing everything in the system I had set up, but lately it had been hard to find a time when he'd let me in to do it. He was always in the middle of something that couldn't be disturbed.

In all the chaos, I couldn't find the most recent statement for our joint bank account, which wasn't in any of the places it should have been. I was flicking through the back of one of his filing cabinets, in a drawer labelled 'Stuff'—not very helpful, but possible—when I came across a file marked 'Amelia'. I'd never seen it before and presumed he'd crammed anything relating to me in there, in an earlier fit of organization.

I opened it to find it was full of notes I'd written to him over the years, which was very touching. There was every Valentine card I'd ever given him, and photographs of us right from the earliest days of our relationship.

I smiled when I found one taken on our very first trip through France together. I remembered Ed asking the waiter to take it after a wonderful lunch at a restaurant in Perigord. We looked so young and so in love. My hair was so long. Oh well.

As well as the photos, there were carefully clipped cuttings from various magazines where we had appeared in the social pages, or in profiles of Ed. Looking at it all made me start to feel rather warm and fuzzy towards him again and a bit ashamed of myself for upsetting him so much. It wasn't like I hadn't known he was going to hate my haircut. I should have done it in stages, I thought, as I had with my new clothes, or at least warned him I was thinking about going for the chop.

Not that I'd had much say in it, I reflected, with Kiki and Oliver bossing me around, but I could see it had been a heck of a shock for Ed—which was particularly unfortunate considering all the extra little strains there'd been on the relationship recently.

I made a resolution, right then, to start working immediately to get things back to normal between us, or perhaps even better than normal. It would be hard with Dervla in residence stirring things up, but it was worth the effort because, despite his undeniable tendency towards selfishness, I still dearly loved my husband.

I leafed through some more of the photos and couldn't help smiling. There was Ed beaming with excitement outside the Krug HQ where he had proposed to me. I remembered taking it when we had first arrived there, and it was funny to think he'd already had the engagement ring in his pocket. I'd had no idea what was coming. No wonder his cheeks were so pink in the picture.

In another snap he was standing outside L'Ambroisie, kissing the sign with the restaurant's name on it and holding up three fingers to indicate three Michelin stars. In yet another he was sitting in Ladurée, with a coffee éclair in front of him, holding Mr Bun up to look at it.

He was such a silly old softie, I thought. Yes, he had his quirky little ways, but still he made me feel secure in a way that nobody else did. He was my rock, my best friend and my safe harbour—or he had been up until very recently. I sighed, remembering the scene in the bathroom the morning before. That had been dreadful and I couldn't just let things slide any further downhill between us.

Perhaps we could get Dervla a fabulous invitation somewhere that weekend, I thought, so we could go down to the cottage on our own. Then I could talk to him about working a bit less and spending more time with me. Tell him how much I was beginning to hate having separate bedrooms. Then move on to another, more measured discussion of the baby issue.

I was still mulling all that over when I found some loose sheets of A4 at the back of the file. They were clearly quite old, as the paper was yellowing and they had been typed on the manual typewriter Ed had still used when I first met him.

Without thinking I might be prying into something private—Ed and I had no secrets from each other, as far as I knew—I started reading:

Marrying Amelia—Pros and Cons

Pro.
Very attractive
Beautiful hair
Good metabolism
Fluent French
Great legs
Good head for alcohol
Not a whinger
Brother a good man
Good company
Loves France
Good appetite
Well groomed
Good manners
Good traveller
Bright
Quick learner
Speaks well, especially considering school
Enthusiastic
Organized
Tidy
Fit
Disciplined

Unknowns:
Good mixer? (Probably)
Good cook? (Can learn . . .)

Con:
Dreadful parents
Suburban background
State school
A little immature

Unsophisticated
Sexually inexperienced
No family money
Dervla not keen

I sank down on to the floor, feeling like I had been punched in the face. He'd really weighed up marrying me like it was some kind of business decision? I thought we'd been in love!

My shock very quickly turned to rage. How dare he say my parents were 'dreadful'—especially considering what his mother was like. OK, so my father was not exactly ideal, but I reckoned Dervla came in at about the same level of nightmare, in her own way, and at least my dad didn't sponge off us. And Ed was always saying how much he loved my mother—was that all lies?

Feeling a bit sick, I read it again. Dervla being 'not keen' had been an issue for him? She hadn't even met me when Ed proposed. Clearly he'd discussed me on the phone with her and she hadn't liked the sound of the package. Obviously, I wasn't rich or grand enough for Dervla. Not enough in it for her.

Then, quite irrationally, what made me become incandescent with fury was the mention of my school in the 'Con' column. I was very proud of my school, but it didn't matter how many times I had told him about the Kent grammar-school phenomenon, as far as he was concerned it was a state school and therefore beyond the pale.

In Ed's view, anyone who hadn't been to one of a small fist of public schools he considered acceptable—which did not include the very minor one my father worked at—had been to a 'ghastly comprehensive'. And so what if I had? Why would that have been so terrible, if I had turned out OK?

All these years I'd told myself Ed wasn't really a snob, that he just had his own quaintly fixed ideas about certain things. He wouldn't drive a Japanese car, or drink wine that had been produced anywhere but France. He wouldn't have instant coffee or tea bags in the house, and he hated pubs, of course, and glass-clinking. And the words 'toilet', 'couch' and 'pardon'.

I'd always told myself these were just his funny little ways, endearingly eccentric, but I hadn't realized that something as petty as where I'd been to school might actually have stopped him marrying me. They weren't 'quirks', I understood in that moment, they were outrageous and ignorant prejudices. He was a snob. A horrendous bloody snob, like his cow of a mother.

And that was it. I couldn't see any way I could spend another night under the same roof as him—especially not with her there.

Had Dervla not been in residence, there was a small chance I could have thrashed things out with Ed, I thought, but as well as being maddening in her own right, she brought out the worst in him. Even in normal circumstances, things were always strained while she was there, and with everything that had gone on between me and Ed already in the past few weeks, she was just one stress too many.

Trembling slightly, I put the pros and cons list back in the drawer and kicked it shut. Then I rang Kiki and asked her if I could come and stay for a while.

Toilets to the pair of them.

21

Kiki certainly knew how to make leaving your husband—or having a break from him, as I preferred to think of it—seem like fun. She was delighted to have me as a 'flattie', as she called it, and started planning our joint social life from the moment I arrived in her spare room that afternoon.

'I'm really sorry things aren't great between you and Ed,' she said, sitting on my bed sifting through a pile of invitations, while I unpacked. I was feeling a bit wobbly, to put it mildly, and it was a very welcome distraction to have her there twittering merrily, as she did. She had a bright-green facepack on. 'I'm sure you will be able to work things out,' she was saying. 'Once you give him a chance to see how much he misses you. Then he won't take you for granted so much.'

I stopped in the middle of the room, holding a shoe in one hand and a T-shirt in the other.

'Do you really think he takes me for granted?' I asked.

'Shit, yeah,' said Kiki. 'I've always thought that. You just need to remind him how much he needs you—how much you do for him. Make him appreciate you a bit more. You're his bloody housekeeper and social secretary and everything else. You've been his live-in clutter-clearer for years.'

I smiled weakly. It was true. Ed was immaculate in his personal appearance and incredibly organized with regard to his work, but actually pretty untidy in every other regard. I didn't think he knew how to put a cup in the dishwasher, and he certainly couldn't turn it on. I'd been doing it all for him for so many years I cleared up after him on autopilot.

It was quite comforting to know that someone else thought Ed took all that for granted but, on the other hand, talking about it so casually made the problems between us a bit too real. I sighed deeply, put the shoe in the wardrobe with its partner and folded the T-shirt on the bed.

'And being entirely selfish,' said Kiki. 'I must say it's perfect timing for me.'

'Why?' I asked, hanging my dressing gown on the back of the door. I was glad I had put that hook there. 'Because now Ollie is so nauseatingly loved up with Sonny and really incredibly boring, you can be my official PIC,' she said, tossing any invites that didn't thrill her on to the floor.

'What's a PIC?' I asked, picking them up and putting them in the bin.

'Partner in crime. Ooh look, there's a party at Shoreditch House tonight, which sounds good. I always like a safari to the East. So we can go to that and then . . .'

It all seemed terribly edgy and exciting after my glamorous yet rather staid life with Ed but, of course, I couldn't have chosen a worse place to stay as far as his reaction went.

I had wondered for a moment, after I had impulsively rung Kiki, whether I wouldn't have been better staying with someone more neutral, like an old schoolfriend, but quickly decided against it.

They all had young children and, even apart

from the associated issues of not having spare rooms and living in places like Forest Hill and Ealing—or in Louise's case, Cornwall—cosy family life was the last thing I needed to be around at that moment. Kiki's hectic and hilarious whirl was the perfect distraction.

So I'd left a cowardly little note on Ed's pillow saying I 'needed some space to think about all the issues which have recently come up between us' and that I was going to stay with 'a friend' for a while.

He got on the phone to me the minute he found it that night, when he and Dervla got back from post-Chelsea Flower Show drinks, dinner and more drinks. She always milked the last possible jolly out of an outing—as long as someone else was paying, of course.

'Is this all because of how I reacted to your haircut this morning?' he said, sounding truly bewildered. 'I know I was upset and maybe I did go over the top, but I had a really terrible hangover after doing all the deliveries, and with Dervla turning up unannounced as well, it was just the end. I'll get used to your hair, Melia, and I promise I won't say another word about it while it grows back, so stop being silly and come home. Please?'

'It's not just the hair, Ed,' I said.

My heart had softened—or rather, weakened— a little when I heard the sincere distress in his voice, but then I remembered that horrible list and it hardened right up again. And his continued arrogant assumption that I would be growing my hair back made it harder still.

'Look, I know Mummy's a pain . . .' he

continued.

'It's not about her either,' I snapped, 'although she doesn't help. I just need some time to think about how things stand between us these days, and if you can't figure out what the issues might be, Ed, then I suggest you need to do some thinking too.'

He was silent for a moment.

'You will come back, won't you, Melia?' he said eventually, in a tiny little terrified voice I'd never heard before—although it did occur to me that his bitch of a mother might have heard it when she had dropped him off at boarding school, aged six.

'I don't know, Ed,' I said, realizing in that moment that I really didn't know the answer to that question. 'I'm too confused to know anything right now. Like I said, I need to do some thinking and, when I have, I'll be in touch.'

'Where can I get hold of you, in the time being, if I need you?' he asked, sounding shattered.

'On my mobile,' I said firmly. 'But please don't hassle me. I really do need some space. Goodbye, Ed.'

And I hung up. My phone rang about two minutes later and several times after that, but each time I saw it was him and didn't answer. Shortly after the last call it bleeped that I had a text.

It said: 'He you are staying with lili foot bother coming back.'

I puzzled over it for a moment and then figured it out. What he was trying to say was, 'If you are staying with Kiki don't bother coming back.'

Ed never had mastered predictive text.

*   *   *

267

Living with Kiki was a bit like being in a student flat, I decided, but cleaner. The place was spotless now she had her housekeeper and very nice to be in. Apart from some scary moments of near panic when I was in the bath—there was something about being alone in there that made the anxiety well up—I seemed to spend most of my time laughing.

Kiki made me go out with her practically every night, which was exactly the distraction I needed—not to mention great for business—and on the few evenings we did stay in she usually ended up inviting people over.

But jolly fun though it all was, between going out every night and working long and taxing hours every day with the needy neurotics who were my clients, it was pretty exhausting and, by the weekend, I was always happy to head down to the cottage for a break.

Communicating only by text, at his behest—he was now officially too angry to speak to me—Ed and I had established that for the time being Winchelsea would be mine to use. As he had put it: 'I am going to France. You are welcome to it.'

It's hard to tell the tone of a text, but I had a strong feeling that one wasn't very warm.

Kiki had threatened to come down there with me a couple of times, but I think she could see it made sense for us to have regular breaks from each other, now we were together five days and nights a week.

I also suspected she didn't want to come without Ollie—and he spent every possible weekend at home in London with Sonny these days, holed up in his flat for the entire forty-eight hours, according to Kiki, who was monitoring their relationship like Jane Goodall with some mating chimps. He had even taken to flying Sonny out to meet him if he had to travel over a weekend for work, she reported.

The funny thing was, though, that while even being alone in the bath could undo me in London, I actually started to enjoy being on my own in Winchelsea. On my first solo weekend there, I had made the strange discovery that you can feel less lonely when you are entirely alone than when you are sitting on your own while someone else is nearby in a room with the door closed.

And if I did start to feel isolated, I would go and see Hermione. As the weeks after I'd walked out on Ed went by, her friendship became as important to me down there as Kiki's was in London.

'Ah, you are beginning to appreciate the difference between loneliness and solitude,' she said, when I told her my discovery one evening, when we were enjoying Campari and sodas on my new terrace—old stone slabs beautifully laid by Sonny, who still worked for us when his new travel schedule allowed.

'That's a very good thing to understand,' she continued. 'I've had nearly twenty years to study it, since my last husband died, and while having it forced upon you like that is hard, I have learned to relish it in a strange way. I really wouldn't like to live with anyone now, even if it were offered.'

'How many husbands have you had so far?' I asked, feeling a bit cheeky, but really wanting to know.

It was the most personal question I had ever asked her, but we'd spent the whole afternoon together weeding her garden and I felt I could.

'Four,' she said, her blue eyes shining. 'Or five. I married one of them twice.'

I raised my glass to her. 'Good going, Hermione,' I said, grinning.

'And how many husbands do you think you might have, Amelia?' she asked me.

I laughed with surprise. She really had me there. I hadn't told her anything that had been going on with me and Ed, but she'd clearly worked it out. 'So you've guessed that Ed and I are having a little time apart, then?' I said.

'Yes,' she said. 'And I wasn't surprised really, after that time your amusing friends came down. You didn't seem like a married woman that afternoon. So was it your decision?'

I nodded, a long sigh escaping unconsciously.

'Do you want to talk about it?' she said. 'Is there a particular reason?'

'There are lots of small reasons,' I said. 'Ed is very eccentric, as you've probably worked out, and that is a large part of what I have always loved about him, but recently it's all got much more extreme. He leaves me on my own too much. He works too much. He drinks too much. He's a snob. And he can be very, very selfish.'

As I listed Ed's failings, I felt myself welling up. Hermione reached over and took my hand. I turned and looked at her.

'He made us have separate bedrooms,' I said.

'That's no good,' said Hermione, patting my hand. 'Separate bedrooms are very bad for a marriage unless it's really essential—one of my

270

chaps snored like a dinosaur—and too much spent time apart can unglue even a good marriage very quickly. I lost at least two of my husbands that way.'

Although I was fighting tears, I had to smile. Then something about her sharing such confidences made me want to tell her more about my own situation.

'There was something else, with Ed,' I said tentatively. I was embarrassed to tell anyone about it, but it was so weird I needed another opinion.

'I found a list in his study,' I continued, slowly. 'I wasn't prying, I was looking for something I needed for the accountant, and in the back of a filing cabinet I came across a list of pros and cons he'd made fifteen years ago about whether to marry me or not.'

Once I'd told her about the devastating discovery it all came tumbling out. 'I was so hurt, Hermione,' I said. 'I thought he asked me to marry him because he loved me, I didn't realize it was some kind of business deal to weigh up, like an employment contract. It was horrible.'

'Oh dear,' said Hermione. 'That was an unfortunate thing to find. Very hurtful.'

'He said I was "suburban", that I had "dreadful parents",' I said, my indignation rising as I ticked the insults off on my fingers. 'And you should meet *his* mother—she's a real piece of work. He'd even asked her opinion about me—"not keen" apparently—and she hadn't even met me then! Probably because of "no family money", which was another reason not to marry me. He said I'd been to a rubbish school, that I was unsophisticated . . .'

'That does all seem unkind,' said Hermione,

271

stopping me in mid-flow, 'but what did he say in the pros column?'

I looked at her. I wasn't sure she was reacting with the outrage I was expecting.

'Well, yes, he did say some nice things in that . . . He said I had a good head for alcohol and beautiful hair,' I snorted with contempt, holding up the ends of my chopped-off bob and pulling a face.

'But I take it the pros list was the longer one?' said Hermione.

I looked at her. She really didn't seem to be as entirely horrified by the whole thing as I had assumed. I was a bit put out.

'Well, yes,' I said. 'But it was still a terrible thing to do . . .'

'Yes,' said Hermione, nodding like an old sage. 'Terrible. Men can be very crass when they are overwhelmed by emotion. Especially those who have had to learn to control their feelings at brutal English boarding schools. Now, we need to talk about your raspberry canes . . .'

The deep and meaningful part of the conversation was clearly over—and after her slightly disappointing reaction to my revelation about the list, I realized I was ready for a break from it too. I nipped inside to get a shawl for Hermione and to make a plate of cheese, apples and grapes for us to share.

We stayed outside until quite late that night, grazing on the food, chatting companionably about nothing more personal than our gardens and those of the people who lived near us, and enjoying the late-evening light. It was getting towards the longest day and neither of us wanted to miss a moment of it.

After my earlier outburst I was relieved to keep things breezy and general, but underneath I was acutely aware that while she was the only person who knew about the pros and cons list, I hadn't told Hermione the underlying reason I had left Ed.

The stupid list was just the trigger really, I understood that now; the fundamental cause, I had come to accept on all my nights sitting alone in the cottage, was his intransigent attitude to my desire to have children. And I hadn't told anyone that. Not even Ed. Not even my own mother. As far as she was concerned, I was just staying with Kiki 'for fun', while Ed was on a particularly long trip to France.

Kiki knew more than anyone, but I hadn't been specific to her, and if she suspected the baby issue was the real reason I had left Ed, she had been sensitive enough not to bring it up, which I was very grateful for. It was such a raw subject I could hardly bear to acknowledge it to myself, let alone talk about it with someone else.

Finally, after it had fallen properly dark, Hermione announced she was going to go in.

'Don't be sad down here, Amelia,' she said, patting my hand again, 'unless you want to be, of course. There's nothing wrong with a bit of sadness now and again, it's necessary really— *bonjour tristesse* and all that—but if you ever need someone to talk to, you know I'm next door.'

'Thank you,' I said. 'That means a lot—but before you go, Hermione, can I ask you a question?'

She nodded and I took a deep breath. 'I don't want to be rude, but do you know you have some

273

rather long white hairs on your chin? I could pluck them out for you, if you would Eke me to . . .'

I was a bit nervous how she might react, but I needn't have been. She roared with laughter.

'Oh, you lovely brave girl. Please! Take them out. I know they're there and it's mortifying, but when I try to pull them out I just can't make the tweezers work. My fingers aren't up to that kind of fine movement any more, and I don't have anyone I can ask to do it. I refuse to have one of those humiliating carers they're always trying to send me . . .'

'Stay there,' I said, and ran inside to get my tweezers. Within a few moments I had the lot out and Hermione was admiring herself in the magnifying side of my mirror. She gave me a very warm hug and I walked her home through Checkpoint Charlie.

22

Sitting at the table in Kiki's kitchen one morning, looking back through my diary, totting up how many days' work I had done for a particularly demanding client, I realized with a lurch that it was now exactly six weeks since I'd left Ed.

I was amazed. The time had flown by in a whirl of parties and dinners and work and weekends, but at the same time it also seemed strangely like a dream that I'd ever lived in Mount Street with him. Fifteen years of my life—nearly half of it— seemed to have evaporated into thin air.

I had all my post forwarded to Kiki's place from

there, but my bank statements were now officially addressed to her flat, which had seemed a very significant move. When I asked her if it was OK to do that or whether she would rather I got a place of my own, she had looked horrified.

'Aren't you having a good time here?' she had asked, grabbing both my hands in hers and looking earnestly up into my face. 'Don't go, Amelia! I love having you here.'

So I stayed, but I found I missed Ed in all kinds of ways, particularly his quirky little remarks. We had all those years of ongoing jokes between us, and just one word from him in the right context could make me laugh until my face hurt. Then I'd remember it again at odd times and find I was laughing as I walked down the street, or queued to pay in the John Lewis food hall.

I also missed the more serious conversations we had over dinner. He was obsessed with international affairs and read the paper every day—the way Kiki was supposed to—and was always incredibly well informed about what was going on in the world. Sometimes I used to think it was like having dinner with Jeremy Paxman, or John Humphrys—though Ed was more handsome and better dressed.

It was also strange not going to all the restaurants I was so used to. I was really craving the crayfish salad at the Wolseley, but I did my very best to avoid that part of London, even shifting my hair appointments to the other branch of John Frieda, north of Oxford Circus.

Anything between the area bound by Piccadilly, Park Lane, Oxford Street and Regent Street was out of bounds, because that was his patch.

Bumping into him there would have been too awful, but even walking down the streets where I had lived since I was twenty-one was too much to bear. I had a personal relationship with every paving stone in Mayfair.

I had forced myself to go over to the flat one morning when I knew he was still away in France so I could pick up some more stuff and had found it almost unbearably painful. Before my brain could stop them, my feet had walked me into his bedroom. I needed to feel near Ed.

Mr Bun was sitting in his usual place on the pillow, and I sat down on the edge of the bed and picked him up. He was starting to look very old and faded, I realized, not having seen him for a while, which wasn't really surprising, he was over thirty-five years old.

Not for the first time, I wondered whether it was quite normal for a grown man to be so attached to a small bundle of plush and stuffing, but then I thought, at least it didn't make any emotional demands in return. I sighed, gave the toy elephant a little hug and put him back.

'Look after him for me,' I said, my eyes filling with tears. Then I opened the wardrobe and stroked Ed's lovely shirts, hanging in their perfectly laundered row. Clearly he was managing to stay on top of all that without me, I realized with a pang. I'd organized it for him for years and it made me feel a bit redundant that he could do it on his own after all. I knew his mother wouldn't be helping him.

I took out one of my favourites, a wide pink and white stripe from Turnbull & Asser which Ed considered his 'lucky' shirt. He always wore it when he had an important meeting, or when we were having a celebration. I buried my face into the soft cotton and for a moment I thought about taking it away with me, but forced myself to put it back in the wardrobe.

I left the flat feeling absolutely shattered but, despite all that, I was still resolute I wasn't ready to go back there yet. Dervla was still in residence, for one thing—she'd gone to France with him, but I knew she was coming back—and I suspected my absence would make her stay on longer than usual.

But most of all, I wanted Ed to make an effort to bring me back. Since that last phone call when I'd first left, he'd made none. Any texts we'd exchanged had been purely pragmatic. He clearly thought all the blame for the situation lay with me, and I wanted to give him as much time as he needed to think that through. I needed him to take some responsibility for the problems that had developed between us.

And I suppose, in my way, I was starting to realize that, when it came to something so important, I could be as stubborn as him.

*　　　*　　　*

Really, I should have known better than to go to the Wolseley the following Tuesday night with Kiki and a gang of her sillier pals. We'd been to a private view at a gallery in Jermyn Street, so it did seem the obvious place and I could hardly protest to a group of people I hardly knew that it was currently off limits for me.

And as we bundled out of the gallery at quarter to nine on an unusually warm London summer

277

night, taking the risk of going to what had been one of Ed and my most regular haunts seemed more attractive than going home on my own, especially as I thought Ed was still in France. I found this particular group of Kiki's friends almost too squeally to bear, but at that point in my life any distraction was better than none—or so I thought.

I saw him the moment I walked in, installed on a banquette just opposite the entrance. He was sitting with Dervla, some pickled old chap with skin the colour of stewed tea—clearly her latest target—and Solitaire.

That was the only name for her. She was wearing a plunging halterneck dress, had black hair right down to her bottom and looked exactly like Jane Seymour in *Live and Let Die*—always his favourite Bond girl, after Honor Blackman in *Goldfinger* and Ursula Andress in *Dr No*. The length of her hair making up for it not being blonde. As I froze, Kiki spotted them too, and at the same moment, Dervla saw me. Trust her to be checking out who was coming in. Ed was clearly too rapt in conversation with Solitaire to notice.

'Shit,' said Kiki. 'It didn't take him long. Who's the drag queen?'

In my shock, I couldn't move my gaze away quickly enough, and Dervla and I locked eyes. But she didn't wave at me, just tapped Ed on the arm—and gestured towards the entrance with her head.

I was out of there before I could see his reaction. I ran out on to the street and jumped straight into a taxi which had just dropped someone off outside the restaurant. I heard Kiki calling out to me as I slammed the cab door, but I just ignored her and asked the taxi driver to take me to Holland Park—fast.

I was practically hyperventilating, I was so shocked. I had dreaded running into Ed in any circumstances, but it had never occurred to me that I might see him with another woman. The minute the cab pulled off, the tears came with such force, I was almost frightened, but I couldn't stop them.

I could see the taxi driver looking at me nervously in his rear-view mirror.

'Are you all right, love?' he said, probably worried I was going to vomit all over his interior.

I just put a hand up and shook my head, to indicate that I couldn't speak, and then proceeded to howl all the way back to the flat. So this is what real grief feels like, I thought to myself, even while I was doing it. It hurt so much. I'd had no idea. It was like falling off a cliff.

*   *   *

When I woke up the next morning my throat was raw from wailing, and when I stumbled to the bathroom mirror I looked like some kind of frog, my eyes were so swollen. Grief was not a pretty thing, I reflected, as I splashed cold water on my face, almost as unpleasant to look at as it was to experience.

Still really wobbly, but feeling strangely detoxed, I checked my phone, half expecting there to be a message from Ed. There wasn't, but there were several Kiki had sent the night before, telling me to come back to the Wolseley and face the drag

279

queen out.

'She's a collagen car crash, darls,' her message said. 'Banana lips and Botox to the max. Zero class. And she holds her cutlery like pencils. I bet Ed hates that.'

I smiled weakly. Ed practically had to leave a restaurant if he saw someone eating with their knife and fork pincered between their thumbs and forefingers. It must have been their first date, I thought bitterly. She'd never get a second one doing that.

Kiki appeared when I was in the kitchen staring vacantly out of the window at the garden and holding a cup of forgotten coffee.

'Are you all right, Amelia?' she said, giving me a hug. 'No, you're not, I can see that. But really, she was such a slapper. Did you get my messages?'

'I got them this morning,' I said. 'It doesn't really matter what she was like, it was just such a shock that she was female. I know he's welcome to go out to dinner with whoever he likes, but I really hadn't expected him to start seeing other women, so it was a terrible combined shock of seeing him for the first time since I left and her being there.'

'Poor you,' said Kiki, giving me another hug.

It was a favourite saying of hers and one that I found surprisingly comforting. Sometimes that was all you needed to hear. Not an in-depth study of your situation followed by an ear-bashing of bossy advice, but just an acknowledgement that you had a right to feel sad at that moment.

Kiki may have presented herself to the world as a frivolous fluffbunny in high heels and pink toenail varnish who thought a party was the answer to all problems, but I had come to understand that

280

she was actually a lot more emotionally intelligent than most people I knew. In fact, the only person I knew with greater insight was Hermione.

That morning, though, parties were, as usual, at the forefront of Kiki's mind.

'I know what you need,' she said, as we sat down to have breakfast together in her garden. She'd hired Sonny to fix it up, and it was already looking wonderful, helped by the fact that her budget stretched to fully grown plants from Petersham Nurseries which looked as though they had already been there for years from the day they were put in.

We were sitting at a lovely old metal garden table—also from Petersham—beneath an arbour of fully flowering jasmine, with the July sunshine streaming down around us.

'What do I need, oh, wise woman?' I asked.

'A party,' she said.

'Really?' I said, not very enthusiastically. 'Another drinks party?'

'No, a dinner party, but we'll make it a super fun one.' She leaned towards me excitedly. 'We'll have a mystery-guest dinner—I'll invite everyone and I won't tell you who's coming—and we'll make it a games night. That's always a good laugh.'

I couldn't see any harm in it.

*   *   *

Kiki and I had great fun getting the dinner party organized, and she was absolutely right: it did take my mind off what had happened with Ed. I was doing all the cooking—not Kiki's strong point— and I had a lot of sport while I planned the menu, trying to trick her into telling me who was coming.

'Any vegans?' I asked, as we sat at the dining table one rare night in, surrounded by cookery books. She shook her head. 'Vegetarians?'

'One,' said Kiki. 'But it eats fish.'

'You're not even telling me if it's a male vegetarian or a female vegetarian?'

'Nope,' said Kiki. 'No clues.'

'Anyone kosher, or halal? Macrobiotic? Any dairy or wheat allergies? Anyone avoiding carbs?'

'One fishetarian, that's all I'm telling you.'

'Any teetotallers?' I asked, marking the page for Nigella's gin and tonic jelly recipe. That was always a winner.

'Absolutely not,' said Kiki, laughing. 'But I think there might be a couple of peppermint teas coming along.'

'OK,' I said, picking up my clipboard, which I had got out entirely to torture Kiki. 'I'll add that to my shopping list.'

My curiosity about the guestlist—we were expecting six; that was all she would tell me—was piqued even more on the morning of the dinner, when four beautiful bouquets arrived for us, one after the other.

'Ah,' said Kiki, reading the cards and chuckling. 'I have them all so well trained. So much better to send flowers on the morning, rather than turning up with them when the hostess is running around greeting people and getting drinks.'

I grabbed the cards from her and found they were all signed with code names—unless Kiki really knew people called Shrek, Princess Fiona, Discount Diva, Dr Beat, Secret Squirrel and Amadeus, which wouldn't have surprised me.

By seven o'clock on the big night, I was actually

feeling quite nervous. The food was all ready to go, Kiki had organized the drinks, and I'd had my hair done. I just wasn't sure what to wear.

I popped my head around the door of Planet Kiki. She was sitting at her dressing table in fuchsia-pink see-through knickers and nothing else, sticking on false eyelashes and singing along to Peggy Lee.

'Is that all there is?' warbled Kiki.

'What are you wearing tonight?' I asked her. 'Apart from a smile and tart's pants?'

'That dress,' said Kiki, pointing over her shoulder at the rail I'd had put on the outside of the wardrobe for her to air clothes before putting them away.

My heart sank. The most exquisite dress was hanging there, made of gorgeous frothy primrose-yellow chiffon, strapless, with a black velvet bow tied under the bust.

'Wow,' I said, going over to admire it. 'That looks like some kind of baby-doll nightie Natalie Wood would have worn. It's gorgeous. So you're really going glam, then? I was going to wear my jeans.'

'No jeans tonight,' said Kiki, looking at me in the mirror with one open eye. 'Why don't you get properly dolled up for once?'

'I don't have anything glamorous,' I said, feeling a bit wretched. 'That's why I always wear my jeans, with different tops.'

'I have noticed,' she said, standing up and walking over to me, already wearing towering black velvet shoes. Christian Louboutins—I could tell now.

'Actually, I think you should just wear what you

have on,' I said. 'That would make it a night to remember.'

'Not such a bad idea,' said Kiki, putting one hand behind her head and copping a glamour-model pose before reaching up for her dress and slipping it on with the insouciance with which I pulled on my jogging pants.

She turned and looked at herself once in the big mirror, and that was it, Kiki was dressed.

'Now,' she said, 'what are we going to put Amelia in?'

She threw open her wardrobe doors, and I marvelled at the treasure within. Kiki had such beautiful clothes and, now she looked after them, it was like being on Harvey Nichols' first floor, with the world's best vintage shops thrown in.

She rifled through the rails, pulling out various wisps of silk, lace and satin, but it was clear that nothing of hers was going to fit me. It wasn't that I was fat, we were just built to completely different scales, and my shoulders would have burst out of Kiki's tiny dresses.

'Let's go and look at your things,' she said. 'I should have ignored your protests and bought you that Lanvin dress in Dover Street when we had our shopping day.'

'Oh!' I said. 'I'd forgotten—I bought one that looked very like it in Zara, ages ago. I've never worn it.'

So I put on my backless black dress with the high heels Kiki had given me the night of her drinks party, and I was quite astonished at the result. The haircut really made all the difference. Then Kiki insisted on doing my make-up—much more than I normally wore—lent me a pair of long

284

gold drop earrings, and the transformation was complete.

I had never looked so good in my life, I thought as I stared at myself in Kiki's huge mirror. And Ed would have hated every bit of it.

*   *   *

The first guests to turn up were Oliver and Sonny.

'Well, this is a surprise,' I said, sarcastically to Kiki. 'What a mystery this is turning out to be. Let me guess—Princess Fiona and Shrek?'

She just giggled.

The two of them were such a unit now, it was quite hilarious. Oliver had to be close to Sonny at all times, preferably touching him, if not actually sitting on him. Sonny just smiled his gentle smile and looked at him indulgently. It was like watching a daddy lion and a particularly cheeky cub.

The only disappointing thing about their relationship, as far as I was concerned, was that Sonny had decided to move to London to live with Oliver and had resigned from being my gardener and Hermione's. He'd found a replacement for us, who seemed nice enough, but it wasn't the same.

'Fuck me,' said Oliver, when he saw me. 'Well, don't actually, but you do look amazing, Amelia. You look really sexy. It's mostly the hair, of course. God, I'm good. I amaze myself sometimes.'

'You look beautiful,' said Sonny, giving me a hug that made me blush. 'And so do you,' he said to Kiki moving over to hug her. I caught her eye and she fanned herself theatrically behind his back.

We had often discussed it, but even now we

knew Sonny was gay—not to mention in a serious relationship with one of our best friends—he could still reduce us both to quivering heaps of rampant hormones.

'I've decided, Ollie,' said Kiki, as we sat in the drawing room, drinking our first glass of champagne, waiting for the other mystery guests to arrive, 'that as a service to society, you're going to have to lend Sonny out to rescue failing marriages. He wouldn't actually have to do the deed with anyone, he'd just stand near them for a bit and their sex lives would be magically restored.'

'Piss off,' said Oliver, putting both arms round Sonny's neck. 'He's mine.'

The next two guests to arrive were a bit more mysterious, because I hadn't met them before. But I had heard so much about Dan and Connor—old friends of Kiki's from New York—that the effect was somewhat diminished. She often made me read their emails because they were so funny, so I felt as though I already knew them. They accounted for Discount Diva and Dr Beat.

But the mystery level really cranked up when Charles Dowdent arrived—the mystery being why anyone would want him at their dinner party.

'Amadeus?' I said to her in the kitchen. It was just the kind of unwitty pretentious code name he would choose.

She nodded.

'Whatever did you invite him for?' I asked her.

'I think he's fun,' said Kiki. 'He's so brilliantly indiscreet about his clients.'

Sometimes, I thought, she had very poor taste in people.

'So, let me see,' I said. 'We've got Amadeus,

Princess Fiona, Shrek, Discount Diva, Dr Beat—so that just leaves Secret Squirrel . . .'

Kiki nodded again, grinning, and disappeared back to our guests.

The doorbell rang while I was making the rouille for my bouillabaisse. I had designed the whole menu round the fishetarian, who I now realized was Charles bloody Dowdent—if I'd known I would have made beef Wellington and given him some fish fingers—and when I went back into the drawing room Secret Squirrel was installed and happily chatting to Sonny.

It was Joseph.

23

'Am I a reality-TV star?' said Oliver.

'No!' we all shouted.

'Am I a man?' asked Dan.

'No!' we yelled.

'Am I a man?' I asked. 'No!' everyone screamed.

We were playing 'names', or 'foreheads', or whatever you call it when you stick a Post-It note to everyone's head with a famous name written on it and they have to guess who they are one question at a time.

Round and round we went, the answers getting louder and louder as we got increasingly overexcited, each of us desperately trying to remember the information we'd gleaned so far.

'OK,' I said, a few turns later. 'I'm not a man, I am alive and I'm not a film star, which seems a shame.' I looked at everyone else's heads. 'Am I

Russian?' I asked.

'Yes!' they all said, which was not that surprising, because they all were too.

Kiki had put 'Rasputin' on Oliver's head. I'd seen it and put 'Anna Karenina' on Dan's head to continue the theme, and so it had gone on.

Sonny was 'Nureyev', Connor was 'Dr Zhivago'—which was funny, because he really was a doctor—Charles was 'Putin', Kiki was 'Catherine the Great' and Joseph, of course, was 'Stalin'.

I had no idea who I was, but Charles had put it there, so I expected it to be something dopey. I really wished he wasn't sitting next to me, but he'd jumped into that chair before Kiki had a chance to dictate her placement, so I was stuck with him.

After several more rounds I worked out I was Anna Kournikova.

'Well, you used to be, darling,' said Oliver, 'before I cut your stupid hair off.'

After that we played another game where you went round the table each saying a word which made grammatical and narrative sense following on from the last one but didn't finish the sentence. If you did finish a sentence you were out. It was much harder than you'd think, and Joseph was brilliant at it.

'Typical bloody lawyer,' said Kiki. 'Endless words, all of it bollocks. You're not charging us by the hour for this, are you, Joe?'

He stuck his tongue out at her in response, and I felt a strange little pang when I saw it. They seemed so comfortable with each other, I wondered for a moment whether there wasn't more between them than just a casual friendship. And although I knew it was completely unreasonable, I didn't like the idea of that at all.

It made me feel complicated in ways I didn't quite understand and didn't want to dwell on. I told myself not to be so stupid and switched my attention to the next game.

For that one we paired off into teams and had to take it in turns to guess the identity of the famous person whose name your partner had pulled out of a hat, from minimal clues. 'Big lips. Singer Rolling Stones . . .' 'British woman prime minister. Handbag . . .' That kind of thing.

You had to do as many as possible in sixty seconds, and it had us all completely hysterical. Kiki and Joseph won and congratulated themselves with extravagant high fives. I tried not to mind that—or how rubbish Charles and I had been. He didn't even get: 'Boy band. Stoke-on-Trent. Angels.' What an arse.

'OK,' said Kiki, after we'd all had a bit of a rest. 'I've got another game. Joseph, can you open another bottle? I just need to get some matches.'

Kiki disappeared out of the room, and Joseph went round the table topping up all our glasses. When he got to me he put one hand on my shoulder. My head snapped round to look up at him.

'More champagne, madame?' he said, bowing with mock formality, belied by the smile in his dark-blue eyes.

'Yes, another bottle or two would be lovely, thank you,' I said, hoping I wasn't blushing, but fairly sure I was.

He filled my glass and gave my shoulder an almost imperceptible squeeze before he took his hand away. Once again working on its own private

289

sat-nav system, my head swivelled to look at him as he moved on round the table.

His bottom looked particularly fine in the nicely wrecked old jeans he was wearing, I noticed, before I forced myself to look away, once again furious with myself that I couldn't just relax around him. One bloody kiss, twenty years before, and it seemed I was condemned to feel twitchy around him for the rest of my life.

It was like some kind of curse out of a Hans Christian Andersen story, and I was glad when Kiki reappeared to distract me a moment later, her hands full of restaurant matchboxes. She tipped them all out on to the table and gave us ten each.

'Are we playing cribbage?' asked Joseph.

'Shut up and listen,' said Kiki, smacking him on his upper arm, a limb which I couldn't help noticing looked tanned and attractive under the short sleeve of his pale-blue polo shirt.

'Now, has everyone got a full glass?' continued Kiki. 'OK, this is how you play. I'm going to think of something that I've never done, right? And if any you have ever done it, you have to give me a match each. OK?'

'I don't understand . . .' said Charles.

'Cribbage is great fun, you know . . .' said Joseph.

'Shut up, all of you!' said Kiki. 'We'll just start playing, and you'll work it out as we go along.' She thought for a moment. 'OK. I've never been to India,' she said.

'I have,' said Charles. 'Last time I was there, of course, was for Liz and Arun's wedding . . .'

'Oh, shut up,' said Oliver, chucking a match across the table to Kiki. 'And give her a fucking

290

match.'

I was still a bit confused. 'I haven't been to India,' I said dumbly. 'So do I give you a match or not?'

'Not,' said Kiki. 'You only give a match when you *have* done the thing that the other person says they *haven't* done. OK? Right, Joseph, your go.'

'I've never been to Ibiza,' he said. Oliver, Sonny, Dan, Connor, Kiki and Charles all gave him a match. 'Wow,' he said. 'I'm loaded. How about you, Amelia—got a match for me?'

I shook my head. 'I've never been there,' I said. 'Innocent as charged.'

It was Connor's go. 'I've never been to Scotland,' he said.

'I have!' I said excitedly, and gave him a match. Everyone else gave him one too.

'Ooooh,' said Connor. 'I'm rich in matches.'

'It doesn't just have to be places,' said Kiki. 'Think more laterally.'

'Um,' said Dan. 'I've never had a tooth filling. Does that work?'

'Perfect,' said Kiki, clapping her hands.

Oliver, Sonny, Joseph, Charles and I all gave him matches.

'I knew that would get me a good score with English people,' said Dan. He leaned across the table to Kiki. 'We're the dentally divine divas, baby.'

She bared her perfect white choppers at him.

It was my go next and my mind went blank. It seemed really easy when someone else was doing it, but now it was my turn I couldn't think of anything.

'I've never broken a bone,' I said, inspiration

suddenly striking. I held out my hand to Joseph. 'Hand it over, Renwick. I know you've broken both your wrists, because the tree you fell out of was in my parents' back garden.'

He grinned at me. 'Should I give her two?' he asked Kiki. 'One for each wrist?'

'No, smartarse,' she said. 'Just one.'

I did quite well with that one. Charles, Sonny and Connor all gave me matches too, with Charles going into way too much detail about how he had broken his ankle on a black ski run at St Moritz.

'Shame it wasn't your neck,' said Oliver.

Charles was next up for the game and came out with a typically lame one, saying he'd never been married—not very bright in that crowd. He only got matches from me and Joseph, who caught my eye as I passed my match to Charles.

'Although perhaps we should both only give half a match at the moment, eh, Amelia?' he said, smiling at me sadly. I nodded back slowly. He had a point.

Oliver was next and did quite well saying he'd never had a dog. Sonny had never seen *The Exorcist,* and I was the only other one who hadn't. Kiki said she'd never shoplifted anything, and I was shocked when everyone else gave her a match.

'Joseph Renwick!' I said. 'I'm going to tell my dad.'

'You'd better not,' he said. 'Your brother stole a Yorkie bar from the school tuckshop the same break-time I stole a Crunchie.'

On his turn, Joseph had never watched *Big Brother.* Connor had never been skiing, Dan had never been to a football match and I'd never been to a rave. Charles the arse had never lived North

292

of the Park or South of the River. Oliver had never been on a jet ski—and never fucking wanted to because they were for total fucking wankers. Sonny had never eaten sushi and Kiki had never passed her driving test.

Round and round we went, the stakes getting higher as we racked our brains for things we hadn't done but thought everyone else would have.

Joseph got matches from everyone except me for saying he'd never taken ecstasy, so on my next turn I took his lead and said I'd never taken cocaine. Every single one of them gave me a match. Kiki said she'd never taken heroin and got one match—from Charles. I thought it was quite brave of him and, on his next turn, he actually came up with a doozie.

'I've never had sex with a man,' he said.

Amid much whooping and hollering, we all— except Joseph—gave him a match. Oliver tried to give him all his, but Kiki wouldn't let him.

'Hang on a minute, Charlie,' she said, reaching over as if she were about to take her match back. 'Didn't you go to Oundle?'

Charles threw a cork at her.

'I've never had sex with more than four men at once,' said Oliver, who was next.

Kiki laughed so hard champagne came down her nose and Joseph had to smack her on the back until she recovered. Then Dan passed Oliver a match and we all fell about laughing.

'Kiki?' said Oliver, holding out his hand. 'Aren't you forgetting something? A little night in Ibiza?'

'It was only three!' she said. 'You little shit. And there were girls there too, so it doesn't count. Your go, Sonny.'

He looked thoughtful. 'I've never kissed a girl,' he said.

Kiki and I looked at each other with wide eyes and, before I realized what was happening, Kiki stood up and planted her mouth on his. She had both her hands firmly around his head, and it looked like she had her tongue stuck right down his throat.

Oliver was squealing. He was so outraged he couldn't get any words out.

'Get off him, you fucking slut!' he managed eventually, but Kiki had already finished.

'You have now,' she said, sitting back in her chair and smirking. 'Nice,' she said to me.

I was laughing so much I could hardly breathe.

Oliver had a disgusted look on his face. 'I'll have to get him fumigated,' he said, stroking Sonny's cheek. 'Oh, what the fuck, I'll do it myself.' He sat on Sonny's knee and kissed him for what seemed like several minutes. We all applauded.

'Right,' said Oliver, sitting back on his own chair and smiling happily at us all. 'Who's next?'

'Um, do I get any matches?' said Sonny plaintively.

'Ooh,' said Kiki. 'Tricky. What do you reckon, Joseph? You're the expert in international law.'

Joseph rubbed his chin and looked thoughtful. 'Interesting case,' he said, deliberately peering at us over his glasses. 'No precedents I can think of. So, as I understand it, the party of the first part had not at the time of his initial witnessed statement kissed a girl—is this correct, Mr Sonny?' Sonny nodded. 'Well, then, I think the matches should be assigned according to that statement and the outcome should not be influenced by

294

events further and subsequent to it.'

'So do I give him a fucking match, or not, Yoda?' said Oliver.

'If you have kissed a girl, give him a match,' said Joseph, throwing one across to Sonny.

Charles, Dan—and Kiki—also gave Sonny a match each. Then so did Oliver.

Kiki squeaked like a parrot. Oliver shrugged.

'I was thirteen at the time,' he said. 'Bowie kissed girls so I thought I'd better try it. Didn't like it . . .'

After that the game continued to crank up to new levels of outrage.

Joseph said he'd never rimmed anyone—a term which had to be explained to me—and got matches from everyone except me. Connor said he'd never slept with anyone over forty-nine and got matches from Kiki and Charles—and a play slap from Dan, who was fifty on his next birthday.

Dan said he had never had sex more than six times in twenty-four hours with the same person and got matches from Sonny and Oliver, who was punching the air in triumph, shouting: 'Eeeee-zee-y!'

Then Joseph casually tossed a match over to him, which momentarily shut Oliver up.

'Nice work, straight boy,' he said after a moment, in tones of bald admiration. 'It's always the brainy ones you have to watch. Half their IQ is embedded in their cocks.'

'Oh, do give it a rest, Ollie,' said Kiki. 'That was almost too vulgar even for me.'

Ollie waggled his tongue at her in a supremely obscene gesture. Then it was my turn.

'I've never had an orgasm,' I said.

I didn't think twice before I said it. Everyone else was being so outrageously frank, and it didn't seem a big deal to me, but the table went completely silent. I'd thought it was brilliant, but suddenly no one was laughing.

'What?' I said, bewildered.

'Amelia!' said Kiki, looking horrified. 'Are you serious?'

I shrugged. It was true, I hadn't.

'I told you she was fucking frigid,' said Oliver triumphantly, trying to grab a match from Kiki's pile. 'I want a bonus match.'

'Come on,' I said, still delighted with my triumph. 'Give me your matches then.'

And then, seeming to act as one, they each gave me all of their matches. This time Kiki didn't intervene. In fact, she stood up, got the large box of kitchen matches out of the drawer next to the cooker and tipped them all out on to my pile too.

'Look!' I cried, picking up handfuls of matches from my huge cache and letting them fall back on to the table. 'I'm the Abramovich of matches. I've won! I've won! I've so won!'

Still, there was silence. I looked at Kiki.

'Have you?' she said quietly.

*   *   *

After that, the dinner party broke up pretty quickly. Dan and Connor were first to leave, professing jet lag, closely followed by Sonny and Oliver, who was claiming they had 'shag lag'.

There was the usual ruckus, banter and kissy kissy as they said goodbye, and while everyone else seemed to be back on a high from all the laughs we'd had, I was feeling lower with every passing moment.

They'd all been so outrageous it hadn't seemed a big deal to say what I had at the time. But now humiliation was gathering momentum fast. What had I been thinking to reveal something so personal?

Leaving Joseph and Charles to drink yet more champagne with Kiki in the drawing room, I went out to the kitchen and started loading the dishwasher, hoping they would soon leave and I wouldn't have to see them again that night. Possibly ever.

I was just putting the dinner plates into the lower rack when Charles came in. I carried on stacking, hoping he would take whatever he'd come for and piss off. Instead, he came over and pressed himself against me while I was bending over.

I stood up sharply.

'What are you doing?' I said, turning round and nearly falling backwards over the open door of the dishwasher as I tried to get away from him. He grabbed me as I stumbled and didn't let go.

Then, with one movement, he turned me round so my back was pushed uncomfortably against the kitchen worktop. His horrible orange face was millimetres away from mine and he was rubbing himself against me lower down as he put his mouth right on to my ear.

'I can help with that problem of yours, you know,' he said, wetting my ear with his hot breath. 'I am an artist of cunnilingus. You know what they call me, don't you? The fastest tongue in SW1.' He flicked it in and out of my ear to make his point.

'Will you get off me!' I protested, but he didn't. Instead his hand found its way under my dress and was advancing fast on my left breast while his mouth was clearly on its way over to mine.

I took my chance and yelled. 'KIKI! HELP!'

I heard footsteps running into the kitchen, but it wasn't Kiki—it was Joseph.

'Leave her alone!' he shouted at Charles. 'Let go of her.'

He pulled Charles off me, pushing him away so hard he fell against the kitchen table and sprawled on to the floor.

'Fuck off, sleazebag,' yelled Joseph at him. 'Get out of here, before I kick you out.'

Then he put one arm gently around my shoulder, delicately pulling my dress over my exposed breast with his other hand. I started crying and buried my face in his shoulder.

'What on earth is going on?' said Kiki, appearing in the doorway. 'I was in the loo and I heard all this shouting.'

'That creep was attacking Amelia,' said Joseph. 'Can you throw him out please, before I do him some serious damage?'

I turned my head just enough to see Kiki give Charles a sharp kick in the backside with her Louboutin-clad foot. 'Get up and get out,' she said and, once he was standing, she literally pushed him out of the kitchen.

'Goodbye and good riddance!' I heard her shout, and then the front door slammed. I buried my face in Joseph's warm shoulder again, while he stroked my hair and made soothing noises.

Kiki's shoes click-clacked back into the kitchen, but she didn't speak and neither did Joseph. I felt him move his head—it seemed like he was nodding—and her shoes click-clacked off again down the hall parquet. Then I heard her bedroom door close, and Joseph and I were alone.

I just stood there taking shaky breaths and holding on to him as though he were a life-raft, then I realized I needed some water—and fast. I pulled away and went to the sink, turning the tap on full, washing my face—and ear—in the running water.

'Sorry,' I said to Joseph. 'I had to wash him off me . . .'

He nodded and handed me a tea towel. I dried my face and realized that I really wanted his arms around me again, as soon as possible. I moved towards him.

'Let's get out of here,' he said.

He led me into the drawing room and, without speaking, we just lay down together on one of the sofas. And somehow it seemed completely natural for us to lie there quietly with our arms wrapped around each other. It flashed through my head that I was still a married woman and what I was doing amounted to something close to adultery, but I didn't care.

I was still in such a state of shock about what had just happened in the kitchen—and not forgetting my embarrassing revelation during the game earlier—that petty reality and all its rules seemed to be on hold. I existed only in that moment and didn't want to be anywhere but safe in Joseph's muscular arms.

That state of suspended time continued when, after a while, Joseph put his hands around my face and gazed deep into my eyes. He traced the outline of my mouth delicately with his forefinger, then ran the tip of it back and forth along my lips.

'I really want to kiss you,' he said, 'but I feel I should ask first.'

I replied by pulling his head towards mine, placing my lips on his and sliding my tongue slowly into his mouth. He kissed me back, softly at first and then harder, until I felt like nothing existed except his tongue entwining with mine.

It was just as good as it had been twenty years before, I thought, that night behind the rugby club at my brother's eighteenth-birthday party. And just like then, as Joseph kissed me, so tenderly, so deliciously, I felt something fire up inside me. It was like the gas lighting on the stove.

Whatever it was had clearly ignited in him too, and very quickly that gentle kiss turned into a wild thing. We were grabbing each other, rolling over so I was on top of him and then he was on top of me again, as our bodies bucked and pressed against one another.

Then he suddenly stopped and pushed himself up on his arms, looking down at me. I smiled when I realized he was still wearing his glasses and reached up to pull him down to me again, but he stopped me.

'I want to stay with you, Amelia,' he said. 'Can we go to your bedroom?'

*   *   *

From the moment he pulled my dress over my head and lowered me tenderly on to the bed, I felt as though every nerve ending in my body was on maximum alert.

As he smiled down at me, slowly pulling his polo shirt over his head and then unzipping his jeans, that knowing grin I had seen more than half my life suddenly made complete sense. In that moment I understood that above and beyond everything else—the intellect, the sporting prowess, the social confidence—Joseph Renwick was a profoundly sexual creature. And in his arms, I began to believe maybe I was too.

He took off his glasses and lay down beside me, kissing me luxuriously as his hands stroked lightly down my body as though he were surfing my curves, until one of them landed firmly between my legs.

'Well, you don't seem frigid to me,' he said, smiling wickedly into my eyes as he stroked his fingers along my smooth wetness.

Fixing his mouth on one of my nipples he carried on stroking me there, alternating the firm rhythm with dipping his fingers inside me and pushing hard, until my hips were rising from the bed and I was groaning quite loudly. Seeming satisfied with that result, he kissed me for a while longer, in that dizzying slow way of his, and then pulled away, winked at me and disappeared down the bed.

He teased me gently with the point of his tongue, then started to press more firmly, never breaking his rhythm, and it was as though he were gathering together all the elusive feelings that were humming away down there.

Losing all awareness of anything else, I began to feel them insistently rising up and, just at the point where they normally slipped away from me, Joseph put two fingers inside and started stroking me firmly in there at the same tempo his tongue was working on the outside.

That was when it happened. The tickly feelings which had been growing stronger gradually knitted together into a rope of deeper, more intense pressure which seemed to grow and grow, until suddenly it all exploded.

I heard myself let out a mighty groan, and I was thrashing around on the bed, my hips bucking up as I grabbed hold of his hair. Then I felt like I'd lost consciousness and was only aware of clamping my legs together and squeezing to capture the very last of those heavenly spasms.

As I returned to awareness, Joseph's head appeared next to mine and kissed me tenderly on the lips. I opened my eyes and let out a wobbly sigh.

'You owe me a match,' he said.

24

The next morning I sent a text to everyone I had an appointment with that day saying I would have to postpone it; Joseph rang in sick to LSE; and we spent the whole day in bed. I hardly left the bedroom, except to make cups of coffee—and to gather all the matches that were still scattered across the dining table and put them on Kiki's pillow.

I hadn't heard her get up or go out, let alone come back in and go out again, but she must have done, because around 3 p.m. she sent me a text: 'Gone away back Friday arvo. Housekeeper

cancelled. Have a matchless time. Love you K xxx.'
Moments later another one arrived: 'BTW present
for you in Planet Kiki.'

I went in there and found a rectangular box,
wrapped in her signature shade of bright pink, tied
up with a big pink and white spotted bow.

I took it into the bedroom and found Joseph
leaning back against the headboard with his arms
behind his head, smiling at me. He had the broad
shoulders and muscular chest of a man who had
played rugby from the age of eight and hadn't
stopped exercising since. It was a mighty fine sight.
My stomach—and parts lower—fluttered at the
sight of him.

'I hope it's chocolates,' he said. 'I need to keep
my energy up.'

I climbed back into bed and opened the present.
I wasn't sure what it was at first. It looked like
some weird kind of toy rabbit, made of bright-pink
latex, with a clear bit in the middle full of what
looked like jelly beans. Joseph started laughing.

'Oh, that Kiki,' he said. 'She's such a funny girl.
I hope she's put some bloody batteries in it . . .'

'What is it?' I said, checking it from all angles
and realizing it was decidedly phallic.

'Do you really not know?' said Joseph.

'I'm not sure . . .' I said, suspicions growing that
I had just been given my first sex toy.

'Give it to me,' said Joseph, with a look in his
eye I had come to know well, 'and I will be very
happy to show you.'

The next morning we both cancelled our lives
again. Kiki had clearly gone away specially to give
us this space—putting off the housekeeper was a
masterly touch—and we seized it. I had

discovered, in the thirty-six hours I had spent in Joseph's arms, that there was a whole slice of life I had been missing out on, and now I'd had a taste of it I was hungry for more—a lot more.

Joseph was hungry for some actual food.

'Feed me!' he said in a growly voice when I came back into the bedroom around midday with a plate of toast and Marmite. We'd finished off the dinner-party leftovers the day before, and there wasn't really anything else. Kiki and I didn't keep much in the fridge, apart from champagne, vodka and her facepacks.

'I feel like I've run the Grand National,' he said, 'several times, actually, and this thoroughbred needs more than a bit of manky old toast to keep him going.'

Without need for discussion it was clear neither of us wanted to burst our magic bubble by going out into the real world together, so I threw on some clothes and nipped out to the butcher's by myself. Steak—that was what he needed: man food.

We also needed some more condoms. We'd used the one Joseph had produced from his wallet, I'd found three lurking in the bottom of my washbag—no doubt left over from a trip to France with Ed, but I pushed that thought right out of my head—and I'd unearthed another two on a raid of Kiki's bathroom, but we had no more.

The irony of using the hated things with Joseph was not lost on me, but when he'd asked me, at the crucial first moment, if I would prefer it, I'd said yes. I had to. I'd stopped taking the Pill the day I walked out on Ed, as part of my general rebellion against his rules.

'I'm not on the Pill,' I told him, 'so much as I loathe those horrible stinky things, you'd better use one to be on the safe side.'

Joseph had looked at me with a strange expression on his face, a bit sad, combined with a hint of his more usual mischief. 'It's hell being a grown-up sometimes, isn't it?' he said, as he rolled the wretched thing on. 'If only we were foolish teenagers, we'd chuck the bloody condoms in the bin, I'd get you gloriously up the duff without another thought and we'd worry about the consequences later.'

I was so surprised I just stared at him, but before I could say anything, he was very much out of his head and back into his physical self, and after a couple of moments so, blissfully, was I.

*   *   *

As I practically skipped along Holland Park Avenue to Lidgate's—and the chemist's—that afternoon, I felt reborn, as though I had just discovered that the earth was round, water was wet and if you let go of something it generally fell to the floor.

I was sure I looked different and wondered if I had a giveaway Ready Brek glow. I was sure that anyone looking at me must know immediately I had recently been seriously rogered. Yes! I wanted to shout out to the world. Yes! Yes! Yes! And it was Joseph James Renwick what done it.

'Why did no one tell me?' I asked him thirty-five minutes later as we sat at Kiki's garden table eating medium rare fillet steaks, with a nice rocket salad, some sourdough bread and a bottle of very

305

superior Australian shiraz.

Buying that wine had been another act of pure rebellion but, in the circumstances, it had felt like the only thing to do. I was officially a brazen adulterous hussy, so I might as well drink forbidden New World wine as well.

The strange thing was that I didn't feel remotely guilty about either betrayal. Every time a thought along those lines drifted into my head, I just batted it away again. I felt drunk on sex, with the equivalent loss of responsibility.

'Tell you what?' said Joseph, chewing happily.

'All of it. Cunnilingus, G-spots, vibrators, how great orgasms are . . .'

'Don't you read women's magazines?' he said.

'Not that kind.'

'Well, aren't those the kind of things women talk to each other about? I thought vibrators and G-spots were major topics of girl talk.'

I thought for a while and realized that, until Kiki, I'd just never really had that kind of girlfriend. I'd grown up in such a supremely male household it was as though I hadn't ever learned how to be properly girlie. My one experience of student flat-sharing had been with an equally swotty and uncool girl and two blokes, and then I'd married Ed, who wasn't exactly in touch with his feminine side—or mine, I increasingly understood.

I did have my female friends, from school mostly, but we had never had that kind of intimate conversation. Even with Louise, I'd never talked about things like that. She was a bit of an old-fashioned goody-goody, like me, really. Or maybe they were all like that with other people, it occurred to me, but something inherently prudish

306

about me made them hold back in my company. Probably the same vibe that had made Oliver call me frigid.

I hadn't known how to do any of that stuff until Kiki had given me a crash course in frou-frou. She was, I suddenly realized, my first proper girlfriend—which explained something else too. I had always wondered, when Ed's increasing dislike of Kiki first began to make itself apparent, why I liked her so much and he was so anti, because normally we agreed about people. Now I understood: a close girlfriend of strong character could be a married man's biggest rival, more dangerous almost than another man. He had felt threatened by her—and he'd been right, really.

I looked across at Joseph, leaning back in his chair, steak consumed, holding his glass of wine, a smile of complete satisfaction on his handsome face. Even with two days of beard growth, he was a fine-looking specimen. Not as exquisitely boned as Ed, whose profile always made me think of First World War poets, but with the even features and square jaw that have universal appeal to women.

Sighing deeply, I pushed Ed firmly out of my mind again. He had no place in the erotic never-never land Joseph and I were inhabiting. Real life of any kind could not be allowed to intrude or I might finally start thinking of me and Joseph as the shameless fornicators we were.

I was still married to Ed, after all—and, as far as I knew, Joseph was still married to his wife— whoever she was. But enclosed in our sexual cocoon, we had pointedly shut all that out. We hadn't talked about anything at all to do with his former life in Washington, or mine with Ed. And it

307

was incredibly easy for us to do that, because we already had such a well-established shared history. We didn't need to get to know each other with tentative little questions and discoveries the way new lovers normally do.

I already knew that Joseph had been born in London and moved to Kent with his parents and his two older sisters when he was four. I knew he was an Aries; liked his steaks medium rare; thought *The Young Ones* was the funniest show that had ever been on television; weirdly, didn't like ice cream; and could put a dangerous spin on a cricket ball. And I strongly suspected that he still had a penchant for the music of U2 and the books of Ernest Hemingway.

So, somehow, it didn't matter that I didn't even know his wife's name, let alone why they had split up, or what he had meant by that strange answer he had given me months before at Kiki's drinks party, when I'd asked him if he had children. What was it he'd said? 'Two, or three. Maybe . . .'

It had been most odd, but at that moment I didn't want to know what he'd meant by it. All I wanted to know on a sunny Thursday afternoon in Kiki's garden was how soon I could get back into bed with him again. Which turned out not to be very long at all.

*   *   *

The next morning we both knew our stolen idyll had to end; we couldn't postpone real life any longer, but still it was hard to let go. We stood by the front door for ages with our arms locked around each other, trying to say goodbye. At one point the hug turned into a kiss and it seemed dangerously like we might end up back in bed, until I broke away and took some deep breaths to recover myself.

He put his finger under my chin and lifted it up, so I had to look at him.

'That was close,' he said, smiling broadly. 'I really don't want to leave you, Amelia, but this is not the last time we'll be together like this. I've waited twenty years to kiss you again and I'm not going to let you get away so easily this time.'

I gazed back at him. What he'd just said seemed significant in so many ways, I couldn't quite process it. I had been so determinedly living in the present in our sex bubble, it had never occurred to me to wonder how it might relate to the past or have an impact on the future.

His remark vaulted me so suddenly into a different mindset, I nearly invited him down to Winchelsea for the weekend, but immediately thought better of it.

Kiki's flat was neutral territory, but the cottage was somewhere I had once shared with Ed; indeed, he still owned it. Way too real. For the time being I absolutely needed to keep things suspended in this bubble of unreality, or it would all get impossibly confusing.

'When can I see you again?' he asked me.

'Next week?' I said vaguely, not ready to commit to anything beyond the next breath.

Joseph's eyes crinkled behind his glasses, and he started chuckling. 'Well, you better give me your phone number then . . .' he said.

I started laughing too. It seemed so mad. I was so at ease with this man who I'd known since I was

309

eleven years old and had just spent the best part of two days in bed with, but we didn't even have each other's phone numbers.

*   *   *

Kiki called me when I was on the train down to the cottage that afternoon.

'Mmmmm,' she said. 'A whole box of matches, was it?'

I giggled down the phone at her.

'So you had a good time with Mr Trouser Snake, then?' she continued.

'Yes, thanks,' I sighed. Just thinking about him made my newly discovered G-spot quiver. 'Quite marvellous, actually. And with Mr Love Bunny—thank you so much for him. But why did you call Joseph . . . what you just said?' I didn't want everyone on the train to hear me say 'Trouser Snake'.

'Well, Joseph's obviously a serious pants man,' said Kiki blithely. 'You just have to look at him to know that. Any man that confident has got to have it seriously going on down there. Am I not wrong?'

'You are most definitely not wrong.'

'Well, there you are then . . .'

And then she continued to tell me the explicit details of her own latest romantic adventure, a subject into which I felt I now had a much deeper insight.

*   *   *

Hermione was pleased to see me, as always, when I got to the cottage, and we spent a very pleasant

310

time walking around our gardens, her arm companionably linked through mine, admiring developments. A great bush of honeysuckle I didn't even know I had was in full bloom over my back wall, and it smelled heavenly.

'You're looking terribly well, Amelia dear,' she said, as we settled on to her terrace for our now customary Campari and soda sundowner.

'Am I?' I said, slightly too quickly.

Hermione was looking at me intently with those bright blue eyes of hers. They were set very deep within the folds of her wrinkled face, but the intelligence shone out of them. I was sure she had spotted my afterglow.

'Yes,' she said. 'You have been looking a little weighed down by care of late, but this evening you have your radiance back.'

Bingo! She knew. She was looking at me with the hint of a question on her face, one eyebrow slightly raised.

I grinned back at her. I couldn't help it. 'I, er, ran into an old boyfriend,' I said, and then just burst out laughing. Rather a girlish giggle.

She laughed too. A silvery tinkle of a laugh that told me I didn't need to be any more explicit. Hermione of the four husbands knew exactly what was going on.

I went back to the cottage from Hermione's place earlier than usual that evening, about seven thirty, because I'd hardly had any sleep the previous two nights with Joseph and desperately needed to catch up on my zeds. As I lurched slightly through Checkpoint Charlie, I realized I was starting to feel quite light-headed from it, especially with the Campari on top.

311

I went straight to bed and fell into a dead sleep, only to be woken in what seemed like the middle of the night by my mobile ringing. Feeling extremely disoriented, I answered it without checking who was calling, thinking it might be Joseph. It wasn't—it was Ed.

'Amelia?' he said, his voice very quiet and tentative.

My stomach turned over giddily. It was weeks since I'd heard Ed's voice, and it was so very familiar it made my heart surge in a peculiar way. I also felt a concurrent pang of extreme guilt about how I had spent the last couple of days. My heart felt as dizzy as my head.

'Are you there, Amelia?' he asked, when I didn't answer.

'Yes,' I croaked out. 'Sorry, Ed, I was asleep. I'm still half asleep.'

'I'm sorry I woke you, but I can't stand it any longer, Amelia. This has gone on long enough. We need to talk.'

I really couldn't think of anything to say. It was such a shock, and I was so sleep-fuddled I felt like a zombie.

'When do you want to do that?' I said, dully, still not able to think straight.

'In about ten minutes,' said Ed. 'I'm coming to see you.'

That woke me up.

'You're coming to see me now?' I said. 'In Winchelsea? In the middle of the night?'

'It's ten o clock,' said Ed.

I put my head in my hands and shook it. 'Why now?' I asked him.

'I got back from another trip to France today,

and the flat seems so desolate without you in it,' he said, sounding sincerely upset. 'I miss you so much, Amelia . . .'

What could I do? It was his house: I couldn't tell him not to come. Well, I could have, but I was so zonked out from lack of sleep—and other factors—I couldn't think straight enough to do something that drastic. And he sounded so sincerely upset, I didn't have the heart.

So I got up, put on my dressing gown and stumbled downstairs to make some strong coffee, hoping to get my brain half in gear before he arrived.

I hadn't even finished drinking it when he tapped on the back door. It was weird to have him knock, but somehow right in the circumstances. I opened it, and there he was, looking particularly dashing in a white linen shirt which showed off his suntan. He had a bottle of Krug in each hand and his most winsome smile on his face.

Before I knew what I was doing, I was hugging him. It was a completely automatic response to seeing someone who had been the most important person in my life for the last fifteen years after the longest separation we'd ever had.

His smell was so familiar, my body just seemed to melt against his, and he hugged me tight, kissing me repeatedly on my neck in a way I realized he always had but which I'd long ago stopped even noticing. He nibbled my ear and I felt something starting up inside me. Something sexual.

'Oh, Melia,' he said, a catch in his voice. 'I've missed you so much. I've been so lonely.'

Suddenly, hearing him speak, in that slightly self-pitying tone, snapped me back to reality. What

313

was going on? Just twelve hours earlier I'd been clinging on to Joseph at Kiki's door; now I was hugging Ed at mine. Or ours—whatever it was. I pulled away.

'Come in,' I said, consciously putting the kitchen table between us and picking up my mug of coffee, like a shield. I was worried that if Ed looked closely at me in that moment, he would know exactly what I had been up to.

Instead he was looking at me with rather pathetic puppy-dog eyes, which had a strangely hardening effect on my heart. I now deeply regretted giving him that confusing hug, but it was too late: he was coming round the table towards me, his arms open, clearly expecting some more. I put my hand up and backed away.

'I'm sorry, Ed,' I said. 'Just give me a bit of space here. I need to take all this in. I was asleep when you rang and I'm still in shock. Just let me be for a while.'

He looked extremely disappointed, mixed with a hint of irritation, presumably that it hadn't all immediately worked out exactly as he wanted it, but he quickly rallied himself.

'Well,' he said. 'I'm so happy to see you, Amelia, I'm going to open one of these bottles to celebrate.'

I let him busy himself getting glasses out while I sat at the table and finished my coffee, still trying to get my brain in gear. I clearly didn't do a very good job of it, because when he handed me a glass of Krug I took it and practically knocked it back in one. He quickly filled it up again.

'So,' I said, the champagne buzz almost audible in my ears. 'How come you've got in touch with me now? You've had nearly three months to do it and nothing—so why now?'

'As I told you, I got back from France again, and the flat feels so horribly empty, I really can't bear it. And then I had dinner tonight with all these happy couples, and it reminded me so painfully what we had. I miss you so much, Amelia. I had to come and talk to you immediately and try to sort this out. I was too angry and hurt to do it before, but now I realize we have to. We can't go on like this, or we really will split up, and neither of us wants that, do we?'

'Don't you have Dervla for company?' I asked him, deliberately changing tack, because I was intensely irritated by his assumptions about what I might want but didn't feel up to discussing it.

A strange look crossed his face. 'She's gone to stay, er, somewhere else,' he said.

He put his head back and ran a hand through his hair. As always, I thought how refined he looked in profile. He had such an elegant neck.

'Oh, I'm going to have to tell you sooner or later,' he said, sighing deeply and looking at me again. 'I've had a bit of a falling out with Mommy dearest.'

I said nothing, just raised my eyebrow as Hermione did when she knew there was more to be said.

'She was going to come to France with me on this last trip,' he continued, 'but at the last moment she had a subsequent and better invitation—something smart in Hampshire—so she didn't come with me. When I got back, I found that, while I was away, she had moved into your bedroom. She'd dumped all your things in the

315

spare room and just moved in. I'm afraid I lost my temper with her.'

I shook my head. It didn't surprise me; it was exactly the sort of thing I'd expect Dervla to do—but I was surprised that I didn't mind more.

'But you can't stop her staying in what is partly her flat, can you?' I said.

'No,' said Ed. 'She did remind me of that. In fact, she threatened to call her lawyers in, so I'm putting her up at Claridge's until she goes home. That's the only deal she would accept, and it's costing me a bloody fortune, but I can't have her in the flat any longer. I want you to come back, and I quite understand that you won't while she's there. She's been dreadful to you and it's time for her to let her claim on the flat go. I think I am going to try and buy her out of her share of it, for the sake of our marriage.'

I just looked at him, amazed—did he still think it was all about his mother?

'Ed,' I said gently, 'I can't seem to make you understand—this is not about your mother. As you well know, I have a truly dreadful father of my own, so dealing with psychotic parents is second nature to me. I can't pretend I love having Dervla to stay, but I can handle it for a few weeks each year—especially now I've got this place to escape to. She's not the overriding problem in our relationship, Ed. I moved out because of issues between us which have been building for a long time, and I'm really disappointed if you still haven't figured out what they are.'

'Well, I suppose you had better tell me, then,' he said, looking quite beaten.

He refilled both our glasses and I drained mine

316

again. Where the hell should I start? The horrible snobby list? The separate bedrooms? The rubbish sex? The general world-according-to-Ed lifestyle? Or the big one—the baby issue?

Ed stood up and opened the second bottle of champagne. I took a big gulp the moment my glass was full. He sat down next to me.

'Well?' he said.

I took a deep breath. 'We have separate bedrooms, Ed,' I began.

He looked incredulous. 'We've talked about that before,' he said, looking quite relieved, as though that was sorted. 'Is that such a big problem for you?'

'Yes . . .' I started.

'Well, we'll start sleeping together again. As I said before, it was only because I didn't want to disturb you coming to bed late, but now you're working for yourself, you don't have to get up so early anyway. We can start sharing a bed again immediately, I don't have a problem with that at all.'

He raised his glass and then clinked it against mine, smiling broadly as though it were a great joke to break his own rule about glass-clinking. I really wasn't in the mood for his Bertie Wooster snob humour.

'That's not the only thing, Ed,' I said, becoming more impatient with the way he was looking at me so cheerfully, clearly thinking it was all going to be as easy to resolve as he'd assumed it would be.

'Fire away,' he said. 'What's the next point on the agenda?'

I was so frustrated by his stubborn obtuseness, I really couldn't think what to say. The fact that he

317

didn't know what we needed to discuss said it all. Just seven little words summed up the major problem between us, I worked out: YOU WON'T HAVE A BABY WITH ME! And if that still hadn't properly sunk in with Ed, I wondered if there was any point me saying anything to him again at all. Ever.

Making it even harder, my head was really starting to spin. With the lack of sleep, the black coffee and now the champagne, I was feeling almost faint—and even before Ed appeared I'd already been cranked up to an emotional fever pitch about what had happened over the days before with Joseph. It was all too much.

'You know what?' I said, putting my fingers on my temples, taking a couple of deep breaths and trying to compose myself. 'I'm not up to having this conversation right now. Can we talk again in the morning?'

'OK,' said Ed cheerfully, as if everything was going perfectly to plan. 'Let's crash out and we'll resume at breakfast.'

I stood up, swaying a little, and made for the stairs.

*   *   *

I fell into bed and sank immediately into a strange state of semi-consciousness. I felt paralysed with tiredness, but at the same time my head was racing. It was like my brain knew my body was asleep, but I was conscious of it, so I couldn't be asleep. I kept slipping in and out of that feeling, and time became all loopy and confused.

I don't know how long it was before I felt Ed get

into bed beside me. Maybe he'd been there for ages and I'd only just realized, but he was definitely there and he had his arms around me. I was lying on my side and I could feel what was clearly an erect penis pressing into my buttock. Immediately, it awoke all the intense sexual feelings of the last few days. I was fired up in an instant.

In my asleep/awake state my body took over and without thinking twice about the implications I reached behind me to grasp Ed's hard-on. Then, before I knew what I was doing I had rolled over and started kissing him, and then I was on top, riding him hard, pressing myself down on to him, pushing my breasts in his face, one hand between my legs to increase the sensation.

In what seemed like a very short time, Ed shouted out and I knew he had come—seconds later, so did I.

I collapsed back on to the bed and fell immediately into a blessedly deep sleep.

25

The next morning I woke up to sunshine streaming through the window. I glanced at my clock and saw it was nearly eleven. I felt completely disoriented. Had Ed really appeared at the cottage the night before—or had I dreamed it all?

Then, with a lurch, I remembered everything that had happened. Ed had turned up when I was fuddled with sleep and coffee, we'd had the best part of two bottles of champagne and I'd had hot sex with him. And it had been that way round—I'd had sex with him. He hadn't had that much to do with it. Otherwise, there would have been a condom involved.

Oh my God! I thought, sitting up suddenly, as an unfamiliar sticky feeling between my legs confirmed it. We'd had unprotected sex—one of the very few such incidences in the whole time we'd been together. Quite ironic really.

But as I took that on board, I started to feel really confused—and more than a little ashamed. What I had done with Ed didn't seem right. Had I been unfaithful to Joseph with him? But Ed was my husband, so that didn't add up. And why did I feel more guilty about betraying my adulterous lover with my husband than the other way around? I turned my face into my pillow and groaned. What a mess.

Then my phone rang. Of course, it was Joseph. I saw his name on the screen and immediately turned the phone off. I really wasn't ready to talk to him. Now, that whole scenario was starting to feel like some kind of a feverish dream.

Had I really spent three nights and two days making love to Joseph James Renwick—the first boy I had ever kissed, best friend of my brother, Captain of the First Fifteen, legendary teenage consumer of tequila slammers? Or was I still married to the man downstairs? I didn't know what was real any more.

I lay there a bit longer, feeling increasingly panicky and muddle-headed, and then I heard noises in the kitchen. Ed was clearly up. I forced myself to get out of bed and pulled on my dressing gown.

Working as always by my father's rule, I reckoned it was better to face him and get it over with—although I didn't have a clue yet how I was going to explain that, while I had ravaged him sexually just a few hours before, I wasn't ready to move back in with him yet.

Ed was sitting at the kitchen table when I came down the stairs, immaculately groomed and dressed as usual, in a fresh blue linen shirt, with two cups of coffee and the *Saturday Telegraph* on the table in front of him, everything as normal—except I hadn't seen him at breakfast for well over two months. And it was usually me who made the coffee and got the papers.

'Morning,' I said, as casually as I could. I bent down to kiss him on the cheek, but he put his hand up to stop me. 'It's OK, Amelia,' he said. 'You can dispense with the amateur theatrics.'

I sat down at the other end of the table and looked at him. Now I was even more confused.

Ed folded his arms and looked at me with the coldest expression I had ever seen on his face.

'So,' he said, 'who are you fucking?'

I stared at him, truly lost for words. Not just at what he had said—but how he had said it. Ed never spoke in such vulgar terms.

'What do you mean?' I said, feeling a treacherous blush rising up my neck.

Ed nodded. 'I'm right then,' he said, a bitterly triumphant look on his face. 'That blush always did give you away, Amelia—but not as much as your whorish behaviour last night. I'm speechless.'

You were pretty speechless at the time too, I wanted to say, apart from the odd orgasmic groan. But I could see that making smart remarks was not going to help the situation, so I said nothing.

'I am so disappointed in you, Amelia,' he said, very quietly. 'I didn't think things could get any worse between us, but never for a moment did it occur to me that, while we were having what I had assumed was a brief separation, you were going to start shagging around town. Presumably Kiki is your guide in these matters, as in all else these days.'

Probably because there was more than a grain of truth in what he was saying—at least in the Kiki part—my astonishment was fast turning to indignant fury.

'Hang on a minute, Ed,' I said. 'What about that Jane Seymour lovely I saw you dining with at the Wolseley a couple of weeks ago? How come it's OK for you to "shag around town", as you so elegantly put it, but not me?'

He frowned for a moment, looking mystified, and then he started laughing. Not a nice laugh.

'Irina?' he said.

'I don't know what she was called,' I said, 'but she was certainly your full Solitaire fantasy. Did she read your tarot after dinner? Did you enjoy fondling her hair? Frankly, I couldn't believe how quickly you found her. Did you get her through an agency? Bond Girls-to-go?'

Ed stood up and put on his jacket. He fished his keys out of a pocket, threw them up into the air and caught them again with casual mirthlessness.

'I think this conversation has just come to an end, Amelia,' he said. 'Possibly for good.'

I stood up too, now absolutely furious. Fully shouting. Hello, Daddy.

'So that's it?' I said. 'It's fine for you to sleep

with someone else, but not me—so now you're just going to walk out without further discussion? Without even being man enough to find out why I left you in the first place.'

He looked at me for a moment with pursed lips, almost as if he were trying to memorize my face. 'What you don't understand, Amelia,' he said finally, as I stood there, fairly certain my face was bright red and my eyes were bugging out, but still too cross to care, 'what you don't grasp is that Irina—and her hideous leather-headed husband, Sergei, who you would also have seen that night— were potential new clients for Bradlow's. Courtesy of my meddling mother who had met them at the Grosvenor House antiques fair. While he is indeed a billionaire, it was not a business relationship I chose to pursue.'

He paused before continuing. 'And now, as you have made it quite clear what you have been up to in the time we have been separated—spelled it out, really—I am leaving. I had at least assumed my wife would be faithful to me, as I have always been to you, until we worked this out. So that leaves us with nothing else to discuss. Ever.'

Then he walked out—leaving the door open, more devastating than slamming it—I heard his car start, and I knew in that moment that this was it. It really was over between us. No way back.

A wave of panic swept over me. I wasn't ready yet. We still needed to talk. We'd never properly discussed the real reasons I'd moved out in the first place and, if he left now, it would be too late.

I ran to the door to try and stop him, but his Bristol 406 took off in a large gust of noxious exhaust just as I got there.

A sense of hysteria rising inside me at the thought of fifteen years of a loving relationship going up in a similar puff of smoke, I ran straight up to the bedroom and turned my phone on, stabbing at Ed's number in my contacts list. The phone connected, but the connection was immediately cancelled. I tried again twice and it was the same. Ed was not taking my calls.

I lay down on the bed and closed my eyes, the events of the past few days swirling around in my head like some kind of psychedelic minestrone. Three of the most momentous happenings of my life—kissing Joseph Renwick again, having my first orgasm, and properly breaking up with my husband—had happened within the last four days. I felt nauseous with shock. And I'd had sex with Ed without a condom. That was an event in itself.

For a moment it flashed through my mind that I might be pregnant. That's how it happened—it only took one little squirt of sperm to do it. That was a thought so confusing, I held my head in my hands and shook it.

In the end I couldn't stand it, so I got out of bed again, grabbed my bag and checked my diary to see when my next period was due. It was in three days' time, which made it much less likely I was pregnant.

I sat there for a moment, looking at the ringed dates on the year's calendar, each of them representing a day when I had been desperately sad to be reminded yet again that I wasn't pregnant and wasn't ever likely to be. Oh well, I told myself bitterly, at least I wouldn't have to wait long to find out this time.

On top of everything else, that was way too

much to process. So I turned my phone off, dumped it on the floor with my handbag and pulled the covers over my head.

*   *   *

I don't know how long I stayed there, drifting in and out of a feverish sleep, waking up every time with a lurch, as the events of the past few days flooded in again.

I heard a knock on the kitchen door at one point, which I was fairly sure was Hermione, but I didn't go down to open it. I felt bad knowing how painfully she would have made her way over to see me, with her fragile hips and knees, but I just couldn't face her. Or anyone.

What I'd done with Ed the night before had made the glorious time with Joseph seem soiled and grubby. I felt cruelly cheated of that brief happiness by my own guilt. It had taken me to the age of thirty-six to discover what sex was really all about, and now I felt ashamed of myself for it. That amazing liberated feeling had been destroyed so quickly, and I had nothing to replace it with.

I couldn't see how I could ever make it up to Ed, and I still felt strangely as though I had betrayed Joseph as well. He had been pretty loved up when we'd said goodbye just the morning before, and my response to his tender ardour had been to run off and immediately shag another man. Who happened to be my husband . . .

What kind of a ho was I?

I rolled over and groaned, burying my face in the pillow. It made no sense, none of it. But as I lay there, feeling slightly suffocated by the goosedown, I suddenly felt I'd spent way too much time between the sheets in the past few days, and being in bed another minute seemed unbearable.

I jumped out and ran to the shower, washing my hair and scrubbing myself clean until my skin tingled. Then I put on fresh clothes, stripped the bed and shoved all the sheets straight into the machine on a hot wash. I needed to purge myself.

What would do it, I realized, was a good blast of fresh air, so I got the old Volvo out of the garage and headed down to Pett Level, the nearest stretch of beach. It was a lovely drive through the country lanes, which looked glorious in their early summer mode, and I felt better with every turn of the wheels.

The tide was out, and I scrambled down the steep bank of pebbles to the squidgy mudflats that stretched out to the sea. Picking my way across the slimy seaweed, I found a suitably prominent rock to balance my bright-yellow flipflops on. Then I splashed to the shoreline where the sand was firm, breaking into a run and trying not to think about anything except the cool water around my feet, the surprisingly hot sun on my face and the pure sea air I was breathing in and out of my lungs.

The run sorted me out enough that I felt able to face Hermione, so I knocked on her door as soon as I got back to the cottage and told her I had been feeling unwell earlier—which wasn't so far from the truth—and that I'd decided to go back up to town right away. If she noticed anything different about me she didn't show it.

*   *   *

The train seemed like a pleasantly neutral space, and I closed my eyes and just zoned out as much as I could, grateful for any further respite from thinking. I didn't turn my phone on until we were nearly at Charing Cross, to find there were no messages from Ed, which didn't surprise me, but there were two from Joseph.

The first one—which he had left that morning, when he'd called just before my row with Ed—was so sweet and affectionate, I almost burst into tears, so clearly did it bring back that beautiful little island of time we'd had together.

Scrolling through my phone log I could see there had been several other missed calls from him, and then he'd left another message not very long before I'd turned the phone back on.

'Meals-on-wheels,' he said, using a nickname I hadn't heard for about twenty years. 'Where are you, baby girl? You're turning me into a stalker. I've been ringing you all day. I want to talk to you. I want to hear your voice. I want to hear your body. Grrrrr. Ring me. Soon.'

I smiled at the phone, but I had tears in my eyes. He was still in the blissed-out state I'd been in too, until the ugly events of the last twenty-four hours had turned everything sour.

I desperately wanted to speak to him, but I was sure he would know something was up the moment he heard my voice and I didn't want to burst his bubble the way I had burst my own. So I sent him a cowardly text instead: 'Sorry JR not feeling well. Phone turned off. Will call you Monday. Miss you. Meals xxx.'

It was true: I did miss him. I was actually surprised how much, but I was so afraid that I was pining for something that was already destroyed— by my own stupid behaviour—that I wasn't ready to expose myself to that disappointment in the flesh just yet.

*   *   *

After all the emotional turmoil of the weekend I kept myself deliberately insanely busy with work, catching up with all the admin I had let slide, against all my own professional advice, and re-booking all the clients I had cancelled in favour of being with Joseph.

At least someone was benefiting from my mistakes, I told myself, as I arrived at the large Chiswick doorstep of the fourth new client I had seen that day, who I had been able to bring forward from the waiting fist as a result of my burst of frenzied activity.

This one's problem was clear from the moment I entered her hallway. She could open the door, which was an improvement on many of my clients, but after I took two steps into her house, I found myself suddenly flying through the air at high speed. I hit the floor with a hard thump, the contents of my handbag spilling out all around me.

Immediately, feeling like Dorothy just landed in Oz, I found myself surrounded by small people, who were very interested in the lipsticks, tape measures, mobile phones and other fascinating adult ephemera spread out before them.

'Oh my GOD, I am so sorry,' said my client— Philippa, an actress, who had found me through Rosalyn. 'Finn!' she yelled up the stairs. 'You left your skateboard in the hall again! I'm taking it to the dump! Tonight! You nearly killed someone!'

'Are you all right, lady?' said a small boy with a mop of brown curls, his face exactly level with mine. He was eating a large carrot and wearing nothing but a pair of Spiderman underpants. Twin rivers of green were descending from his nostrils. On autopilot, I grabbed a tissue from my trusty box and wiped his nose.

As I reached for the tissues, I noticed that a much younger person of indeterminate sex, clad in a nappy and a stained vest, was methodically emptying my wallet, pausing only to chew on one of my credit cards.

'Leto!' said Philippa, grabbing it. 'Don't chew that. And put that lipstick down, Miranda.'

I heard a giggle behind my head and turned round to see two little girls. One, wearing what I recognized as a Princess Yasmin outfit, was wiping my favourite Laura Mercier lipstick methodically across her lower face. The other, dressed as Pocahontas, had my phone to her ear.

She'd clearly found someone to talk to on the other end, because I could hear a tinny voice saying 'Hello? hello?', but before she could say anything back, an older boy had rushed at her and grabbed the phone, causing her to scream loudly.

'Put that phone down, Sigmund!' said Philippa.

I managed to grab him as he attempted to leap across my legs towards the bottom of the stairs.

'I'll have that, thank you, sir,' I said, and was relieved to see the number dialled had only been AAA 1 Taxis. I turned the phone off and shoved it back into my bag, with anything else I could reach before small dimpled hands got to it.

'All you children, playroom, now!' boomed

329

Philippa, in a voice that I knew would effortlessly reach the very back rows in Stratford with perfect clarity. 'Or you won't have any pudding tonight! And it's ice cream!'

At her threat, they fled towards the back of the house like a pack of small dogs.

'We had ice cream last night,' whined the boy identified as Sigmund over his shoulder as he went.

'OUT!' screamed Philippa.

'I'm so sorry, Amelia,' she said, turning to me and snapping back into more dulcet tones, her unusually large eyes wide with horror, 'but at least you've seen what I have to deal with.'

She fell to her knees next to me and looked earnestly into my face with an expression I recognized. I'd seen her Portia at the Donmar.

'Do you think you can possibly help me?' she asked me.

I had to laugh. 'Give me a cup of coffee, and I'll tell you,' I said.

We had about three minutes' peace before the children started sneaking into the kitchen one by one, until they were all in there, even Finn from upstairs, and I had to clamp my bag firmly on my lap to prevent tiny fingers continuing the investigations they had started in the hall.

Now in full flow of the story of her fascinating life and how it had led to all these children, Philippa seemed not to notice what was going on.

In the end I was so frustrated by the constant incursions I gave up. I took out my phone, wallet and car keys and shoved them down my bra, as the only safe place I could think of, put my clipboard and pen on the table where I would be able to hold on to them, and then dumped the handbag—a cheap and cheerful tote thing from Topshop—on the kitchen floor.

'There you are,' I said. 'Do what you like with the rest of it.'

'Are you sure?' said Philippa, suddenly snapping back into the present and looking horrified. 'They're vicious destroyers, you know.'

I shrugged. 'Show me the house,' I said.

It was a huge place, and there was mess everywhere, but I could see right away it was superficial. The large playroom at the back was a wonderful room, with the remnants of a very organized storage system, with different areas for various activities.

The kids' bedrooms were also lovely, with four-poster princess beds for the girls and pirate bunks for the boys, just horribly strewn with toys, bits of discarded food and dirty clothes. But, considering how much chaos they had managed to cause in my life in the short time I had been in the house, it didn't seem too bad to me.

'Is there anywhere we can talk for five minutes where they won't find us?' I asked Philippa, and she took us to the master bedroom, which had a bolt on the inside of the door.

'We had to put that on,' she said, as she slid it closed. 'It was the only way we could have any time together, if you know what I mean . . .'

I nodded and sat down on the corner of the bed. I'd heard about that system from my friends with kids.

'So when did the nanny leave?' I asked her.

She opened her mouth and shut it again. 'Is it that obvious?' she said, dropping to the floor in an

331

elegant heap.

'Well, it's obvious that in the not-too-distant past there was someone very organized here, but they aren't here now . . .'

Philippa looked sheepish. 'I had a row with her . . .' she said, eventually. 'I wouldn't give her a payrise. She caught me at a bad moment. I'd just lost a part I really wanted. I was a bit, well, unkind . . .'

'And what about the cleaner?'

'She resigned in protest,' said Philippa in an unusually unaffected, small voice.

'Can you get hold of them?' I asked.

She nodded.

'Call them both, this afternoon,' I said. 'Give the nanny a much bigger payrise than she asked for— and the cleaner—and you won't need me.'

We went downstairs to find the older boy using my handbag for some kind of one-man sack race, the baby happily tearing pages out of my Moleskin notebook, carrot boy measuring his legs with my retractable tape, and the twin girls rapturously absorbed in my make-up bag. I bent down to rescue what was left of the notebook and while I was there, I kissed the baby—I still wasn't sure what sex it was—on its dear little tufty head. Philippa hugged me at the door. 'Are you sure you won't take your fee?' she said, her eyes in full saucer mode.

'Spend it on the nanny,' I said, 'and then you can relax and enjoy your kids. They're gorgeous.'

'Do you want to take one with you?' she said laughingly, and I waved cheerily back at her before turning quickly towards my car, so she wouldn't see the tears in my eyes.

Keeping busy with other people's chaotic lives seemed to work as an excellent form of therapy for my own mess and I managed to get through the days without obsessing on Ed or Joseph more than, say, twenty times an hour each. I was quite pleased with that result.

Using work as an ongoing excuse, I didn't see Joseph until the following Thursday, when we met for dinner at Julie's. He was waiting for me outside, and when he saw me coming down Portland Road, he ran towards me and scooped me off the ground, swinging me round.

I had felt more and more nervous about seeing him again the nearer I'd got to the venue, in case my face somehow revealed what I'd done that disastrous night with Ed, but the moment I was in his physical presence my nerves disappeared completely.

As he kissed me, there on the street, completely oblivious of early evening passers-by, I felt an enormous sense of relief. It seemed the bubble was not entirely burst after all.

Dinner was heaven—not that I ate it. I found it difficult to do anything but gaze at Joseph's face, and I could barely take in what he was saying for watching his mouth move and thinking how much I wanted to slide my tongue over those sensuous lips.

I did become aware of a familiar expression in his eyes, though, as I realized he had stopped talking English and was saying something along the lines of 'Oogley poogely snoogely noogely you're not taking any of this in, are you, Amelia?'

I giggled and shook my head. He laughed and took hold of my hand across the table.

'I was asking about your weekend,' he said, talking exaggeratedly slowly, and smiling sweetly. 'I was wondering how your vegetable garden was coming along and whether I could invite myself down to see it some time soon.'

I felt like a cloud had just blocked out the sun. My blissed-out mood was gone in an instant. My weekend—eeurgh—just the thought of it made me feel ill.

Joseph frowned. 'What's wrong?' he said. 'You suddenly look shattered.'

I sighed deeply. I had to tell him. Maybe not all of it, but I had to tell him some of it.

'Oh, Joseph,' I said, 'I had a hideous weekend. That's why I couldn't speak to you after it. I couldn't bear to break the spell between us.' He squeezed my hand and I took a deep breath. 'Ed turned up at the cottage on Friday night,' I said. 'Almost exactly twelve hours after I had said goodbye to you.'

'Ouch,' said Joseph.

I nodded. 'Ouch is the word. I hate even saying his name to you, it makes me feel so confused. You'll have noticed I haven't mentioned him once since we, er, kissed—and I haven't asked you anything about your situation either.'

He nodded slowly. 'I have noticed that and I have really appreciated it. It's been like having a vacation from real life.'

'That's exactly how I felt,' I said. 'And when Ed turned up, with no warning, I'm afraid the holiday was definitely over.'

334

'Well, now Pandora's box is finally open,' said Joseph. 'I suppose I have to ask you—what is the situation between you two? I have been wondering . . .'

'Until Friday night it was a stand-off. Full radio silence. I left him nearly three months ago, telling myself it was just a break, because there were a lot of issues in our relationship that he wouldn't even acknowledge, let alone address, and I wanted to shock him into facing up to them. But he has a major problem with Kiki, for some reason, so when I moved in with her, he refused to speak to me at all.'

'That's weird,' said Joseph, frowning. 'How could anyone have a problem with Kiki? She's a one-woman task force for world happiness. What's not to like?'

'I really don't know. I think perhaps he's jealous and sees her as a threat.'

'Bizarre, but tell me, why did he suddenly show up on Friday?'

'He'd just come home from one of his work trips to France and arriving back at the empty flat had made him realize how much he missed me. He came down to the cottage on the spur of the moment to try and thrash it out.'

Joseph looked very serious. I could imagine this was the expression his students saw if they handed in a shoddy piece of work. It was a very grown-up face, and I wanted naughty teenage Joseph back.

I kicked off my shoe and ran my foot along his thigh, nestling it firmly between his legs and wiggling my toes. The corners of his mouth lifted, but his eyes were still grave.

'So how did his effort at a rapprochement go?'

335

he said, reaching down and taking hold of my foot gently with his hand so I couldn't do any more wiggling. Now I knew he really was serious.

'It was a disaster,' I said, slumping in my seat. 'I was so tired from being with you—not to mention somewhat woozey—and it was such terrible timing, because he figured out from the state of me that I'd been seeing someone else and he left in a fury. It felt very final.'

Now I couldn't read Joseph's expression at all. I hoped mine wasn't giving me away.

'How did he figure out you'd been seeing someone else?'

My blush answered for me. Joseph laughed.

'Oh, the blush,' he said. 'I love that blush of yours. I used to do everything I could to make you do it when we were young.'

'Yes, I do remember,' I said, managing to get a last little poke in with my toe before taking my foot away. 'Well, that's what gave me away to Ed too.'

That was enough of an explanation. It wasn't a lie. It wasn't the whole truth, but it was a big part of it.

Joseph leaned across the table towards me. 'Do you know that when you are in bed with me that blush covers a large part of your upper body?'

I felt it spreading down my chest as he spoke and believed him.

'But tell me,' he said, looking serious again, 'how do you feel about things being "very final", as you put it, with Ed—with your husband?'

I put my face in my hands. 'That's what I am finding it really hard to work out,' I said. 'I honestly don't know how I feel about it.'

Joseph nodded. 'I can understand that,' he said.

I saw my opening. 'Can you?' I said. 'So tell me more. What is your situation?'

He flopped back in the banquette and grabbed his head with his hands, as if shielding himself from blows. 'Hideous,' he said. 'I don't want to go into all the gory details, because I just can't bear it. Suffice to say there are two little children back in Washington, who are very dear to me, but who I am unlikely ever to see again.'

'But don't you have legal rights to see your own children?' I asked, mystified.

'That's the problem,' said Joseph. 'They're not my children. Not my biological children, anyway. My wife already had them when I met her. They were two and four then, and now they are nine and eleven, so they feel like my children, but they aren't. And because the famous bloody law academic never actually got round to legally adopting them, I have no rights to see them ever again.'

He looked so sad, I felt tears fill my eyes. Once again I remembered that strange thing he'd said about his children that night at Kiki's party. Finally it made sense, but hadn't he said 'Two, maybe three . . .' when I'd asked him how many children he had? What did that mean in this context?

I desperately wanted to ask him, but something about the way he was looking, all crumpled and defeated, stopped me. It wasn't the moment to push him on that subject.

'I'm so sorry, Joseph,' I said. 'I had no idea.'

'Why would you?' he said, shrugging. 'I don't talk about it. She even took out an injunction that I wasn't allowed to go near the house, or the kids'

337

schools—she claimed I had threatened to kidnap them. It was all absolute nonsense, of course, but for someone who teaches law for a living, that kind of thing is not a good look. I had to get away from there before my professional reputation was ruined as well as my personal life. That's why I came home.'

He laughed bitterly. 'I still pay their school fees though. She doesn't have a problem with that kind of contact . . .'

'But why did you split up in the first place?' I asked.

This time Joseph's expression completely closed up. 'Now *that*, I really don't want to talk about,' he said. He signalled at the waiter to bring our bill, and I knew the discussion was closed.

We were both unusually quiet as we walked back towards Kiki's flat. Joseph had his arm around my shoulders, and I was leaning into him, my arm around his waist under his jacket, finding comfort in his manly bulk, but the sweet dizziness had completely gone out of the evening.

When we got to Kiki's gate, Joseph took my hands and pulled me to his chest. I felt like the wagons were safely enclosed around me and when he kissed me, long and deep, reality disappeared again in a most delightful way.

Eventually, we broke apart and I looked up at him. It was after ten, but there was still a bit of light left. I could see his eyes behind his glasses, dark blue and sexy as ever, but sadness was there now too.

'Goodnight, my lovely Meals,' he said. 'I hope you don't mind but I'm not going to come in tonight. Talking about that stuff really pulls me down, and I wouldn't be good company. I need to go off to my bear cave and listen to boy music and find the place in my head where I file all that away so it can't hurt me again. Do you understand? It's not because I don't want to be with you, I just don't want to expose you to this side of me. It might put you off, and I really don't want that.'

I nodded. I understood, but I was still disappointed. Part of me felt the same—but a larger part wanted to jump on his bones. That kiss had got me going.

'Lucky I've got Mr Rabbit to keep me company,' I said, trying to lighten things up.

'Hmmm,' said Joseph. 'Competition from a rubber rodent—not sure I'm happy about that, but I think it's best this way. Can I see you again soon?'

I nodded and kissed him one more time before running inside.

Kiki was out when I got into the flat, so I made myself a cup of camomile tea and went to bed to read. My attention was wandering from my book to thoughts of Joseph—and his shoulders in particular—and I was just considering whether to get Mr Bunny out of his box when my mobile rang.

It was him.

'Meals?' he said. 'I'm halfway home in a cab and I've been thinking—I'm not sure rabbits are rodents, you know. But I'm not certain, so I think I'd better come over to your place after all and check. Is that OK?'

26

Over the next couple of weeks Joseph and I saw each other practically every night. I still went down to the cottage on my own for the weekends—I wasn't ready to take him back there yet—but most other nights we had dinner, went to the movies, or just stayed in and went to bed early, if not to sleep. All the things loved-up people do.

Whatever we did together, it was blissfully easy and normal-feeling. I felt completely relaxed with him and was really able to enjoy getting to know the adult man as well as I had known the teenager. And I liked him even more, I discovered. Over the years in Washington—and several in New York before that—he had acquired a level of sophistication that I felt matched my own—unlike my dear brother, who was still an unreconstructed rugger-bugger, pub-drinking, politically incorrect, minor-public-school throwback, as I was reminded the evening we had drinks with him. That was a big moment for me. It made my relationship—or whatever it was—with Joseph seem scarily official.

At Dick's request, we met at the Lamb, a lovely old pub in Bloomsbury. He was keen to check out a 'boozer', as he called them, outside his normal patch.

'So you two have finally got it together, have you?' he said, coming back out to where we were standing on Lambs Conduit Street, with all three drinks in his mighty hands. 'And about bloody time too. It's only taken you twenty years.'

He downed most of his pint in one go and

smiled at us. 'Of course, I do feel a bit sorry for old Ed,' he continued. 'He is a good Magdalene man after all, and I will miss having a brother-in-law who's a wine merchant, I don't mind telling you, but you two always belonged together. I never understood what you were playing at, marrying out like that.'

'Well, how about you, Sherbet?' said Joseph, putting his arm comfortably around my waist and squeezing me, as though agreeing with what Dick had just said. 'When are you going to introduce us to a nice girl of your own?'

Dick's face clouded. His single state was one of the many things that wasn't discussed in our family. He was forty and he had never even lived with anyone. He'd had a few girlfriends, but nothing you could really call serious.

'Ah, well, that's the problem, isn't it?' he said. 'There don't seem to be any nice girls left in London. They're all hard-nosed career women or lezzers.'

I looked around the pavement where we were standing outside the pub. There were girls everywhere. Lovely fresh-faced, bright-looking young women, many of them in groups with no men attached. They didn't look particularly hard-nosed, or gay, to me. In fact, I had noticed one or two of them checking Joseph out. It didn't make any sense.

And Kiki seemed to have thousands of single girlfriends, all desperate to meet a straight, solvent, reasonably civilized bloke like Dick. Then there was Kiki herself, also inexplicably unattached, something I found increasingly odd, considering how attractive, social, eligible and

341

sexually rampant she was.

I was about to point all this out to Dick—and not for the first time—but Joseph got in first.

'Are you sure you're not just gay, Sherbet?' he said. It was an ongoing joke between them.

'Not last time I looked at a copy of *Penthouse*,' said Dick, finishing his pint.

'And when was that?' said Joseph.

Dick chuckled, his deep laugh resonating from his chest.

'Lunchtime.'

*   *   *

Kiki seemed delighted that Joseph and I were 'getting all boring', as she called it; her general term for happy couples.

'I mean, it's good boring,' she said one Friday morning, when we had found each other at home by chance and she was painting my toenails scarlet while I lay on the chaise in Planet Kiki. 'But you are getting boring with Joseph incredibly fast,' she continued, sitting cross-legged in her lime-green bra and knickers, black-rimmed glasses balanced on the end of her nose—it turned out she actually did need them. 'You're as bad as Ollie and Sonny these days. So tell me, are you madly in love with him?'

'Gosh,' I said, blowing my breath out between my lips. 'I don't think of it like that. I certainly love being with him, it feels so easy—I have known him most of my life, after all—and I do think he is utterly gorgeous.' I felt a familiar flutter as an image of Joseph naked in the shower that morning flashed across my mind. 'So yes,' I continued. 'I am

342

pretty keen on him, but I just try and take each moment as it comes, because I am still married to someone else, remember, Kiki. I still haven't really officially split up from Ed.'

'Surely that draggy old saga is over?' she said, incredulously. 'You've been here for four months. I thought you would have started divorce proceedings by now. I'm already planning to wear my vintage Azzaro dress to your next wedding.'

I threw a small evening bag at her.

'Stop it, Kiki! I am not getting married to Joseph. We are both separated from our spouses, but neither of us is divorced and we are just enjoying each other's company right now. We certainly aren't making any plans for the future.'

'Well, maybe you should be,' said Kiki. 'Remember that graph I showed you? You don't want to find yourself on the black ski run and still married to Christopher Robin.'

That was her latest name for Ed. And as so often with Kiki's apparently light-hearted teasing, she had a serious point. He might have been Mr Suave Mayfair, with his custom-made shirts and Savile Row suits, but right down to the attachment to a cuddly toy, Ed was still a child in many ways. Rather a spoilt one.

'What about *your* love life?' I asked her, to take the focus off me.

'Well,' she said, instantly perking up. 'Do you remember that gorgeous Imran Khan-look-a-like poshistani bloke I met at the Ivy Club? Well, I saw him again last night at Tim Jeffries' gallery, and it looks like being a happening thing. I'm seeing him on Monday—at his place. Do you reckon he will be skilled in the eastern love arts? Mmmm, chicken tikka cunnilingus . . .'

'But what about something beyond sex, Kiki?' I said.

'Like what?' she said, shrugging.

'A relationship? Motherhood?'

Kiki scowled. 'I've told you,' she said. 'Not interested.'

'Not in either of them? I thought you were a bit interested in the husband part. That was one of the reasons you wanted to sort this flat out, you told me.'

Kiki's mouth hardened. 'Nope,' she said, standing up. 'I can't be arsed.'

She sighed and looked up at me, pushing the glasses up her nose. The momentary hardness had gone, and her eyes were sad.

'Look, Amelia,' she said. 'When everyone knows you've got money, it's hard to trust anyone romantically. He might seem like he's mad keen on you, then it turns out he's more interested in how much is sitting in your Coutts account. That's what happened with that last bloke—the one who took me off to Babington while you were shagging Joseph, remember? Well, at the end of our lovely stay he stood by the reception desk staring into space waiting for me to pay the bill—after he'd ordered vintage champagne on room service every night. I wouldn't have minded splitting it, but the whole trip was his idea, and then he just assumed I'd pay. I'm sick of trying to filter out the bullion bandits so, here on Planet Kiki, girls just wanna have fun, OK?'

'That's terrible,' I said. 'I had no idea.'

She shrugged and her eyes toughened up again. 'And he was not by any means the first. So I'm just sticking to good times.'

'But aren't you a tiny bit interested in having kids, Kiki? You'd be such a wonderful mother . . .'

She rolled her eyes. 'Spare me!' she said. 'How many times have I heard that? Based on what? My immaturity? This is where I live—glamour central, Planet Kiki—and I'm not interested in introducing shitty nappies and snotty noses into it.'

'But there's more to having children than that,' I said. 'You sound Like Ed. . .'

'Not interested, OK?' she snapped and flounced out of the room.

I'd clearly hit a sore spot. Oops. I'd had no idea.

*   *   *

The reason Kiki had been painting my toenails was to get me what she called 'red-carpet ready' for Janelle's charity auction, which was in a few days' time. I was really excited about it—and not a little nervous. The event had turned into something of a media feeding frenzy, especially now that the Honeypots reunion tour was official.

Newspapers, magazines and TV shows were calling me so often it had become a serious distraction from work, until one day—after watching me get all hopeless and flustered in the kitchen when I had *You* magazine on one line and a researcher from *Richard and Judy* on the other— Kiki had volunteered to be my official PR agent.

Since then, all media requests had gone through her, and she was brilliant at dealing with them, setting one magazine against another to get me and my business the best possible coverage. She also had a very clear view of where I needed to be 'placed in the market', as she put it.

'You've got to strike the perfect balance between snob and celeb,' she'd explained to me one day after turning down a rather generously paid interview request from a trashy weekly and agreeing to one with no payment which would take a lot of my time for the *Telegraph* magazine.

'Perfect spot for you,' she'd said, going on to remind me I had to be equally picky about my clients.

'You can do Janelle,' she said, 'because of the charity context, and the media payback is huge— but I wouldn't let you take a footballer's wife below Posh. Even Colleen would be pushing it. You're top end, Amelia, aspirational, like Ed's business, but more fun.'

In just a couple of weeks she had made an enormous difference to me, taking over all the adjacent aspects of the business that I found so alien, so I could get on with my strong point— clearing people's clutter and streamlining their lives for maximum customer satisfaction.

I could already see we were a great team, but I was embarrassed right from the start about how to handle the money side of things. I'd already had to fight to pay her any rent for my room in her flat, and I knew she hadn't cashed any of the cheques I had given her towards bills.

'You've got to let me pay you for doing this work, Kiki,' I said to her one day when we were sitting together in the dining room, which we had converted into ABCC's official HQ. 'Otherwise I won't feel able to ask you to do things for me.'

'But I'm just so happy to have a purpose in life beyond dressing up and chasing dopey men,' she

346

said, speedreading the *Times* feature section.

Now she was a PR she insisted on having all the newspapers delivered again. The difference was, now she had a reason to look at them, she actually did it and they all went out into the recycling bin every night. She tore out anything she thought might be useful and put it into a designated filing tray ready for the part-time office assistant she had recently hired for us to sort each week.

'But you're always telling me to be professional and think like a businesswoman,' I said. 'And I don't think it's very professional to have unpaid slaves in the business.'

'OK,' she said, looking up, but keeping a finger on the last word she had read. 'Here's the deal. If, with my help, by the end of this year we can get your turnover up to £150,000 p.a., we'll legally incorporate ABCC as a limited company and I will be your business partner on a 49 per cent share? How's that? Deal?'

I looked at her, initially speechless. Suddenly the heavy glasses didn't seem so bizarre on her dainty head.

'Deal . . .' I said, finally. 'Ms *Wilmott*.'

She grinned at me and then, as she turned immediately back to her newspaper-scanning, I realized I'd never seen her so happy.

She was even more delighted when I asked her to be my official date for Janelle's auction. My first thought had been to take Joseph, who would certainly look the part in a dinner jacket and who, I rather suspected, was expecting me to take him.

But the more Kiki drilled me on how to pose for the paparazzi who would be outside the venue—her main advice was to stay glued to Janelle, for maximum coverage—I came to realize I couldn't possibly go with him. Ed would see pictures of us together in the paper the next day. *'Celebrity clutter-clearer Amelia Bradlow and friend. . .'* And I couldn't do that to him.

Because, although I was feeling pretty dizzy about Joseph, I still wasn't able to shake off a nagging sense of responsibility about Ed. I might be involved with someone else, but the fact was we were still married, and it really bothered me that we had allowed our relationship to get to that stage of breakdown without ever having a proper conversation about what the original problems had been.

I kept trying to call him to arrange a meeting to have that conversation, but he still wouldn't answer when he saw it was me on the line. One afternoon I even tried ringing him from a phonebox so he wouldn't recognize the number, but when he heard my voice, he immediately hung up.

Shortly afterwards I got a text: 'Please stop phoning me, Amelia. I am not ready to talk to you yet. When I am I will contact you.'

There it was again—all on Ed's stubborn terms. At least his texting had improved, I thought to myself, sticking my tongue out at the phone. Then I rang Joseph's number, when I knew he would be giving a tutorial to his summer school students, just to hear his voice on the message.

It was, I acknowledged to myself, as I hung up, the kind of dopey thing I would have done when I was sixteen. And although I tried to put the thoughts out of my head the moment they popped up, I had also been obsessing on what Kiki had said about Joseph and me and wedding bells.

Mrs Joseph Renwick. Amelia Jane Renwick. Amelia and Joseph Renwick. The names I'd written so many times in my teen diaries were running through my head again as I jogged around Holland Park the next morning. Perhaps, after all these years, my coded teenage declaration would come true: 'AH n JR TRU LUV 4 EVA OK'.

But would it have been like this between us, I wondered, so sweet and easy, if we had got together all the way back then, when we were teenagers?

Probably not, I decided. I would have been like a hopeless little puppy running after him, the dashing captain of the rugby team with his own car and five grade-A A levels, and it all would have ended like a *Jackie* magazine photo-love story when he'd gone off to Oxford—one of the sad ones: 'Joseph was a loner . . .' and all that.

How about later, when we were both students? I'd still seen a lot of him then—until I met Ed—as part of Dick's social crowd, and I'd never stopped liking him. And I'd always been aware of the special way he had looked at me, no matter which of what seemed like an endless succession of pretty girls he'd had on his arm at that moment.

Maybe if I'd had proper girlfriends myself then, I thought, I could have talked to them about it, and I would have known how to read his signals and what to do. They could have checked him out and told me that he liked me, and then I could have made a move. If I'd known Kiki then, I realized, I'd probably be married to Joseph already.

But what would my life have been like if that

had happened? The wife of an academic, no doubt the mother of his children, probably living in an executive home in the suburbs. It might have been New York, or Washington, but it still seemed a little too like my own mother's life for comfort.

So, I asked myself, as I did my cooling-down stretches by the park gate, would I have given up the last fifteen quirky and exciting years with Ed for what would surely have been a more conventional life with Joseph? And I had to be honest with myself however loved up I was about him now, the answer was definitely no. I wouldn't have missed my time with Ed for anything.

I found that very confusing.

*   *   *

Hermione knew something was up. I could see those bright bird eyes looking at me questioningly and I knew I couldn't put her off much longer.

It was Saturday night, the weekend after Janelle's auction—which had been a huge success, raising over £300,000 for what was now a formally structured charity for schools in deprived areas—and once again I was on Hermione's terrace drinking Campari and chatting.

It did occur to me that most women who had a hot thing going like I did with Joseph would probably not have chosen to spend their weekends in the country with a ninety-five-year-old when they could have been in the big city with their own personal love god, but it was where I wanted to be. The bad memory of Ed's visit had lifted, and I found the cottage a great comfort again—and my friendship with Hermione was a big part of that.

350

'I can see you have something on your mind, Amelia,' she said, when I came back through Checkpoint Charlie with some bowls of olives and Twiglets for us to nibble on. 'And I don't mean the blackfly on your roses.'

After five marriages of her own, she was, I had realized, probably the best person I knew to discuss my romantic complications with. My only proper girlfriend seemed a hopeless case when it came to relationships, my brother was even worse and I certainly couldn't talk to my mother about it. The conversation might accidentally turn to her own situation, and then the sky would have fallen on our heads.

Plus, I always suspected that anything I might want to discuss with my mum in relation to Ed would be coloured by her understandably desperate yearning to have grandchildren and his failure to deliver in that regard. Really, I thought, as I sat down again, I was incredibly lucky to have a friend like Hermione, who cared but wasn't involved.

'Oh, things still aren't great in the marriage department,' I said, casually—much more casually than I felt about it.

'Edward came down to see you, didn't he?' she said. 'Was that not a success?'

I turned to look at her, quickly. I hoped she hadn't heard me shouting.

'I saw him out looking at your vegetable garden one morning,' she continued, 'and he came over to speak to me. He seemed very impressed with your *potager*. He said having a garden like that was the main reason you bought the cottage, and he seemed pleased you had fulfilled your dream.'

351

I'd had no idea he'd even seen the garden, because I'd been upstairs sleeping off my fuckfest for most of that morning and, when I had emerged, we'd had that terrible row.

'He seemed rather sad, though,' Hermione continued. 'I couldn't help noticing that.'

'He wasn't sad when I saw him,' I said, suddenly wanting to tell her all about it—well, most of it. 'He was furious, because he'd figured out I've been seeing someone else. So we had a big row and he stormed off, and that was the last time I spoke to him. It's looking more and more like divorce time.'

I was surprised how choked it made me feel to say that. I stuffed a Twiglet in my mouth before a sob could get out.

'Is it the same fellow you were seeing before?' said Hermione.

I nodded. 'You've met him actually, Hermione. It's Joseph. He came down that time with my other friends.'

'Is he the one with the glasses?' she said.

I nodded again. 'Ah,' said Hermione. 'Very attractive, a good intelligent face. I could tell he liked you that weekend. He never took his eyes off you.' She smiled sweetly at me. 'So is that going well?' she asked.

'Yes,' I said. 'He's great. I've known Joseph since I was eleven. He was my brother's best friend at school, so in a lot of ways it feels like comfy slippers being with him but, even beyond that, we just spark each other off we always did—so it's lovely.'

'But . . . ?' said Hermione.

I laughed and shook my head. 'You don't miss a thing, do you?' I said. 'But it doesn't feel quite right launching into a cosy boyfriend/girlfriend scene with him when I'm still married to Ed and I've never had the chance to talk to him properly about what was really wrong between us in the first place.'

'Yes,' said Hermione, firmly. 'That is a mistake I made more than once, going straight from one love affair to another without a break to clear the head. It muddies the new relationship, that's the problem, gets it off on the wrong foot. It was harder in my day, of course, because a woman couldn't be on her own so easily then, even one who earned her own living, as I did, but I do think it is better to let the heart lie fallow for a while, if you can.'

'What did you do for a living, Hermione?' I asked, seizing the opening to ask her. I'd always wondered, plus I wanted a break from thinking about the ghastly complications I had caused in my own emotional life.

'What didn't I do?' she laughed. 'After my father disowned me—a long story, which I will tell you another time—I was a fittings model, for a couture house in Paris. Later I was a war photographer. My first husband worked for Magnum and I just ended up doing it too. After the war I lived in Africa for several years, not working, then I lived in Connecticut and wrote cookery and gardening books. Finally I was a publisher in New York and then in London. And when I gave that up twenty years ago, I moved here.'

'That's amazing, Hermione,' I said. 'What a career. Why do you never talk about it?'

She shrugged.

'It's all in the past. I may be ancient, but I still

353

like to live in the present as much as possible. I'll give you some of my gardening books to look at before you go tonight, I think you will enjoy those—but, Amelia, don't change the subject. What are you going to do about your husband? It seems to me that you need to sort things out with him, one way or the other.'

'But I can't—he won't take my phone calls . . .'

'Do you not have a key to your flat any more?'

I looked at her. Of course I did. I'd never thought of that.

'So, go and see him,' she said. 'Telephones are not always the best way to handle affairs of the heart. Face to face is still the thing for that.'

*   *   *

My conversation with Hermione had really cleared my head, and on the train back to London on Sunday evening I added two unpleasant things to my mental To Do list. I dreaded them both.

Like it or not, I was going to have to go and see Ed and at least try to have a proper conversation about what had gone wrong between us. Even if it was the last one we ever had, we had to have it. What did Americans call it? Closure. That was what I needed.

But before that, I had to do something else I was dreading just as much. I was going to have to tell Joseph that I couldn't see him for a while. I didn't want to do it, I loved my cruise-y times with him—and I was really going to miss the hanky-panky, too, now he had given me such a taste for it—but it was all getting way too comfy-cosy with him way too quickly.

As Hermione had said, starting something you were hoping might develop into an ongoing relationship before you were properly disentangled from the previous one couldn't be healthy. No, I had to sort things out one way or another with Ed, before I let it get any more serious between me and Joseph. She was right—I needed some fallow time.

*   *   *

The train was really slow because of engineering works, and I didn't get back to Kiki's place until after nine that night. The minute she heard my key in the lock she ran to the front door and pulled it open, telling me I had to get changed immediately—we were going to a party, and Joseph was meeting us there. She was already dolled up in her favourite yellow chiffon party dress and seriously hyper.

'Calm down,' I said. 'You're going off like a firecracker. What is this great event?'

'It's an engagement party,' said Kiki, dancing from foot to foot as she did when she was excited. She grasped my hands and pulled me to her. 'Oh, Amelia, it's such good news—Ollie and Sonny are getting married!'

She had tears in her eyes.

'You old softie,' I said. 'You pretend to be such a hard nut about so-called boring relationships and look at you. You're all soppy and misty over this.'

'But, Amelia,' she said, 'it will be my first gay wedding—I'm so excited. I'm going to be the maid of honour. The outfit possibilities are endless . . .'

I went and changed into my own party gear—

355

something I was now capable of doing all on my own—and as I was putting on my make-up it sank in that Kiki had said Joseph was going to be at the party.

I felt distinctly uncomfortable at the prospect of seeing him in a public social context just when I had decided to cool things down with him, but as usual I got caught up in Kiki's excitement at the prospect of a happening and put it out of my mind as we scurried around spraying on perfume and deciding which ridiculously high-heeled shoes to wear.

The engagement party certainly seemed set to be a hoot. It was being held in a new burlesque club in Soho, which had been created out of an old one, keeping a lot of the tacky old fixtures, which added greatly to the atmosphere, and as well as the glamorous women in corsets and seamed stockings doing elaborate stripteases, there were drag queens and beautiful boys doing the same.

Joseph arrived shortly after me and Kiki, and we set off together to hunt down the happy couple. We found them near the stage, holding court on a semi-circular banquette upholstered with purple velvet. Oliver was glowing with pride, and Sonny was as sweet and modest as ever, although looking spectacular in a white suit.

'Here she is!' cried Oliver, when he saw us. 'Here's the girl who made this possible. Get over here, darling.'

He was talking to me, I realized—and I'd never heard him so benign, it was quite unsettling. It didn't last long.

'You lot,' he said, to the people who were sitting with them. 'Fuck off, all of you, I want my real friends sitting with me tonight. This is the girl who introduced me to my darling, and I want to thank her.'

He stood up, a little unsteadily, and put his arms out to me. He hugged me so hard, he nearly winded me. 'Thank you, Amelia,' he said into my ear, 'you uptight old tart. It's all down to you.'

'I only took him on as a gardener because he was so gorgeous,' I said, leaning down to kiss Sonny. He still made me blush.

Joseph and Kiki did their hugging and congratulating and then we all sat happily on the banquette, with me in the place of honour between Sonny and Oliver. He was looking at me thoughtfully, rather as a sculptor might look at his own artwork newly installed on a plinth.

'Looking good, babe,' he said. 'Your hair's great, of course, and it suits you being spunk drunk too. Kiki told me old Speccie Four-Eyes over there is a really dirty fuck and it looks like he's been giving you a seriously good seeing to as well.'

I wasn't sure I was hearing him right. 'Are you talking about Joseph?'

'Yeah. Those brainy straight boys are always big hornheads. Hey, Speccie,' he said, throwing a coaster at Joseph. 'So which of these two is a better shag then? Amelia or Kiki?'

I felt sick. I looked at Joseph, and the expression on his face said it all. He looked shattered, but I didn't care. It was clearly true. Kiki was oblivious to what was going on as she was kneeling on the seat talking to someone behind us.

I looked back at Oliver and my face was clearly giving me away as well.

'Don't tell me you didn't know he was shagging

357

both of you?' said Oliver, not in the least bit concerned that I might be upset. He chuckled with laughter and smacked his hand on my knee, squeezing it.

'That's why she set you up with him, darling. She said he was just the one to sort you out—and that was before you even told us you were actually frigid. How funny was that? Anyway, you know how generous Kiki is. She likes to share her blessings. So is his dick as big as she says, then?'

I stood up and pushed past him and Sonny to get off the banquette. I didn't even look at Joseph again as I walked off. I could hear him calling my name, and he caught up with me at the door, grabbing hold of my arm.

'Amelia!' he said. 'Stop. I can explain. It's not how it sounds . . .'

I turned round and looked at him, saying nothing. If I had spoken it would have come out as a roar, and I didn't want to do that in public. He didn't say anything either and, as I took in that handsome face for what would definitely be the last time, it was as if all the moments I had shared with him over the past twenty-five years flashed before me.

He never had been much good at having one girlfriend at a time, I reminded myself. He'd been at Dick's eighteenth party with another girl the night he had kissed me. That's why it had never gone anywhere that time—except to make all that trouble for me. He was a faithless bastard when he was eighteen and, clearly, nothing had changed. I should have followed my instincts from the time I saw him again at Kiki's party and had nothing to do with him.

I shook his hand off my arm and pushed my way out of the door on to the street, but he followed me.

'Please, Amelia . . .' he was saying again. 'Let me explain.'

'Joseph,' I said finally, turning round to face him and putting my hands on my hips, 'just fuck off. It's all you're good for.'

It felt really good to be so nasty to him, and it had the desired effect. I turned on my high heel and stalked off, and he didn't try to follow me.

27

Ten minutes later I was still standing on Regent Street in my now agonizing shoes desperately trying to find a cab, but at eleven-thirty on a Sunday night it was hopeless—they were all getting picked off by people further up. As I saw yet another yellow light go out as someone got into the taxi I thought I had been hailing, I realized that, even if I could find one, I still had a problem. I had no idea where to go in it.

There was no way I was going back to Kiki's place. What a traitor! I couldn't believe it. She'd said I should be thinking about marrying Joseph, when all along she'd been shagging him too. That's exactly what Oliver had said: 'Don't tell me you didn't know he was shagging both of you?'

I felt physically sick as I remembered it and started to wonder when they did it—not to mention how he found the energy—considering Joseph was with me practically every night, but forced myself to put it out of my mind. I didn't need to know the grisly details; the bare facts were bad enough.

My first proper girlfriend was definitely going to be my last, I vowed, hopping from foot to foot in the stupid shoes she'd given me. Ed had been right about the shoes and right about her. And it turned out I'd been right to avoid those kinds of girly friendships all along. I was so disappointed—but intensely relieved that at least we weren't formally in business together yet. That was a lucky escape.

But as I couldn't go back to her place, where on earth could I go? I was within easy walking distance of Mount Street, even in my crippling shoes, which was pretty funny, but I could hardly turn up there. What would I say? Sorry, Ed, turns out you were right about Kiki and Joseph all along, so can I move back in now please?

The old schoolfriends in Forest Hill and Ealing weren't going to welcome a phonecall close to midnight either. They all went to bed at nine o'clock ready for their 5 a.m. toddler alarm calls. And Louise, who would have been my first choice, was in Cornwall.

How about Dick? I tried him at home and on his mobile, but there was no answer on either. Sunday was a big pub night for him, and at this moment he was probably in a kebab shop in Earls Court, soaking up the alcohol with starch and fat, his mobile lost along the way. Dick was always losing his phone.

I walked towards Piccadilly Circus, wondering if I was going to end up sleeping down in the Tube station. The last trains to Rye and Maidstone had just gone, so I couldn't go to the cottage, or even to my parents.

So here I was. Celebrity clutter-clearer, Amelia Bradlow, so adept at sorting out other people's chaotic lives, and I didn't have a place to lay my own head that night.

I stood on the corner of Piccadilly in a daze, wondering what on earth to do, when suddenly the solution became clear as I saw the lights of the Ritz in the distance. Perfect. Back where I belonged, on the edge of my former Mayfair 'hood.

It would be comfortingly familiar, without being dangerously on Ed's regular beat. We used to have dinner there occasionally, if he suddenly felt the need for serious classical French haute cuisine, but it wasn't on the A list of his regular spots. I actually went there much more often than him, because tea at the Ritz was my mum's favourite treat. It was corny, but she loved it, and I was happy I was able to take her there.

I must have looked like I belonged, because the doorman's eyes flickered with recognition as he held the door for me, and the guy on the reservations desk didn't seem at all surprised to be checking in a lone woman in a silver-sequinned plunge-neck mini-dress with no luggage apart from a tiny clutch bag shortly before midnight.

If I was going to be homeless, I thought, as I filled in the registration card, I would do it in the style to which I was accustomed. And on Ed's black Amex card.

*   *   *

The next morning I woke with a start, very

confused. Then, simultaneously, as I realized where I was, the memory of why I was there came flooding back. I pulled the covers over my head and sobbed, as I remembered what Ollie had said and the stricken look on Joseph's face that had confirmed it to be true.

How could he and Kiki have done that to me? Was it their idea of a hilarious prank? Let's sexually awaken the frigid woman and then toy with her emotions.

That must have been it—and Ollie was clearly in on the joke—but it was bewildering, as I had been certain Joseph's feelings for me went way beyond our physical couplings. It had seemed apparent just in the way he looked at me and how much time he wanted to spend with me. He'd always been asking to have a weekend at the cottage with me . . .

As that thought came into my head, my stomach dropped. For a moment I thought I might be physically sick as I realized that my quiet weekends in the country had left Joseph perfectly available for Kiki. So I must have been his weekday lover, while she covered Friday and Saturday nights.

I knew he had a prodigious sexual appetite— every night and every morning was the minimum with him—but he must be some kind of full-on sex addict, I realized. He was probably having it off with other women as well. I knew several of his students had inappropriate crushes on him, so maybe he was servicing them in his lunch hour, as a little amusement. No wonder he was so fit.

As it all unfolded in my mind, I stopped crying and almost physically felt my despair turning into disgust. What a seedy set-up I had got myself involved in. They thought they were so sophisticated, but really it was just tawdry and tacky—which reminded me: everything I needed to get on with in my immediate life—starting with a clean pair of knickers and my phone charger—was in Kiki's flat. And there was no way I was going anywhere near that place.

She was probably in bed with Joseph there at that very moment. I let out an involuntary groan at the thought. How could I have been so stupid? Ed had been more than right about both of them—he had been almost prescient. There was no doubt about it now: Kiki was a slut and Joseph was a weasel. Official.

Of course, Dick was still friends with Joseph after twenty-five years, which you'd think would mean something, but as my brother had the emotional intelligence of a cricket stump when it came to romantic relationships, I decided his opinion about such things didn't count for much. Joseph Renwick had always been a womanizing bastard, was still a womanizing bastard. End of story.

That would be why he hadn't wanted to tell me why he had split up with his wife, I now understood. She'd probably caught him in bed with the nanny. Really, I should have known that a man with a sex drive like his would need more than one woman to satisfy it.

And as my disgust morphed into anger, my strength returned. I would organize myself out of this horrific situation. Jumping out of bed with almost frenzied energy, I had a hot shower and, after wrapping myself in the thick softness of the Ritz bathrobe, I sat on the bed, grabbed the pencil and notepad from the side table and started to make a list.

My first challenge was clothing. I couldn't leave the hotel room in a sequinned slash-front dress in broad daylight, so I would ask the concierge to find some kind of coat to lend me and, as soon as Zara opened on Regent Street, I'd go over there and buy enough clothes to keep me going for a day or two.

Later, I would get my trusted assistant clutter-clearer, Fiona, to bring me what I needed from the flat, in terms of clothes, my phone charger and laptop, and paperwork relating to the business. She already had a key, and I would arrange for her to do it when I knew Kiki would be out at her yoga class.

I could have gone over myself, but I couldn't bear the thought of seeing the bed where I had spent so many rapturous moments with Joseph, or the rooms where I had had so many happy times with Kiki.

That was easy. A bigger challenge was finding somewhere to live. I chewed the little rubber on the end of the pencil and wondered how to approach that, smiling wryly to myself as I realized there were now two major neighbourhoods off limits to me. Mayfair and Holland Park were both out. Oh well, I thought, that left the rest of London. I reckoned I could find somewhere.

I thought for a moment about asking Dick if I could stay with him for a while, but his scruffy one-bedroom in West Kensington really did not appeal. That place was a testament to his arrested development, right down to Formula One posters and a framed print of that girl in tennis kit with no

364

knickers on, which he considered a major work of art. His only drinking vessels were stolen beer mugs. Really, I reckoned, he needed me in my professional role, not as a flatmate.

No, there was only one thing for it. I would have to get my own place. It was lucky that—for the first time in my adult life—I had enough money of my own to do it, and it wouldn't have to be anywhere flash, because I still had the cottage to escape to at the weekend. I just needed a little toehold in London.

I rang down to the hotel's reservation department and negotiated a deal to keep the room for a week, then I fished the phone book from under the desk and started calling estate agents from my mobile, knowing from all my time staying in hotels with Ed that you never used their phones, unless you wanted to double your bill.

My first few attempts didn't go too well, because there were so many call-waiting tones bleeping over them. I would just be telling some perky-voiced young woman that I was looking for a furnished one-bedroom within walking distance of Charing Cross station, on a six-month lease, when the insistent 'beep beep' would distract me.

It was always Joseph, and I didn't answer.

Later in the morning, after I'd bought something to wear and was up in Highgate making my first visit to a huge house that I was sorting out for three siblings after the death of their elderly father, the calls started to come in from Kiki. I didn't take any of them either, and by midday there were ten messages in my voicemail inbox. I wanted to delete them all without listening, but I couldn't, as there might also have been some from clients and I certainly didn't want to miss those.

So I sat on a park bench on the way back to Highgate tube and listened to a very upset Joseph telling me 'it wasn't as it seemed' and could I please give him the chance to explain. I deleted them all after the first few words. The final one begged me please just to text him that I was OK, because he didn't know where I was and he was 'going mad with worry'.

'Go mad, then, fucker,' I said to the phone, as I deleted it.

Then there were several messages from Kiki, also telling me I had it all wrong and laughingly telling me not to be such a silly sausage and to give her a chance to explain.

I put my tongue out at the phone and deleted those without listening to them all the way through as well.

To my great surprise, there was also a message from Oliver. As it started with the words: 'Stop being a stupid cow . . .' I deleted that without listening further, as I had with all the others.

The last message was from Dick, saying he'd had a rather strange phonecall from Joseph, who was very worried about me, so could I please ring him. I did.

'What's going on, little sister?' he said. 'Don't tell me you and JR have already split up . . .'

'Me and who?' I said in arch tones.

'Oh,' said Dick. 'It's that bad, is it?'

'Yep,' I said.

'Well, he still seems awfully keen on you. He's worried because you're not staying with Kiki and you're not with me—so where the hell are you, actually? You're not back at Ed's, are you?'

'I'm fine,' I said. 'I'm staying in a hotel until I get my own place and, when I do, I'll give you the address on sworn oath that you will not give it to that shit Joseph Renwick.'

'Ten four,' said Dick, reverting as he did in any emotionally charged situation to his childhood settings.

Kiki made a few more attempts to get in touch with me, which I just deleted without listening beyond the first word. Then she started on a new tack, texting me ostensibly about things to do with the business. I deleted those too. I'd had so much coverage after Janelle's auction, I was already overloaded with work. I didn't need any more publicity. But one of her texts did make me sit up:

Vogue wants to feature you in a piece about wardrobe organizing. Please call me about that, if nothing else, you silly stubborn sausage.

I had a better idea. I rang *Vogue* myself, spoke to the features editor, who confirmed it was true— I'd had my suspicions it was one of Kiki's stunts— and asked her to put the writer directly in touch with me.

After that, Kiki finally stopped calling me.

It was very lovely staying at the Ritz, but I was very relieved when, on the fourth day, I found a perfectly nice little one-bedroom to rent in Charing Cross Road. It was in an old mansion block and, because it was at the back, the flat was surprisingly quiet. Barely five minutes' walk from the station, it was perfect for getting down to the cottage and really handy for work too.

I would have liked to have changed my mobile-phone number as well as my address but, for professional reasons, I couldn't. That was the number that was out there for work, so I had to stick to it. But after a few days Joseph stopped calling me constantly—I think Dick must have had a word—and I felt able to start a new life.

One person I did want to give my new address to, though, was Ed, so a few days after I moved in, bearing in mind what Hermione had said about telephones not always being the best way to communicate in 'affairs of the heart', as she called it, I sent him a note, on one of my beautiful new correspondence cards, which I knew he would appreciate. Ed loved good stationery.

Dear Ed
Here is my new address. I have moved out of Kiki's place, and it only seems fair for me to tell you that you were right about her.

I know you are probably still very angry with me, but it has been a very confusing time and I think we have both said things we shouldn't have.

I would truly love the chance to talk to you about all that has happened between us, face to face and in a calm way—preferably on neutral territory.

Do you think that might be possible?
Melia x

It was presumptive of me to use his old pet name for me to sign off, but I wanted to get the message over that I was speaking to him as the person I used to be, when we were still together, not as the slapper about town I had briefly been during my infatuation with Kiki, and my seduction by Joseph, as I now saw it.

He sent me a reply—on one of his own beautiful correspondence cards—in his achingly familiar loopy writing, suggesting we meet in Mount Street Gardens the next day at noon. I texted back my acceptance.

Not that the gardens were entirely neutral territory. They were a little oasis of calm, tucked away between Mount Street and South Audley Street, and something about the huge old London plane trees there made it incredibly peaceful. It was a special place Ed and I had always enjoyed in nice weather, to go and read the weekend papers, or just to sit and chat, to be outside for a while in the years before we got the cottage.

He was already sitting on 'our' bench, when I got there at midday, reading the paper, as usual.

'Hello, Ed,' I said, standing in front of him.

He looked up at me, and I was relieved to see all the coldness had gone from his face. He simply looked pleased to see me.

'Hello, Melia,' he said, putting out his hand to take mine. 'Sit down.'

For a moment we just looked at each other. His tan was even darker than the last time I'd seen him, set off by a very elegant beige and white check linen suit, in a different cut to his usual style.

'You're looking well,' I said, sitting down beside him. 'Have you been back to France?'

'Italy, actually,' he said.

That surprised me. Ed never went anywhere except France, or occasionally Scotland, if a client invited him up for some shooting, fishing, or stalking. He hated blood sports actually, but went anyway for the networking.

'You're looking beautiful,' he said. 'I've got used to that dreadful haircut now.'

He smiled as he said it, and I decided to let it pass without comment. Then he took my left hand in his and played with my wedding ring. I had never taken it off.

'I think we've both been rather silly, Amelia,' he said, gently. 'Don't you?'

I nodded, feeling suddenly teary. I couldn't speak.

'I'm sorry for what I said to you down in Winchelsea,' he continued. 'But I was just mad with jealousy at the thought of you being with someone else—anyone else—and then when I found later it was that frightful weasel Joseph Renwick, I couldn't bear it. So there was no going back. I might have spoken to you before this, but I was just too upset about that.'

I looked at him in amazement. There was no point prevaricating. If we were going to have this conversation, it had to be completely honest.

'How did you know it was him?' I asked, incredulous.

'Leo Mecklin told me,' he said. 'I ran into him at some ghastly party. He thought it was most amusing. Foul little toad.'

'Leo Mecklin!' I spluttered. 'How the hell did he know? He's never even met Joseph—except maybe at Kiki's party . . .'

The words died on my lips. Ed nodded. 'Yes, your little friend Kiki told him. They are quite the buddies those two, you know. Did you know she's selling her Australian art collection through Mecklin's?'

Now I really was speechless. I couldn't imagine why she was doing that, but that wasn't the issue—why on earth would she have told Leo about me and Joseph?

'You were right about her, Ed,' I said. 'I should have listened to you, but I was very impressed by all that girly stuff and her social whirl—I've never done any of that and it *is* good fun, and I'm afraid it clouded my judgement.'

'Don't blame yourself,' said Ed. 'I've had time to do a lot of thinking over these lonely months without you, and I have come to the conclusion you have had quite a dull time with me in a lot of ways over the years. I am a fuddy-duddy, I know that, but it's just the way I am. I'm stuck in my ways, Amelia, and I can see now that perhaps I have been unfair—selfish—imposing that on you. We're still young, and I've made you live like an old person.'

'But it was your quirky little ways that made me fall in love with you,' I said, truthfully. 'I knew what you were like and I chose to be with you but, to be honest, in the last few years it did start to get me down a bit. As I said before, I hated the separate beds . . .'

'And as I said before—why didn't you tell me how much that bothered you? I know we joked about it, but you should have told me that it was a big problem for you, instead of bottling it up.'

I looked at him. I really didn't know why I hadn't been firmer about it. I had always just gone along with all of Ed's little rules and regulations, until those last few weeks, when my sudden rash of acts of rebellion had caused all the problems.

'It's what I'm used to,' I said eventually. 'I've always done what Dad told me to, or risk a clip round the head, so I suppose I always did what you told me to do as well. And to be fair, Ed—when I did try to change things, like your birthday, you went ballistic.'

'Only because you didn't tell me first. If you'd discussed going to that dreadful sushi bar . . .' he laughed. 'No, the food was really good actually, superb, I was just in a foul mood. But if you'd talked to me about wanting to go there, I would have psyched myself up. So talk now, Amelia—tell me the other things that were getting you down.'

I sighed. I finally had my opportunity, and it was scary. Really scary. My heart was pounding. I decided to start with the simple stuff and work up to the big one.

'Well, you work too hard, Ed. I ended up spending most of my time on my own while you were in your study, and I was just really lonely. I think that's why I got so caught up with Kiki and that crowd, it was such fun to have company.'

'You're right, I was working too hard,' he said.

' "Was"?' I said, surprised.

He held the paper up to me. It was the *Times*, I noticed, rather than his customary *Telegraph*, but even more surprising was the headline on the front of the business section:

LAUREL CORP TO UNCORK BRADLOW'S BOTTLES

'I'm selling the business, Amelia,' he said. 'I'm bored with it. Dragging around France on my own. Doing the deliveries, long nights drinking with all those overly wealthy blowhards—it's boring. I'm bored with being professionally hungover, I'm bored with stroking egos to ease another few thousand quid out of people. I'm even bored with obscure French wine and the dipsomaniac freaks who make it. I want a change.'

I was dumbstruck. I couldn't have been more surprised if he'd told me he was having a sex change.

'That's why I went to Italy,' said Ed, grinning broadly. 'I've developed quite a taste for Prosecco . . . Well, I can drink it without throwing up, anyway, and Italian wine is quite interesting when you look into it. But what really interests me is the Italian approach to coffee. I know there are a million cappuccino bars in London now, but very few of them actually make decent coffee. It's all bland garbage. So I might start a new business based on that. High-end coffee for the masses. This suit is Italian, too, do you like it? It's Brioni.'

I had to laugh. Ed never did things by half.

Our talk had gone so well we decided to continue it over lunch, and the maître d' at Scott's was so pleased to see us, it was rather sweet.

'But how can you sell the business?' I asked him, once we were settled at our usual table. 'You *are* the business.'

He chuckled to himself.

'That's what I've been stuck in my study figuring out for the past year. I'll still be involved—for the first three years anyway—but over that time I will train up various wine writers to do the journal for me. What they really want is the brand name, which they are going to exploit in truly horrendous ways. There'll be all kinds of Bradlow's Bottles-branded wine paraphernalia, with concessions in

373

big stores and stand-alone duty-free boutiques selling it. Crap like that. There's going to be a blog . . .' He pulled a face.

'Doesn't that bother you?' I asked, amazed. He had always been so particular about the sanctity of the brand.

'Ten million quid can ease a lot of pain,' said Ed and raised his glass to me.

I raised mine back. 'But why didn't you tell me you had that in the pipeline? I might have understood why you were working so hard.'

'I didn't think you'd be interested. I know the gloss went off the whole wine scene for you a long time ago, Amelia. I was going to tell you when it was all sorted, as a jolly surprise. I had been planning to do it on my birthday, actually. That was why I was so cross when it all went wrong.'

He smiled at me, sadly, and tears pricked my eyelids.

'Anyway, I'm sick of thinking about all that,' he said, clearly trying to cheer things up. 'It's in the past. Tell me about your new place.'

'Well, it's very small, just a *pied à terre* really, within walking distance of the station, so I can go easily between there and Winchelsea.'

'How are things down there? How is your *potager*? I was very impressed when I saw it.'

I had a pang as I remembered the happy afternoon I'd spent with Sonny and Oliver and Kiki and Joseph finishing off the raised beds. Although I was desperately hurt by what they'd done to me, it was still hard just to dismiss them. We'd had such good times together. But there was no going back: I had to put them out of my head. They weren't real friends—and the longer I talked to Ed, the more I felt he was.

We carried on chatting right through lunch, so companionably and easily I almost forgot that there had ever been a problem between us. I just sank back into the familiar comfort of his company.

He was so original and smart, I realized all over again as he talked about his plans for the coffee business. No wonder all those hedge-fund billionaires loved hanging out with him—and no wonder some big corporation was prepared to pay so much for what was really a piece of his brain. He just wasn't like anyone else. So when the waiter came to offer us coffee and Ed asked me if I would rather have it back at the flat, where he had some rather special single-estate Kenyan beans, it seemed natural to say yes.

It was strange being back there—odd because it was so familiar—but I soon relaxed into it and, as we sat on the sofa talking, drinking amaretto with our espressos—which were amazingly good—I really felt I had come home. So when Ed put his arms around me and started kissing me, it didn't seem inappropriate.

'Let's go to bed,' he said. 'Our bed. We won't have separate bedrooms any more, Melia, I promise. Come home and live with me again, starting right now.'

I didn't answer him, but just let him lead me to his bedroom, where he walked over to the bed and took Mr Bun off it, placing him on the bedside table, facing the wall. Then as I watched him take something out of the drawer, I realized I had made a terrible, lazy-minded mistake letting things get this far.

It was his precious condom which he'd got out ready, and it was a cruel reminder that I still hadn't told him the real reason I had left him.

I was instantly furious with myself for letting it come to this without having discussed the big issue with him. Yet again, I'd let him steamroller over me, seduced by his style, brilliance and charm into forgetting about my own needs. No wonder he was such an amazing salesman, I thought. In his quiet way, he could get you to do exactly what he wanted.

'Ed,' I said, and my heart sank when he turned around and looked at me, his face all bright and happy, clearly convinced everything was now sorted.

I let out a big sigh. I just had to say it.

'Ed, this is all a bit hasty. We need to talk some more before we start behaving like nothing has happened. There is one major issue we still haven't discussed.'

His face fell, and the way he flicked the condom on to the bed indicated his irritation. He had thought it was all going exactly the way he wanted it to, and suddenly it wasn't. I looked at him intently, expecting his expression to darken as he realized what I was referring to, but it didn't. I couldn't believe it. I was going to have to spell it out to him yet again.

Playing for time, I suggested we had some more of that amazing coffee and went through to the kitchen to make it. I was struck by how easily I slipped back into automatic pilot in there. Everything was where it had always been. The same cups, the same French sugar cubes in the familiar box with a parrot on it. The only thing that was different was the coffee. He always used to buy a French blend from the Algerian Coffee Shop in Soho but now the cupboard where we kept it was full of neat canisters of different beans, clearly labelled in Ed's writing. I smiled despite myself.

He came in to join me, as I fiddled about, sitting on one of the high stools by the brunch counter—a leftover from his mother's 1970s decor—and looking brightly at me. He had clearly decided to hide his earlier disappointment to try and keep everything sweet between us. I gave him mental points for effort.

'So come on, then,' he said eagerly, as though it were all a huge lark. 'What is the other issue that's bugging you? Tell me?'

I sighed deeply. 'Oh, Ed, surely you know? It's the family thing. If we don't get on with it right now, I'll be too old. I'm nearly on the black ski run already.'

He looked confused. 'What ski run? What are you talking about? You want to go skiing with your family but you're worried you're too old?'

I couldn't help laughing, but I was getting exasperated. 'No. That's not it.' I took a deep breath. 'I want a *baby*, Ed. Remember?'

This time he did understand. I could tell by the frown that had immediately appeared between his eyebrows. 'Oh, not that again,' he said wearily.

'That's exactly what I'm talking about,' I said, making a Herculean effort not to raise my voice. 'You think it's a boring old subject that's been discussed, dismissed and can now be forgotten— but for me it is very much still a hot issue. In fact, it gets hotter with every day that passes and takes me nearer to my thirty-seventh birthday, which is when my fertility will go into freefall.'

'You mean it would be harder for you to get pregnant after thirty-seven?' said Ed, at least making an effort to understand.

'Yes,' I said. 'And harder and more risky still with every year that follows. I've got a serious deadline with this, Ed.'

'But what about Madonna?' said Ed.

'Statistical freak,' I said, trying to remain patient. 'Not many other women can fill Wembley Stadium either. Or buy Cecil Beaton's house . . .'

He sipped his coffee and looked thoughtful. 'I understand your sense of urgency,' he said slowly, as if he were thinking it out as he spoke, 'but I'm afraid it still doesn't change my position. I don't want to have children, Amelia. You've always known that. I've never indicated otherwise, or done anything to string you along that I might change my mind. You've always known the score, and the fact that your window of opportunity to have them is getting smaller doesn't make any difference to that. I wouldn't want them if we only had one more day to do it. Do you understand?'

'No,' I said. 'I do not understand why a brilliant, intelligent, wonderful person like you, who professes to love me, would not want to celebrate that love by having a child together.'

He put his cup down. He looked serious, but not angry, I was relieved to see.

'Let me try and explain,' he said. 'I think I am an unusually lucky person, Amelia, because I love my life—or I love the life I had with you in it. I know what makes me happy and I am in a financial position to do those things. I have watched all my

378

friends have kids, and I know what happens. If we had a child, I would have to give up my freedom to do what I enjoy when I want to, and I am not prepared to do that.'

I opened my mouth to speak, but he stopped me. 'I'm only going to say this once, Amelia, so please let me finish. I categorically do not want to have a child, so if I give in to you on this point just to persuade you to come back to me, I would be giving my consent to having a child I don't want. As far as I am concerned, it would be an unwanted child.'

He paused, sighing deeply, and looked at me very seriously. 'I was an unwanted child, Amelia,' he said, 'and I don't want to do that to someone else. So—no. No children.'

I could feel the disappointment that had been growing in me turning to anger. I was about to lash out when I saw Ed had tears in his eyes. It had not been easy for him to say that last thing, I realized.

I went over and put my arm around him. 'Has that been the real reason, all this time?' I said. 'And you couldn't tell me?'

'It's a big part of it,' he said.

'But don't you think that having a child of your own could help to put that right?' I asked him quietly. 'By loving your own child, couldn't you somehow love the lonely child you once were?'

'No,' he said. 'It's too late to do that, and I will never change my mind, Amelia. It's not just my rubbish childhood, it's about how I want to live my adult life. I'm sorry, but I have never led you on about this. So if you come back to me—and I dearly hope you will—it has to be on those terms.'

This time, I believed him.

379

*　　　*　　　*

I left the flat in Mount Street sadder than I had ever been. I didn't feel angry with Ed at all. He had finally been completely honest with me and at least I knew exactly where I stood. It just wasn't where I wanted to be.

As I walked once again along those almost unbearably familiar paving stones towards Berkeley Square, en route to my new flat, I felt as though I had been cast adrift with nothing and no one to anchor my life to. I had never felt so lonely.

I could still go back to Ed, I reminded myself. As I left he was still telling me he desperately wanted me to 'come home', but I'd said I needed a lot more time to think about his non-negotiable terms. He'd been very reasonable about that, and we had parted in sadness, not anger. Which almost made it worse.

If we'd had another huge blow-up, I could have fled decisively on the energy of my fury but, like this, I felt every step was carrying me away from the nicest man I had ever known. But, I had to ask myself, was that really love—or was it familiarity?

I felt even more alone when I got back to my little flat. It had seemed like an exciting new phase to have a place of my own for the first time when I had moved in, but now it felt like some kind of nun's cell—a horribly furnished one too. And while being at the back of the building was great for avoiding the traffic noise, it meant my outlook was an ugly lightwell and brick walls.

I knew there was a beautiful summer evening out there, and I felt trapped inside, as if I were missing out on life. I found the sitting room, with the kitchen at one end of it, particularly claustrophobic, so I sat in the bedroom, which felt more homely, with a big pile of my own cushions piled up on the bed.

I leaned back on them and thought about the day's events. Since that morning, I'd had what had seemed like a lovely rapprochement with Ed, then narrowly escaped what would have been a very ill-advised sexual reunion, which had led directly back to deadlock on the big problem in our relationship.

So there I was, all alone, with two men looming large in my life, both of them hopeless. One of them seemed to love the idea of children but couldn't keep his pants zipped; the other was devotedly faithful but absolutely refused to have children. It was too much to take in. Meanwhile, I was another day closer to my thirty-seventh birthday in September.

I wondered what they were each doing now. With regard to Joseph, I put the thought out of my mind again as quickly as it had come in. I dreaded to think what he had planned for a Friday, beyond deciding which of his willing lady friends he would be servicing.

Ed was more predictable. It was just after seven o'clock, and he would be sitting in the bar at Duke's Hotel, sipping one of Alessandro's legendary vodka martinis. That was how he comforted himself when he'd had a particularly bad day and I was sure this one would qualify. It was another of his precious Ian Fleming moments. Then he'd go for dinner at Morton's, where he'd sit at his favourite table and order the steak frites, cooked rare, nursing a glass or six of Pomerol—or perhaps now more likely something obscure and Italian—and it gave me a pang as I realized I didn't even know what kind of Italian wine Ed would drink.

If I had agreed to go back to him I could have shared that whole adventure with him, I realized. We could have learned Italian together, something I'd always wanted to do.

Thinking about that—and imagining him sitting alone in that so-familiar bar, thinking sadly about me, I didn't doubt—it would have been so easy just to get off my bed and go and join him there, taking up my exquisitely comfortable old life where I had left off, to climb back into my fur-lined rut. But I just couldn't.

It was absolutely clear to me now that my choice came down to this: I could have Ed and definitely no children. Or I could give up Ed for the possibility of finding someone to have a child with—and my misadventure with Joseph had already shown me the pitfalls of that path.

The odds of a thirty-seven-year-old woman finding a man who wanted to have children with her in time for her still to be able to have them were very short indeed. So, the way things were, I was most likely to end up with no Ed and no children.

Maybe, I thought, the same old arguments going around in my head again, I should just cut my losses and at least have the lovely man and the enviable lifestyle—even more luxe now he was selling the business—but, even thinking about that option, I felt a stab of pain somewhere in my belly.

Just the day before I'd received an email from Louise with photos from Posy's fifth birthday party. I pulled my laptop on to my knees and had another look at the pictures: Posy shyly holding up a piece of paper with a big pink '5' drawn on it. Posy in a sparkly pink dress waving a wand. Posy's rapt face looking at the lit candles on her birthday cake. A group of little girls in fairy wings chasing each other through an apple orchard. Fat tears poured down my cheeks.

Was it abnormal for a woman to want that? I didn't think so. Really, when you considered it, there was probably nothing more normal.

I kissed Posy's little face on the screen. I had held her the day she was born, and I'd always felt such a special connection with her. But since they'd made the big move to Cornwall, I'd only seen them all once, right after the twins were born. Now it was just emails and photos like this and the odd treasured drawing through the post.

Was that going to be as close as I would ever be to children in the years to come? The way Dick was going, I wouldn't even have any nieces and nephews. It was all so wrong—and I was beginning to understand why my parents were increasingly frustrated about it.

I lay back on the cushions with my arms behind my head and thought about Kiki and her strange antipathy to having children. I couldn't imagine what made her so against the idea. She should have been married to Ed, not me. Shame they loathed each other, because they could have had a life of untrammelled, childless pleasure together— although it seemed a pretty empty prospect to me.

I wondered what she was doing that lovely summer evening. No doubt she was at some glamorous party, caught up with her brittle crowd, laughing too hard at nothing, drinking too much and spilling out of the venue on to the pavement with all the smokers, where the action was these days.

And then, of course, that made me wonder again what Joseph was doing. This time, I let myself think about him. Perhaps he was with her. Maybe they were an official item now I was out of the picture. Suddenly I felt a physical yearning for him so strong I grabbed hold of a pillow and hugged it to me, pretending it was him. It wasn't just a sexual thing—I missed his physical presence, his reassuring bulk, the broad shoulders I could cling on to.

If he hadn't been such an arsehole, maybe we could have become an official couple and had a baby. He could have got me 'gloriously up the duff', as he'd called it. It was obvious from that— and from how cut up he was about the separation from his stepchildren—that he loved kids and pregnancy and the whole package of reproduction and family life. What a contrast to Ed's attitude. Whenever I'd told him a friend was expecting a baby he had pulled a repulsed face.

I looked at my mobile on the bedside table and willed it to ring. Suddenly, I desperately wanted Joseph to call me. In that moment, I knew, however hurt and angry I had been, I would have begged him to rush over right away. So why didn't I just ring him? Give him that chance to explain that he had pleaded for?

My hand reached out for the phone, but I stopped short. What possible explanation could put it right? He'd behaved like there was something special between us, but all along he'd been sleeping with Kiki too. What was it Oliver had said? 'Don't tell me you didn't know he was shagging both of you?' There was no way to make that acceptable.

No wonder his wife had kicked him out, I reminded myself. He was a bastard, he always had been, that was all there was to it. The sooner I could stop thinking about him, the better. What I needed was a faithful, reliable man, I told myself . . . Someone like Ed. Which brought me right back to the start of the argument.

I nearly yelped with frustration as I realized the mental merry-go-round had done its full circuit for the umpteenth time that day. I knew I had to get out of the flat before it started off again.

I stepped out into the soft air and crossed Charing Cross Road. As I wandered aimlessly into Leicester Square I felt more like some kind of alien spaceperson with every step. Everywhere I looked there seemed to be couples strolling along hand in hand, smiling and laughing.

I'd better get used to this thing called being single, I thought. I'd hardly had a chance to find out what it was like, going straight from home to university, to being married to Ed, to dating Joseph.

Maybe it wouldn't be so bad, I told myself firmly. It did have its advantages—I could see that already—and I did really need to have some fallow time, as Hermione had said. And if she'd learned to be happy on her own after all those husbands, I could jolly well get to like it too.

So, to educate myself in the ways of the twenty-first-century single woman, I bought the entire boxed set of *Sex and the City*. Then I picked up a bottle of Tasmanian pinot noir and a tub of Ben and Jerry's Cherry Garcia ice cream—Ed would have been appalled, I thought happily—and headed back to the flat with something like a spring in my step.

Thinking of Hermione made me want to just keep walking down the hill to Charing Cross station and get on the train to Winchelsea, where I had already grown to enjoy being on my own, but I knew I wouldn't be able to go for a while.

I still had that huge job on, sorting out the house in Highgate. It was a big place—seven bedrooms—and an absolute tip. The man who had died had been a well-known historian, and he had lived and worked there for forty years, so there were Jurassic layers of clutter to clear.

Even with my assistant and a specialist archivist I had recruited to do his study, preserving all the papers for posterity, according to his children's instructions, it was going to take at least another couple of weeks. And they were paying extra for me to do it as quickly as possible, so I was going to have to work all that weekend and probably the next two as well. What a bore.

So I wasn't going to be able to see Hermione and have one of my comforting chats with her for ages, which was a royal bore, but as I was in the rickety lift going back up to the flat, I suddenly had a great idea. I would ring Hermione. I needed to tell her I wasn't coming down that weekend, and there was no reason I couldn't have a chat to her on the phone. We didn't have to have all our conversations sitting on her terrace.

'Amelia, dear,' she said when she answered. 'How lovely to hear from you. Is everything all right?'

Well, that did it. Just when I'd thought I'd reached some kind of equilibrium about my situation, it took one kind enquiry and I let out what I knew was an audible sob.

'Oh, I'm sorry, Hermione,' I said, recovering myself. 'It's just I am desperate to come down to the cottage, but I won't be able to come this weekend, or probably the next one either.'

'Tell me about it,' she said, simply.

So I told her about my near-reconciliation with Ed and his final pronouncement on the baby issue. Then I heard my voice wobbling treacherously again as I outlined my situation as I had analysed it.

'What I find so hard to cope with, Hermione, is the awful choice between Ed and no kids—and no Ed and still possibly no kids. I just don't know what to do. I do still love him, but I think he is being so unfair. Surely if he really loved me, he wouldn't let me be so unhappy about something?'

'Hmmmm,' said Hermione, 'that is a very difficult dilemma.' She paused. 'Have you considered writing a pros and cons list about Ed?' she said.

*　　　*　　　*

One hour and several glasses of the Ninth Island pinot later, and my list was finished. I sat up straight and stared at the blinking screen of my laptop until my eyes started to smart.

Staying Married to Ed—Pros and Cons

Pro.
Can be the sweetest man in the world (Mr Bun)
Really loves me
Fifteen years' shared history
Very loving
Very funny
Very clever
Very successful
Highly respected
Glamorous lifestyle
Financially secure
Flat in Mount Street
Beautiful profile, hair, hands, feet, etc.
  £10 million . . .

Con.
Can be the most stubborn man in the world
Quirky to the point of eccentricity (Mr Bun . . .)
Doesn't like me having girlfriends
Can be a silly snob
Tendency to selfishness
Sulks if doesn't get own way (e.g. haircut . . .)
Works too much
Wine obsession gets boring
Keeps anti-social hours
Heinous cow of a mother
My dad hates him
Crap in bed
Absolutely refuses to have children

And there it was. I counted up and there were thirteen points in each one, which didn't seem to augur well but, as I looked at them, I knew the issue wasn't quantity anyway. It was content. I took another big swig of my wine, read through the lists again and then highlighted the last one and put it in thirty-six point, and the boldest font I could find:

Absolutely refuses to have children

That said it all. The other pros and cons all pretty much balanced each other out, but there was nothing to compensate for that. Even if I never met another man, I couldn't stay with Ed if he insisted on imposing that restriction on me. It just wasn't right.

I would just have to learn to love being single and hope for the best.

28

I was missing my weekends in Winchelsea desperately and longing to see what the new gardener had done, but I was actually very happy to be frantically busy at work, because it was such a useful distraction from thinking.

But the day I had a surprise call from Janelle, saying she needed me to pop round for a 'follow-up' visit, I began to wonder if I would need to clone myself to cope. If all my clients were going to expect this kind of aftercare as well as the initial clutter-clearance, it was going to mean twice as much work again.

Settling back in the rackety Northern Line tube carriage on my way up to see her, I wondered if I should promote Fiona to do some of the first appointments to try and clear some of the backlog.

The waiting list just kept getting longer and I had understood from my very first experiences with Kiki and Janelle that getting on to the job as soon as possible was of paramount importance to the desperate client.

But that pressure was almost too much at times—especially now I no longer had Kiki there to field all the calls from the media, which were still coming thick and fast. Perhaps, I pondered, I would need to take on a PR company to look after that side of things for me.

As I sat there looking at the ridiculously busy day I had ahead of me on my iPhone schedule, I keenly wished I still had her and Ed to discuss such important business decisions with. I tried to imagine what each of them would say if I asked them about splitting the first consultations with Fiona.

I could almost hear Ed's voice in the rattling of the train. 'You *are* your brand, Melia, my darling,' he would say. 'They are paying for you and what you represent. Never water that down. If you physically can't do more, you have to charge more instead for the real thing. That's what I've always done.'

And what would Kiki's take on it be, I wondered. Similar, just put differently. 'Shit no, darls,' she'd say. 'They're paying for the glamour associated with Amelia Bradlow. They want the woman they've seen in *Grazia* not some superannuated chalet girl in Marks & Spencer's jeans.'

So, gathering up my bags, ready to get off at Hampstead, I decided to abandon that idea, wondering whether I had quite made the decision myself or not, but fairly sure it was the right one.

*   *   *

Janelle was waiting at the open door of her flat when I got there, smiling broadly. Her eyes were a startling violet colour now, I noticed.

''Allo, darling,' she said, giving me a big hug. 'How are you? You looked great in the mag. Were you pleased with it?'

I promised her I was, although I had no idea which one she was talking about, and looked round the hallway, puzzled. It was immaculate. Perfectly clean and tidy.

'The flat looks great, Janelle,' I said. 'So what can I do for you?'

'Well, come through to the lounge and I'll show you,' she said, grinning mischievously.

I understood why when I walked through the door. Ollie was sitting there, clearly waiting for me, legs akimbo, his arms spread along the back of the sofa.

'Hi, babe,' he said, not bothering to get up.

'Surprise!' said Janelle, like it was all a great hoot.

'Hello, Oliver,' I said coldly.

'Oh, don't start with that old arctic-knickers shit,' he said. 'Sit down here and let me talk to you.'

'No, thank you,' I said, and turned to Janelle, who was looking crestfallen.

'Did you want to discuss anything with me?' I asked her, as warmly as I could muster. 'Because I am happy to help you in any way I can, but if this is just a social visit with Oliver, I think I'll be off. I

391

have an awful lot of clients to see today.'

'Oh, come on, Amelia,' said Janelle. 'I'll put the kettle on and we can all have a nice cup of tea. Ollie said he needs to talk to you about the wedding. He said he can't get married until he sorts things out with you, so I thought we could all go through it together. I love weddings . . .'

I turned back to Oliver.

'So that's what this is all about, is it?' I said, feeling the anger rising up inside me like a geyser. 'This is all about me salving your conscience so I will come to your wedding and everything will be lovely for you. Unbelievable. And quite despicable of you to involve Janelle in it . . .'

'Oh, come on, Amelia,' said Ollie, sounding pretty angry himself. 'I said a lot of stupid things that night—I was drunk, OK? And over-excited. But get off your fucking high horse for a minute and listen to me. You are such a stubborn cow and you are breaking Sonny's heart with this—and Kiki's . . .'

'What about my fucking heart?' I screamed at him, and I fled from the room, the flat and the building.

I could hear Janelle calling after me as I left, but I kept going. I'd ring her when I recovered, I promised myself, as I ran up Hampstead High Street towards the tube.

At that moment I just needed to get away from everything that reminded me of Joseph and Kiki and the entire sordid scene I'd got myself so unfortunately tangled up with. They were revoltingly tacky, the lot of them, as that little scenario had reminded me.

By the time I reached the tube station I was

panting heavily, not just because it was uphill, but from the tidal wave of emotion that had crashed over me. It was as though I had managed to put that whole episode—and the people involved in it—where it belonged, in the past, but seeing Oliver had made it all real again. And that made Kiki real and Joseph real, and that was what I couldn't bear.

The only way I knew how to cope with the hurt from what those two had done to me was to carry on like none of it had ever happened—the good or the bad—but now I had been forced out of that artificial mental refuge, and it was so damned painful.

I sat down heavily on a bench and sobbed. As the tears came pouring out of me I felt quite out of control—it was a public place after all—but strangely it felt good to let it all go. After a few minutes, a kind older lady stopped to ask if I was all right, and lifting my head to thank her and say I would be fine nudged me back into the here and now.

I took some deep breaths and groped for my trusty box of tissues, always ready for weepy clients in my tote bag and at that moment very useful for weepy me. Then, once I had recovered enough to breathe properly, I went into a nearby florist and ordered a large bunch of flowers for Janelle, attaching a non-specific note of apology.

After that unpleasant outing, I was happier than ever to lose myself in work. I stayed at the historian's house in Highgate late every night, mainly to get the job done but also to be somewhere that wasn't on my own in the flat, or on my own surrounded by those goddam happy couples, who seemed to be everywhere else.

I hadn't noticed them when I was in a happy couple myself, but now I couldn't seem to escape them. It almost became a private joke I had with myself, because if I wasn't following them around the supermarket as they stocked up for another joyous weekend together, no doubt filled with picnics and afternoons strolling around art galleries, it seemed they were off to the myriad theatres or cinemas near my new flat, sharing confidences over coffee, or just bloody holding hands everywhere I looked.

I felt awful to think that for so many years I had been half of one of those happy duos, quite unaware of how much pain my very existence might be causing single onlookers. I sent them all a mental retrospective apology.

There wasn't even any escape when I was home alone. I was watching quite a bit of television to pass the time, and even the adverts were full of neat little pairs. I did actually laugh out loud every time another lot of them appeared, but there was a bitter edge to it.

And, of course, every time I saw another Mr and Mrs Happy Couple, the thought would come tripping into my mind that I only needed to pick up the phone and I could be back in one myself, with Ed, but I couldn't let myself do that. Thanks to Hermione's brilliant advice, I had made my decision in a very considered way, and I wouldn't let myself go back on it, just to run away from being lonely.

My conviction that I had made the right choice was renewed again one morning when I had what I had come to think of as my monthly low moment, waking up with that telltale dull ache in my belly, and the bright-red reminder in the loo.

I knew in my rational brain that I couldn't be pregnant—I hadn't had sex and I hadn't had a visit from the Angel Gabriel—but now I understood that through all the years with Ed there had always been a tiny kernel of irrational hope buried deep inside me that somehow it might happen.

Even though I'd known it was extremely unlikely—if not actually impossible with the Pill and condom combo—my lower brain had always secretly nurtured the idea. It only took one sperm and one egg, after all.

What would Ed have done if I had? I wondered, as I ran myself a bath one morning, having woken up yet again with the bright-red reminder in the loo that I still wasn't a mother.

Maybe it would have changed his mind, having fatherhood presented to him as an implacable fact—but then, maybe it wouldn't have. Either way, now I would never know. And to remind myself why I had left him and why our marriage had to end, after I finished my bath, I printed out the last sentence from the cons list and stuck it up on the wall in every room in my flat.

My plan was that, every time I had a wobble and was tempted to call him, just to get away from the gut-tearing sadness of being on my own after so many years with him—and my brief, ill-fated romance with Joseph—I could make myself read it. I had to remind myself that I was better off alone than with the wrong man. I wasn't going to go back to Ed on his brutal terms.

I still hadn't finally told him that though. I just couldn't. He had been ringing me every few days—

ostensibly to see how I was, but clearly really to see if I was ready to go back yet—until in the end I'd had to ask him, nicely, to leave me be until I contacted him. He took it pretty well, considering.

'Barkis is still willin',' he'd said. 'Maybe not for ever, but he's still willing at the moment.'

I felt a bit guilty stringing him along like that, but although my mind was now made up, I just wasn't quite ready to make it official by telling him that. I couldn't quite understand what was making me hold back until a visit to a new client spelled it out for me.

Celia lived in a tiny Kensington flat and, as with so many of my first visits, there was a problem even opening the front door. In her case it was because the place was stacked up with furniture piled to the ceiling like some kind of storage depot.

I didn't say anything as we picked our way via a circuitous—and probably quite dangerous—route through bookcases piled on top of sideboards, to a corner of the sitting room where there was a small table and two accessible chairs. Then I accepted her offer of a cup of tea, so I could have a think and suss it out.

She seemed to be taking an awfully long time making it, so I peeped through the serving hatch into the kitchen to check she was all right, and saw what appeared to be several sets of china piled up around her on every work surface. One of them had a special Christmas pattern, I noticed. There was also an inordinate amount of general kitchen equipment in there, including a whole set of copper pans, and a fish kettle big enough for a whole salmon.

Then, on my way back to my seat, I spotted a photograph in a large silver frame, which gave me the clue I needed. It was a family group, with a younger version of Celia—she was now in her early sixties—and three young children. There was a man in the centre of the photograph next to her, but his face had been carefully cut out. Other frames contained pictures of the same people in different parts of what looked like a lovely house and garden. The man's head was missing in all of them.

She eventually appeared, carrying an enormous tray laden with a silver teapot, matching milk jug and sugar bowl, tongs, strainer, two beautiful teacups and saucers and a plate of biscuits. The tray was actually bigger than the table and we had to be careful not to tip it over. What an impossible way for anyone to live, I thought.

Having checked my tissue situation—I had plenty—I decided to use my shock-tactics method. If I played the middle-class English game of pretending everything was lovely with this lady, I would get nowhere. I knew that because she reminded me keenly of my own mother.

I took a sip of tea and launched in. 'So who did your husband leave you for?' I asked her. Bingo! Her teacup clattered back on to the saucer and she looked at me, horrified, her mouth hanging open. 'It will be better if you tell me the whole story,' I said, words I was rather regretting an hour later, when she was still—between sobs, sniffs and nose blows—relating the entire sorry scenario of her divorce.

Her husband, an accountant by profession, had left her for his secretary, who was some thirty-five

397

years younger, and they were now living together in Australia, with a new baby. Having set things up carefully in advance, with most of his money hidden offshore, he had managed to settle Celia with the bare minimum.

All she'd really come away from forty years of marriage with were the contents of the family house. She only had the flat because she had recently inherited it from an aunt.

'The children want me to sell it all,' she said, dabbing her eyes. 'But I just can't. It's all I have of my life since I was twenty-one. All I ever did was devote myself to my house and my family.'

I noted that she had put the house first, which told me a lot about her priorities. It wasn't going to be easy to persuade her, but it was obvious her children were right. It was either sell most of it or move to a larger place in a much less prestigious part of London. There were no other solutions.

From what she'd told me about her financial situation, she'd have to sell something even to pay me, which made me feel very uncomfortable, but I really believed letting some of it go and staying in the nice area was the healthier option for Celia. Being surrounded by reminders of her former gracious home was actually the last thing she needed.

Relating the details of the court case—which sounded gruesome—had left her very shaky, and I didn't want to put her through too much on the first visit, so I decided to concentrate on the kitchen. By the end of the afternoon, I had persuaded her to reduce it to just two out of the five sets of china and had also convinced her that, with the splendid Marks & Spencer food department on Kensington High Street, she really didn't need the fish kettle. It was a start.

When I left, feeling desperately sorry for Celia, so cruelly abandoned, battered and bewildered, I decided to walk home through Hyde Park in the afternoon sun to clear my head. She was clearly so traumatized by the experience of her divorce it made me think properly for the first time about what might be in store for me once I told Ed my decision.

I certainly wasn't interested in forcing some kind of huge revenge settlement from him—really I just wanted the cottage. I just hoped that hurt and bitterness didn't make him turn on me and try and block me having it out of spite. He could bring up the affair with Joseph, I realized, and paint me as a shocking slut, if he really wanted to be nasty.

Of course, now he was going to be so wealthy, I could hold out for half of it, like so many of the dumped first wives of his clients seemed to do— the men were always moaning on about it, as though they were the wronged parties—and I'd be a very rich woman. And I could certainly claim in all honesty that I'd helped him build up the business over the years we had been together. I had all the evidence of Heady Bouquet in the journals to prove that—but going all out for what I could get was not my style.

It would have been different if I'd still been working at Mecklin's, I thought, breathing deeply as I walked along the tree-lined path near the Serpentine Gallery. I would have needed a decent payout just to continue living in London at all, let alone in the style I was used to, but now I was earning very good money of my own and it felt great. I didn't need Ed's cash as well.

With that in mind, when I got home, I went straight into the kitchen, took out my wallet and cut up all Ed's credit cards. I hesitated for a moment over the black Amex—I had so enjoyed plonking that down in front of snotty waiters and shop assistants—but then, snip, it was done.

In that instant I became a financially independent woman—and my split from Ed finally felt official. I just had to tell him.

*   *   *

In the meantime, without him, or Kiki, to turn to, and Hermione available only on the phone for the time being, the person I came to rely on in those first dismal weeks as a single woman in her late mid-thirties was my brother.

'How do you not get desperately lonely, Dick?' I asked him one Wednesday night when we were having a curry in Charlotte Street, his choice of restaurant.

'Oh, that's easy, sis,' said Dick, raising his bottle of Kingfisher beer to me, 'I drink.'

'Are you serious?' I said. 'I know you have always been fond of a pint, as you put it, but do you really consciously drink to block out your feelings?'

'What other reason is there?' said Dick, looking deadly serious. As if to prove his point, he drained his bottle and signalled to the waiter for another.

'To have fun?' I said, thinking of all the hilarious nights I'd had with Kiki after drinking way too much champagne. We'd laughed and laughed, which had felt great at the time, but perhaps there was something slightly desperate about the way Kiki determinedly had an alcohol-fuelled good time. I wasn't sure whether she could really have one without the bubbles to get it going.

'Or,' I said, still pondering, 'how about for the experience of the drink itself. Like Ed with his wine.'

Dick laughed very loudly. Not a pretty sight with a mouth full of lamb vindaloo.

'You are joking, aren't you?' he said. 'Do you really think Ed drinks for the taste of his precious wine?'

I nodded. 'Of course. He's widely considered to have one of the finest palates in the world . . .'

'He's also one of the finest pissheads in the world,' said Dick. 'I like your ex-husband, or whatever he is these days, but he is a bit of a wino, Amelia, you must admit that. I've known him since we started college together, remember, and he was bad enough back then. Whenever I got up myself about being a rugby Blue, he always used to joke he was a drinking Blue.'

I thought about it. Ed did drink too much, but it was such a part of our life together I had just accepted it as normal. Ed drinking every day—or 'tasting', as he called it—had seemed part of his job, the same way other women's husbands worked long hours in the City or travelled all the time. I didn't think he was a full-blown alcoholic, but he definitely drank over the healthy limit.

I had another point for my cons list, I realized. And it tipped the balance, so there were now officially more cons than pros. I tried to tell myself that was a good thing.

'Anyway,' Dick was saying. 'Tell me what's going

on with all that. Are you actually getting a divorce? Are you really single, like me, or just playing at it? Because if you have got the chance to go back to Ed, I would, if I were you. It's pretty bleak here in outer space where I live.'

'I'm supposed to be having this time away from him to make my mind up,' I said, 'but really, I have decided. I'm not quite ready to raise the "D" word with Ed yet, but it is over. Definitely. I'm not going back to him.'

It made my stomach churn to say it out loud like that, but at the same time, I knew I had to start thinking in those terms.

'What's the problem?' said Dick.

'He doesn't want to have children,' I said.

Dick laughed wryly. 'I think Dad could have told you that,' he said. 'Have you only just found out after fifteen years? Well, I agree that is a valid reason to leave him, but have you got someone else lined up to have them with?'

I smiled at him sarcastically. 'Oh yeah,' I said. 'I had a T-shirt printed saying: "Desperate woman, nearly 37, seeks perfect man to have child with immediately." I had to fight them off. Of course I haven't got anyone. That's the problem. I could be leaving Ed because he won't have kids and then not find anyone else to have them with and die alone, eating cat food in a basement bedsit . . .'

Those were the images that haunted me in the middle of the night when I couldn't sleep.

Dick was shaking his head and sighing. 'We really have fucked it up, the lot of us, haven't we?' he said. 'We are like a whole generation of retards when it comes to having a normal family life. Here's me, nearly forty, nearly fat and no hope of finding a decent woman, because I just don't know how to do it. I seem to have a bit missing where all that's concerned. Then there's you, married to a charming but selfish rich git who won't have children. Then there's poor old JR, who thought he had a family and then found out the hard way that he actually didn't.'

'Joseph?' I said, my stomach churning all over again.

'Yes,' said Dick. 'It would have saved a lot of heartache for all of us if you two had just got together back in the day and got on with the breeding thing.'

'But what did you mean about Joseph finding out the hard way?'

'Didn't he tell you why he left his wife?'

'He told me about not being allowed to see his stepchildren . . .'

Dick looked really surprised. 'He didn't tell you about the other child?'

I shook my head and dropped the piece of naan bread I had been eating. Suddenly I had no appetite whatsoever. Finally, the mysterious third child.

'Oh, well, I'd better tell you then,' continued Dick. 'As you know, JR's wife had two small kids when they met. He took them on, and he loves them like his own, but he really wanted one or two that were his own as well, to complete their family. Pretty normal. So the year before last, she got pregnant, and he was ecstatic—but when she was seven months gone and they'd been for all the scans and all that, she told him it wasn't his baby. She'd been having an affair for nearly two years, and she was leaving him for the other guy and taking all three kids with her. Nice, huh?'

I was appalled. 'Oh, poor Joseph,' I said. 'No wonder he didn't want to talk about it. That's horrendous.'

'Yes,' said Dick, draining his beer and raising his hand to the waiter for another. 'Pretty humiliating for a macho man, eh?' He paused for a moment and looked at me with narrowed eyes, then he stuffed in a large piece of chapatti and crunched it loudly while still talking. 'It's amazing, really, when you think about it,' he said, between crunches. 'There's the two of you idiots, my sister and my best mate, both single for the want of a baby. How bloody ironic is that? So tell me again—why did you and JR split up? You never told me why, and you looked so happy together I was quite nauseated.'

'He was shagging Kiki as well as me,' I said. There was no nice way to put it.

Dick was nodding slowly. 'So that was what he was going on about then,' he said. 'The last time I saw him he kept droning on about how you'd got it all wrong about him and Kiki. I wasn't really listening actually. It was late and we were watching the cricket live from the West Indies. I had to tell him to shut up and watch the bloody game in the end.'

He chuckled to himself. I felt a bit sick. His casual chat was making me picture Joseph all too clearly, an image I had spent the past few weeks doggedly putting out of my mind.

'Oh, well,' said Dick, picking some bits of stray food out of his teeth. 'JR the cockmeister strikes again—that is disappointing, I must say. Especially with my own sister. I should knock him down

404

really, except he's fitter than me, so forgive me if I don't. But I am surprised. I mean, he never could keep it zipped when we were young, but I thought he'd grown out of all that. He told me he'd always been faithful to his wife.'

I rolled my eyes. Joseph never had been able to do any wrong as far as Dick was concerned.

'And it was Kiki he was shagging you say?' he said.

I nodded irritably.

'Well, there's another sad story for you,' said Dick. 'She can't even have children, can she, poor thing?'

I stared at him. 'What do you mean?' I said.

'Don't you know that either?' said Dick, frowning like a confused dog. 'I thought you were friends with these people. She was born with some kind of abnormality in the woman-y bits and she's known since she was very young that she can't have kids. No chance. I assumed you knew.'

I shook my head in amazement. Poor Kiki.

'Whoever told you that?' I asked him.

'JR,' said Dick, shrugging.

I said nothing. It was almost too much to take in on top of everything else, and I felt rather hurt all over again that she hadn't confided in me about it when we were talking about my baby issues.

I couldn't believe she had told Joseph about it and not me—but even as I had that naïve thought, I realized how stupid it was. Of course Kiki would have confided in Joseph about such things. She'd probably told him when they were in bed one Saturday afternoon while I was weeding with Hermione in blissful ignorance.

I was trying to think of something else to talk

about, anything to take my mind off all that, but Dick had other ideas. He took a deep drink from his bottle and nearly choked on it, trying to speak at the same time.

'I've just remembered something,' he said, spluttering, as he pulled his dreadful old attaché case on to his lap and scrabbled through the contents. 'JR gave me something for you. Now where is it . . . ah . . .'

He pulled a bent and grubby envelope out of the case and handed it to me. 'Sorry it's a bit of a mess. I've had it a while. I forgot about it. Sorry.'

I looked down at the writing, which simply said 'Amelia' in a very familiar bold script. My stomach did a triple somersault with pike, but my hands were already tearing the letter up.

'Bloody hell, sis,' said Dick, looking quite shocked. 'That's a bit harsh, isn't it? Aren't you going to see what the poor heartbroken bugger wants to say to you?'

'Nope,' I said, shredding the last pieces and dumping it on top of the remains of the chicken tikka masala on my plate. I glanced down and saw what looked like a corner of the word 'loved' on one of the scraps. I put some rice over it quickly. 'Not interested.'

'God, you're stubborn,' said Dick, appalled. He leaned across the table towards me. 'Don't go getting all twisted and bitter on us, Meals,' he said, in a quiet voice. 'Because right now you've got an expression on your face that is all too familiar to me.'

'What are you talking about?' I said tersely. He was beginning to annoy me.

'You look just like Dad,' he said.

406

The combination of the rich curry, the gassy beer and all the revelations kept me awake most of the night. I felt desperately sorry for Kiki and suddenly her concern, all those months before, about me and Ed sleeping separately made sense. It wasn't just interfering nosiness. She couldn't bear to see someone who ostensibly could have children throwing the chance away.

And it made me understand a lot of other things about her. The relentless partying and her resistance to being in a settled relationship, plus the angry way she had reacted that time when I had pushed her on the baby issue, all fell into place now—although it still didn't excuse the way she had behaved with regard to me and Joseph.

I felt terribly sorry for him as well, now I knew his full story—the thing about the baby not being his was really awful—but that still didn't excuse his behaviour to me. 'JR the cockmeister', Dick had called him, and that nickname said it all. And Kiki had called him a 'pantsman', I remembered. There was no getting over it. Joseph Renwick had been a shocking Lothario at eighteen and he still was at forty.

He may have told Dick he had been faithful to his wife, but I didn't believe it for a minute, and while I might feel sympathy for his situation, I still didn't want any part of him. Well, I did, and one part in particular, but I wasn't going to let myself go near it. He was used goods.

*   *   *

By the end of that week the house in Highgate was finished, and I could finally go down to Winchelsea again. It was the first time for a month, and I was so happy at the prospect I spent most of the journey gazing out of the train window at the beautiful Kent and Sussex countryside speeding past in its full high-summer glory.

I sighed with relief when I opened the back door and stepped into my lovely familiar kitchen with its window looking over to Hermione's house, with her wonderful pink roses scrambling over the hedge.

Before I even changed into my weekend clothes, I rushed out to see what was going on in my garden and was amazed to see I had a mass of runner beans up the bamboo wigwams, where only leaves and stems had been before. I remembered putting the seedlings in with Hermione months ago, and now there was this great harvest.

I rushed through Checkpoint Charlie to share my excitement. She wasn't in the garden, so I ran up to the house. The French windows were open as usual, but when I called out, she didn't answer. I went inside and could see her lunch plate, with a half-eaten cucumber sandwich on it, on the counter, so she was clearly around.

I found her eventually in the greenhouse, and I knew immediately she was dead. She was lying on the floor, her gardening gloves on, her hat fallen off to one side, her blue eyes open but the spark entirely gone.

I crouched down to touch her face. It was stone-cold. I put my head to her chest, and there was nothing there. I think I let out something like a howl of shock and then I bent down to kiss her lovely old face. My tears wet her cheek.

'Oh, Hermione,' I said, smoothing her white hair. 'I'm going to miss you so much. Thank you for being my friend, the best girlfriend I've ever had. I love you so much.'

I sat there sobbing over her until I realized I had to do something. I stood up, turned around and then sat down again. So this is panic, I told myself, trying to take a few deep breaths to recover my senses. I'd left my mobile phone back at my place, but I didn't want to leave her to get it.

'I'll be back in a minute,' I said stupidly, after a moment, and then rushed into her house to call the police. I didn't know what else to do. They told me not to move the body and to call her doctor.

While I was waiting for someone to come, I went round to tell her other neighbour, Joyce, the one who did her shopping, and I was very relieved to find she knew where Hermione kept everything, perfectly filed ready for this moment, right down to her preferred undertaker. Joyce came back to the house with me and took over the arrangements, while I sat in the greenhouse with Hermione. I couldn't bear to leave her on her own.

I lit a candle, in her favourite lily of the valley scent—*muguet*, she always called it—and sat with her, stroking her cold hand and telling her all that she had done for me and why I would never forget her.

After a while the doctor came and officially declared her dead, the police came and took a statement from me and the neighbour, and then, finally, I sent Hermione off in the undertakers' van with a bouquet of her favourite roses next to her. I stood outside, tears coursing down my face, watching it drive away.

It was after six when I went back to my house, and I knew I couldn't spend the night there alone. I needed a friend more than I ever had, but who to call?

Ed? So tempting, but too complicated. There was too much going on with all our other issues for him to be a comfort with this one. And if he was too nice to me, I would probably cave in, and all my hard work trying to adjust to life without him over the past few weeks would be for nothing. I'd be back where I started.

Dick? It was Friday, so he was probably already in the pub and, even if he did come, he'd be useless. He was not great in any area that involved intense emotion, apart from England rugby matches.

Louise would have been great, but she'd need to charter a helicopter from Cornwall, not to mention the childcare issues. Joseph? Forget it. I might need to call another ambulance after I attacked him with a carving knife. My mum? It was Friday night, Dad would be tired and expecting his dinner on the table. I wasn't going to risk making trouble for her.

That left one person: Kiki.

I had felt so desperately hurt by her, but I still knew she would be the perfect support in this situation. My hands shook a little as I dialled her number, and I was relieved when she answered immediately. Although I shouldn't have been surprised. Kiki never missed a phonecall—it might be an invitation.

'Kiki?' I said in a very small voice.

'Amelia?' she said, clearly amazed. 'Is that really you? At last. Are you OK?'

'No,' I said. 'And I know I've got a cheek ringing you out of the blue like this, but I really need a friend tonight, and you are one, in spite of everything.'

'Whatever's happened?' she said, sounding genuinely concerned. 'Where are you?'

'I'm at the cottage,' I said. 'I came down earlier and I found Hermione—you remember, my lovely neighbour? She's dead, Kiki.' I burst into tears.

'Oh, baby girl,' said Kiki. 'That's terrible, I know how much you loved her. Do you want me to come down? I'll get the next train.'

'Please, I'd be so grateful.'

'I'm on my way,' said Kiki. 'I'll call you from the train.'

She rang me again about forty minutes later.

'OK, sweetie, I'm on my way. I'll be with you in another hour and a bit but, before I arrive, I have to clear something up with you. I want to be there for you tonight in your sadness and I don't want any of that other bullshit getting in the way. OK?'

'OK,' I said, in a really tiny voice. I wasn't sure I wanted to hear whatever it was she was going to tell me, but I needed a friend so badly I couldn't really object.

'What happened that night at Ollie's party . . .' said Kiki. I started to speak, to tell her not to worry about all that now, but she interrupted me. 'No, Amelia. You need to know this. You have to let me tell you. I did sleep with Joseph, that's true, but only once. The night of that party, when I first met him, he stayed that night—and only that night.'

So that was who she had been with that morning when I rang her from the park, I realized. Even in my shocked state, it all fell into place.

'But that was the only time, and it meant nothing to me, Amelia. You know what I'm like with men. Each one is just a new toy for me. I play with it non-stop until I am bored and then I want another one. So I did root him, but only the once, and he never bloody stopped talking about you the whole time. It was really boring.

'So whatever Ollie said that night at his engagement party—he was drunk and just trying to stir things up, as usual, he feels awful about it—Joseph wasn't two-timing you with me. It was a one-night stand ages before you got with him, when you were still very much with Ed. So forgive me—and forgive him, Amelia. Give the guy another chance. He's a good man.'

I promised I would, although he was really the last thing on my mind at that moment. I just wanted my girlfriend to be there to hug me and make me laugh—especially as now I knew I had been wrong about the Joseph thing, I could love her unreservedly again.

29

It seemed like forever waiting for Kiki to arrive, so I busied myself getting a tray of drinks ready—Campari and sodas and a bowl of Twiglets in honour of Hermione and our weekend evening ritual.

I shed a few more tears as I cut up slices of

orange to go in the drinks; Hermione had always made them with orange. It was still barely sinking in that I would never again sit on that terrace with her, drinking our sundowners and chatting so happily. There was so much I hadn't asked her, and now I never could, but I was just grateful for having known her at all. If I was going to be alone for the rest of my life, she had shown me how to do it in style.

I sat down heavily at the table and was about to pick up my glass when I heard an unmistakable sound: the clip clip clip of high heels on the brick path.

'Cooee, Meelie girl,' called Kiki. 'I'm here.'

I rushed out to meet her, practically knocking her over in my enthusiasm.

'Oh, Kiki,' I said, giving her a huge hug. 'Thank you so much for coming. I've been so awful to you, and you were my friend all along. I had it all wrong and I'm so sorry.'

'That's all ancient history,' she said, hugging me back. 'I'm just happy you finally know the truth, you obstinate old sausage. We all tried so hard to get the message through to you, but you just wouldn't listen. Anyway, you know now. I *am* a total ho, you were right about that, but Joseph is not a bastard. Anyway, let's forget all that. Tell me everything about Hermione. I am so sorry, I know how fond you were of her.'

We sat at the table and, after raising a toast to girlfriends—young and old, living and dead—I told Kiki the whole story about coming down and finding Hermione in the greenhouse. And then, somehow, in that way she had, Kiki managed to get out of me everything that had happened in the months since I had last seen her at Oliver and Sonny's engagement party.

I told her how I'd found a place to live on my own and how I'd tried one last time to sort it out with Ed, but that his stubborn intransigence about having kids had finally made it impossible and I was just working up the courage to tell him I wanted a divorce.

Kiki looked very serious as she listened, and I suddenly remembered what Dick had told me about her not being able to have children. Some time I would ask her about that—but this was definitely not it. I had other, more pressing questions for her.

'That's enough about me, actually, Kiki,' I said. 'I'm really sick of me—and I've got something I desperately want to ask you.'

She nodded encouragingly. 'Ask,' she said.

'OK—why the hell did you tell Leo Mecklin about me and Joseph? He only bloody told bloody Ed. And why on earth are you selling your beautiful art collection through him and his heinous father?'

Kiki threw back her head and roared. 'Oh, that all got back to you, did it? Genius. The jungle drums—they never fail me. Except they did this time . . .'

'What do you mean?' I asked, even more bewildered than before.

'I had tried everything else I could think of to make you listen to me—did Ed give you the letter I sent you via him, by the way?' I shook my head. 'Hmmm,' said Kiki. 'I wondered about that. Anyway, I was trying everything, then I thought, what can I do that would make you so furiously cross you would ring me up to abuse me and then I could tell you the truth about me and Joseph and everything would be all right again?'

I had to laugh. 'Well, you certainly succeeded in making me cross,' I said, 'but that just made me *less* likely to ring you. I don't think you understand the English as well as you think you do, Kiki. But tell me, are you really selling your beautiful paintings through those creeps? They'll rip you off, you know.'

'No, of course I'm not,' she chuckled. 'I was just stringing them along. I thought I'd get two for the price of one. Piss you off enough so you'd phone me—and teach that slimy piece of shit Leo Mecklin not to mess with me. You should have seen him preening about having acquired "The Wilmott Collection" for dispersal. I so enjoyed ringing his father to say I'd changed my mind because of Leo's incompetence.'

'How did Leo mess with you?'

'He told a lot of people that he'd slept with me.'

'Yuck!' I said.

'Quite,' said Kiki. 'I might be a ho, but I'm not a desperate ho.'

I laughed, so happy to be enjoying her lively company again. Then, as I looked at her dear, familiar face, something else occurred to me that I really needed to ask her.

'Kiki,' I said. 'I need to ask you another serious favour.'

'Ask,' she answered, spreading her hands in a gesture of giving.

'Will you come back into business with me?'

She jumped up and ran around the table to hug me. 'You bet,' she said. 'I have been sooooo

415

bored.'

'But there's one condition,' I added, in a pretend serious voice, when she sat down again. 'You've got to come back as a formal 49 per cent partner, right up front or no deal. OK?'

'Deal!' said Kiki, clinking her glass against mine.

She drained it and made panting noises like a thirsty dog, so I took the hint and got up to mix some more drinks. I glanced over at her from the dresser where I was cutting more orange slices and saw she was looking around the room with narrowed eyes.

'What?' I asked her. I knew Kiki well enough to know she was framing one of her big questions.

'So now you and Ed really are in separate beds . . .' she said.

I had to smile, but I sighed deeply at the same time. 'Yes,' I said. 'And separate flats, like I told you, and separate lives for ever.'

'Are you very sad about it?' she asked, with uncharacteristic gentleness, as I sat down again and passed her drink across the table.

I thought for a moment. I had been ineffably sad about it, but somehow now that Hermione had died I felt like a whole chapter of my life had formally ended—which made it possible that a new one could begin. As I took a deep drink of my Campari, I felt the first glimmer of a possibility that it might be a happier one.

So much had changed in my life in the brief few months since I had first sat in that kitchen with Kiki, I now understood how stagnant it had been for so long before that. I had really needed things to change, although I hadn't known it then.

'Yes,' I said eventually, 'I am sad. Desperately

sad. Ed has been my best friend since I was twenty-one, and I really miss him. But I'm also sad that he is so intransigent about things that he won't risk the one change that might make things better in the long run—so it has to be this way.'

'Do you think you can really move on now?' said Kiki.

'Yes, I think I can,' I said with all honesty.

'So are you going to give Joseph another chance then?' she asked, with her usual bluntness.

I slumped slightly. Kiki always pushed it one notch further than I was ready to go. 'No,' I said, determinedly. 'I need a break from men. It's all too confusing. I need to lie fallow for a bit longer.'

'Oh, that's a pity,' said Kiki, and as she took another drink I could see a dangerous twinkle in her eyes over the rim of the glass. I knew that look all too well.

'Why?' I said, getting wary.

Kiki giggled. 'Because he's waiting in the car outside . . .'

'What car?' I spluttered, focusing in my shock on the least important part of her statement. 'You said you were coming on the train. And anyway, you can't drive . . . and you haven't got a car and neither has Joseph.'

'No,' said Kiki. 'But your brother Dick has. It's his car. He lent it to us to come down here.'

'Well, you arranged that quickly,' I said, my brain still stuck in the inconsequential details of the situation.

'Oh, for God's sake, look out of the window,' said Kiki, hoicking an ice cube out of her glass and throwing it at me.

I stood up and looked out over the front lawn to

where I could see Dick's ridiculous four-wheel-drive truck parked by the garden gate. And back-lit by the evening sun, I could clearly see Joseph's profile on the driver's side.

At the moment I looked out, he put his head back and moved it from side to side, rubbing his neck with his hand. The sight of his extended, vulnerable throat, the Adam's apple standing out, made me emit something close to a whimper. Another ice cube whizzed past my head.

'Stop it!' I yelled at Kiki.

'Well, go out and see him,' she said.

I picked the wet dishcloth up from the side of the sink and threw it at her. 'I'm just getting over the shock,' I said.

The third flying ice cube jolted me out of it, and I raced to the back door, pausing to kiss Kiki on the top of her hair as I went past.

As I ran up the path I saw Joseph's head shoot round. His handsome face broke into a broad smile when he saw me, which he immediately tempered down, presumably as he remembered why he was down there.

By the time I had reached the car, he was out of it, and I ran straight to him and flung my arms around him. It had been too emotional a day for any lesser show of feeling.

'Meals,' he said, softly, pulling me into his broad embrace. 'I'm so sorry about Hermione . . .'

'I'm so sorry about everything,' I said, looking up at him. 'Kiki has told me the whole story, and I shouldn't have jumped to such stupid conclusions. I should have given you a chance to explain.'

'I should have told you right at the start what had happened between me and Kiki. I was an idiot, but I'd already fucked it up with you once, twenty years ago, and I was so scared of spoiling what we had this time . . .'

'It doesn't matter,' I said. 'I was unbelievably stupid not to listen to you guys but, as Kiki said, it's all ancient history. I'm just so pleased to see you now.'

I leaned my head against his chest and just breathed for a while, feeling a sense of contentment that had been missing in my life since the last time I had been in that exact position. He put his arms more tightly around me, and I turned my head up to look at him again.

His dark-blue eyes were gazing at me so tenderly through those funny old John Lennon glasses. I sighed deeply, my heartbeat pounding in my ears, as I realized he was just about to kiss me.

At that moment, I heard what sounded like a fighter jet screeching around the corner into the tiny lane where the cottage was. Seconds later, car doors slammed and Sonny came running over to us, closely followed by Oliver.

'Is it really true about Hermione?' said Sonny. His beautiful face was all crumpled, and his eyes were full of tears. I nodded and felt my own eyes well up again. Sonny flung his arms around me and sobbed on to my shoulder. Joseph stepped discreetly back.

'I never got to say goodbye to her,' said Sonny, as I patted his back. 'I never got to thank her. I just pissed off to London . . .'

'It's all right, Sonny,' I said. 'She was thrilled that things were going so well for you.'

He straightened up again and looked at me, tears streaking his cheeks. 'I'm so glad you were here,' he said, wiping his nose on the back of his hand and taking a couple of gulpy breaths. 'I'm going to look at her garden.'

He ran off in the direction of Checkpoint Charlie, and Oliver stepped forward and kissed me on the cheek very gently, his hands resting softly on my shoulders.

'Hello babe,' he said, looking at me sadly. 'Can you finally forgive my foul ugly mouth? I'm really sorry, Amelia. I didn't mean to make such a mess for you.'

I just shook my head and hugged him. 'There's nothing to apologize for, Ol,' I said. 'You have got a gob like a sewer, but I was incredibly stupid and mad about the whole thing. I acted like a crazy lady. I'm sorry too. Now go and be with your boy, he needs you.'

He smiled at me again, and then his eyes narrowed. 'You need a trim,' he said, touching the bottom of my hair with his fingers. 'I'll do it for you later.' And after giving me another kiss on the cheek, he disappeared off towards the back garden.

I turned around to look at Joseph, who was leaning against the boot of the car, smiling gently. He stood up and came towards me, taking both my hands in his and leaning his forehead against mine, gazing into my eyes.

I was feeling almost dizzy as his lips moved towards my mouth, when I heard a noise like a warthog being strangled and pulled back in surprise as my brother's face, red and a bit sweaty, suddenly appeared out of the back door of the car.

'Arewetherethen?' he asked. 'Fuck, feel really rubbish . . . Bloody winding roads down here . . .

Ah! Sis . . . Sorry. Hi. Sorry about the bad news.'

He patted me on the shoulder with his huge paw, staggering slightly, his eyes shifting into focus and out again. 'Really bad luck . . . Think gonna hurl . . .'

As he stumbled down the garden path towards the back door, I hoped he would make it to the loo before unleashing whatever he had consumed since leaving work that afternoon.

'Have you met my brother?' I asked Joseph, who was shaking his head indulgently.

'He's such a messy fuckwit,' he said. 'But he's our messy fuckwit, isn't he, Meals?'

I nodded and rested my head against his shoulder.

'Do I finally get to kiss you now?' he asked me, lifting my chin up with his hand.

'That depends,' I said. 'On who else you've brought with you . . .'

'Well, as you mention it . . .' he said, 'there is someone else. Dick rang your mum from the car to tell her what was going on, and your dad answered. They're on their way over. They should be here any minute.'

I froze in horror. The prospect of having my father and Oliver in the same room was too horrendous even to contemplate. Then I wondered what Kiki might say to him and physically shuddered. It was all too terrible: I had to intervene immediately while there was still time and get them all to scarper.

I took a step towards the house, but felt Joseph's hand on my arm, as he gently restrained me. In my panic, I'd almost forgotten he was there.

'Amelia,' he said, pulling me to him and resting

421

his hands on my cheeks so I looked up at him again. 'I was joking.'

I just blinked at him stupidly.

'It was a joke,' he repeated. 'Your dad is not about to turn up here, but even if he was, you wouldn't have to worry, because I'm here. I can deal with him. Even if they were coming it would all be fine—it *will* all be fine.'

And in that moment, as his lips touched mine, I finally understood that it would be.